THE

BILLIONAIRE'S

LAWYER

by

Cordell Parvin

Prologue

Roberto Sanchez's heart was racing like it never had at the counsel table while waiting to hear the verdict. He needed his daughter to succeed and hear the jury declare Sparks Duval "not guilty."

Roberto remembered the day Gabriela told him she wanted to leave his law practice in McAllen. He had started to protest, but her eyes were alive when she talked about becoming a top litigator in a big Dallas law firm. Gabriela had a burning desire to prove herself on a bigger stage. He couldn't stop her.

Roberto watched nervously as Judge Comstock studied the jury's verdict. He was always calm and collected when waiting to hear a jury verdict in his own cases, but today was different. It wasn't his case. It was his daughter's.

"Will the defendant please rise?" Judge Comstock asked, even though they all knew it wasn't a question.

Sparks Duval, Gabriela, and Roberto stood.

A movement to the right caught Roberto's eye. Jason Daniels, the D.C. Department of Justice prosecutor, had turned to the reporters in the gallery with a smirk on his face. To his right, Duval shifted from one foot to the other. Roberto looked down at his own hand and discovered he was clicking his pen. He put it down on his legal pad.

Roberto couldn't look back at Deborah Snow and Steven Graham, the public relations experts who had recommended Gabriela defend Duval, but he was sure they were squirming in their seats in the front row. They should have been. They were the ones who had convinced Duval to testify over his and Gabriela's strong objections. He stifled a sigh of impatience.

Roberto believed Duval was at least technically guilty. He suspected there was no way Duval Energy could drill for oil and gas in Mexico without paying someone for the opportunity. But early on, Roberto had told Gabriela that he thought Duval was innocent. She needed to believe he was. "Why," Roberto had asked, "would a man who started with nothing, who built a top energy company from scratch, risk it all just to win a fracking contract in Mexico?"

He wasn't sure, even now, that his daughter believed him.

Roberto looked at Judge Comstock, trying to guess what the judge was thinking. He seemed puzzled by what he was reading. Roberto glanced over at the jury. None of the jurors was looking at the defendant. Always a bad sign.

Roberto felt helpless.

Chapter 1

A make-or-break career opportunity was the last thing on Gabriela Sanchez's mind as she stepped out of the rain into the cold marble entrance of the Earle Cabell Federal Building. Passing through security, she stuffed her dripping umbrella into the worn brown leather briefcase her father had given her when she passed the bar exam. Running her fingers through her black curls, she glanced at the time on her phone. *I'm going to be late.*

Slipping around an elderly Hispanic couple, Gabriela hurried toward the shiny elevator doors and pressed the up button for the tenth floor, home of the Dallas Federal Immigration Court.

As she exited the elevator, her phone vibrated. She ignored it. Five seconds later it vibrated again. Sighing, she pulled it from her pocket and read a text from her assistant, Lucia:
Wainwright & Green want to see you now! Get back here pronto!

If Jack Wainwright, Parker & McEvoy's managing partner, and Chuck Green, head of litigation, wanted to see a young lawyer *pronto*, it was usually to read them the riot act. She couldn't think of anything she had done to warrant their wrath, but there had to be something.

She looked at her phone and exhaled audibly, wondering if she should ask the immigration judge for a continuance. Scanning the courtroom, Gabriela finally saw her young Honduran client. Despite being only twelve, Teena de la Cruz could have passed for a college

3

student. She looked more like a frightened young adult facing deportation than the innocent child Gabriela knew she was.

Gabriela shook her head, opened her text messages, and typed, *I'm in court. Be back right after.*

Gabriela helped immigrants, especially children. She empathized with those who were undocumented and afraid of being sent back to violence. She had grown up in the Rio Grande Valley, where more than a third of her high-school classmates were undocumented. Many of those classmates became pregnant, thinking it increased their chances of staying in the United States. Others, who wanted college, attended the University of Texas Rio Grande Valley because they feared being stopped at the Border Patrol checkpoint north of the Valley.

Her eyes returned to Teena. It had taken time to earn the girl's trust. Gabriela smiled and told her in Spanish that everything would be okay.

The twelve-year-old bit her lip and rubbed her face with trembling hands. Apprehension covered her like a wet blanket.

Gabriela had seen that anxiety many times. Despite her best efforts, she had yet to find words that comforted the panicked children in that cold courtroom. She hugged Teena instead. When she pulled back, she looked into Teena's watery eyes and held her again.

"Teena, you can count on me," Gabriela whispered in Spanish. "I will take care of you."

When she arrived in Dallas in 2015, Gabriela immediately offered her assistance with the humanitarian crisis involving 60,000 children illegally crossing the southern border when she learned that the Dallas Bar Association had begun collaborating with Catholic Charities Dallas to provide volunteer attorneys for immigration court support. Teena was one of the thousands of faceless children with no home to call their own.

After Teena's mother witnessed a murder in Honduras, her parents had gathered their savings and paid for their only child to be taken, unaccompanied, alone, and afraid, to a place she had only read about: the United States. Teena had traveled without her loved ones, tired, hungry, and terrified. She was one of the many young girls sexually abused on the journey.

As she waited, Gabriela watched a young Honduran mother with two malnourished children cling to her legs before the Honorable Jefferson Davis, the immigration judge. The woman had no attorney and no knowledge of courtroom procedure. Her son climbed the steps, waving at the judge, as another young Hispanic girl squealed from the gallery, "No niño, no!"

The judge waved scornfully. The boy, sobbing, was guided back to his trembling mother.

Gabriela heard the judge bark, "If you can't control your children, the marshal will escort you from the courtroom. Now, why can't you return to Honduras?"

Because she's afraid for her children! Can't you see? Gabriela screamed silently.

The small boy wailed in his mother's arms. The woman set him down and tearfully told the judge in Spanish that she wanted a better life in America for her children.

Dismissively, the judge ordered that she and her children be deported immediately.

Gabriela's stomach turned as the authorities led them out. She wondered how she could save Teena from such a harsh judge.

"Ms. Sanchez, are you ready to address the court?" Judge Davis asked without looking up from his laptop. She guessed he was checking his stocks.

Gabriela rose, took a deep breath, and began her remarks. "I am, Your Honor. Teena De La Cruz is only twelve years old." She gestured toward her client. "She has been the victim of gang and cartel violence, human trafficking, and crime in Honduras, It is the murder capital of the world. Before she left, one gang member wanted her to be a 'girlfriend,' which is code for sex slave. Teena escaped before they could attack her.

"Teena endured great hardship and danger on her journey. She began by bus, rode on top of the train known as *La Bestia* through Mexico, and somehow made it to the Rio Grande Valley. Many children didn't survive. Some fell from the train. Some were kidnapped. Others, like Teena, were abused in so-called safe houses.

"For the last month, Teena has slept on the floor of a detention center. She spends her days watching television, playing cards, and passing time with new friends. Teena's great-aunt in Irving is willing and able to care for her. We ask that she be allowed to stay with family here, where she's safe. If she returns to Honduras, she will likely face molestation, degradation, and possibly death."

Gabriela stood straight, her face calm but her eyes pleading for empathy. The Immigration and Customs Enforcement lawyer had agreed not to pursue the case, so it should have been an easy hearing. But in Dallas, it all depended on the judge.

A year earlier Judge Davis had deported a child in Gabriela's first immigration case. This time she had invited writers and television reporters to the hearing so that whatever Davis did would become public knowledge.

"Case dismissed," Judge Davis said with a wave of his hand.

Gabriela exhaled, hugged Teena, and told her in Spanish that she could stay in the United States.

Teena smiled and grabbed her around the waist. Afterward, her great-aunt hugged Gabriela and whispered a thank-you. Before leaving, Gabriela told the aunt she would check up on Teena. The girl smiled again and hugged her one more time.

As she left the courtroom, Gabriela texted Lucia: *Tell Wainwright & Green I'm on my way.*

News reporters cornered her in the hallway, shouting questions. "I want anything I say to you to be off the record," she said.

A reporter she knew called out, "Can you tell us about the need for lawyers representing children in immigration court?"

"If anyone in our country needs the best lawyers money can buy, it's these children," Gabriela said. "Having a great lawyer who cares is more important than their actual eligibility. These children came here to escape unthinkable violence. We have a moral obligation to help them. *Give me your tired, your poor, your huddled masses, yearning to breathe free.* Those words on the Statue of Liberty are as true today as they were when written. We can't let the government deport these children and families. It's immoral and un-American."

"Why aren't they provided top-notch lawyers like you?" another reporter asked.

"You're kind to think of me that way," she said sincerely. "That's a great question—one we all ought to ask. The rich have the best lawyers. Even the poor have court-appointed lawyers. Yet these immigrant parents and children rely on volunteers, and there are nowhere near enough of us."

She started walking again but was blocked.

"Why aren't the children entitled to a lawyer?"

"Ask Congress. Ask the immigration judges. You might be shocked to know that one judge said in a deposition that children as young as three or four—who couldn't even speak English—were competent to represent themselves."

"What?" another journalist exclaimed.

Gabriela raised an eyebrow. "Oh yes. He claimed he had taught immigration law to three- and four-year-olds. That even though it took time and patience, they understood it."

"Can you name the judge?"

She shook her head.

Her phone vibrated again. *Wainwright/Green upset. Get back pronto. Go directly to Green's office.*

Damn, she thought. *Are they going to fire me?*

"I have to go," she told the reporters. "I hope you'll highlight the plight of these children. They need your support."

As she left the building, she texted, *What do they want? Don't know. Upset you're not here. Just get back.*

She put her phone away and traded her heels for running shoes. She jogged through the rain from Commerce Street to the Ryan Office Building on Ross Avenue, then took the first elevator. She slipped her heels back on, grateful to be alone as it climbed to the thirty-fourth floor. When it arrived, she swiped her entry card and stepped inside.

Approaching the corner office, she was met by Green's assistant. "You look like you just ran five miles in the rain."

"It wasn't five miles, but I did run from the federal court building."

"Do you want time to take care of your hair?"

"They don't care about my hair."

"Okay," the assistant said. "They're waiting for you."

Gabriela took a deep breath and knocked.

"Come in," a deep voice said.

As she entered the expansive office, a jolt of fear settled in her stomach, like the first climb of a roller coaster. Chuck Green stood with Jack Wainwright, arms folded, both men frowning. Goosebumps rose on her arms.

"Gabriela, sit down," Green said in a serious tone.

"Yes sir," she said but didn't move. The faint scent of Polo aftershave reached her. She and her friends were convinced Green owned stock in Ralph Lauren.

"You look like you've seen a ghost. You've done nothing wrong," Wainwright said.

During her first week at the firm, Wainwright had mistaken her for a secretary. When they met, he'd asked, "Which lawyers are you assisting?"

She had smiled and replied that she didn't know yet. Ever since, Wainwright had been uncomfortable around her.

"We're not planning to fire our rising star today," Green chuckled.

Gabriela smiled weakly. Parker & McEvoy's marketing director had recently nominated her as one of *D Magazine's* "Top 10 Most Beautiful Women in Dallas." Gabriela had protested, suggesting they instead nominate her for "Best Women Lawyers in Dallas." But they moved forward anyway. *D Magazine* pegged her as the "Latina Rising Star" in Dallas's legal profession. Since the issue hit newsstands, Green and several partners had delighted in teasing her.

Like many large Texas firms, Parker & McEvoy had developed a reputation for driving away their top minority and women lawyers. To improve its image, the firm hired Gabriela, making her the first Latina attorney at the firm and one of only a handful in big Dallas firms.

Gabriela knew she was a "two-fer." She checked both female and Hispanic boxes—a prize in diversity hiring. She knew, and they knew—though no one would say it aloud—that her gender and nationality mattered more than her credentials, class rank, or federal clerkship.

Over the past seven years, women had left the firm one by one, worn down by long hours and office machismo, until Gabriela was the only young lawyer left from her class. The firm placed her photo on its website, appointed her to diversity and recruiting committees, and sent her to law schools nationwide to interview minority students.

Even though Chuck Green rarely assigned her major cases, she had more trial experience than any other junior partner—thanks to her early work with her father and her willingness to take small cases no partner wanted.

"I hear you're doing outstanding work on your cases," Green said casually, as if avoiding the real reason for the meeting.

Gabriela searched his face. "That's good to hear," she responded nervously, glancing at Wainwright.

"I echo what Chuck said. You're doing very well," Wainwright added.

With his flat top and horn-rimmed glasses, Chuck Green looked more like a rocket scientist than a trial lawyer. What he lacked in charisma, he made up for in preparation, his ability to read jurors, and his cold heart. Gabriela suspected part of his success came from jurors being intimidated enough to rule for his clients.

In Texas, Green was known as the "Bet-the-Company" trial lawyer, a title the American Trial Lawyers Association gave him in 2010. He was the lawyer companies called when survival depended on winning in court. *Texas Monthly* and *D Magazine* had both put him on their covers, praising his record. He charged $1,200 an hour—but clients who needed him gladly paid it.

"Gabriela, did you hear what I said?" Wainwright asked. "You look like you were daydreaming."

"Oh, I'm sorry. No, I didn't. What did you say?"

After a pause, Wainwright spoke. "We have a sensitive case, and our client has specifically requested that you help Chuck defend him. Take a seat so Chuck can fill you in."

Stunned, Gabriela did as she was told.

Chapter 2

Green sat down across from Gabriela. He held her gaze for a few moments, his lips slightly pursed. "When you clerked for Judge Comstock, you worked on Foreign Corrupt Practices Act bribery cases, right?"

"Yes," Gabriela answered.

"Did you save all the research you did for those cases?"

Gabriela remembered each case by name and what the court held. "Yes, I still have it. I know every nuance in the cases."

Green handed her a stapled document from the Department of Justice, dated November 18, 2016. She quickly scanned the text. It was a press release for a criminal complaint filed against Duval Energy and William Thomas "Sparks" Duval.

"I've read all about this," she said. "And I've seen that video of Duval being led away in handcuffs from his jet. The media seems determined to see a conviction without a trial."

"Yes, and that's a big problem."

"So, will you defend him?" Gabriela tried in vain to read his facial expression.

Green leaned forward in his chair. "Yes. And Sparks Duval wants to interview you to help me defend him."

"How does he even know who I am? We certainly don't move in the same circles."

"He read the *D Magazine* article. Who wouldn't want one of Dallas's most beautiful women lawyers on their side?" Green replied with a roll of his eyes he didn't attempt to hide.

Gabriela's face turned red. She hated having been featured in that magazine and the seductive pose the photographer had directed her to make.

"Well, there's more to it than that," Green said.

Gabriela clenched her jaw. "He's never met me. He has no idea whether I'm a good trial lawyer. What more could there be?"

"Frankly, It's because you're Hispanic and Judge Comstock treats you like a daughter, and yes, you're easy on a juror's eyes."

That wasn't what Gabriela wanted to hear. Women trial lawyers in the firm had rarely been assigned to big cases. Even the most experienced women partners had never been part of the firm's inner circle. The firm was dominated by white male partners who had made it clear to Gabriela that she was easy on their eyes.

She stood up and looked at him, waiting for him to make eye contact before speaking. "So, I'd be window dressing. I wouldn't have any meaningful role in the trial."

Before Green could respond, Gabriela said, "You've been on the cover of *Texas Monthly*. They named you a top trial lawyer. *D Magazine* wrote that you are 'the go-to lawyer for bet-the-company cases.' I've proved time and again that I know how to try cases. I've been in court more than any young lawyer in this firm. But what does the firm think of me? I take a good photo. How flattering." She turned and headed toward the door.

"Sit down," Green said sternly. "Yes, but that's why we'll be a good te—"

"You can't think Duval is innocent!" Gabriela interrupted. "Mexico is one of the most corrupt countries in the world. No top U.S. company is doing business in Mexico without paying someone off."

"Yes, Mexico is corrupt, but Duval doesn't believe he did anything wrong, and his politics should make no difference to us. He sought the advice of his general counsel and relied on it. His lawyer assured him the deal was clean."

"Oh, please. That's what rich CEOs always say. Duval's rich. He hired you. He should find it easy enough to cut a deal."

"I agree. But the career Department of Justice lawyers in Washington who hate President Trump plan to make Duval a poster child since environmentalists say he's wrecking the planet. That's why the media has mounted this campaign to convict him before the trial."

"So what? All he needs to do is write a check and walk away."

"I've done everything within my power to convince him to write the government a check and go about his business. But he won't settle. Says he's innocent and will do whatever it takes to clear his name."

"Which is why he needs you. None of this has to do with me."

"Normally, I'd agree. But there's never been a worse time for a rich oilman to be accused of a crime and face a jury."

"But you've never lost a big case like this, even the tough ones no one thought you could win. Sparks Duval can afford to pay you over a thousand dollars an hour to save him. Ask someone else to be your pretty face."

"Gabriela, quit the bullshit. Aren't you the lawyer who told me you aspired to be the top litigator in Texas? To be on the cover of *Texas Monthly*?"

"Yes."

"Now I give you the chance to work on a case that will be in the news every day, and you don't want it? Please." Green sat back in his chair, irritated.

"Why should I? A billionaire, who we both know is guilty, sees my photo and decides he wants me with no knowledge of whether I'm a top trial lawyer. And I should be thankful for that?"

"Take my word. He's checked you out far beyond *D Magazine*. This is your big chance," Wainwright interjected.

"Maybe so. But Chuck says we have to settle the case."

"Even if we settle, you'll be in the news," Green responded. "People will start to know who you are. What, you'd rather spend your career defending immigrant children for no pay?"

There it was. The dig Gabriela had expected. "Maybe I would. They genuinely need my help. Duval doesn't need me to sit with you and smile. And I don't want to do it."

"Gabriela, open your eyes," Wainwright said. "Only the rich defendants who work a deal get treated with kid gloves. The feds crucify and bury those who dare to put up a fight."

"But you just told me you don't want to fight. You want to settle the case," Gabriela said.

"I've tried to tell Duval that the risk of any white-collar defendant going to trial is too great, even if he is innocent," Green said. "But he insists. And he's convinced that having you sitting at the counsel table alongside me will give him the best chance."

"Just sitting there with you?"

"Yes. Duval believes there will be three or four Hispanics on the jury."

"So, I'm the Hispanic prop?"

"No, I didn't say that. Duval believes you'll connect better with the jurors and Judge Comstock than I will. He's willing to pay us to have you help defend him."

"And I won't have any role at all in the trial?"

"Good lord, Gabriela," Green said, exasperated. "I'm not asking whether you want to back me up. I'm telling you that you'd be my second chair. Get used to the idea and quit making assumptions about our client's guilt. We want to settle. But if we have to try the case, I'll win."

Gabriela paused.

"Gabriela," Wainwright said. "As managing partner, I want you to work with Chuck. If he's forced to defend Duval, you'll have a role. You'll share in the credit for the win."

"Chuck, it wouldn't matter if we won. I won't get any credit for it if all I am is a prop. You've got to give me more responsibility than just sitting there for the judge and jury to see."

"Fine. I will. You've got my word."

Bingo.

"Sit here and read more of the file. Get acquainted. Ask me questions."

Gabriela could hardly concentrate.

As she read, she learned that the government accused Duval Energy and Sparks Duval of bribing PetroMex officials to win oil and gas contracts in the newly opened free market in Mexico. According to the complaint, in 2014, shortly after the Mexican Congress passed a bill paving the way for foreign companies to enter the Mexican oil industry, Duval had hired a well-connected contractor and a broker named José Lopez as a middleman. He allegedly paid Lopez a thirty percent fee when he successfully negotiated the oil and gas contracts with the state-owned oil company PetroMex. Lopez set up an elaborate chain of offshore trusts and companies, including ones that funneled millions of dollars to PetroMex officials and their families.

That took her by surprise. She looked up at Green. "How did the offshore accounts come to light?"

"That's a big mystery. We don't know how the government found out."

"Was there a whistleblower?"

"We haven't heard of one. But someone knew José Lopez had set up offshore accounts. Duval thinks the NSA was spying on Lopez."

"Ah, the classic government conspiracy theory. He's just paranoid."

"Yes, but it's not as far-fetched as you might think. Edward Snowden made that pretty clear."

"Proves what I said about doing business in Mexico," Gabriela said. "What about the accounts?"

"Someone discovered Lopez set up offshore accounts for two PetroMex officials. The career DOJ upper management couldn't resist when they discovered that Sparks Duval had paid a commission to Lopez, which he supposedly passed on as bribes."

"Did the DOJ indict Lopez?"

"No. Lopez is an unindicted co-conspirator."

"That's odd. Lopez is the guy who bribed the PetroMex officials."

"You've caught on to the irony," Green said. "DOJ may want him to be a witness against Duval. After all, Lopez could testify that Duval paid him the commission knowing he would use part of the funds to bribe PetroMex officials."

"That would be a killer."

"Which is just one more reason we need to settle the case."

Gabriela thought for a moment and asked the question she asked all her clients when she was stuck. "What else should I know?"

"The feds arrested Duval at DFW Airport. Don Lawrence, Duval's former general counsel, pleaded guilty to his role in the bribery scandal. It was supposed to be under seal, but someone leaked it to the press the day before Duval was arrested."

"Leaked by whom?"

"We don't know. All we know is Lawrence's guilty plea was on the front page the day the feds arrested Duval. They orchestrated the arrest for maximum negative publicity."

"Don Lawrence. Isn't he an international oil and gas lawyer?"

"That's the one."

"I thought he was with a firm. How did he end up as general counsel for Duval Energy?"

"Christopher Duval, Sparks Duval's son, wanted to do international deals. Sparks likely made him an offer he couldn't refuse."

Gabriela continued reading while Green added, "Jason Daniels, the main Justice lawyer from D.C., claims this is a slam dunk case for the government."

"Sounds like a kid on the playground bragging that he could kick your behind."
Green looked startled.

"I laughed at Daniels when he said it. That didn't go over well. Then I asked what made him so confident he would win."

"What did he say?" Gabriela asked, looking up from the files.

"It's what he didn't say that I found more interesting. He didn't mention that Lopez would be a witness. If they don't want to call Lopez as a witness, that must mean they're afraid of his testimony."

"What did he say?"

"That Don Lawrence will testify that he made the payments to Lopez for Duval Energy at the direction of its owner, Sparks Duval. Lawrence also wore a wire and a button video camera for the FBI before he resigned as general counsel. No telling what Duval said on the recording. According to Daniels, Lawrence is going to bury Duval."

"Lawrence videotaped his conversation with Duval while employed as general counsel? Isn't that unethical?"

"We'll argue that if we have to. But there's something else about this case…" Green trailed off, his forehead creased with worry.

"What? Just tell me."

"For only the second time in history, the DOJ has indicted the company as well as its owner."

"Why?" Gabriela asked. "Do they plan to put Duval's company out of business?"

"The government indicted Duval Energy to punish Sparks for not making a deal. They'll only make a deal for the company if he pleads guilty."

"What does Duval say?"

"He says that any U.S. energy company that wants to do business in Mexico has to go through Lopez because he has a long-standing relationship with PetroMex."

"That wouldn't be unusual. There are plenty of connected middlemen in Mexico. Is he right?"

"I'm sure he's had to go through Lopez. But as I said, Duval claims he had no idea that any money paid by Lawrence to Lopez was for bribes to get the contracts. He even asked Lawrence for an opinion on any potential legal problems with the deal. That's our ace in the hole."

"Well, that should be helpful, since they have to prove Duval's intent to win the contracts through bribery," Gabriela said, half-muttering to herself. "What did he think he was getting for the thirty percent fee?"

"The chance to be the first to do horizontal drilling in Mexico."

"You believe that?"

"Duval believes it, and that's what matters."

Gabriela shut the file folder. "Okay. What do we need to do?"

"If we can find Lopez, we'll want you to go to Mexico and talk to him. We need to know what he'd say if he's called to testify. In the meantime, you should explain to Duval what he's risking if he goes to trial. He wants to interview you before he makes the final decision for you to be on his defense team."

"Well, at least he realizes you should interview your lawyers rather than just choose them based on fluff pieces in *D Magazine*."

"Yeah, but he also doesn't listen to his lawyers, and he won't listen to you. Duval thinks he knows more than any of us, even though he never went to law school. He makes up his mind and wants his team to go along with him."

"He wants a yes-man like he got with Lawrence."
"Stop putting words in my mouth. I didn't say that. Sparks Duval single-handedly made Duval Energy what it is today. He's a legend, and his company is our biggest client. We need to keep him out of jail and keep his company alive. And if he approves, I want you to help me make that happen."

Gabriela took a deep breath. "What am I supposed to say when he interviews me?" She had ideas, but she needed to know the party line.

"Make sure he knows your job is to dig into all the facts. We want to give him our best advice, not just tell him what he wants to hear."

"I understand."

"He'll ask you what you think his chances are. Tell him you haven't spent enough time with the case yet to advise him. Don't let him talk you into any position."

"Suppose Duval decides after my interview that he doesn't want me to help you defend him?"

"He won't. I'm confident Duval and his son will both like you. There's one last thing you need to know. American Oil paid a twenty-eight-point-five-million-dollar fine for bribing the same PetroMex officials through payments to Lopez. Then the DOJ indicted Ralph Farmer, American Oil's Texas general manager, for arranging and authorizing those payments through Lopez. The same DOJ prosecution team is prosecuting Farmer in Houston. They think that if they convince Sparks Duval to make a deal, Ralph Farmer will cave. You might want to chat with Farmer's legal team."

"Got it. If that's all, then I'll be going. I've got quite a workload ahead of me," Gabriela said, grinning ear to ear, having totally abandoned her negative thoughts about representing a billionaire who was the president's friend.

Chapter 3

When they finished, Gabriela stepped out of Green's office, sprinted down the hall, and rushed down one floor to her office. She continued down the corridor to greet Lucia, her trusted assistant, whom she had hired when she made partner. They had both grown up speaking Spanglish, the hybrid mix of English and Spanish.

Gabriela was both nervous and excited when she told Lucia, "It's my big day, Lucia! My big opportunity is here!"

"Stay calm, Gabriela," Lucia said in Spanish. "Slow down, girl. What opportunity?"

"Sparks Duval wants me to help Chuck Green defend the richest man in Texas. I'll help defend Duval in one of the most sensational courtroom spectacles in Texas since the Enron trial. All my hard work has been for this. Life is good!"

"I'm happy for you. But I never thought I'd see you excited to defend a billionaire."

"I'm excited because this is the big opportunity I've waited for since I joined the firm."

"Okay, okay! Tell me what they said! How did Duval select you?"

"I know it doesn't sound good, but he saw my photo in the *D Magazine* article."

"He chose you because he thinks you're attractive?" Lucia asked. "I thought you hated that article."

"I do, but it got Mr. Duval's attention. And now I get to work on the highest-profile case in our firm's history." She caught her breath. "Green says Duval thinks I'll appeal to the **Hispanics and men on the jury.**"

Lucia rolled her eyes. "Well, take advantage of your advantage! Soak up all the positive press you can get. You're in a perfect position. If he's found innocent, you were part of the team. If he's convicted, you were riding the bench. Lots to gain, little to lose."

"That's a good way to look at it. But honestly, I also feel selfish," Gabriela said with a sigh. "Representing a billionaire is a far cry from helping young children stay in the United States."

"Be selfish. You deserve the chance to shine! The Duval trial is your one chance to become famous on a national stage. Think of how many more you can help after that."

"Well, I'm not officially on the team yet. Duval wants to interview me."

"Then you better be prepared for the interview."

"I will be. But I'm also a little nervous."

"Gabriela, Duval wants you on his defense team. He knows you'll be focused on getting the job done. When do you plan to visit him?"

"*Pronto*," Gabriela said with a little wave as she stepped into her office.

She closed the door and leaned back against her desk as a memory from law school flashed into her mind. *Ms. Sanchez, with your accent, you need to e-nun-ci-ate. Speak up and speak slowly, or no one will understand you.*

That criticism had pushed her to try harder—to overcompensate. She had projected self-confidence that irritated some of her classmates. She closed her eyes. *Am I ready for this?*

She had plenty of trial experience, but they were one- or two-day trials with only a handful of people watching. Helping defend Duval would be different—a much longer grind, a packed courtroom, and media coverage every day.

Gabriela had dreamed of defending a high-profile defendant in a trial the *New York Times*, *Washington Post*, and cable news networks would cover daily. Her heart raced as she visualized the packed courtroom.

She heard a knock and stepped forward just as Lucia opened the door.

"Do you want me to set up an appointment for you to meet Mr. Duval?" Lucia asked.

"Um… what?"

"Earth to Gabriela! Do you want me to set up an appointment for you to meet Mr. Duval?" Lucia repeated with a big smile.

"Oh! Yes. Yes, please."

"I'll get on that now," Lucia said and closed the door behind her.

Gabriela walked over to her large cherrywood desk and sat in the brown leather chair she'd been so proud to buy for herself when she first got this office. She rotated toward the window, gazing at the fountains below, and let her thoughts drift backward.

Gabriela had read that Justice Sotomayor once said that when she was at Princeton, she constantly looked over her shoulder and wondered if she measured up. Gabriela felt that perfectly described how she had felt—not only in college but through law school and well into her career at Parker & McEvoy, even up until this very moment.

She thought about the English professor at the University of Texas who told her she didn't write well enough to be a lawyer. She hired a writing tutor, practiced, and improved.

She thought about her first semester at Notre Dame Law School, where she was suddenly surrounded by wealthy classmates from elite private schools. She was the only Hispanic in her class. In her first semester, she overheard students saying that affirmative action was the only reason the law school admitted her. One student asked if she was "legal." Another student she dated told her she was "exotic." She grew accustomed to ignoring the stereotypes.

When Gabriela applied for the law review during her second year, the editors rejected her. That hurt, especially since firms and judges favored first-year lawyers who had been on the law review. She had wanted professors to tell her she was a good law student. She needed her litigation professor to tell her she could become a top trial lawyer like her father.

Her intense desire to excel in the courtroom led her to regularly read biographies of famous trial lawyers. Several months after her moot court trial, Gabriela asked the Notre Dame trial advocacy professor what he thought of her trial skills. "You have the empathy and heart of a woman," he said. "But you think and act like a man. You're a gladiator, and you learned from watching your father. You must gain confidence in yourself and believe you can win in the courtroom."

Gabriela's extra writing lessons paid off, and when she graduated, she was offered a clerkship with Judge Comstock. After her clerkship, Gabriela went back to the Valley to work with her father, Roberto. She tried more than a dozen jury cases in that year. Then, at Judge Comstock's request, Parker & McEvoy interviewed her for their Dallas office.

Chuck Green had a good memory. He was using that interview to push her. During it, he'd asked about her career goals. She had replied, "I've been raised to be an extremely humble person. My father told me never to act like I'm special just because I'm a lawyer."

"You didn't answer my question," Green had said.

"I'm uncomfortable telling you what I want to accomplish."

Green pushed her. "Don't be uncomfortable. Tell us."

Gabriela took a deep breath. "I want what you've achieved. That's why I'm here. I want to be a top Texas litigator and on the cover of *Texas Monthly*."

Green had smiled.

"Quite ambitious for someone from the Valley who has never set foot in a Dallas courtroom," one of the partners had replied, not bothering to hide his skepticism.

"Ambitious, sure," Gabriela had replied, raising her chin. "But I have more courtroom experience than any sixth-year lawyer in this office, and I'll work harder than any lawyer in this firm to get where I want to be."

Another partner in the interview said, "If you can match Chuck Green's billable hours, you may just achieve your goal."

Gabriela thought she had convinced them she was a valuable asset to the firm. With her trial experience and her history with Judge Comstock, she expected partners would assign her to high-profile cases. But that never happened. Year after year, those cases went, without exception, to the young male lawyers. Gabriela thought of leaving and starting her own law firm, focused on fighting for the civil rights of Mexican Americans. But she needed the salary Parker & McEvoy paid her to help support her family.

"Well," she said aloud to herself. "This isn't getting me anywhere." With a quick clap of her hands, she turned her chair back to her computer and did a quick search to learn more about Sparks Duval.

Gabriela was impressed by his story and rise to success. Duval had built his business from the ground up, starting from nothing. His father, Lucas, had been an alcoholic, gambler, and womanizer. He abandoned the family when Sparks was young after one of his oilfield projects failed, leaving them with no money and a heap of debt. Some said Lucas was why Sparks was so intent on becoming a billionaire.

Sparks Duval had started in the oil and gas business nearly forty years ago, driving tank trucks before he went to college. After graduating from Texas A&M with the help of local oilmen, he started his own company. Just a few months after he turned twenty-five, he had his first hit. That was the beginning of what would become the Duval Energy empire. He became a multibillionaire after revolutionizing the industry by being the first to successfully use hydraulic fracturing and horizontal drilling in massive shale oil deposits in Texas, Pennsylvania, and North Dakota.

She learned that Duval was a conservative Republican and proud of it. When President Obama took office, Duval refused to invest in any alternative energy projects. When Mexico's president and Congress opened the Mexican market, Duval Energy was one of the U.S. companies to submit proposals through José Lopez.

Gabriela also found plenty of negative blog posts about Duval Energy and Sparks himself. Environmentalists had posted numerous attacks focusing on the damage caused by fracking. Those posts were picked up by major newspapers and television outlets. There was even a National Public Radio segment called "Anatomy of a Careless Fracker."

She found many damning tweets, mostly linking to those environmental blogs, but one stood out among the rest. The handle *@nofrackingtx* seemed to have a particular grudge. When the grand jury indicted Duval, *@nofrackingtx* immediately went on the offensive:

TX fracker conman brought to justice … finally.
TX fracker paid to play.
TX fracker Sparks Duval indicted for payola in Mexico.

Sparks Duval used backhander to play in Mexico.
Sparks Duval caught in kickback scheme.
Sparks Duval illegal Mexico oil deal.

Gabriela sat back in her chair and stretched her arms over her head. Why would Donald Lawrence, one of the top energy lawyers in the U.S., leave his law firm to work for Sparks Duval? What was the real reason Duval hired him? And why would a lawyer like Lawrence risk going to jail and being disbarred?

It makes no sense. I'm missing something. Something big. Who risks their entire career for one deal? There has to be something dark at play. Why did Duval want to drill in Mexico, and what made Lawrence willing to risk everything?

Chapter 4

The next day, Gabriela got up early and put on her running gear and a waterproof windbreaker. She walked outside and saw that the streets were still wet, but it was not raining. She started running while listening to Selena's last concert from the Houston Astrodome.

After her shower, Gabriela surveyed her closet, looking for her most conservative business suit. She put on a white sleeveless blouse with a ruffled neckline and tassel tie closure, along with a dark gray skirt and heels. She picked up a pair of hoop earrings, then set them down and chose instead a pair of pearl-drop earrings.

At 9:30 a.m., Gabriela stepped into the elevator at the Renaissance Tower and pushed the button for the top floor. Nothing happened. She stepped out and walked to the security guard's desk.

"Excuse me, I'm Gabriela Sanchez. I'm here to see Mr. Duval. I couldn't get the elevator to go to his company's floor. Is there a special code or something?"

"I'm sorry, ma'am. You should have been told to check in with us. Can I see your driver's license or another photo ID?"

She should have known. Her own office building required guests to check in with security. Gabriela pulled out her driver's license and watched as the guard scanned it, then picked up the phone.

"We have a Ms. Gabriela Sanchez here. She says she has an appointment with Mr. Duval." After a pause, he said, "Okay, I'll give her a pass to your floor."

He looked at Gabriela and handed her the printed pass. "Keep this with you at all times. Now please come with me, and I'll get you to Mr. Duval's floor."

He walked with her to the elevator, waved his pass, and the top floor button lit up.

"Have a nice day, Ms. Sanchez."

Gabriela took another deep breath. She caught herself tapping her foot and humming Selena's *Si Una Vez*. She pictured meeting the billion-dollar man, and more than anything, she just wanted the interview to be over. She tried to look calm on the outside, but inside her heart was racing.

When she stepped out of the elevator, she looked around at the artwork. Each painting showed a different oilfield with a small plaque identifying the site.

"Each one tells a story of a Duval Energy project."

The fashionable Duval Energy receptionist had startled her.

"That's fascinating."

The receptionist stood and smiled. "You must be Gabriela Sanchez."

"Yes. Mr. Duval is expecting me."

"He's on a call right now and should be ready to see you in about fifteen minutes. Can I get you a cup of coffee?"

Gabriela looked at the nameplate in front of her—*Chantel Grant*. She considered coffee but knew caffeine would make her heart race even more.

"No thank you, Ms. Grant." She paused. "I have a question while we're waiting. How well did you know Don Lawrence?"

Chantel hesitated before answering. "I didn't know him well. Early on, he asked me to go for a drink, and I declined. He pretty much ignored me after that."

"Did you think he was hitting on you?" Gabriela kept her tone light. She didn't want Ms. Grant to think she was cross-examining her, but she wanted to learn as much as she could.

Grant crossed her arms. "He just liked attention. I don't know if it went beyond that, but he certainly thought he was a good-looking guy. He had the **swagger**: the hand-tailored Italian suits, the Porsche convertible."

Gabriela didn't push further. She was pleasantly surprised by how much Chantel had already shared.

"You should ask Christopher. He and Mr. Lawrence spent a lot of time together on the golf course and at bars."

"Thank you. So Christopher and Lawrence were friends?"

"Yes. Christopher isn't like his father. You'll understand when you meet him. He's a ladies' man. Be careful. Christopher wanted to hire Lawrence. His father didn't, but he gave him a chance."

Gabriela was surprised that Chantel was sharing so much with a stranger. She shook her head. "Christopher's married with two children."

Chantel grinned. "Being married has never gotten in his way."

"How long was Lawrence here?" Gabriela asked, changing the subject.

"I think he started in 2010."

Gabriela understood why Christopher might have wanted a friend, but was Sparks Duval also a ladies' man?

"Other than giving in to Christopher, what did Mr. Duval see in Lawrence?"

"That's easy. Lawrence was the first lawyer Mr. Duval met who truly understood the energy business. Plus, he was cocky and would do whatever it took to get a deal done. Mr. Duval's tough. Lawrence wasn't intimidated by him. That impressed him."

"I understand."

"One other thing you should know about Mr. Lawrence. Even though he and his wife didn't get along, he loved his two boys and daughter. He made time for them and even coached their soccer teams."

"That's interesting. Thank you for sharing that."

The phone on the reception desk rang, and Chantel answered. After a short exchange, she stood. "Mr. Duval is ready to see you. I'll take you now."

I want Ms. Grant to be my friend. She's the gatekeeper and my best source of information.

As the two women walked down the hall, Chantel stopped by an office with a large glass-topped desk.

"This was Mr. Lawrence's office."

Gabriela wanted to know more. "Did he clean it out when he left?"

"I think so. He left with several large boxes."

"How about his computer?"

"He took that with him, too."

Darn.

"Your company has a server, right?" Gabriela already knew the answer.

Chantel hesitated. "Yes."

"Is there any way Lawrence could have wiped his files from the server—or added documents—on his way out the door?"

"I don't know. I don't think he's a computer guru, so I doubt it."

"I'll want to talk to your IT department."

"His name is Craig Martin. I'll let Mr. Duval know you want to speak with him."

When they reached the corner suite with sweeping views of east, north, and west Dallas, Chantel said, "Gabriela, this is Vivian Dandridge, Mr. Duval's executive assistant. She'll take good care of you." Before Gabriela could reply, Chantel turned and walked away.

Vivian Dandridge stood. She was an elegant, dark-haired woman dressed in a tailored black suit. Gabriela guessed she was in her late forties. Vivian glanced at Gabriela, then looked away, biting her lip.

Gabriela knew why. Chuck Green had told her that Jason Daniels had threatened to prosecute Vivian Dandridge. No wonder she seemed uneasy.

"Ms. Sanchez, let me see if Mr. Duval is ready to meet with you now."

Gabriela waited for what seemed like five minutes before Vivian reappeared.

"Mr. Duval can see you now. Would you like anything to drink? Iced tea, coffee? I can also get our kitchen staff to fix you a latte."

"I'll have ice water," Gabriela said.

"Coming up. Go ahead, and I'll bring it to you."

You've got this, she reminded herself.

Gabriela walked into the largest office she had ever seen, with floor-to-ceiling windows. She stood, staring up Central Expressway almost to

635. Looking north, she saw the towers at the Galleria. Looking west, she saw where Texas Stadium once stood and the towers in Las Colinas. It felt as if Duval ruled over Dallas.

She turned and took in the manly furnishings: dark leather chairs, a massive desk, and heavy bookshelves. On one shelf were photos of Sparks Duval with several Republican presidents, including both Bushes and Donald Trump. On another were photos of Kyle Field and the Texas A&M engineering building bearing his name.

Like most A&M grads, Sparks Duval was first and foremost an Aggie football fan.

"Ms. Sanchez. Ms. Sanchez."

"Oh, I'm sorry, Mr. Duval. I was admiring the view and trying to pick out landmarks."

She walked over and shook his hand firmly, warmly, looking him straight in the eye.

"Yes, Ms. Sanchez, we love the view up here. Seeing how far I can see reminds me how far I've come."

Gabriela smiled, hoping he'd return it. His blue eyes widened as he looked her over from head to toe.

"This is my son, Christopher. I wanted him to meet you. Please, sit on the couch."

Gabriela looked at the two of them. Sparks moved behind his desk. His white, curly hair and tanned face made him look as if he'd just stepped off a movie set playing a Texas oilman. She noticed his diamond-studded Rolex and the Stetson hat resting on the corner of his desk.

Christopher leaned against the desk between her and his father. He looked a lot like Sparks, but polished, Mr. Ivy League. Tall, handsome, with short dark hair and two days of stubble that somehow suited him. He wore a navy sport coat, a blue shirt, gray slacks, and expensive alligator loafers with no socks.

Gabriela had Googled him. She knew he was one of the top amateur golfers in Texas. He'd grown up playing at the Dallas Country Club and, likely to spite his father, had played college golf at Oklahoma State. He'd tried three times to qualify for the PGA Tour but never made it through Q School. At thirty-three, he was still the reigning club champion at DCC.

Christopher smiled, and that put Gabriela on edge. She instantly understood why people liked him. He had the *it* factor. When their eyes met, he leaned toward her.

"Ms. Sanchez, thank you for coming. Chuck Green told me you're an overachiever and driven to succeed. I'm confident you can help us."

Gabriela felt awkward and cleared her throat. Green had never paid her a compliment in all the years she'd worked for him. "Thank you. That's nice of you to tell me."

"I'll leave the two of you to get to know each other." He placed his hand on his chest. "This is personal to me and to our employees who are afraid of losing their jobs. I'm confident you can convince Sparks to settle this case and put it all behind us."

As he stood, Christopher smiled again, a gleam in his blue eyes. He grabbed her hand with one hand and her shoulder with the other, moving closer. Gabriela froze. His touch was more than friendly.

"It was nice seeing you," he said, his eyes still locked on hers. "I hope I can get to know more about you."

Gabriela had trouble meeting his gaze without blushing. She suspected he used the same moves on every woman he met.

Sparks Duval walked out with Christopher. To calm herself, Gabriela looked out the windows again, marveling at the panoramic view.

When Sparks returned, he said, "I enjoyed the view from here more when I could look west and see Texas Stadium."

Gabriela looked that direction.

"Now that the new stadium is in Arlington, I can't see it. I told Jerry I was upset he didn't build it in Irving. Ms. Sanchez, let's sit down and chat. Would you like more water?"

"Yes, thank you."

For a minute, they sat in silence. Gabriela caught the woody scent of his cologne. When the water arrived, Duval began.

"Christopher wants us to settle with the government to save the company. He's also concerned about our employees, especially Vivian. They browbeat her in front of the grand jury."

"I'm sure Chuck will want to interview Vivian and get the full story."

41

"It might go better if you interview her."

"Okay. With all that's at stake, why aren't you willing to settle with the government?"

"I'm more interested in saving my reputation than the company." He pounded his fist on the desk, and Gabriela jumped. "I feel for our employees, especially Vivian, but I'll be damned if I admit I did anything wrong."

"Yes, sir. I understand why Christopher wants to settle. Getting this behind you is important for his future. I also understand why you don't want to admit guilt."

Duval stood and paced the room. Finally, he said, "I want you to help Chuck defend me."

She wondered what role he envisioned for her. "Mr. Duval, I'm excited, but why do you want me to help Chuck defend you?"

"Because I believe the jurors will like you."

Gabriela crossed her arms. "Mr. Duval, I won't be window dressing. I want to have an active role in defending you."

"No need to be upset," Duval replied. "I like your honesty. You won't be window dressing. I promise."

"Chuck told me you asked to interview me after seeing my photo in *D Magazine*. That's not a good reason to want me on your defense team."

Before Duval could respond, Vivian stepped in.

"I'm sorry, Mr. Duval, you have an important phone call you need to take."

Gabriela stood to leave, but Duval motioned for her to stay.

"I'll take the call next door."

Five minutes later, he returned. Gabriela looked for clues in his expression. His furrowed brow suggested bad news.

He exhaled and forced a smile. "I had to take that call. We're negotiating a contract. Christopher wanted my approval. Where were we?"

"I told you that seeing my *D Magazine* photo wasn't a good reason to want me on your team."

"*D Magazine* is where I first learned about you. Afterward, I did some research and discovered you're an experienced trial lawyer, and Chuck told me you work harder than anyone in the firm. I wanted to meet you."

Chuck Green said that about me? Or is Duval making it up?

Gabriela thought about the phone call and made a note to find out why Christopher needed his father's approval for a U.S. deal but hadn't shared the details of their first deal in Mexico.

She was startled by Duval's voice. "You've already made a splendid first impression. Christopher gave you his seal of approval."

Gabriela smiled, uncertain what to say. "He did?"

"Yes. He liked you. In 2017, some jurors will take pride in knocking Chuck Green off his pedestal as Texas's top trial lawyer. You can convert those jurors."

"Have you ever visited the Mexico site?"

"No. I stayed away. Don Lawrence and Christopher handled our work there."

"Has it been profitable?"

"It's been a pain. We've had labor problems, and the cartels steal the gas."

"You wish you hadn't agreed to drill in Mexico?"

"You know the answer."

"What more do you want to know about me?"

"I know more about you than you think."

"You do?"

"Yes. You're like me. Nothing ever came easy for you."

How does he know that?

"That's true."

"You believe you have something to prove because you grew up in the Rio Grande Valley, and people have made you feel you'll never be a successful lawyer in Dallas. I saw where you once said you were too light-skinned in the Valley and too brown-skinned in North Texas."

Where did he read the light-skinned, brown-skinned comment? I only told a handful of people, and they all lived in the Valley.

Gabriela grinned. "You're right. Since I was a little girl, I've worked hard to prove myself."

She started laughing.

"Why are you laughing?" Duval asked.

"Since I joined Parker & McEvoy, I've been mistaken for a secretary, court reporter, interpreter, even the cleaning lady. I have more to prove because Dallas lawyers stereotype Hispanic women."

"I understand. The seasoned lawyers in Dallas underestimate you. I faced the same thing when I started."

"Thank you, but did you want to know anything else about me?"

"No. I don't have time. I'm already confident you have the physical, mental, and emotional strength to help Chuck Green get me through this ordeal. That's all I need to know."

"Mr. Duval, there's one more thing we need to discuss."

"What's that?"

"You're one of President Trump's biggest supporters. I can't stand him. He's vulgar, he hates immigrants, and he's hurt the immigrant children I defend. I thought you should know we couldn't be further apart politically."

"Ms. Sanchez, President Obama was no friend of immigrant children either. You're one of my lawyers. I expect you to put politics aside. Are you capable of doing that?"

"Yes, sir."

He stood. "I have other meetings scheduled today. I'm confident you'll do a good job. I'll have Christopher tell Chuck I want you on my defense team."

When they reached the reception area, Sparks said, "Did you meet Chantel when you came in?"

"Yes. Ms. Grant took great care of me."

"I guess you heard about Chantel's movie career."

"No, she didn't tell me."

"Chantel played a receptionist when they brought back the TV show *Dallas*."

"Chantel, please send me a link to your TV debut. I want to watch it. *gsanchez@parkermcevoy.com*," Gabriela said.

Gabriela saw Chantel smiling, her computer already open to YouTube. Gabriela bet she wouldn't be the first to receive the video.

She walked out of the office uneasy about her meeting with Duval. Supposedly, he'd wanted to interview her, but he'd spent little time asking questions. He'd been impatient and controlling. She already knew Sparks Duval would be a difficult client, and worse if he took the stand.

Chapter 5

Sparks Duval knew his son Christopher wanted to settle the case with the government. He questioned whether Christopher had known that José Lopez planned to use part of the thirty percent commission Duval Energy had paid him to bribe PetroMex officials. When he asked, Christopher denied having any knowledge, and his father believed him.

When Duval returned to his office, Christopher was waiting.

"What did you think of her?" Sparks asked.

"She's stunning. She looks like Eva Mendes."

"Who?"

"Eva Mendes. She's a well-known Latina actress. Have Vivian do a Google search and look at the images. Gabriela looks like her."

Duval threw his hands in the air. "Son, I wasn't asking you about her looks. I want to know if you think Sanchez is the right lawyer to help Chuck Green defend me."

Christopher shook his head. "She's an ambitious woman. She cares about her success. For that reason, I doubt she's interested in settling the case and saving our company."

Duval stepped closer and lowered his voice. "Son, that's what makes me want her on our defense team. It doesn't matter how much she cares about me. What matters is how badly she wants to win my case."

Christopher took a step back. "Dad, I've done some research. Sanchez is a fine lawyer, and she seems to be a fine person. I want her to help Chuck, but only if you'll let them settle the case."

Duval scowled. "I've told you I'm not pleading guilty. Sanchez has more trial experience than Daniels, and she needs for us to win more than Chuck Green does."

"That may be true, but Daniels can crush you and our company. He has the weight and resources of the entire U.S. government on his side. Your freedom and the future of our company are at stake. We can settle and save both."

Duval stared at his son. "If I plead guilty, I'll destroy the reputation I've spent a lifetime building. I'm not doing that. I never wanted to do the PetroMex deal. I let you and Don talk me into it."

"Dad, that's nonsense. You agreed that if American Oil wanted to be in Mexico, we should be there too. So don't put this on me."

"You weren't indicted. I'm the one on trial, and I'm the one who'll go to jail if I'm convicted. I'm the one who'll lose my reputation forever if I plead guilty. I get to decide whether to go to trial or not. End of discussion."

"Like you always say, it's your company, Pop."

Christopher started toward the door.

"Son."

"What?"

"Call Sanchez and tell her she passed the test. Then call Chuck Green. Tell him I want Sanchez to help defend me."

Christopher sauntered out of his father's office. On the way to his own, he thought about Gabriela Sanchez. Christopher believed she was a good lawyer, but his thoughts turned to her looks. She had Eva Mendes's soft chocolate-brown eyes, the small mole on her cheek, and stunning curves. She deserved to be named by *D Magazine* as one of the "Top Ten Most Beautiful Women in Dallas."

At his desk, Christopher found her business card and dialed her direct number. He was surprised when she answered, "Gabriela Sanchez."

"Sanchez, you passed the test. Sparks wants you on the team."

He heard her breathing. "Thank you," she said, her voice bright with excitement.

"I liked how you looked today. Has anyone told you that you look like Eva Mendes?"

He heard her laughing. "You don't know much about Hispanic women. The only thing I share with Eva Mendes is dark hair and a mole on my cheek."

"That's not true. You're both very attractive."

"You're digging a deeper hole for yourself."

"Okay, Sanchez," he said with a laugh. "I give. May I call you by your last name? It's a habit that's hard to break."

"Sure."

"Christopher," she said after a pause. "May I call you Christopher?"

He laughed again. "Sure."

"Get your mind off what I look like and focus on how I can help you and your father."

"Okay, Sanchez. I'm counting on your help to convince my father to settle the case so we can save the company. I have great confidence in your ability to do that."

"I'll do my best. And if I can't convince him, I'll work till I drop to help Chuck Green defend him."

After a pause, Christopher said, "Sanchez, your one job is to convince him. I don't care how you do it. Just do it."

Chapter 6

Chuck Green sat in his office reviewing the depositions in a civil case he was defending. It was the part of his practice he hated the most. Other trial lawyers delegated deposition review to younger lawyers. Chuck Green had never done that. He believed a young lawyer might miss something he could use in cross-examination during trial. So, he painstakingly studied transcripts, looking for a mistake or an opening the deponent had made.

As he focused on a transcript page, his phone rang. Green saw Christopher Duval's name.

"Chuck, Gabriela made a great first impression. She's hot. I liked her."

Green had expected Christopher to make a comment about Gabriela's looks. "What about your dad?"

"He liked her. He thought she had a chip on her shoulder and something to prove. He liked that."

"I knew the two of you would be impressed."

"We were, for different reasons. Sparks is delusional. He thinks if an attractive Latina woman sits next to him, the jury will see him differently. Did you tell him you could successfully defend him?"

"No, I told your father about the recent trials of top CEOs. Hotshot lawyers represented each CEO, and the jury found most of them guilty."

"He believes that somehow a Dallas jury will reach a different result, in part, because you have an attractive woman sitting next to you?"

"Gabriela is more than just an attractive lawyer. I told your father that I'd seen her in court. She's one of our top young lawyers and has the most trial experience. Before she joined us, she tried dozens of cases with her father, Roberto. She's a quick read and has an unmatched memory for details. Plus, she clerked for Judge Comstock."

"I concede all that. But I don't want to roll the dice in a trial. Why did the government indict the company? I thought they only went after individuals."

"You've likely answered your question. The Department of Justice believes indicting the company will force your father to plead guilty to save Duval Energy and you."

"He hasn't pleaded guilty and says he won't. If the DOJ destroys our company, our employees will all be out of a job."

Chuck Green believed Christopher genuinely cared about the Duval Energy employees, but he also suspected Christopher wanted to keep up his lifestyle after his wife got finished with him in their divorce.

"I understand, Christopher," Chuck said. "I've told your father he'll save money if he settles the case. I even argued he should make sure your employees have a place to work. I fear he's stubborn and has made up his mind."

There was a long silence on the other end of the phone.

"Christopher, are you still there?"

"Yes, Chuck. I've begged him to retire, spend time with his grandchildren, and let me run the company."

"Christopher, Sparks isn't the kind to retire. He'd be bored in a week."

"Maybe so."

After he hung up, Chuck Green heard a knock on his door.

"Come in."

Gabriela came in and made a thumbs-up sign.

"I'm excited. This opportunity could change my career forever. Thank you."

That was not what Chuck Green wanted to hear. He rose from his seat and walked around his desk. "Get this straight. Stop focusing on your career and start focusing on how we can take care of our client. We need to convince Sparks Duval to settle with the government. His freedom and company are at stake here."

"I told Christopher I would do my best to convince his father to settle with the government. But Sparks Duval doesn't want to settle. He contends he's done nothing wrong. He was against the PetroMex deal and gave in only after the company lawyer gave it his seal of approval."

"Innocent executives plead guilty or no contest every day to stay in the game. Sparks Duval will save money if he settles his case with the government, and his company will survive."

"He said he will not settle with the government, and I believe we have to prepare to defend him," Gabriela said.

"Sparks Duval would settle if Daniels didn't demand he plead guilty. He says he's innocent, and pleading guilty would ruin him."

"We need to meet with Jason Daniels and convince him to settle without having Duval plead guilty."

"Would Daniels let the company plead guilty and pay a fine?"

"Daniels doesn't want to lose this case. The question is whether the company paying a large fine is a big enough scalp for him to go back to DC a winner. I want you to collect a list of all the cases the government has lost, and let's convince Daniels that he could easily lose."

"When do you need it?"

"Sunday. I want to call Daniels first thing on Monday."

"I'll prepare a memo for you by Sunday." She already knew she'd cancel her weekend plans. Green expected perfection, and she wasn't about to give him any reason to doubt her work ethic.

On Sunday, Chuck Green was up before his wife, Charlotte. Over coffee, he began reading *The Dallas Morning News*. He had expected to see a feature story on Sparks Duval and was pleased when he found none.

Before he finished the first section, it was time to drive Charlotte to the First Baptist Church. She was a faithful member and major contributor. Green rarely went to church and had never let his Baptist upbringing get in the way of a Maker's Mark over ice.

After church, Green took Charlotte to brunch at the country club. After dropping her off at home, he went to the office, expecting to find Sanchez's memo on his desk.

It wasn't there. He picked up the telephone and called Gabriela's cell number. When she didn't answer, he left a heated voicemail demanding that she call him immediately. Green was angry with Sanchez, and he wanted to make sure she knew it.

Finally, at 7:00 p.m., Sanchez sent an email and attached her memo with a review of all the cases the government had lost. He read her analysis of each case and thought she had made a point that might carry the day.

Chuck,

Attached is a summary of recent DOJ losses and a draft motion to dismiss the case against Duval, along with a supporting brief. The PetroMex officials were not government officials, so we have grounds to challenge jurisdiction.

I've also attached a motion to suppress Don Lawrence's video conversation with Sparks Duval, based on attorney-client privilege. While I know Judge Comstock will likely deny the motion, it's important to plant the seed now to preserve the issue for trial.

—Gabriela

He picked up the phone and called Gabriela again. This time she answered.

"Sanchez?"

"Yes, sir."

"Did you get my voicemail?"

"No, I put my phone on Do Not Disturb while I was working on your assignment. I just changed the setting."

"I want you to come to my office, pronto. We need to talk."

Twenty minutes later, Gabriela was standing in front of Chuck Green's desk.

"Why did you prepare a motion to dismiss that Judge Comstock will not grant us?" he asked.

"Chuck, I know Judge Comstock. He won't throw out the case now, but at trial, he'll consider it when he instructs the jury or reviews our motion to dismiss after the prosecution rests."

"Damn it, Sanchez. How many times do I have to tell you we don't want to go to trial? I've busted my behind to convince Jason Daniels to consider a deferred prosecution agreement with the company and Duval. It's been hard because American Oil agreed to a deferred prosecution immediately after the government found the Lopez accounts. If we file your motion,

"Chuck, Sparks Duval doesn't want to settle. He told me that over and over. He claims he's innocent and expects us to defend him. You'll see in my memo that the government doesn't have a good track record when the defendant refuses to settle."

Green didn't look up from the brief she had written. "I know that, but this is only the second time the government has indicted both the individual and his company. It's also the first time the government has the company's lawyer testifying against both."

"Have you ever considered Lawrence might be lying to avoid going to prison?"

Green finally looked up at her. "Why would a lawyer lie and cop a plea, knowing he'll be disbarred? That makes no sense."

"Lawrence doesn't need to practice law. He has enough money to retire. Duval says he's lying about Duval's involvement in the deal. He thinks Lawrence may not have known what Lopez was doing with his commission and that Daniels put pressure on him the same way he did with Christopher and the other Duval employees."

Green grimaced. "Does Duval think Lawrence will just confess on the stand like a *Perry Mason* episode?"

Gabriela laughed.

"Duval will change his mind when he fully understands his lawyer could send him to jail and put his company out of business."

"Chuck," Gabriela replied. He's more afraid of losing his company because of oil prices than he is of losing this case. You're the master at preparing a case. Shouldn't we get ready to try it, even if we want to settle?"

"Sure, I'll be prepared if Duval doesn't wise up. But we can't file a motion that will cut off negotiations with the government. I want you to set up one last meeting with Daniels to see if we can settle."

"Yes, sir."

Chuck Green calmed down a bit. He didn't know what to make of Sanchez.

"Sanchez, you don't have the experience in white collar criminal cases yet to really understand the problem."

Gabriela resisted the urge to argue. She had tried more than a dozen cases in The Valley. But, he was right. None if them were like this one.

"What problem?"

"The most dangerous client is a white-collar defendant who believes he has to go to court to save his reputation. Juries don't presume those defendants are innocent. They presume they must have broken some law to become rich. That's how they'll view Sparks Duval."

Chapter 7

Jason Daniels loved coming to Dallas. He told himself it was for the cases, but it was really for the women. Dallas women tried harder, whether in heels or cowboy boots. They knew how to make an impression, and he liked that. On most trips, he spent one night in a country-music bar and another in an upscale lounge, watching for his next conquest.

At six foot five, with curly brown hair and a gym-built frame, Daniels drew attention wherever he went. He played basketball with younger players just to prove he could still beat them. He hated to lose, and everyone who played him knew it.

Now he sat in first class on an American Airlines flight from Washington National to DFW, finishing his first drink. The government did not pay for first-class tickets, but Daniels, raised in privilege, had never flown coach in his life.

He smiled, picturing himself rubbing Chuck Green's face in defeat once Sparks Duval pled guilty. Green, the flattop, the horn-rimmed glasses, had beaten him once in Dallas. This trip was payback. He could already taste the victory, that delicious moment when power crushed the arrogant defense lawyer and his rich client.

"Mr. Daniels, you look like you're having a great day. May I bring you another drink?"

He looked up at the flight attendant, her hand on his arm. He placed his hand lightly over hers. "Yes. Bring me another before dinner."

As she walked away, he stood and headed toward the lavatory, mind spinning again on Duval. He had been in Dallas when FBI agents cuffed the billionaire and marched him past cameras. The national press loved it, and Daniels had helped by feeding liberal bloggers dirt, knowing mainstream reporters would repeat anything once it went viral.

He was flying back now to meet Green. *Fuck you, Chuck Green.* He grinned at the thought. *I've got your client by the short hairs, and you'll pay to make it stop.*

Daniels was ahead of every defense lawyer on both the Duval case in Dallas and the Farmer case in Houston, thanks to his partnership with the FBI from day one. He had coached witnesses, shaped grand-jury testimony, and nudged Special Agent Thomas Barnes to "clarify" that Christopher Duval admitted his father did not want to know what José Lopez did with his thirty-percent commission. That was not what Christopher had said, but it was close enough, and no one would ever check.

He had been surprised when Green demanded a speedy trial. White-collar defense lawyers delayed everything, hoping witnesses vanished or forgot. *Fine,* Daniels thought. *If Green wants fast, I'll bury him in paper until he drowns.*

The flight attendant returned with his drink. He studied her face, saw the wedding band, and turned away. "No, I'm fine." He lifted the glass and leaned back, picturing the upcoming meeting.

He had bullied every Duval Energy employee who touched the PetroMex contract. Most cracked under pressure. Vivian Dandridge, Duval's executive assistant, was his favorite target. Daniels was sure she and Duval were lovers. How else could she earn two hundred fifty thousand dollars a year after starting at sixty-five? He would make the jury see what he saw, another rich man buying silence.

He had never prosecuted a foreign-bribery case, but that did not stop him from calling himself an expert. Twenty-three FCPA settlements, two-point-seven billion dollars recovered. The press loved his "tireless efforts." The deputy attorney general had even turned him into a poster boy for corporate accountability. Daniels believed every word of it.

From the moment he got the file, he was convinced Sparks Duval was guilty. The man had hired López to bribe PetroMex officials, either knowingly or by willful blindness. It made no difference. Daniels could win on either theory.

He remembered his first meeting with his boss, Sandra Fenton.

"You know, Duval's an enemy of the environment and therefore an enemy of the country," she had said. "Indict him and his company before President Trump takes office. No settlement unless Duval pleads guilty."

He had asked, "What about American Energy?"

"Public company. Big donors. Let them pay a fine and give you Farmer."

Fine with him. American Energy had folded quickly, settling for thirty-four million. He'd gladly drop that pursuit, because he knew securing a guilty verdict in the Duval case would make him famous, and earn him over one million dollars at a top D.C. or New York law firm.

When the grand jury returned its indictment, Daniels made sure the *Wall Street Journal* got a quote from a "former DOJ insider," his friend, declaring that Justice never indicted a man like Duval unless conviction was certain. The story spread everywhere. Daniels retweeted it from burner accounts to make it trend.

Later, to protect himself, he hedged with Fenton. "These cases are hard to prosecute."
She lifted her chin. "If they were easy, we would not need you. Get convictions. Do whatever it takes, and don't leave a trail that bites your ass."

Do whatever it takes. He liked the sound of that.

Still, losing again to Chuck Green would be ruinous. His Harvard classmates already whispered about the last trial he lost in Texas. A second failure and he could forget the two-million-dollar offers waiting at white-shoe firms.

The weak link was Duval's general counsel, Don Lawrence. The man was a drunk, a woman-chaser, and the government's reluctant star witness. Caught hiding two million in untaxed income from López, he had first denied knowing about bribes, denied even receiving the bonus. He had said Duval opposed doing business in Mexico and demanded assurance there was no corruption. Daniels made sure those exculpatory statements never appeared in the FBI's reports.

Then there was that damned email: *Don, you know I've been against this deal… I want you to assure me there are no legal problems, no corruption.*

It read like innocence, and Daniels could not have that. He had leaned on Lawrence hard, twisting every hesitation into guilt.
"Mr. Lawrence, you're lying. We can put you away so long you won't see your kids graduate. Tell the truth. Duval sent that email to cover his ass."
Lawrence's voice had broken. "That might be true."
"Then it better be your testimony."

Daniels never trusted him. Barnes did not either. Lawrence's racy texts had disgusted the straight-arrow agent. When Daniels ordered Barnes to "build rapport," Barnes hung up. Daniels did not forget the insult.

He had told Barnes to make Lawrence wear a wire. When Lawrence balked, the agent threatened him with twenty years. Daniels waited for the confession that would end Duval, but it never came. Duval had been too smart or maybe just too careful.

There were other problems. The money López used for bribes came from American Energy, not Duval Energy. Daniels knew it, and he knew it did not matter. Guilt was perception. If Duval settled, no one would ever see the difference.

He had even ordered the FBI to prepare a chart showing payments from both companies without distinguishing which money went where. It looked damning, and that was what counted.

If the defense ever uncovered the truth, he could spin it. Until then, he would keep leaking to the media and turning up the heat. He did not need a conviction, only Duval's surrender. A guilty plea would be as good as gold.

And if Duval refused? Daniels smiled at the thought. Then he would crush his own witness, Don Lawrence, on the stand. Someone always broke first.

He finished his drink and stared out the window as the plane began its descent over North Texas. Dallas shimmered in the distance. He could already the headlines, the cameras, the smug Texas lawyer silenced.

Let's see how Chuck Green and his rising-star associate handle me this time.

Chapter 8

How did José Lopez become the major dealmaker in Mexico? Gabriela started digging to find out.

She searched José Lopez's name on Google and discovered he was born in Monterrey, moved to McAllen at eight, and became a naturalized citizen. He maintained dual citizenship. She found photos of Lopez with Mexican presidents, governors, actors, and actresses. He knew the movers and shakers throughout Mexico, and that made him invaluable for any U.S. company wanting to do business there. A business article in Spanish claimed Lopez was worth fifty million dollars.

When U.S. investment in Mexico surged in the 1990s after NAFTA, the Mexican economy took off and Lopez was right in the middle of the boom. But how had he gotten there?

Gabriela discovered Lopez had married the daughter of a former PetroMex CEO. That gave him access no one could match. Even after their divorce, he kept his influential position. He could tell any U.S. company he had tight connections at PetroMex and knew how they planned to award oil and gas contracts.

Companies throughout Latin America went to Lopez when they wanted to do business with PetroMex. The U.S. firms followed suit. Gabriela found several photos of Lopez. He was good-looking, with dark curly hair, a mustache, and a neatly trimmed beard. In the photos he was always smiling.

Her father, Roberto, knew José Lopez. He had represented Lopez in a contract dispute in McAllen, and the two had stayed in touch ever since. Gabriela raced to tell Chuck Green.

She opened his door without knocking and saw Green hang up the phone. "Chuck, I have great news about José Lopez."

Green did not look happy. "You are late. We do not have time for that. We have an appointment to meet Jason Daniels, the DOJ lawyer from Washington. He is only in town for a few days. We need to leave now."

"But I have something important to tell you before we go."

Green checked his watch. "No, Sanchez. It will not impact our discussion with Jason Daniels."

She blurted it out. "My father knows José Lopez."

Green stood and waved a dismissive hand as he headed for the door. "That is great, but it will not help us get the case settled today."

It was humid, so Green had a staffer drive them six blocks to the Earle Cabell Federal Building and wait for a text when they were ready to return. The young man's eyes widened when he saw Green's BMW 750iL.

At the courthouse, Green put on his clip-on sunglasses as he stepped from the car. Inside the lobby, they put their briefcases on the X-ray belt. The metal detector buzzed loudly when Gabriela walked through and a female U.S. marshal gave her a pat-down.

"Are you wearing an underwire bra?" the marshal asked.

"What?" Gabriela stared in disbelief.

"You heard me. Are you wearing an underwire bra?" Now everyone in the lobby knew about her problem.

"Yes."

"Then I recommend you go to the ladies' room, remove it, and walk through the detector again."

Gabriela smiled to avoid a scene. The marshal pointed to the restroom. Green walked ahead, glanced back, and shook his head.

Two minutes later Gabriela reappeared with the bra in her purse and passed through the detector. She smiled and gave the marshal a thumbs up.

When the elevator opened on the third floor, Gabriela looked at her watch. It was 10:29 and their appointment was at 10:30. She decided she would rather be late than meet Jason Daniels braless. She told Chuck she needed to go to the ladies' room again.

"We cannot take the time now. I told Daniels we would be here at 10:30," he said. "I cannot wait for you."

"Chuck, I really need to go."

"Okay, but I am going in so we are on time. I do not want to lose this last chance to convince Daniels to settle."

Not wanting to be left behind, Gabriela walked into the U.S. Attorney's office with her bra still in her purse..

The receptionist escorted them into a small conference room. A man who looked to be in his early forties sat with a younger woman across from him.

"Gabby, glad you can join us. I'm Jason Daniels, and this is AUSA Melinda Swanson,"

Gabriela glared. No one had ever called her Gabby. She looked at Swanson, who was smiling. "I've never seen you in federal court before."

"That takes me by surprise," Gabriela said. "I clerked for Judge Comstock in 2008."

"Maybe I did appear in his court," Daniels said, "but I do not remember you."

"Let's get down to business," Daniels said. "I understand your client wants to make an offer. Since we have an open-and-shut case, we want a lot of money, a deferred prosecution agreement for the company, and a guilty plea from Duval."

Green looked at Daniels. "Isn't that the same thing you told me the last time you prosecuted a case against one of my clients?"

Daniels swatted the air. "We persuaded jurors to convict your client until you confused them so much that they could not tell up from down. I will not let you do that again."

Gabriela decided to test him. "Mr. Daniels, as much as you think your case against Sparks Duval is a sure thing, you do not want to try this case."

Daniels smiled condescendingly. "I did not quite hear you. Is that your Spanish accent? Does it surface when you make a point you do not believe? If so, I will remember that."

Gabriela felt a flush of embarrassment and anger. Daniels laughed. "I'll be able to tell each time you are blowing smoke."

"Mr. Daniels, the government has a terrible track record in these bribery cases. That is not blowing smoke. It is a fact."

He sneered. "Señorita, I did not prosecute those cases, and none of them had the defendant on video. I've been told you and your father have never won a bribery case in the Rio Grande Valley. Is that because your politician clients were guilty, or because you and your father are not very good lawyers?"

Gabriela smiled. "We are not in the Rio Grande Valley. Aren't you the lawyer who came to Dallas with a swagger and got his rear end handed to him by Chuck Green?"

Daniels tightened. Green brushed her wrist and muttered, "Damn."

Daniels scowled. "That's bullshit. I do not have much time. Tell me what you want to offer."

"Duval is willing to settle for the company, but he is innocent and he will not plead guilty."

"If he is innocent, why settle the company?"

Gabriela laughed. "You know why. You made sure the grand jury indicted the company. He does not want his company to become the next Arthur Andersen."

"Ms. Rising Star, I cannot do that. Read this." Daniels tossed a memo across the table dated September 9, 2015, from the deputy attorney general. The title read "Individual Accountability for Corporate Wrongdoing"

On the first page she read, "The most effective way to combat corporate misconduct is seeking accountability from the individuals who perpetuated the wrongdoing." Gabriela read the first directive: "To be eligible for cooperation credit, corporations must provide to the Department all relevant facts about individuals involved in miscondu\\

She frowned. The memo prevented Daniels from settling with Duval Energy unless Sparks Duval pleaded guilty.

"Needless to say, we are not willing to settle with Duval Energy without Duval admitting he is guilty. Do you see why?" Daniels asked.

Before she could answer, Green said, "Gabriela, let me talk to Mr. Daniels just the two of us."

Why is Green dismissing me from the meeting? Gabriela thought. She rose with Melinda Swanson and left the room. Neither spoke.

"May I get you anything?" the receptionist asked.

"No. I just need to go down the hall. I'll be right back."

When Gabriela returned with her underwire bra back on, she opened her briefcase and found her phone missing as she expected. She took out her iPad. "Is there a guest login?" she asked the receptionist, who handed her a sheet.

She logged in and sent a quick text to Green about her phone. She made an internet search of Jason Daniels and found he was not on LinkedIn, Facebook, or other social media. Gabriela wondered what that meant.

When Green and Daniels were alone, Daniels said, "Your new assistant is quite sexy and exotic. Even her accent is sexy."

"What did you just say?" Gabriela asked when she returned.

"Your rising star is exotic, and I like the slight accent. Is that why you selected her to assist with Duval's defense?"

Green cringed. "Mr. Daniels, that comment is sexist, racist, and demeaning."

"Do not leave now. I was kidding," Daniels said.

Green got back into his seat. "If you insist. Convince me why we should settle with Duval."

"That's simple. You do not want to try this case."

"What makes you say that?"

"For one, you are on my turf. Judges and juries in Dallas are not fond of liberal, Ivy League lawyers from Washington. You do not fit in here."

"I do not need to fit in to convict your client," Daniels snapped.

"You think a Dallas jury will convict a man who has given so much to this city?" Green asked.

"You mean the man who has raped the land and air in Texas, Oklahoma, Pennsylvania, and North Dakota and likely put toxins in their drinking water? The man who donates millions to right-wing candidates who only help their rich friends? Duval is not a paragon of virtue. He is a pariah."

"That is where you will get in trouble," Green said. "The jury will hate you for attacking a hometown hero. People here love the rags-to-riches story, and they hate the Washington establishment."

"Is that what Enron lawyers thought when the Justice Department came down to Texas to put their clients in jail? Times have changed. With Californians and New Yorkers moving here, jurors might relish the idea of jailing the president's friend."

"There you go again. Do not compare Enron and Duval Energy. Enron's collapse harmed almost everyone in Houston. Duval Energy did not hurt a single Dallas resident. If anything, people here may have benefited."

Daniels shook his head. Green cut him off. "Enough. How about Duval Energy pays a significant fine and both the company and Sparks Duval enter a deferred prosecution agreement?"

"Green, you know we do not offer deferred prosecution agreements to individuals. My boss has been clear: we focus on individuals, and

Sparks Duval is a prime example. If you want the company to settle, Duval must plead guilty."

"He is not going to do that."

"He should, to save his company. If he refuses, we are wasting our time."

Green thought a moment. "Suppose Christopher Duval pleads guilty, and his father walks away. Would your boss accept that?"

"We may indict Christopher if his father refuses. Is Christopher guilty?"

"Does it matter?"

"Yes. If Christopher is guilty, the company is guilty."

"I am not his lawyer, and his lawyer says he is not guilty. Like Sparks, Christopher relied on Don Lawrence's legal advice. He did not know company money Lawrence paid Lopez would end up in accounts and gifts for PetroMex officials."

"Leaving aside whether he is lying, why would he consider pleading guilty?"

"He is a pragmatist. He cares more about the company surviving than about avoiding a felony."

"There is no way my boss will approve that. If you want to take a fifteen-minute break to get coffee with Ms. Sanchez, I'll call and find out."

After an hour, Green and Daniels returned to the conference room.

Daniels spoke first. "Sorry to keep you waiting, Ms. Rising Star. We had important business. Don't be so feisty and maybe next time Chuck will let you sit at the adult table."

Gabriela stared at Green. He did not respond. She bit her lip.

She stopped him as he rose. "I think my cell phone fell out of my briefcase. Let me go back and get it."

"We can get it when we go back to meet Daniels. Let's get some coffee."

"Why?"

"I will tell you when we are alone."

Gabriela hoped they would not have to leave the building to get coffee so she would not have to go through security again without a bra. No such luck.

"Chuck, I do not need more coffee. Let's find a quiet place outside a courtroom where we can talk privately."

He smiled. "You win."

Two minutes later they sat side by side on a bench outside a courtroom.

"I suggested an idea to Daniels. He is calling his boss to see if it will fly."

"What did you suggest?"

"That Christopher pleads guilty, Sparks walks away, and the company pays a fine."

"What?"

"I wanted to see if Daniels would take the proposal to his bosses. He did. That tells me he is afraid of trying the case. I am sure his boss in Washington will not go for it."

"I still wonder why they did not indict Christopher."

"Maybe Daniels wants a second bite at the apple if the first one does not go as planned."

"You look upset. What's the frown about?"

"Are you serious? You cannot imagine why I would be upset?"

"No."

"Chuck, a great trial lawyer like you cannot be that out of touch. Why did you excuse me from the meeting? You humiliated me."

Green leaned in and whispered, "You should have kept your damn mouth shut. What you said infuriated Daniels. I needed you out so I could work on him without you being a foil. Let's drop it."

"What did you say to him?"

"I told him he was not welcome in Texas, and we would kick his ass if he forced us to trial. Let's get back to his office."

"Do I get to sit at the adult table this time?"

"As long as you keep your mouth shut," Green said, flushed.

Gabriela smiled.

"Why are you smiling?"

"It has been that kind of day. Remember what I wanted to tell you before Daniels?"

"You said your father knows Lopez."

"That was not all."

"What else?"

"I found a photo of José Lopez and Don Lawrence taken before the Duval-PetroMex deal at an oil and gas reception. They were close during the time Lawrence persuaded Duval to enter Mexico and pay Lopez."

Green raised his eyebrows. "That will taint Lawrence's testimony."

"There is one problem."

"What is that?"

"Christopher is also in the photo."

When they returned to the conference room, Gabriela found her phone under the chair where she had set her briefcase. She picked it up, turned off the recording, put it away, and zipped her briefcase.

"Chuck, it is okay for the Rising Star to sit with us now?" Daniels asked.

"Yes, Mr. Ivy League man. We got our business done while Gabriela was gone."

Daniels glared.

"Well, Chuck, I have bad news. Washington does not give a rat's ass about Christopher Duval. He could plead guilty and offer to go to jail for five years and they still would not agree to let his father go."

"Okay, what do you have to offer?"

"DC says we can offer a Deferred Prosecution Agreement for the company."

"What are the terms?" Green asked. "I assume Duval must cooperate, the company must pay a large fine, and it must reform. What else?"

Daniels looked down. "I am happy you recognize we want more."

He paused for effect. Gabriela felt the theatrics. Finally, he said with a contemptuous smile, "Sparks Duval must plead guilty to conspiring to pay bribes to a foreign official in violation of the FCPA, serve twelve months in prison, and step down and leave the company for three years."

"Is that all?" Green asked.

"Actually no. You gave us an idea."

"What is that?"

Daniels grinned. "The company must provide full disclosure of wrongdoing by Christopher Duval and Don Lawrence. Then we will nab Christopher, and he can plead guilty to save the company."

Green cleared his throat. "That is laughable, Jason. Sparks Duval will not agree to plead guilty."

"That is up to him. If he wants the company to survive, I suggest you convince him to reconsider."

"This reminds me of what your Justice Department did to Arthur Andersen. The Supreme Court overturned that conviction unanimously."

"By the time that happened, Arthur Andersen was out of business. The same could happen to Duval Energy."

Green shook his head and stood. "Welcome back to Texas. You will be spending a lot of time here with our case and your Houston matter. Want advice on where to buy western wear so you do not look like a New Yorker?"

"I do not need western wear," Daniels said.

"You would still look like a New Yorker on his first day at a dude ranch," Green said, chuckling.

Daniels smiled. Green continued, "I do not think you want to try this case in Dallas. I beat you last time and you have not learned."

"And I know your client needs to settle this case more than I do. We will file motions to keep you busy and reconvene a grand jury to look into other Duval Energy and Sparks Duval matters."

"What?"

"You heard me. You will find out soon enough."

Chapter 9

Sparks and Christopher Duval sat waiting for Chuck Green and Gabriela Sanchez to arrive.

Sparks glared at his son. "Why didn't you tell me they met with the DOJ?"

"I wanted Chuck to tell you about the meeting."

Sparks turned when he heard a knock at the door. Vivian Dandridge stepped in. "They're here. Do you want me to bring Mr. Green and Ms. Sanchez back?"

"Yes, Vivian, do that," he said, still angry.

When Chuck and Gabriela entered, Sparks watched his son greet her. Christopher grasped her hand, then her arm, holding on for a moment. She pulled away. Duval made a note to ask later why his son seemed so taken with her.

He rose from his chair and stared at them before finally speaking. "Chuck, why didn't you tell me you and Gabriela met with Daniels about our case?"

"Daniels claimed he had orders from Washington not to settle with the company unless you pled guilty," Green said. "I wanted to see if that was true. So, I suggested Christopher might be willing to plead guilty."

"What did Daniels say?"

"He took the proposal to his bosses. That told me he doesn't really want to try this case. But the only way his bosses will let him settle is if you plead guilty."

"Could he settle with the company and still take me to trial?"

"Only if Christopher or your employees turn on you. That's what he's doing in the American Oil case. The company settled, paid a big fine, and threw Ralph Farmer under the bus."

"Screw Daniels. I hope you told him we plan to kick his ass."

Green grinned. "I did. He made another offer, but it's no better than the first."

Duval got up and walked toward him. "Then why would I even consider taking it?"

"Because when they made the first offer, we didn't know Daniels planned to indict both you and the company. And we didn't know the FBI had wired your lawyer and taped a conversation designed to sink you while he was still working for you."

"I'm not afraid of anything on the tape. When I figured out what was going on, I even told Don to make sure everything was legal."

"You should be. You were being set up. And it's not just the tape. Don Lawrence, the lawyer you trusted, is now the government's chief witness against you. And he'll lie because he has to."

"If Lawrence claims I knew Lopez planned to bribe PetroMex officials, he'll be lying. He'll only do it to save himself."

"Sparks, Don may be lying through his teeth, but at trial, what matters is whether the jury believes him. He was your lawyer. If he says he bribed PetroMex officials for the company, that puts the company at risk."

"Isn't that your job, Chuck? I'm paying you over a thousand dollars an hour to convince the jury he's a liar."

"Sure, but why take the chance?"

"What's the government's offer?"

"The company must agree to a deferred prosecution agreement."

"What's that?"

"It means the government won't prosecute the company if it meets the conditions in the agreement."

"What conditions?"

"The company pays a thirteen-million-dollar fine."

"And?"

"The company must cooperate."

"And me?"

"You have to plead guilty to conspiring to pay bribes to a foreign official, serve twelve months in prison, and step down from the company for three years."

"There's no way I'll plead guilty, no way I'm going to prison, and no way I'm leaving the company for three years," Duval said, his voice rising.

"But, Dad, with good behavior, it's only six months," Christopher said. "The company pays the fine and keeps operating."

Duval pointed at him. "Damn it, Christopher. You don't get it. I'm innocent. I won't plead guilty to a conspiracy I didn't know existed. I've spent a lifetime building this reputation, and I'm not ruining it."

"That's the difference between us," Christopher said. "I'd plead guilty to save the company. Innocent executives do it every day."

"Son, if I have to choose between losing the company and losing my reputation, my reputation is more important."

"If you go to trial, you may lose both. And we've already paid Parker & McEvoy over a million dollars. We've paid lawyers for me and our employees who testified before the grand jury, and Chuck says taking this to trial will cost two to three million more."

"I'll take my chances," Duval said. He turned to Gabriela. "You've been quiet. What do you think?"

She glanced at Green. He stepped closer to her—a signal. Duval noticed.

"Mr. Duval," Gabriela said, "I understand how you feel. I'd feel the same way. My reputation matters to me too. But—"

"I've been doing a lot of thinking about how we'll win against a prosecutor hell-bent on putting me in jail," Duval interrupted. "Christopher, I need to speak to Chuck and Gabriela alone."

"What?"

"I said I need to speak to them alone. Having you here may waive our attorney-client privilege. Right, Chuck?"

"Right," Green said.

"Okay, Dad." Christopher turned to Gabriela with a smile that lingered too long. He winked and walked out quickly.

Once he was gone, Sparks gestured for them to sit. "I have big news. I've hired a public relations firm. They have strong opinions on how we can win this case and counter the god-awful publicity I'm getting from the media."

Gabriela covered her mouth and looked at Green, who was shaking his head.

"You hired a public relations firm? For what?"

"Media strategy, print, broadcast, and online. They'll help us convince the jury I'm innocent. This firm is the best trial consulting firm in the country. They're like Dr. Bull."

"Who is Dr. Bull, and what does he have to do with your defense?" Green asked.

"It's a TV show. Michael Weatherly plays a psychologist who helps lawyers select jurors and strategize. Dr. Phil helped create it. You might remember he saved Oprah in a civil case here in Texas."

Green raised his eyebrows at Gabriela.

"Sparks, this is not television. Your trial is real life," Green said. "Dr. Phil convinced Oprah to be authentic, not to let the other side define her. That's different."

"I know it's real life. But the environmentalists and liberal media have already tried to convince the public I'm not who I say I am. I have to counter that."

"You can be authentic without a PR firm manufacturing your image," Green said.

"I found a firm that helps lawyers select jurors and shape trial arguments, just like Bull on TV. They'll develop a pre-trial media strategy and help with arguments, presentation, even what to wear to court."

Green could hardly believe what he was hearing. "Sparks, we're your lawyers. We know Dallas juries. You don't want a consulting firm dictating your defense."

"I disagree. They've already tested ideas with mock juries and the public. You should hear what they found."

"Like what?"

"First, they told me that in 2017, juries will more likely convict rich businessmen defended by high-priced lawyers in fancy suits."

"That's the reason you shouldn't go to trial."

"I'm going to trial," Duval said, staring at Gabriela. "They recommended that Gabriela defend me."

Green stood. "You can't be serious."

"I'm as serious as a heart attack."

"Sparks, you want Gabriela to defend you as a PR move?" Green asked. "What do they know about defending a billionaire in federal court?"

"They've worked on political campaigns. They've crunched the data and know how a Dallas jury will think."

"Sparks, your trial isn't a political campaign."

"I know. The consultants believe Gabriela gives us two advantages."

"Two?"

"Yes. Hispanic and male jurors, and a judge who will treat her better than his own daughter."

Green buried his head in his hands. Gabriela rolled her eyes.

"Mr. Duval," Gabriela said, "I'm a trial lawyer, not a beauty-pageant contestant. Your consultants have the wrong idea. Studies show male jurors prefer male lawyers, and female jurors prefer female lawyers."

"The consultants did their own studies."

"Other than selecting Gabriela, what else are they doing?" Green asked.

"They'll handle pre-trial messaging, counter environmentalists' attacks, and help with jury selection and imaging. They'll also advise on what Gabriela and I should wear to court based on the image they've created. They even suggested acting and voice lessons."

Gabriela gasped. "They don't want Chuck Green at the counsel table with me?"

"That's right. If Chuck sits there, the jury will expect him to take over."

Chuck rose. "Don't tell me it's the same firm Ken Lay and Jeffrey Skilling used."

"They weren't involved in Enron. Things have changed since then. Social media is everything now. You've seen what the bloggers are saying about me."

"Sparks, you rarely use email," Green said. "Now you're trusting social media to persuade jurors? Who gave you this idea?"

"The consultants. They told me we need a social media and traditional media plan. They'll get Gabriela interviews and positive press about our community contributions. They may even get me an interview on *60 Minutes* or launch a website to get our story out."

"Yeah, Ken Lay did *60 Minutes* too. We know how that ended," Green said.

"I relate to people better than Ken Lay."

"I do not believe communications with a PR firm are covered by attorney-client privilege," Gabriela said. "That's a problem."

"Daniels already beat us in the media," Duval said. "He had me handcuffed in front of every camera in Texas. The story was everywhere. Jurors have already been tainted. Saying 'no comment' won't fix that."

Green sighed and removed his glasses. "Sounds like they convinced you, Sparks. Did they tell you to find Jesus and join a Hispanic parish?"

"Quit being sarcastic."

"I'm skeptical, not sarcastic. Creating a PR campaign is risky, and you don't even use social media."

"Not creating one is riskier," Duval said. "They plan to use media power to counter the attacks. Let's bring them in. I'll introduce my PR team."

Gabriela looked at Green and whispered, "I'm not taking acting lessons or letting anyone tell me what to wear."

He whispered back, "That's the least of our problems. He thinks this is a presidential campaign—him running, you as his VP. This just got worse than I ever expected."

"And I'm supposed to fix his juror problem," Gabriela said. "It's tough enough to defend him with your help, but to answer to a PR firm makes it impossible."

Still stunned, Gabriela looked toward the door as Vivian Dandridge entered with a blonde woman in her forties and a younger man. Neither of them had any idea how much control they planned to take.

Chapter 10

"Chuck, Gabriela, I want you to meet Deborah Snow and Steven Graham."

Gabriela nodded and stepped back so she could size them up. They didn't look like they were from Texas.

She could feel everyone's eyes on her as she tried to process what she had just heard.
Did Duval say he wanted me to defend him?

Gabriela was a private person, an introvert, and she didn't want anyone prying into her life. She hated the thought of exposing her personal life as part of an online public relations campaign. Gabriela had built her career by letting her work speak louder than her image. The idea of becoming a media prop made her stomach turn.

She looked over at Green nervously. He was shaking his head. Gabriela assumed he was also trying to process what he had just heard.

Finally, Sparks Duval said, "Deborah, tell Chuck and Gabriela a little about yourself."

"I'm sure you can tell by my accent that I'm a New Yorker. My undergrad degree was in theater, and I started my career after college acting. Then I went to NYU law school and became a litigator with a mid-sized firm in Manhattan. Over time, I realized my real passion was communication and psychology, so I became a jury consultant and started a public relations firm that specializes in litigation. If you watch the TV series, I'm a real-life version of Dr. Jason Bull. Like Bull, we understand the lens through which jurors and judges view a white-collar criminal case."

Gabriela thought, *There's no way this New Yorker has a clue what it's like trying cases in Dallas, Texas.*

"Neither Chuck nor Gabriela have watched the show," Sparks Duval said.

"Dr. Jason Bull is a TV series Dr. Phil helped create," she replied.

"Thank you, Deborah. Please explain why you recommend Gabriela to defend me."

"Yes, I'm eager to hear your reasoning," Chuck Green said.

"Sure, Sparks," Snow replied as she looked at Chuck. "Chuck, we know you've won every case you've handled for Duval Energy, even some unpopular environmental fracking cases."

Gabriela knew *but* would be the next word.

"Right."

"But that was a few years ago, and all those cases were civil cases where the argument was over money. This trial is a criminal case."

At least she knows the difference between a civil case and a criminal case, Gabriela thought.

"I've successfully defended rich guys before, including a case against Daniels."

"We know that, and we discovered just how much that loss sticks in Jason Daniels' craw. He hates you, and he'll do anything to win this case, even if it means crossing the line."

Gabriela understood what she meant by *the line*. Federal prosecutors have incredible power over the lives, liberty, and reputations of people. In a win-at-all-costs environment, many cross the line with malice, violating a defendant's constitutional rights. Jason Daniels would do whatever it took to obtain a conviction because convicting a billionaire Republican was more important to him than obtaining justice.

Usually, those so-called errors involved failing to turn over documents or testimony favorable to the defense. Just recently, a Dallas federal judge had railed against prosecutors for withholding favorable evidence in a high-profile politician's case.

"That makes it more likely Daniels will make mistakes," Chuck Green said.

"We can accomplish the same thing by Daniels knowing you're mentoring Gabriela. You can sit in the front row and intimidate him."

"Mentor? You're kidding, right?" Green replied. "Trial lawyers don't have mentors sitting in the courtroom to comfort them each day. You don't even want me at the counsel table?"

"No. How would we spin having the top trial lawyer in Texas assisting his younger Latina partner?"

"This makes no sense. It's okay for me to mentor Gabriela from the front row, but you don't want me to be her co-counsel sitting beside her?"

"No, we want you in the front row to intimidate Daniels while the jury doesn't know you're part of the team."

"That's crazy," Chuck replied.

"No. Gabriela isn't aggressive like you are. Daniels is afraid of you. He'll blow her off."

Gabriela bit her tongue. Strength didn't always have to sound loud. She'd learned that silence, used right, could rattle a man like Daniels more than any outburst. She started to defend herself, but before she could, Deborah continued.

"Chuck, think Ken Lay and Jeffrey Skilling in the Enron case. Think Bernie Ebbers in the WorldCom case. Top lawyers defended each of them, and juries found every one guilty."

"That's true, and Lay's public relations team didn't help his case. If anything, their efforts hurt him," Green said. "Plus, Lay and Skilling both made a terrible impression while testifying, and the jurors hung them for it."

"Chuck, you're making my point. We learned from watching the Enron trial. Plus, those trials were over ten years ago, and the world has changed a great deal."

"How is it different?"

"After the 2008 recession, the Occupy Wall Street movement, the Great Racial Divide, and the 2016 election, jurors who are poor, Black or brown-skinned, or even liberal Democrats are more likely to convict a wealthy man. The fact that Sparks and Duval Energy may be innocent of any wrongdoing is largely irrelevant."

"It can't be irrelevant," Gabriela said. "It dictates how we defend the case."

"I'm speaking about how juries look at cases involving billionaires. Our job as trial consultants is to make sure we get the right jurors and that you deliver the right message to them," Snow replied.

"And who are the right jurors?" Green asked.

"We want jurors who believe the indictment and trial are a gross abuse of government power and who see Daniels as a Washington lawyer who wants to win at all costs. We want hard-working, middle-class jurors who feel the government has forgotten them. In a nutshell, we want jurors who voted for President Trump."

"How will you know if any particular juror feels the government has forgotten them, or voted for the president?" Gabriela asked, knowing the court would never allow those questions during voir dire.

"It's pretty easy to figure that out. If a juror is white, middle class, and doesn't have a college degree, he or she is most likely part of the forgotten middle class and most likely voted for the president. The problem is we can't exclude every suburban wife or Black or brown-skinned person in the jury pool, and Daniels will try to keep our best jurors off the panel."

"And you think Gabriela will appeal to the young and minority jurors?" Chuck asked.

"Yes. Gabriela will appeal to the young jurors, the Hispanic jurors, and the men. We'll create a media campaign to highlight her work with immigrant children."

"That all seems contrived to me," Gabriela said.

"Gabriela, studies show media influences prospective jurors and even judges. It certainly did in the Enron case. You litigators focus on the judge, the jury, and the other side. You sometimes miss that the communication taking place before the trial can carry the day."

"You can't win a case with a PR campaign," Chuck said with disdain.

"That may be true, but you can lose a case without one. Sparks Duval is innocent, and our work will ensure the jury acquits him."

"Amen to that. Did you tell Sparks a PR campaign may not work in a city as diverse as Dallas?" Chuck asked.

"The Dallas population is diverse. That's why we created focus groups and showed them your photo and Gabriela's photo and asked who they liked more at first glance. Ninety-three percent chose Gabriela. That's an off-the-charts percentage."

"Just based on photographs?" Chuck asked.

Gabriela thought she knew why. Chuck looked more like a rocket scientist than a lawyer, but they would be defending a billionaire, not competing in a popularity contest.

"No, we played one-minute audio clips of each of you and asked who sounded more trustworthy. Slightly over seventy percent of the people found Gabriela more trustworthy. We trimmed the audio to fifteen seconds, then to eight seconds. Each time, the vast majority found her more trustworthy."

"That's why Deborah believes it would be better if you're not at the counsel table with Gabriela," Sparks said.

"We want every potential juror to view her as the underdog," Deborah added.

"This isn't a presidential debate. None of your focus groups can predict what will happen in a trial," Chuck said. "Gabriela has tried several cases. I've tried hundreds, including some of the most high-profile cases in Texas history. That experience allows me to change course in the middle of a trial."

Gabriela waited for a reaction from Duval or Snow. None came. Green's argument had fallen on deaf ears.

"Focus groups can and do predict what will happen. That's why we've scheduled mock juries before trial. We'll test and decide on Gabriela's opening statement, her closing argument, how she should cross-examine Don Lawrence, and whether Sparks should testify."

Gabriela looked at Chuck. She saw his eyebrows rise and his forehead crease. He took a deep breath. "You'll decide? We can't defend Sparks if you're deciding those things."

"You claim to have thought of everything, but you don't know me," Gabriela said.

"Yes, we've even thought of your trial clothes and how loud you should speak. Steven is an expert on those things."

"I'm sorry, Ms. Snow, but you've done all these studies where potential jurors chose me for just the way I am, and now you want to change me. That makes no sense. Jurors want lawyers to be authentic."

"Change is too strong a word. We want to fine-tune your performance. The top athletes in the world have coaches who fine-tune their skills."

"We'll also mount an online social media campaign and a television campaign. You'll post daily on social media, and we plan to get you daily interviews on cable news and local networks. It'll be tricky because we want you to appeal both to minorities and young jurors and to the president's most ardent supporters."

Gabriela shook her head.

"I'm not on social media, and I don't want to be. And it's impossible to appeal to everyone."

"You're on social media now. We've already created accounts for you. We've crafted different messages for different audiences, just like candidates do in an election."

"You created social media accounts without asking me?" *How could they open accounts without asking?*

"We asked Mr. Duval. He's your client."

Gabriela felt her face grow hot with anger. "¡No manches!"

The room went silent. For the first time, Deborah and Sparks saw that Gabriela Sanchez was nobody's puppet.

"What?" Deborah asked.

"No way. There's no way I'll agree to having social media accounts or to being interviewed on television every day. I'm a private person, not a TV personality. I won't be the vibrant person you want for television, and I won't agree to messages that are contrary to my values."

"Ms. Sanchez, you're a trial lawyer, not an evangelist. Your values aren't as important as successfully defending your client."

Gabriela thought she was having a bad dream. She hoped Chuck would intervene. When he didn't, she asked, "How can I be on television every day and prepare a defense?"

"We want your father to assist you."

"My father?" Gabriela's voice rose. "He can't just leave his law practice and come up here to assist me."

Sparks raised his hand and rubbed his thumb and first two fingers together. "Gabriela, I'll make it more than worth his while."

"Mr. Duval, with all due respect, if my father was motivated by money, he'd be doing something different and wouldn't still be helping clients in the Rio Grande Valley."

"I bet he'll want to help his daughter succeed," Deborah said.

For the next twenty minutes, Gabriela tuned out while Deborah continued describing her plans to make her the face of Sparks Duval's defense team.

As they left Duval's office, Gabriela looked over at Vivian Dandridge. She was staring at her computer screen and didn't look back.

They rode back to the office in silence. When Chuck parked and turned off the car, he looked at Gabriela, swallowed hard, and asked, "Do you think you're ready to defend Sparks Duval?"

Gabriela didn't know how to respond. After a moment she said, "A public relations firm selected me, and you've already told me I'm not ready. So I'm trying to process what just happened."

"What just happened is a disaster. Sparks just put his defense and freedom in the hands of two New York public relations people he trusts more than his lawyers."

"Chuck, even if I were ready for a big-time case, I wouldn't want a public relations firm to dictate what I wear, how I speak, and nitpick what I do. You've got to convince Duval to have you defend him and quit listening to the PR firm. I'll back you up like your original plan."

"You don't know Sparks Duval. He thinks he knows more than any lawyer, and now he's hired a PR firm to prove it. Now he's counting on you to save him and his company."

"No pressure, right? A New York-based PR firm is sending me out at the last minute, facing government lawyers who'll do anything to win, and defending a billionaire who thinks he knows more than me about how to defend him."

"Go home and talk to your father. He's defended more bribery cases than any lawyer in Texas. Having him assist you will boost your confidence."

"I'll do that. I have to go to the Valley anyway this weekend for my niece's quinceañera."

"Remind me, what's a quinceañera?"

"In our culture, it's as important as a wedding. It's a ceremony on a girl's fifteenth birthday marking her passage to womanhood, giving thanks to God for his blessings, and presenting her to the community. It's like a sweet sixteen or debutante party, only more important. My brother and his wife have been saving money for fifteen years."

"Convince your father to come up here and help you."

"That'll be a tall order."

Gabriela's phone vibrated. She looked down at the screen. *@nofrackingtx* had tweeted again: *#crooked #con #colluder #sparksduval one month from prison.* Within a minute, more than fifty followers had retweeted it.

@nofrackingtx must have a large group of followers always ready to pile on. Every one of them seemed determined to put Sparks Duval in prison.

Chapter 11

Vivian Dandridge was glad to see the lawyers leave. They had reminded her that she was living through the biggest nightmare of her life.

It had started after the government arrested Sparks Duval. She was called to an employee meeting where Christopher announced that the company had hired Don Mitchell to represent them in case any employee received a subpoena to testify before the grand jury or if the FBI requested an interview. At the time, Vivian couldn't think of anything she knew that would interest the FBI or the grand jury, so she wasn't worried.

Don Mitchell stood after Christopher introduced him. He was a short man with red hair and a neatly trimmed beard. His gray pinstripe shirt and flashy gold watch looked out of place in the Duval Energy conference room. He told the employees there was no reason to worry, but everything he said afterward made everyone in the room uneasy.

Mitchell explained that he had informed Jason Daniels he would represent the employees and had agreed to accept service of any grand jury subpoenas. If any employee was subpoenaed, Mitchell would accompany them to the courthouse, but he would not be allowed in the grand jury room while they were questioned. There would be no judge in the room, he said, so they would be on their own. Vivian remembered the uneasy sighs that spread around the table.

A week later, she received a call from Mitchell's assistant. Vivian's chin dropped when the assistant told her that Mr. Mitchell had accepted a subpoena for her to testify before the grand jury.

She ran into Mr. Duval's office, her hands trembling. When she told him about the subpoena, he assured her she had nothing to worry about. All she had to do, he said, was tell the truth.

Over the next two weeks, Vivian met twice with Mitchell and a younger lawyer whose name she quickly forgot. She learned she had been granted immunity, which meant that as long as she told the truth, nothing she said could be used against her.

Vivian explained to Mitchell that she knew nothing about the PetroMex deal because Christopher and Don Lawrence had handled all negotiations in Mexico. Mitchell told her to give that same answer if asked. The less she knew, he said, the less interest Daniels would have in her testimony. He even suggested the questioning would take fifteen to twenty minutes at most.

On the day she testified, Vivian was running late. Still, she believed she was ready and expected to be back at her desk within the hour. She dressed neatly and professionally and rode in a Lincoln Town Car to the federal courthouse. When she entered the witness waiting room, she saw Mitchell and four other Duval employees, each sitting with their lawyers.

For the next two hours, she watched one employee after another called to testify. Finally, an assistant U.S. attorney named Melinda Swanson entered and asked Vivian to follow her.

The moment Vivian stepped into the grand jury room, her stomach turned. She was led to a chair in the center of the room, surrounded by two dozen people staring at her. At the podium stood a man she recognized from news photos—Jason Daniels. A court reporter sat beside him.

Daniels introduced himself and reminded her that she had been given "use immunity." As long as she was truthful, he said, nothing she told the grand jury could be used against her.

After a few preliminary questions, he asked, "Ms. Dandridge, how long have you worked for Sparks Duval?"

She thought for a moment. "I believe I've worked for Duval Energy for ten years."

"How did you first meet Mr. Duval?"

"I was a waitress at The Mansion."

"A waitress?"

"Yes. It was my second job. I worked there on weekend nights."

"Did you have any experience as a personal assistant to a company CEO?"

"No. But I had plenty of experience serving CEOs. They dined at The Mansion."

"How much were you paid when you started working for Mr. Duval?"

"As a waitress at The Mansion or as a paralegal?" Vivian asked.

"Paralegal."

"I believe it was sixty-five thousand dollars a year."

"How much are you paid now?"

"Two hundred fifty thousand dollars."

"To be an administrative assistant?"

"I'm more than an administrative assistant."

Jason Daniels chuckled. "I bet you are."

Vivian's pulse quickened. She didn't like his tone, but she kept her expression neutral.

For several minutes, Daniels questioned her about the PetroMex deal. Vivian told him she knew very little because Mr. Duval had little involvement.

That answer seemed to irritate him. For the next hour, he brought up deal after deal, demanding to know why she could discuss other contracts but not PetroMex. Vivian repeated that Mr. Duval had not been directly involved in the PetroMex transaction.

Daniels turned toward the grand jurors. "You want these people to believe that Mr. Duval didn't care enough about his company's first international drilling contract to be deeply involved?"

Vivian's mouth went dry. After a moment, she said, "Mr. Duval cared deeply about this company. He was dead set against entering a drilling contract in Mexico."

Daniels shook his head. "He knew Duval Energy planned to pay José Lopez a thirty percent commission, correct?"

"I'm sorry, Mr. Daniels, I don't personally know anything about a commission, and I've never heard of a man named José Lopez."

"Did you ever hear Mr. Duval complain about paying a commission to a middleman?"

"I heard him complain repeatedly to Christopher and Don Lawrence about entering a contract in Mexico. I thought it was because expanding outside the country made no sense for our company."

"Ms. Dandridge, you failed to answer my question."

He handed her a document. It was an email from Christopher to Don Lawrence. It read: *Don, Sparks is against the deal because we are paying José Lopez a thirty percent commission. He believes that amount is unreasonable.*

"You never heard Mr. Duval complain about the commission Duval Energy planned to pay José Lopez?"

"Mr. Daniels, I've never been invited to sit in on private meetings between Mr. Duval and Christopher or between Mr. Duval and Don Lawrence."

"Ms. Dandridge, if Duval Energy paid José Lopez a thirty percent commission knowing that part of it would be used to bribe PetroMex officials to award the contract, that would be a crime, wouldn't it?"

Vivian froze. She assumed bribing officials was illegal, but she didn't want to agree to his loaded question.

Finally, she said, "Mr. Daniels, I know Mr. Duval. He would never do anything he believed was illegal. So I don't believe what you're suggesting happened."

Daniels walked closer, raising his voice. "Ms. Dandridge, I want you to go back and search your computer for any documents that mention José Lopez or the PetroMex deal."

"Documents?" she asked.

"Yes, Ms. Dandridge. Documents."

Vivian sat stunned, unsure how to respond.

"Did you hear me, Ms. Dandridge?"

She shook her head slowly. The government already had access to the company's servers. She didn't know of any documents on her computer that weren't already available to them.

Daniels took another step toward her, pointing his finger. "Ms. Dandridge, you can shake your head all you want. Other Duval Energy witnesses have testified that not all company documents are on the server."

Vivian didn't speak. Daniels had shaken her confidence. She worried that if she said the wrong thing, she might make things worse for herself—or for Mr. Duval. She believed she was telling the truth, but it wasn't the truth Daniels wanted to hear.

Finally, Daniels told her she could step down. Vivian glanced toward the grand jurors, expecting at least one of them to be offended by his bullying. None of them seemed to care.

When she left the grand jury room, Don Mitchell was waiting in the hallway. Daniels followed her out and pulled Mitchell aside. Vivian watched Daniels gesture animatedly as he spoke to her lawyer.

When they finally walked outside, she asked, "What did Jason Daniels say to you?"

Mitchell adjusted his tie. "He believes you lied to the grand jury when you testified that you knew nothing about the PetroMex deal. He wants you to come clean before it's too late."

Even shaken, Vivian promised herself she wouldn't let Daniels twist her words or break her loyalty to Mr. Duval.

Vivian's throat tightened. "I have nothing to tell him," she said, fighting back tears.

Chapter 12

After her morning run, Gabriela Sanchez sat outside to cool down and opened her *Dallas Morning News* app. When the front page loaded, she did a double take. Her color photo filled the screen beside the headline:

"Billionaire's Rising Star Defense Lawyer"

She read on.

Just weeks before his long-awaited trial for allegedly bribing PetroMex officials to win a fracking contract, Sparks Duval has shocked the Dallas legal community by replacing the state's top trial lawyer, Chuck Green, with a young Hispanic attorney, Gabriela Sanchez, known more for her supermodel looks and her work for immigrant children than her trial experience.

Mr. Duval's defense may depend on whether Ms. Sanchez can convince a federal jury that her billionaire client did not know his company paid a bribe to win the PetroMex contract. His greatest challenge will come when his own general counsel, Don Lawrence—who has already pleaded guilty—testifies that he warned Duval about the bribery and Duval went forward with the deal anyway.

Raised in Justin, Texas, William Thomas "Sparks" Duval became a rags-to-riches story when he began drilling shale. The News has learned that before elevating Ms. Sanchez to lead counsel, Duval and his son, Christopher, made substantial contributions to Dallas and Fort Worth Catholic Charities, the Rio Grande Catholic Charities, and Sacred Heart Catholic Church in McAllen.

Gabriela grabbed her phone, which had been charging overnight. She listened to ten voice messages from reporters, each Dallas television station, and Fox News. She erased each one without listening. Talking to reporters was the last thing she needed. Even in the chaos, she refused to let anyone else tell her story until she had written it herself in the courtroom

Her heart racing, she called her father.

It rang twice before he answered. "Papá."

"Yes, Gabriela. You sound excited."

"I am. Can you and Mamá pick me up when I come down for Camila's quinceañera?"

"Of course. Why?"

"I want to tell you something in person."

"I assume from the sound of your voice that it's good news."

She hesitated. "It is, Papá, but not entirely. I'll tell you when I get there."

"Not entirely? What does that mean?"

"Papá, just bring Mamá and pick me up at the airport."

"Okay. Love you."

"Love you too, Papá."

At 6:15 p.m., Gabriela rolled her bag out of the Harlingen airport. Her father stood beside his car; her mother waited in the passenger seat. Gabriela climbed into the back.

As soon as she sat down, her father asked, "What do you want to tell your mamá and me?"

Before she could answer, her mother turned and said, "Have you found a husband?"

"No, Mamá. I have no time to find a husband."

"You should take the time, Gabriela, before you are too old to have children."

"Mamá, first things first. I have to build my career. Then I'll find the right man and get married."

Her father interrupted. "What do you have to tell us?"

"Let's go to La Roca. I'll tell you over dinner."

La Roca was the Valley's most elegant Mexican restaurant. Roberto opened the hand-carved wooden door and led his wife and daughter into the dimly lit dining room. Gabriela loved the seafood, especially the red snapper prepared three ways. She always ordered the Red Snapper Mojo de Ajo with lemon and garlic sauce.

When her father's Pacífico, her mother's Diet Coke, and Gabriela's mojito arrived, her father looked at her. "Tell me your big secret."

"Papá, Sparks Duval chose me to defend him."

"I know. You told me you're working with Chuck Green. Great opportunity to learn from a master."

"No, Papá. Sparks Duval chose me to be his chief defense lawyer."

She watched her father lean back, mouth open, eyes wide.

"Why?" her mother asked, unable to hide her disbelief.

"A trial consulting firm told him that it's harder than ever for a rich man to get a fair trial. They believe jurors will resent him for his wealth and convicting him could be their chance at fifteen minutes of fame."

Gabriela waited for praise, for him to say he was proud, for any sign of approval. Instead, he asked, "Are you sure you have the experience to defend him? You've never tried a high-profile case."

Her stomach tightened. He could read her too easily. She sat straighter and rested her hands on the table. "Papá, I grew up watching you try cases. I've tried a dozen myself in the Valley. I know what it takes, and I have it." *If I can't convince my own father, how will I ever convince a jury?*

"Gabriela, watching me and trying small cases down here hardly prepares you to defend Sparks Duval in what the media calls the trial of the century. The government will throw everything it has at you, including dirty tricks."

"You're right. It's high-profile, but it's not complicated. Don Lawrence admits he knew José Lopez would use part of his fee to bribe PetroMex officials. Sparks Duval denies knowing anything about it. It's a simple he-said-she-said case."

"Simple? Your client is the richest man in Texas in the most publicized trial since Enron. You're an outstanding young lawyer, but you've never faced pressure like this."

"I can win this case," she said firmly. "I plan to win."

"You look disappointed," he said quietly.

She took a breath. "Papá, I know you're trying to protect me. But this time I need your support."

He reached across the table, his voice softening. "You have it. I've seen you in court, and you're good. Juries like you." He paused. "Your mother and I believe you can do anything you set your mind to. I believe you'll defend Sparks Duval successfully."

Gabriela smiled.

"Tell me about this consulting firm," he said.

"They handle pre-trial publicity, jury selection, and image coaching. They plan to use focus groups to decide what I wear, how I should look, and what themes to use at trial."

"What? That's absurd. You can't do your best with people second-guessing every move. The PR firm gives you the perfect reason to back out."

"I can't back out now."

"Sure you can, and you should. Tell Duval you won't defend him with that firm dictating strategy."

"You want me to tell the richest man in Texas I can't defend him? My career would be over."

"Then tell him you won't do it under those conditions. That kind of pressure breaks good lawyers."

Gabriela stared at him. He was right about the pressure. She had never faced this level of scrutiny. Her future depended on winning.

"I appreciate your confidence. I can handle the case, but I was doing better before you reminded me about the pressure." She exhaled. "Papá, I'm committed to defending Sparks Duval. He's counting on me. I need you by my side to keep me steady."

"You'll have my support. And you'll have Chuck Green to back you up so you don't make any big mistakes."

"That's the problem. The PR firm doesn't want Chuck Green at counsel table."

"What are they thinking?"

"They believe the jury will see me as the underdog against the government."

"And Duval as the underdog client? That's ridiculous. All the prosecutor needs to do is ask how much money he made last year."

"They think I'll make him more appealing to Hispanic and African-American jurors."

"Assuming there are any. You can't defend a case like this alone. You need a team."

"That's where you can help. I need you at counsel table with me."

"I can't just drop my work and move to Dallas for months. Besides, your niece's quinceañera is tomorrow. Focus on her for her big day."

"I'll focus on her tomorrow, but I still want you to help me prepare. You have the experience I need, and will give me unfiltered feedback.."

He closed his eyes for a moment. "Gabriela, I'm old school. I don't even know how to work the courtroom electronics."

"I can handle that. I need your strategy and calm. Will you think about it while I'm here?"

"Okay, I'll think about it. One thing I will do right away."

"What, Papá?"

"I'll find Lopez so you can talk to him. And I'll tell you the secret to going into trial with confidence."

She smiled. "What's the secret?"

"You'll out-prepare Jason Daniels. He'll stare at his notes. You'll look at the jury. And you'll walk into that courtroom believing you'll win."

It wasn't only what he said that gave her confidence—it was the tone. Her father believed something about her she hadn't yet believed about herself. For the first time, she began to believe that courage wasn't the absence of fear but the decision to move forward in spite of it.

"I'll be ready, Papá," she said. "But I still want you next to me in court, and at night to keep me calm. Mamá, convince him to come to Dallas."

Chapter 13

The next morning, after coffee, they drove to Francisca's Restaurant, her favorite place to eat breakfast in Harlingen. There were several Mexican restaurants in Dallas that made tortillas on-site, but none compared to Francisca's warm flour or corn tortillas.

Gabriela recognized at least one person at almost every table, so she spent the first fifteen minutes carrying her coffee cup from table to table, chatting with high school classmates. None had gone to college, and none had left the Valley. Once again, she felt uncomfortable. They looked content in a way she never quite managed. A house, a husband, a simple life. She wondered when ambition had started to feel like isolation.

As she returned to the table, she thought about growing up in the Rio Grande Valley and later attending the University of Texas and Notre Dame Law School. Each had been a different world, yet they all had one thing in common: she had never quite fit in.

When she was in high school, very few white students attended. They went to private schools. Her classmates, mostly poor, treated her differently because she was the daughter of a lawyer, her skin was lighter, and her family had moved out of the barrio into a gated community. Very few of their parents had gone to college, and none planned to leave the Valley. Many of her friends were U.S. citizens raised by at least one undocumented parent.

Gabriela had tried to fit in with the poorer students, which got her into trouble and created constant conflict at home.

Even though she hadn't been accepted by her classmates, she had still been part of the majority. That changed when she went to college. In Austin, she became a minority. She was the only Latina on the University of Texas golf team. She didn't feel comfortable socializing with the girls on the team, so she kept to herself, studied hard, and practiced her game. In the Valley her skin had been too light; in Austin, it was too dark. In the cafeteria, students often mistook her for one of the workers.

At Notre Dame, she was the only Hispanic student in her class. When first-year students formed study groups, no one asked her to join. Once again, she felt alone.

In Dallas, some lawyers at her firm thought her skin was too dark to be assigned to certain corporate clients. She had faced bias at every level of her journey. Instead of letting resentment harden her, Gabriela turned every slight into fuel, every exclusion into quiet resolve to prove she belonged.

Even though her father was a lawyer, Gabriela and her brothers had grown up relatively poor. When she became a lawyer, she realized many of her father's clients had never paid him. Roberto devoted his life to helping people who couldn't afford him. He was rarely home, missing several of her birthdays, often working late and sleeping in his office.

Her mother, Alita, had started college but quit when she married Roberto. Since he was seldom home, Alita became the disciplinarian. She rarely disciplined Gabriela's brothers, but Gabriela was another story.

Luis and Robert both studied engineering at Texas A&M and now worked for the largest highway contractor in the Valley.

Gabriela, on the other hand, had been the rebel. She got into trouble with the police more than once. Her mother often told her in Spanish that she was at her wits' end.

Despite her rebellious streak, Gabriela was an outstanding student. She took AP classes in middle school, excelled in sports, and became passionate about golf. Her father once told her she could be the next Lorena Ochoa. But while she loved golf, she had always wanted to become a lawyer, if only to prove she could be as good as her father.

"Gabriela!" a voice called sharply. "I've been calling your name. You were daydreaming."

She blinked. "Oh, sorry, Blanca. I was daydreaming."

Blanca and every other classmate who stopped by asked if she was married and had children. When she answered no, and saw the pity in their eyes, Gabriela realized how hard it was to come home.

Unlike Dallas, conversations in the Valley shifted easily between Spanish and English. Her friends couldn't finish a sentence without mixing the two.

On the drive home, Gabriela and her father talked about the case.

"If you have to go to trial, you'll need to humanize the richest man in Texas for a working-class jury," Roberto said.

"That was my first thought too. How do I do it?"

"Start with his rags-to-riches story."

"I can only get that in if he testifies, and I'm not sure he should."

"You might weave parts of it into your cross-examination of the government witnesses."

"What's second?"

"Go after the big, bad Washington establishment. The jury needs a villain, and you want it to be the government."

"Papá, see why I need you sitting next to me?" She smiled when she said it, though inside she already knew the answer. She'd learned long ago not to rely on anyone for too long.

Loud Spanish music blared from ahead. An Elote truck was parked by the curb. The smell of roasted corn filled the air. Gabriela's mouth watered. She asked her father to stop. In Dallas, trendy restaurants called it *street corn* and charged ten times the price, but it never tasted like this. She wasn't hungry, but she devoured the corn in a cup, covered with lime juice, chile sauce, crema fresca, cotija cheese, and Tajín.

That afternoon, Gabriela joined Luis and his family at South Padre Island. Watching her nieces and nephews build sandcastles, she wished she could spend more time with them. But after seeing her old friends that morning, she understood the cost of chasing her dream. She had left the Valley behind.

At four o'clock they hurried home to get ready for the big event.

Gabriela, her mother, and her father arrived at St. Francis Catholic Church, where the quinceañera Mass was scheduled for seven o'clock Valley time, meaning closer to seven forty-five. Sure enough, at eight o'clock, fourteen attendants, or *damas*, and fourteen escorts, or *chamberlanes*, walked down the aisle and filled the front pews.

Sofia, Mario's daughter, carried the altar pillow where Camila would kneel.

Gabriela looked back and saw Camila entering with her parents, Robert and Alexa, wearing a floor-length white satin dress with lace overlays, rhinestone accents, and a tiara.

It was a special Mass in which Camila reaffirmed her dedication to God and received a blessing from Father Ronaldo.

Afterward, photographs took nearly an hour. Then, the two hundred invited guests and several uninvited ones moved to Casa del Mar for the reception.

The ballroom was bright and colorful, each table decorated with pink balloons, the number fifteen at the center, and quinceañera spelled below.

The carnival theme continued with a large four-tier cake, each layer adorned with a mask and the top crowned with a glittering fifteen.

As the party began, the lights dimmed. Angélica Cepeda announced, "Please join me in welcoming Camila Sanchez, our dazzling and stunning quinceañera."

The crowd rose, cheering and whistling as Camila walked to the stage. She looked twenty-five, not fifteen. There she gave her doll to her mother as Robert knelt dramatically to replace her flats with the silver heels Gabriela had bought her.

Robert grimaced at Gabriela as he buckled them. Then he and Camila danced their first dance to *Amor Eterno.*

Moments later, Alexa stormed toward Gabriela.

"¿Qué crees que estás haciendo? What in the world are you doing?"

Gabriela froze as people turned to watch. "What do you mean?"

"You know she can't wear those heels after tonight."

"When I asked what she wanted, Camila said she wanted heels like mine. So that's what I bought her."

"You haven't been gone that long. You know if she wears those heels, boys and men will assume she's available to them."

Gabriela winced. "Alexa, I'm so sorry. I should have thought beyond tonight. Please forgive me."

Alexa scowled and walked away.

Later, Camila danced with her court as disco lights flashed. Gabriela was stunned. Camila moved like a professional.

When the dance ended, Gabriela asked, "Where did you learn to dance like that?"

"Mamá hired a choreographer. We've been practicing for six weeks."

Gabriela's eyes widened. "A choreographer?"

"Yeah. Mamá's been planning this since I was born."

"And your father approved?"

"Mamá never told him."

Gabriela smiled faintly. Alexa was honoring their Mexican roots while embracing American extravagance.

They danced until midnight. Finally, Roberto and Alita drove Gabriela home, where she fell asleep thinking about her niece and her own quinceañera, which felt like another lifetime.

The next morning, after Mass, Gabriela volunteered to hand out clothing at the parish hall of Sacred Heart Catholic Church in downtown McAllen.

She was matched with a mother and two children. As she helped them pick out clothes, she noticed photographers taking pictures.

"What are you doing?" she asked one of them.

"We've been hired to take photos and video of you helping families here."

"Who hired you?" she asked, though she already knew. "How did you know I'd be here?"

"We just work for the studio," he said. "We don't know who hired us."

"Then how did you know I'd be here this morning?"

He didn't answer.

The mother beside her looked lost, her hand pressed to her head. Gabriela switched to Spanish, gently guiding her toward the showers and clean clothes. When they finished eating, the family left for the bus station. Gabriela hugged them goodbye, tears stinging her eyes.

As she turned, she saw the photographers still filming. "Why are you taking pictures of me?"

"We were told to capture you doing good deeds and with your family this weekend," one said. "We took photos and video at your niece's quinceañera. We have great shots of you."

Gabriela pulled out her phone and found Christopher Duval's number. On the third ring, he answered.

"Christopher, tell your father I quit. I'm not putting up with this anymore."

"Slow down, Sanchez. What are you talking about?"

"Your father's PR firm has photographers following me."

"How do you know they're following you?"

"Because they took photos at my niece's quinceañera, and today they're taking photos of me at Sacred Heart. How did they know I'd be here when I only decided yesterday?"

"They must be following you. I'm not surprised. The consultants told Sparks they want to make you the Mother Teresa of the Hispanic community in Dallas and the Valley."

"Christopher, I'm not Mother Teresa, and I'm no angel. I grew up in the Rio Grande Valley, went to UT and Notre Dame, and moved to Dallas to work. I didn't sit at home praying the rosary every day."

"You have skeletons in your closet?"

"I don't know what that means. I just value my privacy." Her voice steadied. She wasn't angry now, she was resolute. "If they want a saint, they hired the wrong lawyer. What they're getting is someone who fights back."

Chapter 14

When her flight landed at Love Field, Gabriela turned on her phone and saw a text from Christopher and a voicemail from her father. She listened to her father's message first. "Gabriela, count me in, but I have to come home on weekends to be with your mother."

Relief washed through her. She opened Christopher's text.

The Energy Conference is in Houston this week. Come to Houston Tuesday. We can corner my father over dinner at Vince and Tony's. You can spend the night at the Four Seasons and fly back Wednesday morning.

Houston's rich and powerful dined at Vince and Tony's. Gabriela enjoyed people-watching, and that, along with the ambience, made it her favorite restaurant in the city.

She replied, *Are you inviting me to spend the day or just dinner?*

A couple of minutes later, her phone vibrated. *Just dinner. No PR photos.*

Amen, she texted back.

Still, she hesitated before putting her phone away. Pride kept her from asking for help, even when she knew she needed it. Gabriela debated whether to tell Chuck Green about the invitation. She didn't want to seem dependent on him, but convincing Duval to drop the PR firm would be easier with Green's help.

"Are you actually working on a Sunday night, Sanchez?" Green asked when she called.

Gabriela ignored his teasing. "When I was helping refugees at Sacred Heart Church this morning, there were photographers sent by Positive PR taking photos and video of me working with a family. I was upset. They're following me."

"Did you tell Sparks?"

"No, I told Christopher, and now I'm telling you. One of you will get his attention better than I can."

"What are you asking me to do about it?"

"I'd like you to call Sparks Duval and tell him to stop the photographers from following me. I don't need a spotlight to do my job."

"I'll do that for you, but I'm not sure he'll listen. Anything else?"

"Yes," she said, her tone softening. "My father agreed to work on the case with me."

She heard a deep breath on the other end. "I'm sure that will make Duval and his PR team jump for joy."

"Quit being sarcastic."

"Sorry. Having a PR team dictate how to defend Sparks Duval is ridiculous."

"I understand. One more thing—when I got off the plane, I found a text from Christopher. He wants me to join him and his father for dinner

Tuesday in Houston to convince Sparks to stop the PR firm from following me. Did he invite you too?"

"No."

"I want you to join us. Duval is more likely to listen to you than to Christopher and me."

Silence followed. Gabriela waited, pacing the length of her office. The silence stretched, reminding her how often men in power made her wait for a simple answer.

Finally, Green said, "Gabriela, if Christopher had wanted me there, he would have called. He probably thinks you can convince his dad that the PR firm is messing with the quarterback he's chosen to bring home the win."

"I doubt that. Christopher already told me we're too late. His father has decided to fight. You need to convince Sparks that settling with the government is the better option."

"I've tried. If I tell him to settle now, he'll think it's because he booted me off the defense team. Go to Houston and give it your best shot. We'll talk when you get back."

The next morning, Gabriela came into the office and told Lucia to book a flight to Houston for Tuesday afternoon and back first thing Wednesday.

Lucia raised an eyebrow. "You're spending the night in Houston?"

"It's my best chance of getting photographers to stop following me. Why do you ask?"

"Men breathe heavy around you. What's your plan when Christopher Duval goes *hombre macho* on you?"

"He's married."

"He's separated and looking. Plus, he's handsome, charming, and you seemed impressed when you met him."

"I have to go. I can handle him."

"You don't have to spend the night. There's a Southwest flight at ten. You'd have time to eat and still make it."

"Sparks Duval will be there. Christopher won't try anything in front of his father."

"They won't be together all night. Suppose you're back at the hotel and Christopher calls to invite you for a drink?"

"I'll tell him it's late and I have work to do. I have to catch the six a.m. flight."

"They say Christopher has a way with women. He seduces them with his eyes. Are you sure he can't tempt you?"

"No. He's married, and I don't care how charming he is. That's where I draw the line. He's a player, and I'm not hurting his family."

Lucia crossed her arms. "That may be your intent, but I'm sure he has plans for you."

"I'm a grown-up. I can take care of myself."

"Then I recommend you not drink any alcohol."

Gabriela smiled. "I won't. And if I'm wrong about him, I'll still have my self-respect."

Lucia grinned, unconvinced. When she left the office, Gabriela sat for a moment staring at her reflection in the dark window. She wasn't worried about Christopher Duval. She was worried about what her ambition could make her ignore.

Chapter 15

After working out in the morning, Gabriela dressed and got ready for work. As she packed for the Houston trip, she heard her phone and saw it was a call from Chuck Green.

"Come see me as soon as you get to the office. I want to go over ideas for getting the case settled."

"Yes, sir."

She finished packing a black dress and heels, then added a dark gray business suit.

She stayed in a great mood all day, got plenty of work done, and never mentioned her shopping spree to Lucia. She knew what Lucia would say. *"¿Qué estás haciendo chica?* What are you doing, girl?"

The black Lincoln Town Car picked her up and dropped her off in time to catch the Southwest Airlines four o'clock flight to Houston Hobby. Thankfully, the plane landed on time, and a Duval Energy limo driver greeted Gabriela in the lobby and took her to the Four Seasons.

Growing up in the Rio Grande Valley, Gabriela rarely arrived on time to meetings or dinners. But she realized it was important to be on time for a dinner with Mr. Duval and his son. She opened her suitcase and saw what she had packed. Her pulse quickened. This wasn't just dinner; it was her chance to push back against the PR firm and prove she could handle Sparks Duval on her own terms.

Gabriela put on her black dress and looked in the mirror. She liked how she looked, but since she had no plans to impress Christopher, why should she wear it? Gabriela looked at her watch. She had no time to change.

She hurried downstairs and climbed into the black Town Car Mr. Duval had sent for her.

When she entered Vince and Tony's, she told the hostess she was meeting Sparks and Christopher Duval.

As they walked through the restaurant, Gabriela saw heads turn, looking at her. Soon they arrived at a table in a dark corner of the restaurant where Christopher Duval got up from a black leather chair to greet her. There were only two chairs at the table, both facing out from the corner. Gabriela shook her head. Maybe Lucia was right. Maybe Christopher had other plans for her.

Christopher clasped her arm and leaned in, kissing both cheeks as if they were meeting in Paris. Gabriela stiffened and stepped back.

His eyes opened wide. "That dress should come with a warning label," he said, smiling. "You look incredible."

Christopher still had hold of her arm and hand. He looked deliciously handsome, in a gray pinstriped suit. She noticed men at nearby tables watching, some openly, some pretending not to.

Gabriela withdrew her hand and stood back. She looked and saw a man standing in the far corner with a camera.

"Christopher, someone's taking photos of us. I told you, no PR shots," she said, her voice rising.

"Where's the photographer?"

When she pointed, she saw the photographer walking briskly away.

"He's gone."

"Where?"

"I don't know. I asked you to make sure no one followed me, and no one took photos of me."

"I'm sorry. I had nothing to do with it. Let's sit down, have a drink and enjoy ourselves."

Gabriela scoffed. "If you think we're going to have an overnight date, you're mistaken."

"No, what makes you think so?"

"What did you imagine? Where's your father? Talking to him about the PR firm was the only reason I agreed to be here."

Christopher ignored the question. "I like the perfume. What is it?"

Gabriela ignored the question and thought about one of her mother's favorite expressions for her. "*Calladita te ves mas bonita, mijita*" ("When you are quiet you look prettier, sweetheart.") She couldn't be quiet now.

"Christopher, I'm here for a business dinner to discuss the PR firm, and all you are talking about is my looks and perfume. Where's your father?"

"When I told Sparks that we wanted to talk about firing the PR firm, he had a last-minute call on an urgent business matter and had to go back to Dallas."

"Why did you tell him what we wanted to talk about firing the PR firm?"

"Because he asked why I had invited you to come to Houston for dinner when we could easily meet at our office. I had no choice."

Gabriela smiled, getting the picture. "Why didn't you call me to save me the trip?"

"Because you were already on the plane coming here."

"So, is your father missing the rest of the Energy Conference?"

"No, assuming he even left Houston, he'll fly back in the company plane in the morning."

Lucia called it.

"What are you drinking?" Christopher asked when the server came to the table.

She started to order iced tea, wanting to stay sober. Then, she changed her mind. "I'll have a Grey Goose lemon drop martini, but first, I want to call and book a flight to return to Dallas tonight."

"And I'll have a Bombay Sapphire martini up, olive, and no vermouth."

She stood up to make the phone call.

As she expected, Christopher stood up and took her arm, pulled her close to him, and said in a soft voice. "Your bags are back at the hotel. Stay tonight, so we don't have to rush through dinner."

Gabriela wasn't sure there would be enough time to get back to the hotel, pick up her bags and make it to the airport in time for the last flight. She sat back down.

A few minutes later, the waiter brought ice cold martini glasses and two shakers. After shaking her lemon drop martini, he poured it into her glass. Afterward, he shook the Bombay Sapphire and poured it into Christopher's glass.

"Look, I want to explain to you why I think it's so important that we resolve this with the DOJ. Sparks can plead guilty. We can pay a large fine and walk away."

She leaned in toward him and whispered. "You know your father won't plead guilty."

"Why are you whispering?"

"This is a terrible place to have a private conversation."

"Okay." He lowered his voice. "I understand he doesn't want to plead guilty. But I want you to appreciate the problem."

"What's the problem? You knew about the bribe?"

"I didn't know for sure, but since it was Mexico, Don and I thought Lopez might bribe the PetroMex officials."

"Did you ask him?"

"No."

"Is any of that in writing that made you suspicious?"

"No, this is the only deal we've ever done with no discussions in writing or email. Doesn't that show we knew what the deal was and purposely didn't discuss it?"

Gabriela looked over at the next table. She thought one man was leaning to overhear their conversation.

"Christopher, the man to our left is either staring at me or he is trying to overhear our conversation."

Christopher stopped their waiter and asked if they could move to another table. A few minutes later the waiter returned, picked up their drinks and led them to another table in a different corner.

"Let's talk about your family," she said.

"We can do that another time. I'm here with you tonight, and I want to give you my full attention. You don't look Mexican. Your skin is lighter than most Mexicans."

"Christopher, has it ever occurred to you that we are different colors? We don't all look alike."

He blushed. "Sorry, you've got me there."

Gabriela looked back at the table, and the men were getting up to leave. Had they heard anything? Were they following Christopher, or maybe following her?

They had two more drinks while eating their appetizer and salad. Gabriela was feeling a little tipsy by that point.

Suddenly, his eyes locked on hers for an instant too long. "Sanchez, you are a beautiful woman."

She had heard that line so many times that it had lost any meaning.

"Christopher." She straightened in her chair. "If you want to flatter me, call me a brilliant lawyer. I'm leaving now to catch the last flight tonight to Dallas."

Before she could get up, he reached over and put his hand on her forearm.

"I don't know yet if you are a brilliant trial lawyer. I know you are beautiful. You don't have enough time to go to the hotel and make it to the airport in time. Let's have a good time."

His hand was still on her arm. She reached over and removed it.

She took a deep breath. "Christopher, stop right now. I'm not here to have a good time. You're married and have children."

He smiled. "I'm separated, on my way to a divorce, which means I'm available."

She took his hand from her arm and said, "Being a rich guy with children in the middle of a divorce proceeding is a good reason to be on your best behavior. I saw a man taking photos of us when you were holding my arm. Your wife's lawyer may have sent him to take photos of us."

"My soon to be ex-wife cares more about my money than who I am seeing. As long as I am generous, she won't put up a fight on the kids."

He sat more rigidly in his chair. "You're not married." He held his hand out and gestured."

"You're making it easy for her to take you to the cleaners."

"That's okay."
Gabriela straightened. "No, it's not. You're reckless, and I'm not playing this game."

"Quit trying to play me. I'm your father's lawyer and your company's lawyer. I will not be in a relationship with you. End of story."

He finally stopped.

"You're right. Let's go back. Maybe, we can spend more time together after the trial."

She wasn't sure he was serious.

Finally, he said, "I watched every man stare at you as you approached our table. They were envious when you stopped at my table."

"There you go again. Flattery will get you nowhere. You can stop now."

They left the restaurant and Christopher opened the door to the limousine for Gabriela and came around to the other side. On the way back to the Four Seasons, he put his arm on the back of the seat and touched her shoulder. She pulled his hand away.

When they pulled into the hotel entrance, Gabriela spoke first, "Christopher, I enjoyed dinner, but I didn't appreciate the passes you made at me"

He frowned. "Give it time. You'll warm up to me."

She grinned. "You can think that all you want. But it isn't going to happen."

As they walked into the hotel, he grabbed her hand and interlaced their fingers. Gabriela saw a flash from a camera and quickly pulled her hand from his.

He smiled as Gabriela hurried toward the elevator. Unfortunately, Christopher got in before the doors closed. They rode up in silence. When they got to her floor, he took her arm, stood close to her, and said. "Take care, Sanchez. I need for you to win for my father."

As she walked away, she turned back and saw he was holding the elevator doors open. Gabriela picked up her pace. If she had followed Lucia's advice to not drink, she would have had time to come back to the hotel and get to the airport in time for the 10:00 p.m. flight home.

After drifting to sleep, she woke up to her phone's vibration. It was another tweet from @nofrackingtx. This one included her photo with Christopher Duval holding her hand. She read *#sultry #spicy #sensuous #latina lawyer spending nite with @christopherduval.* Her phone kept vibrating as Twitter followers retweeted over and over. Gabriela felt a knot in her stomach.

Who is @nofrackingtx, and how does he know I'm in Houston with Christopher?

She set the phone face down, but the image stayed in her mind. It wasn't fear she felt; it was humiliation. The one thing she'd sworn would never happen again was happening now, and the whole world could see it.

Chapter 16

Gabriela left Houston the next morning. After landing, she walked from gate sixteen to the baggage area where her driver waited.

On the way to the office, she speed-dialed Sparks Duval's number, not expecting him to answer.
To her surprise, he did.

"Mr. Duval, do you want me to defend you?"

"Of course. I selected you. What's wrong?"

"Then I need to be direct. The PR firm that recommended me has people following me and taking photos. I'm a private person, and I don't like it."

"What?"

"They followed me to the Valley, then to the Sacred Heart Church while I was helping a refugee mother and her children. For all I know, they photographed my niece's quinceañera. Last night, I caught them taking pictures of Christopher and me at dinner in Houston. It's invasive."

"I'm sorry. I didn't know."

"That's why I called. I didn't sign up for this kind of attention. I'm angry, and I wanted you to hear it from me."

"I'll take care of it. I'll make sure they stop."

"It disappointed me that you came back to Dallas and missed dinner with Christopher and me."

"What are you talking about? I never went to Houston."

"Christopher lied to me."

She'd trusted his word, and now she'd have to question everything he told her about the case.

Fifteen minutes later, the limo stopped in front of her office on Ross Avenue. Gabriela stepped inside, rode the elevator up, and saw a missed call from her father.

She redialed.

"I've found Lopez," Roberto said. "He's willing to meet with you, but he also said travel in Mexico is more dangerous now than it's been in fifty years. I want to go with you."

"No way, Papá. I'll be safe."

He started arguing in Spanish. Finally, she said, "Papá, I have to go," and hung up.

When Gabriela reached her office, Lucia was waiting.

"¿Cómo fue la cena? How was dinner?"

"Everything you predicted."

Lucia smiled. "Oh, I'm sorry to hear that."

"Nothing happened. But I understand why women are drawn to Christopher. He made me feel like I was the only one in the room. He listens that way."

"I told you he'd try to charm you."

"He tried. But I can still say I've never slept with a married man."

Lucia laughed. "Gabriela, you're fuego. Remember Shakira's 'Hips Don't Lie'? That's you."

"I've seen the video. I'm not Shakira. I'm a lawyer."

"You're both. A beautiful lawyer. For now, people notice before they listen. Use it."

"Christopher tried to use it to his advantage."

Lucia grinned. "Are you interested in him?"

"No. Absolutely not. I'm not interested in married men, especially ones who cheat."

"If he weren't married?"

"He still wouldn't get the time of day. A man who cheats on his wife will cheat on his girlfriend."

"I understand. Anything else happen?"

"I tried to confront the photographers at the restaurant and hotel, but they disappeared before I could."

Lucia changed tone. "Oh—someone delivered a package for you this morning."

"A package?"

"Yes, a box."

Gabriela walked to her desk and eyed the box for a long moment before slicing the tape. Inside were a bottle of Grey Goose Vodka, a bottle of Limoncello di Capri, a recipe for lemon drop martinis, a thousand-dollar Neiman Marcus gift card, and a handwritten note. She read it aloud to Lucia.

" 'Sanchez, you lit up the room last night. Enjoy the lemon drops and something new from Neiman's. I want to share some things you should know about Don. —C. Duval.' "

Lucia shook her head. "Christopher's on a mission, and he won't stop."

Gabriela frowned. "What mission?"

Lucia smirked. "The one where he tries to make you his next conquest."

"He's a distraction I don't need. I only care what he knows about Don Lawrence."

"Whatever you say."

"Send the box back. All of it."

She knew accepting the gifts from Christopher would only encourage him.

"Even the Neiman's card?"

"Especially that. And before you go, I need a flight to Puerto Vallarta next Wednesday."

Lucia froze. "What?"

"This is top secret. I'm meeting with José Lopez. He's sending a driver to take me to his home in Sayulita."

"Sayulita?"

"Yes. It's a small surfer town about an hour north of Puerto Vallarta."

"Is it safe?"

"He says it is. I checked the State Department site—no warnings." Gabriela changed the subject. "Also, contact Vivian Dandridge. I need to interview her and learn what she told the grand jury. She'll probably want her lawyer there."

"I'll handle it."

Gabriela's phone buzzed. Christopher Duval.

Lucia arched an eyebrow, smirking as she closed the door on her way out.

"Did you get the gift I sent?"

"Yes. I'm sending it back."

"Don't do that."

"I can't accept it."

"Can't—or won't?"

"Both."

He chuckled. "At least keep the card."

"No."

"All right, then. But I meant what I said—I have information you'll want about Don Lawrence."

"Tell me now."

"Not over the phone. Meet me at six in the bar downstairs in your building."

"What's this big secret?"

"You'll find out at six."

At six, Gabriela rode the elevator to the main lobby and walked to *The Bistro* at the far end of the building. She chose a quiet table in back, hoping no one from Parker & McEvoy would see her.

Five minutes later, Christopher appeared. He leaned down and kissed her cheek. She flinched.

Out of the corner of her eye, Gabriela caught a flash—someone taking a photo with their phone.

She stood. "What are you doing? I work here. I don't want anyone thinking we're a couple."

Christopher smiled. "Are we?"

She glared. "No."

A waitress hurried over. "Hi, Mr. Duval. Hello, ma'am. What'll you have?"

Christopher gestured toward Gabriela. "Lemon drop martini, Sanchez?"

"No. I'm not drinking. I have work to do. Topo Chico with lime."

"Yes, ma'am. Mr. Duval?"

"Corona, lime."

When the waitress left, Gabriela asked, "How did she know your name?"

"I come here a lot. I tip better than your partners."

He reached for her hand. She pulled away.

"How did you know they serve Topo Chico?"

"I asked the manager to add it. Tell me what you know about Don Lawrence."

"You first," she said.

Christopher smiled, unbothered. "Everyone knows he's a top energy lawyer. What they don't know is that he's a drunk, a gambler, and a womanizer."

"How do you know?"

"I've seen it. Vegas, Dallas, you name it. And one of his assistants filed a complaint before we hired him."

For the next twenty minutes, he told her stories about Don Lawrence, including his gambling losses, women, and late-night bar deals. As he spoke, Gabriela pictured her cross-examination. The government's star witness was starting to look less like a witness and more like a weakness she could exploit.

Chapter 17

When Christopher left, Gabriela took the elevator back up to Chuck Green's floor. When she walked by and stuck her head in his door, he was still working.

"Do you ever eat dinner at home and hang out with your wife?"

"Dinner at home rarely, but sometimes she comes here, and she works on her business while I work on mine."

"In total silence?"

"No, not total silence. Since you are single, you likely haven't considered you can be together without talking. Enough of my life. Why are you still here, and what's on your mind?"

"I left Christopher downstairs at The Bistro. He told me Don Lawrence has the trifecta — gambling, drinking problems, and he's a womanizer. He harassed women in his law firm."

"How does he know?"

"They've been to Las Vegas many times and hung around singles bars here in Dallas."

"They're both married."

"Yes, but Christopher and Lawrence both play around, even in their backyard. They make no effort to keep their dalliances secret."

"Does the government know?"

"Christopher doesn't think so. He says they were discrete."

Green grinned. "And that's why he's getting divorced? He must not have been discrete enough. They both were pretty stupid."

The difference was, their stupidity could cost her client everything and her career along with it.

"I agree."

"You need to become an expert on why powerful men do stupid things to nail Don Lawrence when you cross-examine him."

Gabriela spent that night doing research on narcissism and on famous people who risked and lost all doing stupid things.

She also researched ways to get rid of emails. She suspected Christopher and Don had exchanged emails on the PetroMex deal. She also believed they had exchanged emails with José Lopez.

The next morning, Gabriela walked back into Chuck Green's office.

"I think Christopher Duval erased the PetroMex emails using BleachBit."

Green laughed. "I bet you never even heard of BleachBit until it was in the news during the presidential campaign."

"True, but it is the only explanation for why there are no emails."

"Ask Christopher."

"I did, and he's not talking."

"We can ask Sparks."

"Maybe, but I don't believe the FBI can easily recover the deleted emails."

Gabriela believed Christopher was hiding something, and she was afraid whatever it was would bite her in the behind right in the middle of the trial when an FBI agent testified to what he had found in the emails Christopher had deleted.

She left Green's office thinking about what she would learn from Lopez and Dandridge and contemplating what to do about Don Lawrence's mental condition.

***

She hated flying into the unknown, but this meeting could change everything. If Lopez was telling the truth, she might finally have a way to clear Duval's name. Two mornings later, Gabriela boarded a flight at DFW bound for Puerto Vallarta International Airport. Two hours and forty-five minutes later her flight landed. After clearing immigration and customs, she stepped outside and saw a man holding up a card with her name on it.

He greeted her in English. "Good afternoon, Ms. Sanchez. I'm your driver, Oscar Morales."

Morales looked more like a bodyguard than a driver. He looked like a professional athlete with broad shoulders, a barrel chest and a slim waist. He wore a fitted black suit with a white shirt and a blue striped tie.

She couldn't see his eyes behind his dark sunglasses. Outside, the glare off the concrete made her squint. The air was still and heavy, already hotter than Dallas at noon.

They walked quickly to a black Cadillac Escalade parked near the terminal.

She asked, "Will I be safe traveling in and out of Puerto Vallarta?"

Morales opened his coat, and she saw a revolver. "I picked you up to keep you safe."

If her driver needed a gun, she decided she wasn't safe.

"So, how do you know José Lopez?"

"I do more than drive for him. I've worked for José many years. I make sure he and his guests are safe."

It took thirty minutes to get from the airport to the Sayulita town bridge. Five minutes later, Gabriela was walking up the hill to her hotel room.

She opened the door and walked immediately to the terrace to take in the spectacular Sayulita Bay coastline, Sierra Madre jungle, and the city. "You should take photos of the sunset on the hillside across the bay," the young man who had brought her suitcase up said in Spanish.

Gabriela unpacked and walked down the hill to Morales's car. She glanced toward the building and saw two American men in suits. They turned as she passed, their gazes sharp and deliberate. Gabriela kept walking, but the back of her neck prickled. Whoever they were, they weren't tourists, and they were watching her.

Chapter 18

Gabriela rushed to Morales' car.

Gabriela spotted the two men again near the parking lot. Same suits. Same steady eyes. She hurried to Morales's car. "I think someone followed me," she said. "They look like FBI."

"You saw two American men in suits?"

"Yes."

"They are not FBI agents. They also work for Mr. Lopez."

"Why do they wear suits?"

"To intimidate people who see them. Like you, most people believe they are US government agents."

Gabriela thought that made no sense, but she let it drop.

Morales drove her to the north end of town, where he pulled up in front of a large luxury villa with separate casitas.

Gabriela thought the two-story home rivaled mansions owned by the wealthy in Dallas. Only Lopez's home overlooked the Pacific Ocean.

"Does Mr. Lopez own this villa?"

"You can ask him."

Lopez looked older than she expected, fit but tired, the kind of man used to giving orders and having them followed

"*Hola,* Ms. Sanchez. *¿Alguna vez has visitado Sayulita?* Have you ever visited Sayuliat?" Lopez asked.

Gabriela paused until he finished. "No, I had never heard of Sayulita. May we speak in English?"

"Absolutely. Are you a surfer?"

"I've never surfed."

"This, *señorita*, would be a great place to learn."

"I won't have time this visit."

"You should make time. Stay an extra day. I could also take you out fishing."

"I've got to get back to Dallas to get ready for the trial."

"Okay, but next time you must go fishing with me. I'm the co-owner of one of the top Sayulita restaurants. My partner, Ernesto, who runs the restaurant, went fishing today, and he's fixing snapper, Veracruz style. Have you ever eaten it fixed that way?"

"Yes, but not in Mexico."

"In Dallas?"

"Yes, at our most fancy Mexican restaurant."

"You're in for a treat. The fish is fresh, and Ernesto cooks it with garlic and capers, jalapeños and cayenne pepper for spice."

"That's the way I like it."

"Do you want your tequila straight or in a margarita?"

"I prefer bottled water." Gabriela said.

After pouring a bottle of Topo Chica mineral water into a glass and adding a lime, Lopez poured himself a glass of straight tequila.

After two drinks, they walked along the beach to the restaurant. Gabriela took off her shoes as they walked. She saw the restaurant with a thatched roof in the distance and heard the band playing on the beach.

When they arrived, Lopez introduced Gabriela to Ernesto in Spanish.

"*Ernesto, te presento* a Gabriela Sanchez."

"*Mucho gusto*, Ms. Sanchez."

"*Igualmente*"

Ernesto seated them outside, where Gabriela could view the sunset. A couple of minutes later, he reappeared with a bottle of tequila and ceviche. Gabriela once again asked for mineral water and a lime.

After they finished dinner and Lopez finished three shots of tequila, they sat and listened to the band. Finally, they walked back to Lopez's house, and Gabriela began asking Lopez about the PetroMex deal.

"How did you become so connected with the Mexican government?"

"I married the daughter of a former PetroMex president. While married, he introduced me to many top Mexican company leaders, including those who worked with him at PetroMex. I used those connections to broker many business deals while giving my father-in-law a share of the money I earned. Over the last ten years, my companies have brokered close to one billion US dollars of contracts with government-owned companies."

"And what is your connection with the current Mexican president?" Gabriela asked.

"We're friends. We travel together. I know his wife."

"Did you set up an offshore account for the president and his wife?"

"That is something I want to keep to myself."

"I know that you set up the offshore accounts for kickbacks to PetroMex officials."

"Yes, I never dreamed the US government would find the accounts. That discovery is the only reason Mr. Duval is facing a trial."

"How did the DOJ discover the offshore accounts?"

"Either someone who knew about the accounts told them, or they found out by having me under surveillance."

"Why would they have you under surveillance?"

"I can't tell you the reason. I can only say that the NSA wants to keep track of what I am doing."

Why can't he tell me?

"Why weren't you indicted?"

"I told your father that I believe the Department of Justice declined to indict me because I could ruin their case against Duval and the company."

"How can you?"

"When we closed the deal, Sparks Duval specifically asked Donald Lawrence if everything was legal about the deal, and Lawrence said it was."

"Duval was there at the closing?"

"Yes."

"He claims he never met you."

"He met me more than once. I'm not sure why he is lying about that."

"Would you be willing to come to Dallas and testify to your conversation with Lawrence and Duval?"

"No, but I'd be willing to give you an affidavit saying that. Maybe that would convince the government to drop the case against Duval."

"I'll have my secretary prepare an affidavit and email it to us for you to sign."

Gabriela sent Lucia a text with the affidavit language. Ten minutes later her phone pinged.

"If I email this to you, can you print it?" Gabriela asked.

"Sure," Lopez replied.

Pop! Pop! Pop! Gabriela heard the gunshots. She leaped to her feet and hid behind the sofa. She looked over the back of the sofa and saw Lopez still sitting in his chair.

"Why aren't you hiding? Someone out there is shooting at the villa."

Lopez laughed. "No, Ms. Sanchez, it's only fireworks," Lopez said, chuckling. "In Sayulita, people shoot them for birthdays, weddings, anything. The loud ones are called palomas. They only make noise."

"Whew. That's good to know."

Lopez told her Duval was innocent. When she asked what made him say that, Lopez replied, Follow the money."

"Follow the money? That's it?"
"That's it," Lopez said. "Every peso leaves a trail. You just have to prove where it goes."
She wrote the words in her notebook. Simple advice, but it could change everything.

"I'm afraid a jury wouldn't understand what tracing the funds means. I need for you to tell the jury that none of the Duval Energy commission was used to bribe the PetroMex officials."

"I told you, I can't be a witness for you."

"Why?"

"You know why. If I testify, the FBI will arrest me before I leave the courtroom. Daniels would have a grand jury indict me in a heartbeat."

Gabriela wanted more details. "How can I show that you never passed on Duval money to the PetroMex officials?"

"Look, the government must prove that a portion of the commission paid to my companies by Duval Energy ended up in the offshore accounts I set up for the PetroMex officials. Find an accountant and have him or her trace the funds. Where they came from and where they went. Look at the dates I transferred money. I believe your accountant can prove that I did not transfer any of the Duval money to any of the PetroMex offshore accounts."

"You said companies. You own more than one company?"

"Yes, which is part of the reason I have told you to follow the money."

Gabriela changed the subject. She asked Lopez about the two million dollars he had deposited in an account for Lawrence. Gabriela learned that Lawrence had asked for the bonus after Sparks Duval had expressed no interest in doing business in Mexico.

Lopez told Gabriela he had met with Lawrence at least a dozen times.

"Did you introduce Lawrence to PetroMex officials?" Gabriela asked.

"Yes. Lawrence is an experienced energy lawyer. He wanted to know all about them before he advised Duval to go forward. But he only met

Garza. Villa didn't get promoted until late July. He didn't participate in the Duval deal."

"Anything else you can tell me about Lawrence?"

"He's arrogant and selfish. He didn't care about Sparks Duval or Duval Energy. All he cared about was making money for himself."

Lopez picked up the shot of tequila he had poured for himself. Once again, he moistened the back of his hand, poured salt, licked it, downed the tequila shot, and bit into a lemon.

"Why lick the salt before drinking?" Gabriela asked.

"It lessens the burning sensation from the tequila."

"I thought the top-shelf tequila was smooth, not burning."

"It is, but I grew up drinking the lower shelf tequila and I have never lost the habit."

"Are you sure Duval didn't know that you might use part of your commission to pay bribes to the PetroMex officials?"

"I seriously doubt he knew. Duval didn't want to pay any commission to me."

"Did he ask what the commission covered?"

"No, I could tell that Duval thought I charged an excessive amount because I was the only one who could deliver the PetroMex deal."

"Did Duval know you planned to pay a bonus to Lawrence?"

"Only if Lawrence told him. Can we call it a night? I'm exhausted from answering your questions. I'll take you back to your hotel."

"Oh, sure."

"If there is anything else to cover, we can talk tomorrow on the beach. I'll come by and take you to breakfast at my favorite restaurant. Gringos from California own it, and they have a top Mexican grill man."

"I can't. I have to get back and prepare for trial."

In the car, Gabriela asked, "May I ask a couple more questions?"

"What do you want to know?"

"First, do you use email?"

"Sure."

"When I went through Don Lawrence's and Christopher Duval's email, there were none from you. Why didn't you communicate with them by email? That seemed odd to me."

Lopez raised his eyebrows. "We had no reason to communicate by email. We communicated by telephone or when we met in person."

"Not even an email to set up a meeting or phone call?"

"Text."

"Lawrence didn't want to leave any record?"

"Maybe so. What was your other question?"

"Did Christopher know the secret accounts you set up for the PetroMex officials?"

"Yes."

Gabriela sat stunned for a moment.

"Christopher wanted to drill in Mexico as much as Lawrence wanted his bonus. They were in it together. Christopher wanted his own operation, separate from his father's. That's why he hired Lawrence."

They arrived at Gabriela's hotel. Lopez got out and opened her door.

"Before you go," Lopez said. "I want to warn you that if the US government is surveilling me, they are also surveilling you."

"No way. They wouldn't do that to a defense lawyer."

"Whatever you want to believe, Ms. Sanchez."

Early the next morning, Oscar Morales greeted Gabriela as she walked out of her hotel. One hour later, he dropped her off at the Puerto Vallarta airport. Before boarding Gabriela called her father and told him to meet her at her office at 1:30. As she spoke to her father, Gabriela surveyed the other passengers. Only one male passenger wore a suit. Gabriela caught him staring at her. *Is he a government agent?*

Three hours later, Gabriela's flight landed at DFW. After clearing Immigration and Customs, Gabriela met her driver in the Terminal D lobby. Gabriela watched the man in the suit use the app on his telephone to call for an Uber driver and decided he was not likely a government agent.

Forty minutes later, Gabriela exited the elevator, and saw her father standing in her doorway talking to Lucia. They both smiled.

After Gabriela closed her office door, her father asked, "What did he say?"

Gabriela spent the next thirty minutes going over what Lopez had told her. Roberto quizzed her, especially about Lopez telling her to follow the money.

"If only Lopez could testify," she said. "He could clear Duval."
Her father nodded but said nothing. Gabriela stared past him toward the window. Lopez had given her the path forward. Now she had to find the proof.

Chapter 19

Over the next four weeks, Gabriela spent day after day in green rooms and television studios answering softball questions from local and national reporters. She had become the face of the Sparks Duval defense. But the constant appearances left her little time to work on the case, and the interviews had shifted from questions about Duval to questions about her—her background, her rise, her looks.

When Judge Comstock issued a gag order, Gabriela felt a rush of relief. For the first time in weeks, she didn't have to smile for a camera. But she had traded bright lights for fluorescent ones. The quiet of her office felt strange, almost too still.

She decided to focus on the case and file a motion to dismiss. Later that evening, she began reviewing the motion and brief an associate had prepared.

Her father walked in carrying a latte.

"And what is that?" he asked.

"The FCPA defines the term 'foreign official' as:

'Any officer or employee of a foreign government or any department, agency, or instrumentality thereof, or of a public international organization, or any person acting in an official capacity for or on behalf of any such government or department, agency, or instrumentality, or for or on behalf of any such public international organization.'"

Gabriela decided to argue that PetroMex was not part of the Mexican government and that its officials were not foreign government officials. Even if she didn't convince Judge Comstock to dismiss the indictment, she wanted to plant the idea in his mind for trial.

As she read, one word in the definition bothered her—*instrumentality*. Congress had never defined it. Would Judge Comstock consider PetroMex to be an instrumentality of the Mexican government?

She dug through statutes and cases but found little guidance. Congress had enacted the FCPA to make bribery of foreign officials a crime, and knowing Comstock, she doubted he would rule that bribing PetroMex officials was somehow outside that prohibition.

After hours of research, Gabriela crafted three arguments she believed had a chance and refined them carefully in her brief. Before filing, she asked Roberto to review it. He pointed out a few spots to tighten but told her the judge would take the motion seriously.

With that encouragement, and his signature on it, she filed the motion to dismiss. When the government responded, Judge Comstock set it for oral argument.

This would be her first time arguing before the judge for whom she had once clerked. She practiced for days in front of a mirror. Deborah Snow wanted a video crew to film her rehearsal, but Gabriela refused and asked her father to critique her instead.

On the morning of the argument, adrenaline surged after her run. She entered the courtroom with her father, confident and ready. Jason Daniels was already seated at the prosecution table, smirking.

"If it isn't Dallas' own Latina Rising Star," he said. "I've been following your TV career. You must be the darling of Fox News. Let's see what the press says after you get crushed on your ridiculous motion."

Gabriela thought Daniels had taken a page from Donald Trump when he invented nicknames for opponents. She stood tall, shoulders back, and smiled.
"Good morning, Mr. Daniels."

He glanced at Roberto. "And I see you brought your daddy to console you after you lose."

Before Gabriela could respond, Judge Comstock entered and called the courtroom to order.

When the judge invited the defense to argue, Gabriela stepped to the podium. Her voice was steady. She argued first that the FCPA's text and legislative history showed that employees of state-owned entities were not foreign officials because no corporation could qualify as an instrumentality. Second, she argued that if the court found any ambiguity in that term, it must resolve it in favor of the defendant. Third, she argued that even if the court included state-owned entities under the FCPA, the statute was unconstitutionally vague when applied to Duval.

When she finished and turned to sit, Roberto gave her a quiet nod. That was all she needed, win or lose.

Daniels rose to respond, repeating predictable points: the motion was premature, PetroMex officials were clearly foreign officials, and the statute was clear. Gabriela watched Judge Comstock's expression but saw no hint of how he would rule.

When the hearing ended, Comstock promised a ruling within a week. Exhausted but relieved he hadn't ruled from the bench, she sank into her chair.

As she gathered her notes, Daniels approached.
"So, Gabby, I hear you've been traveling."
"What?"
"To Mexico. Surfing, wasn't it?"
She froze. "What gives you that idea?"
"I tried to reach you, and the person I spoke with mentioned it."

Her pulse quickened. Who could have told him that? Did Daniels talk to Lopez? No one in Texas would have mentioned surfing.

She walked past him without responding. Her mind raced. Was Lopez setting her up with the offer to lie in an affidavit? Was Daniels behind it?

Then Daniels added, "I saw a photo of you having dinner in Sayulita that someone posted online."
Her stomach dropped. *Sayulita.* He knew exactly where she had been. The connection was clear now. It had to be Lopez.

Daniels smirked, his tone smug and condescending, just like the last time he'd mocked her during the settlement meeting. She said nothing, clutching her files tighter.

Outside the courtroom, reporters swarmed.
"Ms. Sanchez, are you trying to get Mr. Duval off on a technicality?"
She hadn't expected the question. "I'm sorry. Judge Comstock ordered that we not talk about the case."

"Doesn't Mr. Duval want to tell his story and clear his name?" another shouted.

Their phrasing sounded rehearsed. Like Daniels had given them the questins.. So much for the gag order. Gabriela stopped and turned toward them.

"No person, including Mr. Duval, should have to face trial when they are innocent. Put that on your evening news. I have to get back to the office."

She knew immediately she'd gone too far. Daniels would drag her before the judge for that one.

On the walk back, cameras trailed them. Gabriela said nothing until Roberto took her hand, like he had when she was little.

"Next time, I'll arrange a car to take us to and from the courthouse," he said.

She laughed softly.

Back at the office, Roberto hugged her.

"You made the important points in court, and I was proud of you for staying strong with the media."

But?"

"Since you clerked for him, I'm sure you knew we'd lose this motion."

"I suspected as much. But why are you sure?"

"In all my years, I've never seen a white-collar case dismissed on a technicality. Still, you gave him something to think about for trial."

Gabriela nodded. "Papá, I think Jason Daniels tried to set me up—and maybe the government is spying on me."

"How so?"

"Lopez offered to lie for us. I think Daniels told him to make that offer and record it."

"You think Lopez was wearing a wire?"

"No, I think he used his phone. When I changed the subject, he picked it up and acted like he was reading a text. I think he was stopping the recording."

"If Lopez was trying to trap you, why tell you to follow the money?"

"He said that after I didn't take the bait. After he stopped recording."

"And why do you think the government is spying on you?"

"Daniels knew I'd just returned from Mexico—and from Sayulita. If they aren't watching me, how else would he know?"

Roberto frowned. "I've seen prosecutors pull dirty tricks, but setting up defense counsel would be a new low. And I know Lopez. If he's part of it, I'm disappointed."

Later that night, @nofrackingtx was back on Twitter. Gabriela, who had set up an alert for his tweets, watched as they appeared one after another:

#Nojustice if #crooked #con #colluder Duval gets off on a technicality.

#Disgusting #deplorable #disingenuous argument by #sparksduvalguilty fiery #risingstar Latina attorney.

She replayed the reporters' voices in her mind. Their questions matched his phrasing almost word for word. Maybe one of them *was* @nofrackingtx.

A week later, Judge Comstock issued his ruling in one sentence:

A government-owned corporation may be an "instrumentality" of a foreign government within the meaning of the FCPA, and officers of such a government-owned corporation may therefore be foreign officials within the meaning of the FCPA.

Chapter 20

Roberto Sanchez looked up from reading the decision.

"Gabriela, I told you that you made a good argument."

"You also predicted we would lose, and we did."

"Read the ruling one more time. It's a bit confusing, but what's the most important word in the sentence? He said it twice."

Her face lit up. "May."

"Bingo. The door is still open."

Before she could reply, Scottie Johnson, the associate Chuck Green had assigned to work with her, stepped into her office.

"I've prepared a motion to suppress the video and audio recording of the conversation between Lawrence and Duval on September fifteenth."

"How do you like our chances?" Gabriela asked.

"I'd bet that we lose. I based the motion on attorney–client privilege. Lawrence was still Duval's general counsel when he wore the wire for the FBI."

"Exactly. He was giving Sparks legal advice while recording him."

"We're also claiming it violated Duval's due process rights. The problem is what's on the tape. Duval mentions that he and Lawrence each hired a lawyer and suggests Lawrence's lawyer contact Chuck Green. The government will argue that by then Lawrence was no longer acting as Duval's lawyer."

"He was still his general counsel while trying to trap him," Roberto said. "The jury will hate him for that."

Johnson nodded. "True. Gabriela can use that when she cross-examines him. The government argues that even if Duval sought legal advice, he lost the privilege by trying to obstruct the investigation. They claim he told Lawrence to change his memory and get their stories straight."

"Duval says he only reminded Lawrence to keep everything above board," Gabriela said.

"Daniels calls that obstruction too. They haven't charged it, but they're laying the groundwork. The tape isn't that damaging—Duval never admits anything—but we'll file the motion anyway to get parts excluded."

"What about the motion to get information on Lawrence's gambling and drinking problems?" Gabriela asked.

Roberto folded his arms. "Does Daniels know about those problems?"

Gabriela thought for a moment. "I doubt Lawrence told him, but Daniels could've learned from Duval employees."

"In the brief, I start with *Brady v. Maryland*," Johnson said. "If Daniels knows about Lawrence's substance abuse and hides it, that's a due process violation."

Gabriela leaned back, tired of playing by rules the prosecution ignored. "I don't want to take the chance. File a motion for the rehab records. What will Daniels argue?"

"He'll say we already know about Lawrence's issues and that they're irrelevant."

"It is relevant," Gabriela snapped.

"Absolutely," Roberto said. "The government's star witness was a drunk and a drug abuser during the PetroMex deal. The jury deserves to know that. Otherwise, Daniels will cross the line again."

"Once again?" Gabriela asked.

"He crossed it from the beginning, starting with the search warrant."

"What was wrong with the warrant?"

"The government falsified affidavits to get it."

"How can you be sure?"

"I've seen it before in the Valley. They were hellbent to indict, and now they're hellbent to convict. But that's not the only time they crossed the line."

"What else?"

"FBI witnesses may have lied to the grand jury. So we filed a motion for the government to identify all *Brady* material, anything showing weaknesses in their case. Judge Comstock granted it."

"Does Daniels know about these problems?"

"He knows, but he needs to win at all costs. I'm sure he believes the ends justify the means."

"What else is he doing?"

"He's intimidated Duval employees, threatened to prosecute them if they didn't give him the story he wanted."

Gabriela frowned. "What if they knew nothing about the story he wanted to hear?"

"He told them they were lying and covering up for Duval. Their lawyer said they're all scared to death."

"I met Vivian Dandridge. She's terrified."

Roberto nodded. "And one more trick. They dumped 1.9 million pages on us, ninety-nine percent of it is irrelevant. They're burying the truth."

"Are we really in America?" Gabriela said. "How can they get away with that? Duval says he sent Lawrence an email before going forward, asking him to confirm there were no legal problems. I wonder what Lawrence told Barnes about it."

"Because judges let them," Roberto said. "They say the defense should've found it on their own. That gives prosecutors permission to hide the ball."

Gabriela stared at her notes. When she was young, she'd believed courthouses were where fairness lived. Her father's clients had taught her otherwise—the poor never got equal treatment. She had expected a billionaire would. But the government was punishing Duval simply for fighting back instead of pleading out.

"The Constitution requires prosecutors to ensure fairness," she said quietly. "That doesn't happen when they bend the rules to convict a billionaire."

Roberto sighed. "Most prosecutors mean well, but some will do anything to win. Think about the Stevens case."

"What's that?"

"Ted Stevens, the Alaska senator. Indicted a hundred days before his election. After the trial, the judge discovered prosecutors had concealed evidence helpful to the defense. He said he'd never seen such misconduct."

Gabriela shook her head. "I thought things were different here. Maybe Dallas isn't so different from Washington after all."

Johnson cleared his throat. "I've drafted a motion asking Judge Comstock to make Daniels identify what's favorable to Duval in that mountain of documents."

"Anything specific?" she asked.

"Yes. We're also asking for every statement Don Lawrence made to the FBI. You'll need everything they have to destroy him."

Gabriela knew those reports would show only what helped the government—that's why the FBI hadn't recorded them.

Johnson continued, "After a while, only one agent handled Lawrence."

"Is that normal?"

"No. At first several interviewed him. Then only Thomas Barnes, with rotating note-takers. Maybe they wanted him to build rapport—or maybe they were hiding something."

"Like what?"

"My guess? Early on, Lawrence said something that exonerated Duval. They made no record or buried it in the dump of documents."

Gabriela felt the old frustration settle in. "What can we do?"

"Not much. Once trial starts, we'll be locked into our theory. If Daniels produces something that contradicts it, it'll be too late to change course. We're demanding every FBI 302 report from the American Energy investigation and the company's internal records."

"How does that help Duval?" Johnson asked.

"Because I believe the bribes came from American Energy, not Duval," Gabriela said.

Johnson frowned. "That won't show up in their 302s."

"It might," she said. "If we can show Lopez used American Energy's money to pay PetroMex officials, not Duval's, we'll destroy the government's theory."

"I'll add it to our request."

"What do I have to prove to get the 302s and the Lawrence materials?"

"That the prosecution suppressed evidence, that it's favorable to Duval, and that it's material to the trial."

Gabriela exhaled. "How do I show that when I don't even know what they're hiding?"

"You can't," Roberto said. "That's why you demand everything. Make Comstock force Daniels to identify what he's withholding."

Gabriela looked at both men, feeling the fatigue settle behind her eyes but refusing to show it. "Then that's what we'll do. I'll make him play by the rules, whether he likes it or not."

Chapter 21

The following Tuesday, Gabriela Sanchez walked with her father through the metal detector at the federal courthouse. This time she didn't set it off. When she stepped through, the female U.S. marshal gave her a quick thumbs-up.

She drew a slow breath and steadied herself, the same kind of focus she'd relied on through dozens of high-pressure golf tournaments, back when everything depended on one perfect shot.

Inside Judge Comstock's courtroom, Jason Daniels and Melinda Swanson were already seated at the government's table.

"If it isn't Dallas's own 'Rising Star' and Fox News darling," Daniels said. "Has your client taken you to Washington to meet your two Texas senators?"

Gabriela started to answer but stopped when she heard, "All rise." Judge Comstock entered and took his seat on the bench.

"Ladies and gentlemen, in all my years on the bench, I've never had a case with more motions and disagreements," the judge said. "Almost every day you're before me with something new. Have you tried to resolve any of this before coming to me?"

Gabriela caught the edge in his voice. The judge sounded impatient, and a tired judge was the last thing she needed before trial.

Gabriela stood. "Your Honor, before filing each motion, we called Mr. Daniels's office to discuss it. Sometimes he said no, and often he didn't return our call."

"Your Honor, that's not true," Daniels replied. "I've responded to every legitimate request. Ms. Sanchez's problem is that the only answer she recognizes is one that agrees with her."

Judge Comstock frowned. "We're here today to hear several motions. The defense has moved to suppress a video of a conversation between the defendant and a government witness and also to compel the government to produce discovery documents. Let's begin with the suppression motion. Ms. Sanchez, the floor is yours."

Gabriela delivered her argument, steady and measured. When she finished, Comstock nodded. "Thank you, Ms. Sanchez. Mr. Daniels?"

Daniels made the points she expected. When he finished, the judge began reading from his notes.

"Let's review what's required for attorney–client privilege. First, a client must be seeking legal advice. Second, the communication must be with a lawyer or representative. Third, it must relate to a fact disclosed by the client. Fourth, strangers may not be present. And finally, the client must expect confidentiality."

"Anything else, Mr. Daniels?"

"No, Your Honor."

Judge Comstock looked toward Gabriela. "Ms. Sanchez, I agree that your client and Mr. Lawrence had a lawyer–client relationship. But that alone isn't enough to exclude the video. I've watched and listened more than once. Mr. Duval isn't seeking legal advice, and Mr. Lawrence isn't giving it. In fact, it sounds like Mr. Duval is the one offering advice. The government may introduce the video at trial, and you may argue the nature of their relationship to the jury."

"Yes, Your Honor."

"Thank you, Your Honor," Daniels said, with a grin she ignored.

Comstock continued, "Next, the discovery motions. Mr. Daniels, your office listed seventy-five witnesses."

"Yes, sir."

"Do you intend to call all seventy-five?"

"We're not sure yet, Your Honor. We're erring on the side of disclosure."

Gabriela rose. "Your Honor, we all know Mr. Daniels doesn't plan to call seventy-five witnesses. He's trying to send us on wild goose chases."

"Is she right, Mr. Daniels?"

"No, Your Honor. We would never do that."

"Sure, Mr. Daniels," the judge said. "Two weeks before trial, you'll provide Ms. Sanchez a list of witnesses you actually intend to call. If you don't call all of them, I'll want to know why."

"Yes, Your Honor."

Gabriela stood again. "We also don't believe the government has given us all of Agent Barnes's grand jury testimony."

Daniels rose. "Your Honor, we've turned over all relevant evidence, including Barnes's testimony."

"Mr. Daniels is playing games again," Gabriela said. "His office dumped one-point-nine million pages on us, most of it irrelevant. He expects us to find the needle in the haystack before trial."

"This is a complex case, Your Honor," Daniels replied.

Judge Comstock leaned forward. "Mr. Daniels, consider this fair warning: don't bring new evidence to trial that you haven't disclosed. If you do, after Ms. Sanchez finishes with you, you'll hear from me. Understood?"

"Yes, Your Honor."

"Now," Comstock said, "the defense requests all FBI reports, grand jury testimony, and documents from American Energy's internal investigation. The government claims those aren't material. Is that right, Mr. Daniels?"

"Yes, Your Honor."

"Ms. Sanchez, you argue they're material because they might show payments from American Energy, not your client, funded the bribes. Do you have information suggesting that, or is this a fishing expedition?"

"I have information suggesting it."

"Would you care to share what that information is?"

Gabriela looked at her father. His eyes widened slightly. "I'm not at liberty to disclose that at this time, Your Honor."

If Comstock pressed her again, she would have to decide whether to reveal Lopez's name or protect him. Either choice could backfire.

Daniels pounced. "You see, Judge? Fishing expedition. She can't identify anything material."

"Your Honor," Gabriela said evenly, "if those documents don't show what we expect, Mr. Daniels should have no objection to producing them. There's no way to prosecute or defend this case without tracing the funds. Both sides must know where the money went."

"Mr. Daniels?"

"Those are separate deals, Your Honor."

"Then you have nothing to hide," Comstock said. "I order that you turn over the information to Ms. Sanchez. Any other motions?"

Daniels sighed audibly.

"Yes, Your Honor," Gabriela said. "We have another matter."

"Very well. We'll take it up after lunch."

When Comstock left the bench, Daniels walked over. "Gabby, you're maybe breaking even today. Not bad for someone who's not ready for prime time. Is Chuck Green taking over soon to save your client?" .

Gabriela turned toward the door without responding.

"Do you really think the jury will believe your billionaire client didn't know about the bribes?" Daniels called after her.

She didn't turn back.

Outside, she looked to her father. He smiled faintly. "Daniels wants to rattle you. You frustrate him when you don't react."

"I've learned from you that arguing with him only gives him what he wants."

"Exactly. Let him keep underestimating you. Save your fight for trial, where the judge can keep him in line."

At lunch, Roberto asked, "How do you think Comstock will rule?"

"It's a mixed bag," she said. "We lost the suppression motion—it was a long shot—but I think he'll let us exclude part of the tape. If he orders Daniels to produce the American Energy documents, we'll get another document dump. But at least it'll be ours."

At 1:30 p.m., both teams assembled in Judge Comstock's conference room.

"Given the sensitivity of what we're discussing," he said, "we'll handle this in chambers. Ms. Sanchez, you may proceed."

Gabriela rose, but the judge motioned for her to stay seated.

"Yes, Your Honor. We've learned that Mr. Lawrence, the government's star witness, was in rehab for alcohol and drug abuse. It's entirely possible that during the PetroMex deal, he was under the influence. We seek his medical and rehab records to test his perception, credibility, and motivation. The government has refused. The Supreme Court and Fifth Circuit have both held that the defense has the right to examine a witness's addiction history when it bears on credibility."

"Mr. Daniels?"

"Your Honor, Ms. Sanchez wants to use psychiatric evidence to impeach a witness. The defense can't do that. And releasing Mr. Lawrence's medical records would violate his privacy and doctor–patient privilege."

Gabriela met the judge's eyes. "At the relevant time, Mr. Lawrence was an alcoholic and drug dependent. His memory and judgment were impaired. We have the right to test that."

Comstock paused. "You've both given me a tough one. I'll weigh the defendant's right to confront a witness against the witness's privacy rights. Mr. Daniels, provide me copies of Mr. Lawrence's rehab and medical records. I'll review them in camera and issue an order."

"Is there anything else?"

"Yes, Your Honor," Gabriela said. "We've also requested all correspondence between FBI agents and Don Lawrence, including all emails, texts, or other messages. The government refused, but those communications may contain exculpatory or impeachment material."

Daniels rose. "Your Honor, this is yet another fishing expedition. The defense is speculating that something helpful might exist."

"Mr. Daniels," the judge said, "provide all emails, text messages, and related documents between Mr. Lawrence and the FBI."

Gabriela glanced toward Daniels. He was shaking his head, jaw tight.

Something in his expression unsettled her. He looked less angry than confident, as if the emails he was forced to hand over would hurt her more than help.]

Chapter 22

After her run on Wednesday morning, Gabriela Sanchez made a latte and sat down to read the Dallas Morning News on her iPad. When she got to the local section, her color photo was on the front page. It had been taken while she was helping the family at Sacred Heart Church in McAllen.

The headline: *Duval's Lawyer Helps Immigrant Families*. She started reading the story. For a moment she smiled. It was good press, the kind that might remind the jury she was more than a defense lawyer.

Billionaire Sparks Duval has picked Gabriela Sanchez, a Dallas lawyer, to defend him. Sanchez is known throughout Texas for her contributions of time and money to provide humanitarian relief and legal assistance to Hispanic immigrants and children. A few weeks ago, the DMN caught up with Sanchez when she spent Sunday at an immigrant assistance center in Parish Hall (Welcome Center) of the Sacred Heart Church in McAllen.

Over the last few years, large numbers of immigrants from Honduras, El Salvador and Guatemala have entered the country and been picked up by the US Border Patrol. After being processed, they are dropped off at the McAllen Bus Terminal, where they wait before leaving for their destination. The bus terminal is located two blocks from Sacred Heart Church. At the Welcome Center, Ms. Sanchez has helped families, mostly mothers and children, get a bath, fresh clothing, and a meal before the families go to the bus station.

As Gabriela read on, her cell phone rang. She didn't recognize the number.

"Hello, this is Gabriela Sanchez."

"Ms. Sanchez?"

"Yes."

"This is Aubrey Gall from the *National Tabloid Journal*."

"*National Tabloid Journal*?"

"Yes."

"Why are you calling me?"

"We are planning to run a front-page story about you, and I wanted to contact you before we go to press."

"What kind of story?"

"Let's put it this way. Our story will show you're not the angelic one the media has portrayed you since you were named Sparks Duval's lawyer."

"I thought you published articles about celebrities. I can't believe your readers would care about me?"

"Oh, I think they would. The media has made you a celebrity."

"So, why are you calling me?"

"I just want to share with you what we have and offer you the chance to comment."

"What do you think you have?"

"Well, we know that when you were in high school, you were caught shoplifting and smoking marijuana."

Gabriela raised her voice. "What are you saying? I was never caught shoplifting, and I've never smoked marijuana. Who told you that?"

"A source who knew you. You know I can't divulge our sources."

"I need to know who is lying about me."

"I'm sure you'd like to know, but we promised the source we would not divulge their name. We have another source who told us you are bisexual and had lesbian relationships both in high school and college."

"At least that is not a total lie. I experimented then. Nowadays, do you think anyone cares about that?"

"We do. Many Christians still believe homosexuality is a sin. We also know you've had intimate relationships with several married men."

"That's not true. I've never, and would never, have an intimate relationship with a married man."

"We have photos of you and Christopher Duval on your overnight date in Houston. You are walking with his arm around you. He held your hand at the table. The two of you look like young lovebirds. We have a photo of the two of you in the back seat of the limo. It looks like he is kissing you."

"Nothing happened other than we ate dinner together."

"Our photos look like it was more than dinner."

Gabriela felt her body tense. In an angry tone, she said, "I told you nothing happened between us!"

Gabriela waited for a response, and when she didn't hear one, she said, "Look, Christopher Duval is a good guy. He's married. If you publish those photos, you'll hurt his family."

"We'll check with Christopher to get his version of what happened before we go to press.

"We also know about your affair with Kevin McNally when you first joined the Parker & McEvoy law firm. McNally's ex-wife claims you broke up their marriage when you and her husband started working closely together during your first year. She claims she found his car parked at your apartment."

For the first time, Gabriela understood the fake news concept. "There was no affair. He was my first mentor. We spent a lot of time working on a case together, and his wife became suspicious. He may have been interested in me, but he was a gentleman."

"His wife claimed otherwise in the divorce."

"Kevin denied it. I denied it when her lawyer questioned me. We didn't have an intimate relationship." *Not that Kevin hadn't tried.*

"Then why did Mrs. McNally accuse you, if there was nothing to it?"

"I have no idea. You'd have to ask Mrs. McNally."

"So, you claim Mrs. McNally's accusation is wrong?"

"Yes. I worked on two cases helping Kevin McNally and that's it. People like you make it ever so much more difficult for women to succeed."

"As a result of your relationship, your law firm forced McNally to leave."

That's not true. There was no relationship. One of the firm's female partners got wise to him and saved me from him. "That's not true. He left to become the general counsel of one of the firm's largest clients."

"But he left right after his wife accused the two of you of having an affair."

There was silence as if Gall stopped to process what she had told him.

"We have photos of you dirty dancing with your boss Chuck Green."

"Dirty dancing? We danced the salsa. There was nothing dirty about it."

"Did Connie Schmidt interview you? We understand she was quite upset and told the firm your behavior reflected badly on all the women lawyers in the firm. What do you have to say?"

"She interviewed me, and I told her Chuck Green had been drinking, and I had tried to help him leave the firm event."

"What about your affair with Steve Kraft, the Cowboys quarterback in waiting? You were sexting with him, and we plan to publish the photos and the banter back and forth. You have to admit your text messages to Kraft were a little kinky."

Gabriela's heart sank. If they had the photos she had texted to Steve Kraft when they dated, publishing them would devastate her mother and father. Over their year-long relationship they had texted back and forth "Why do you want to hurt me and embarrass my family? What can I do so they won't be hurt and embarrassed?"

"You've put yourself in the spotlight being on TV every day. You should have thought about embarrassing yourself and your family when you were sexting with Kraft. We have a text he sent you: 'Hello my spicy Latina lover. I've been thinking about what we did last night and want to know when we can do it again because you have the best ass I've ever seen.' Were you his Latina lover?"

"I didn't think anything about it. He sent the text and I didn't reply. You shouldn't publish it."

"It's too sexy to keep out of the story. We have another text Kraft sent you: 'Yes, my exotic one, I loved you undressing for me in your stilettos, garter-belt and nylons. Big turn on looking at what was hidden between your thighs!' You must have been the hot-blooded Latina?"

"He was joking. Please don't publish Kraft's texts. I beg you."

"I'm sure you do, but the texts tell the story of your relationship with Kraft and it goes with the photos of yourself that you sent him."

Gabriela didn't know what to say. She couldn't just say the photos were meant to be private. Before she could speak, Gall continued, "It must have been quite a lurid affair."

"Kraft was single, so I would hardly call it an affair. His texts and my sexting were meant to be kept between the two of us. How did you get a copy of the text messages? Did you hack my phone?"

"No, no. An anonymous source brought us the texts."

"Anonymous?"

"Yes."

"I don't have anything more to say, other than your story is mostly full of lies. I never thought I would become the subject of fake news."

"You make the news almost every night and the entire country is watching the trial coverage. So, you deny the affairs with Christopher Duval and Kevin McNally?"

"Absolutely, and I don't think anything you've said, even the small part that is true, has a bearing on my defense of Sparks Duval. In fact, if you run the fake news story, you'll be doing a grave disservice to Mr. Duval."

"I don't think so."

Gabriela's mind was focusing on who started the story. Was it someone trying to hurt her, or someone trying to hurt Sparks Duval? "Who is encouraging you to run a story about me?"

"You know I can't tell you that. I can only tell you that the source is certainly not one of your friends."

That night Gabriela couldn't sleep. All night she dreamed about the look on her father's face when she first saw him after he saw the story. She woke up the next morning and called him.

"Papá, I have some bad news."

"Bad news?"

"Yes, Papá. *The National Tabloid Journal* is printing a story about me with a lot of lies in it."

"The newspaper at the check-out counter in grocery stores?"

"Yes, Papá."

"Why do they care anything about you?"

"They say I have become a celebrity because I'm defending Sparks Duval."

"What are the lies?"

"That I've had affairs with married men."

"Why are they printing that if it's a lie?"

"Papá, I believe they are trying to destroy Sparks Duval's defense and embarrass me and our family."

"Since you were on TV, this is the way to do it?"

"Yes, Papá. You better prepare Mamá."

"*No hay manera de preparar a tu madre*. I'll do my best."

Two days later the tabloid was on the newsstands in grocery stores throughout America. On the cover was a big color photo of Gabriela Sanchez walking with Christopher Duval into The Four Seasons. More suggestive photos were inside. The headline: *Sparks Duval's Fiery Latina Lawyer Revealed.*

Gabriela read on.

They say she is the Latina vixen and they may be right. Everything about Gabriela Sanchez exudes sex. Her accent, her full red lips, her long brown hair, her stiletto heels accenting her long bronze legs and ample behind. When she walks into any Dallas courtroom, heads are sure to turn. Reportedly, several male judges have jokingly told colleagues that she is the hottest lawyer in Texas, a reputation the Rising Star Sanchez does nothing to discourage.

One judge reportedly told colleagues that he's caught male jurors with mouths wide open just staring at Sanchez.

Since she was named the lawyer to defend Sparks Duval in his Dallas criminal case, the media, in a carefully orchestrated public relations campaign, has tried to convince the public that Gabriela Sanchez is the next coming of Mother Teresa.

In a bombshell article, The Tabloid Journal reveals for the first time that Gabriela Sanchez is far from being a saint.

When she opened the newspaper to the page where the story continued, she saw a selfie photo she had taken of herself in a black bra and the text messages from Steve Kraft. That was embarrassing enough, but thankfully, none of her fully nude photos were there.

The article went on to report that she had been arrested twice when she was in high school. In the next paragraph, she was outed as a bisexual who had been in intimate relationships with a high school classmate, two college girls while she was a student at the University of Texas, and a female fashion model in Dallas.

As she read further, she discovered the Tabloid Journal also questioned her legal ability.

The Tabloid Journal has learned that while defending cases with her father, Roberto, the two of them never successfully defended a client accused of making or receiving a bribe. So, many Dallas lawyers question why Sparks Duval chose a lawyer with a history of losing to defend him.

That made Gabriela even more angry. She had never defended an innocent client when she tried cases with her father.

Who said those things about me? How did they get the photographs of me? I'm as capable of defending Duval as any lawyer in Dallas.

She continued reading.

Roberto Sanchez dreamed that his daughter would become the next Lorena Ochoa, so he had her playing golf as soon as she could hold a golf club. It looked like

Sanchez's dream for his daughter would come true until she choked and blew a two-up lead with three holes to play in the NCAA Championship and lost after she missed a two-foot putt on the first playoff hole. At that point, Sanchez decided not to pursue an LPGA golf career.

"That is not true." She muttered to herself.

I didn't choke. I made one bad shot on sixteen, but while I made par, she birdied seventeen and eighteen and the first play-off hole to win. I missed the putt because it was downhill at lightning speed and broke right the entire way. I don't call that a choke.

Gabriela continued reading.

Growing up in the Rio Grande Valley, when Sanchez was a student at the University of Texas, she had to take a remedial writing course. At Notre Dame Law School, she was called the affirmative action student.

Guess they missed that I finished in the top ten percent of my class.

The National interviewed law school classmates and lawyers in Dallas. All tell the National that Gabriela Sanchez has taken advantage of her good looks to get ahead in law school, and more recently, in her career. Certainly, that was the case when she had an affair with her mentor, Kevin McNally, whose wife identified Sanchez as the other woman in her divorce proceedings. When they were out together, McNally reportedly told Sanchez to not dress like Shakira.

A former partner in her law firm told the National that Sanchez, "Used her Latina sexuality to attract the attention of the senior lawyers in the firm." He says, "It worked, show a lot of leg, in tight skirts with some cleavage showing at the top, and all of a sudden the firm promotes her to partner."

Sparks Duval selected Sanchez to be the second chair to renowned lawyer Chuck Green on his defense team after seeing her photos in D Magazine. After Duval's public relations firm submitted soundbites of Sanchez and Chuck Green to mock juries, he selected her to lead his defense, have her father assist, and told Green to sit behind the rail in the courtroom.

We know that the lawyer Sparks Duval has made the face of his defense has had affairs with four men, two of whom were married, and a dirty dance in public with her married boss. Gabriela stopped reading. She was sick to her stomach. She knew she could no longer be a role model for girls in the Rio Grande Valley, or anywhere else. She saw the call was from Deborah Snow. Before answering she took the sedative her doctor had prescribed.

"I know it was worse than you expected, but we will have a rebuttal blog post and try to get Fox News and the Washington Times to rebut what they have said."

Gabriela didn't know what to say. She could barely speak.

"Are you there, Gabriela? Gabriela are you there? Are you okay?"

Finally, Gabriela replied. "That's nice, but it won't help me when I see my father. You can't know what it's like when you father is ashamed of you."

"Tell him you are sorry, and you hope he will forgive you."

"I'm not sure you understand. He'll forgive me, but I will forever be his girl who brought shame to her family. I will forever be the imposter for the young Hispanic girls."

"Even role models have flaws," Snow replied.

The Tabloid Journal article went viral on Twitter, with her almost nude photo and a link to the article. The general theme of the Twitter posts slut-shamed Gabriela and claimed she caused the divorce. The same tweeters who had been slamming Sparks Duval were now slamming her.

@nofrackingtx tweeted the link to the article twice. In one he tweeted, *#sparksduvalguilty attorney's #salacious #scandalous #shameful tabloid journal cover story*. In the second he tweeted *#sparksduvalguilty attorney's #tawdry, #titillating #trashy @nationaltabloidjournal cover story*. Tweets from others called Gabriela a #slut, #whore, #bitch #otherwoman, and those were just the tame names.

Is Aubrey Gall @nofrackingtx on Twitter? Why would a tabloid reporter care about fracking? He wouldn't, but he might care about destroying Sparks Duval.

Gabriela drove to DFW airport to pick up her father. She parked in the one-hour lot and went in the door at terminal A 21. After about ten minutes, she saw him walk through the revolving door and walk toward her.

When Gabriela saw her father, her eyes teared up. She had never cried in front of him, and she was determined not to cry now. She forced herself to look at him and not look away.

I can't lose it now. She took a deep breath to calm herself.

"Papá, I'm so sorry."

Gabriela expected her father to lecture her. Instead he said, "I know you are. Are you okay?"

"I'm okay, but I'm worried about Mamá.

"With good reason. Your mother is beside herself. She hasn't left the bedroom and refuses to go to the grocery store. She's afraid to show her face outside our house."

Gabriela pictured her mother sitting at the kitchen table with her rosary, a cup of coffee growing cold beside her, staring at nothing in particular.

They walked outside and crossed the street into the parking garage. When they got in Gabriela's car, Gabriela asked, "What can I do to make it better?"

"Call your mother. Be prepared for her to say it's too late to make it better. You can't take back the damage you have done to your family."

Gabriela waited for the gate to go up at the exit. She said, "All I can do is ask for Mamá to forgive me."

"That will take time. Your mother has asked me to come back home and not work with you on the Duval case."

Gabriela turned on to the highway. "Papá, please. I have to win this case to vindicate myself, and I need you to keep me calm and focused now more than ever."

"I thought you were confident you can win on your own."

"No, Papá. You give me confidence. I realize it now. I have to win this case, and I need you more than ever to be at my side."

"Okay Gabriela. But your mother needs me more now. She is anxious and depressed. I'm worried about her."

Gabriela took a breath. "Papá, I understand how Mamá feels. Would she come with you to Dallas? That way she could get away from believing everyone she sees is judging her."

"I don't know. I tried to protect you from the beginning. I told you this case was too big and the government would do whatever it takes to win. You didn't listen. When Duval hired the public relations firm, I tried to protect you again. You didn't listen. Now you've proved I was right on both counts."

Gabriela frowned. "Papá, I don't need your protection. I need your help. We need to win now more than ever."

"We aren't defending Duval. You are. You need to win. Get Chuck Green to help you. I don't want any part of a case for a man who relies on a public relations firm."

Gabriela held back the tears and took another deep breath. "I trust you and want you, and at this point, I'm not sure I can win without you."

"Gabriela, I love you. The article and your photos haven't changed that, but I also want the best for you. There's something I must tell you."

"Sure Papá. What is it?"

"You've changed since you moved to Dallas."

She wanted to argue, to say he was wrong, but the words caught in her throat. "In what way?" she finally asked.

"When you came back from law school, and worked with me, you were humble, and you were focused on the person you wanted to become."

"I'm still focused on that, Papá."

"You may think so, but you act differently."

Gabriela gasped and sighed. She felt her heart racing. "What, Papá?"

"Since you moved to Dallas, you've been focused on you, what you want to achieve, what you want to wear, and what you want people to think of you. The Tabloid Journal was right about that. It's like you are constantly putting on a show for an audience."

"I don't understand. When I was growing up, you encouraged me to dream big dreams and work hard to achieve them."

"I did. I encouraged you to dream big dreams and do your best to excel at whatever you wanted to achieve. That's different from being more focused on your ego, your work and how you look, and less focused on who you are on the inside."

"Papá, I do focus on what I am on the inside. I work to help children stay in our country. I contribute money each month to the Sacred Heart Church in McAllen so they can provide clothing for immigrant families."

"Maybe when you are helping children, but other times, you're not. You need to remember who you are, or maybe, re-discover who you are. I can tell you what I think, but it will be more powerful if you think about it."

She smiled for the first time. "Thank you, Papá. What after that?"

"Look at what you are doing, and even ask why you are doing it. Does what you are doing fit your vision of the person you want to be?"

"Yes, Papá. Thank you."

She saw her father's face soften.

With that, Roberto Sanchez looked away. Gabriela couldn't hold back the tears any longer.

Wow, I'm crying! I've never cried like this before. How can I make him proud of me again?

Two hours later Gabriela Sanchez read the blog post about *the National Tabloid Journal* article. The title: *National's Duval's Lawyer Affair Story is Crap.*

She read on.

I recently read the National's *article about Sparks Duval's defense lawyer, Gabriela Sanchez's lesbian relationships in high school and college, her current affair with Christopher Duval, and affairs with a married Parker & McEvoy partner and with the Dallas Cowboys back-up quarterback.*

I recognize that the National *has been right on other occasions, but it also has been wrong far more often. But my initial thought was why would the* National *publish this article?*

Who cares if she had intimate relationships with girls and women? I don't. Gabriela Sanchez is a single woman, and Steve Kraft is also single and sits on the bench. She allegedly also had an affair with a married partner in her firm. But that partner and his wife divorced, and he moved on to a different firm.

I'm not sure that it matters, but the National *never identified the women with whom Ms. Sanchez had an intimate relationship and in his divorce case, lawyer Kevin McNally denied having an intimate relationship with Ms. Sanchez. That leaves Steve Kraft. Does the public have a right to know, and more importantly, does the public care if two single people living in Dallas are sleeping together?*

So, how did the article get into the National Tabloid Journal? *Who wanted to smear Sparks Duval's defense lawyer? The* National *hit piece failed to answer that question.*

Is it just a coincidence that Gabriela Sanchez is defending Sparks Duval in one of the most highly watched trials this century? I doubt it.

Someone is digging deep into Gabriela Sanchez's personal life and flinging arrows at her, with the goal of derailing the Duval defense. I find it interesting that the National *published the article less than a month before the scheduled trial date and within a week of an article about Ms. Sanchez's work with immigrant families.*

Gabriela dialed Deborah Snow.

They talked at length about combating the National Tabloid Journal story. Gabriela was thankful the blogger had attacked the story, but she realized that would never placate her mother who would be reminded every time she checked out at the grocery store.

Gabriela worried that people wouldn't find the blog post, and Deborah assured her they would because it had been tweeted by over ten thousand people on Twitter and the blogger had created a YouTube video attacking the article.

Deborah shared that she had contacted Fox News and had set up an interview for Gabriela to answer questions about the article and show it was a hatchet job. Because she would not be asked about the case, the interview would not violate Judge Comstock's gag order.

Their conversation then turned to changing Gabriela's appearance.

"Given your nearly-nude photos that were made public, we're going to have to work on your wholesome appearance for the courtroom. Steven has some ideas to share with you, and we have some wardrobe suggestions. No pencil skirts or anything tight that shows off your bottom."

"I don't want to change my appearance," Gabriela said, raising her voice.

"I didn't create your image problem. You did and you must change it. I'll schedule a meeting for you with Steven."

"Before I meet with Steven, I need to talk to Chuck Green."

"About what?"

"I may need him to replace my father as co-counsel. When my father read the tabloid article and saw the photos, he quit."

"Your father can't quit. It's too late for that."

It was clear that Deborah did not know her father.

Chapter 23

Chuck Green shook his head. "Your father can't quit. Sparks Duval expects him to support you, and you need his help."

"Well, Chuck, I'm afraid he did."

For the first time, she couldn't picture trying a case without her father sitting beside her.

"Duval will go ballistic."

"True, so he needs to persuade my father."

"He will make an offer your father can't refuse."

Gabriela got up to leave.

"Where are you going?"

"To my office. Afterward I'm going to Starbucks, for the meeting I've been dreading. What can a white guy from New York City know about the best image for a Latina lawyer in Dallas?"

"I guess you'll find out," Green replied, smiling as he reached over and picked up his telephone.

When Gabriela returned to her office, Lucia stopped her.

"What's wrong?" Lucia asked.

"You know what's wrong. The article."

"Sure, but there must be more to it than that."

Gabriela sighed. "I expected my father to read me the riot act. Instead, he asked me how I was doing and told me he loved me."

"That's good. So, what's wrong?"

"I could tell by his tone I had disappointed him. That feeling is worse than if he had acted upset. He also told me he would not help me with the trial."

"Oh."

Gabriela thought about all the times she had assisted her father. He made her feel like she was the best lawyer in the Rio Grande Valley. She was always afraid of losing because she knew if she lost, it would severely impact her client and his family.

Her father's belief in her had helped her overcome whatever anxiety or fear she had felt going into a trial. He had once told her that it was okay to be anxious or nervous, and he could see that the prosecutor was more afraid and nervous. Roberto explained she would become an outstanding trial lawyer because jurors could see she was real and a caring.

"I can't defend Sparks Duval without him. He knows how to bring out the best in me," Gabriela said. "The stakes are too high."

"You may have no choice. If he is unwilling to help, you'll have to prepare like never before. Your fear is of the unknown. If you are totally prepared for anything, you will do well."

"You're wrong. I need my father's support. He keeps me steady and focused."

"May I offer some advice?"

"You usually do without asking. Not sure what you think will matter this time."

"Maybe not. But here's what you should consider. Your father is awesome, but you don't necessarily need him sitting next to you to win a case. You're mentally tougher and more confident than that. Take your nervous energy and use it to your advantage."

Gabriela thought for a moment. He had always been by her side for the most difficult cases. She said, "Thank you. I needed you to kick in the behind. Eventually I have to deal with my fear of losing on my own."

Thirty minutes later, Gabriela sat across from Steven Graham, sipping on her vanilla latte.

Graham started by explaining that the judge, the jury, and , public through television cameras would have their eyes riveted on her and would be judging her appearance.

Gabriela agreed and told Graham she was judged every day and that was one reason she chose to work out and stay fit.

Graham then hit a hot button when he claimed that Gabriela's clothing choices, like those of many Latina women, showed she lacked confidence in herself. Her patience was wearing thin; every word out of his mouth sounded like another rule written for someone else.

They argued over whether Latina businesswomen and news reporters dressed too provocatively.

Gabriela could not believe what she was hearing.

"We want you to dress demurely so jurors won't be distracted by your appearance," Graham said.

"I am not a demure woman. If I dress that way, jurors will think I'm a fake."

"Keep your voice down, people are staring at us."

"You know nothing about me, much less what I wear to court. You know nothing about the Hispanic culture and how women dress. I dress professionally, and it is part of my unique image. It draws attention to me and away from my adversary."

She saw him roll his eyes. "Ms. Sanchez, I don't want to argue with you."

"So stop arguing."

"Let's just say you don't want to be known for your cleavage, hips, or your shoes in the courtroom. All the jury will think about are your near-naked photos they saw in the article."

Gabriela quit arguing, hoping she would be done with him sooner.

"The one thing we can agree on is that women lawyers have many more choices to make than men."

"I agree. Men just need to make sure their tie matches their suit and shirt, and they don't wear light brown shoes with a navy blue suit."

Steven Graham spent the next fifteen minutes discussing his research, describing interviews with jurors and judges, focus groups, and surveys. Jurors often commented on how female lawyers dressed and rarely on how men did. At the end, he argued that what he had told Gabriela was not just his opinion but was based on research.

Gabriela had done her own research. She found jurors were impressed by authenticity and that included how they dress.

"May I ask you a few questions about your research?" Gabriela asked.

"Sure."

"How many Dallas Federal Court jurors did you interview?"

"Well, none, but I don't think geography changes my findings."

"And none of the focus groups were here in Dallas?"

"No, but again geography should not make a difference."

"Were any of the lawyers whose image was judged by jurors or focus groups, Hispanic women?"

"No."

"African-American women?"

"One or two."

"Out of thousands?"

"Yes."

"Go on with your findings on what image jurors and focus groups expect or want from white female lawyers."

"Their expectations aren't just of white female lawyers. Plus, given the unfortunate stereotyping of Latinas as looking sultry, I believe if anything, Latina lawyers should present an even more wholesome image."

Gabriela clenched her fists and raised them to pound on the table. She caught herself, unclenched her hands, and placed her palms on the table.

"We're sultry? I'm a little confused."

"About what?"

"You and Deborah decided I should be Sparks Duval's defense lawyer because I am Hispanic, right?"

"That's only part of it."

"And now you want me to abandon my Hispanic identity. That makes no sense."

Graham turned to her hairstyle and told Gabriela she should get her hair cut and should pull it back. He told her that her skirts should be at least knee-length and should not cup her rear end, and that her heels should be no more than two inches.

Gabriela told him she would not change her hairstyle and because she was tall, she didn't own any skirts that were knee-length, and she planned to wear heels like she had on that day.

They were at an impasse, but Graham made matters worse when he said, "You're fighting me on this, but what I'm telling you is important. Your heels should be no higher than two inches and should be closed-toe. We don't want the judge or members of the jury to confuse you for a hooker."

That was the final blow. "Hooker?" Gabriela stood up to leave. She looked at Graham. "Do you have firsthand experience of a hooker's heels?"

"Sit down, Gabriela. If you want to be treated like a professional in the courtroom, you have to dress more professionally."

Gabriela sat down. "You're saying if I want to be treated like a professional in the courtroom, I need to dress the way a white female lawyer would dress. That makes no sense. I am not a white female lawyer. Plus, you and Deborah expect me to appeal to the men and the Hispanics on the jury."

"No, I'm suggesting how any female lawyer appearing in court in one of the most visible and publicized trials in years should dress. Your ethnicity has nothing to do with it."

"But it does. I'm Latina. We dress differently. I have to be me, not an Americanized version of me you're trying to create."

"Which is partly to blame for the negative stereotypes you've been trying to avoid."

"Jessica Pearson doesn't dress the way you are suggesting, and her hair is longer than shoulder-length. She's a power dresser, and that's what I am. If you want to pick out a wardrobe for me based on her designer suits and dresses, go for it."

"She plays a fictional character on television. You'll be in a real courtroom in Dallas, Texas. As an aside, all of Jessica Pearson's skirts and dresses are knee-length."

"If that's true, I'll wear mine knee-length. But, beyond that, I'm not letting you or anyone else tell me what to wear."

"Even if it means losing Mr. Duval's case?"

"I plan on winning it."

****

When Gabriela returned to the office, Lucia caught her. "What did he suggest?" Lucia asked.

Gabriela shared what Graham had suggested and her response.

For the next hour, Gabriela searched for photos of Gina Torres and if she liked an outfit, she emailed the photo to Steven Graham.

Lucia stepped into Gabriela's office. "Sparks Duval is on the phone."

She hesitated, then added, "Your dad always comes around, you know. Maybe this time will be the same."

"Tell him I've gone for the day."

"He knows that's not true."

"What?"

"He called from Chuck Green's office, and Chuck told him you were here. He wants to come down to see you."

"I can't wait."

Gabriela was certain she knew what Duval wanted to discuss and she was right.

Two minutes later, Sparks Duval was at her door. He told her that her father had every reason to be upset with her about the *National Tabloid Journal* photos and story, but she had better get him back on the defense team, pronto.

"I already tried," Gabriela said.

"Then I'll have to take care of it myself," Duval said.

"How?"

"I know what will convince him to stay on the defense team. He's broke. Your mother is not well, and he needs the money far more than you. I told Chuck Green that $100,000 of what you charge for your work will be paid directly to your father."

"Don't do that to me. It will make things between us even worse. I'll take care of it. My father just needs time."

"You better take care of getting him back on the team, and fast. One other thing."

"What's that?"

"Deborah called and said you weren't cooperating on the advice Steven Graham offered."

Gabriela frowned. She had expected Deborah to contact Duval.

"I didn't," Gabriela said after a pause, "because he knows nothing about Dallas juries, knows nothing about how Latina businesswomen and lawyers dress and has never had a focus group consider either."

"Gabriela, I'm telling you to listen to what Graham is saying and follow his advice, especially after the *National Tabloid Journal* article. I have confidence in Deborah and him. You need to be on board."

I don't have any confidence in them.

"Mr. Duval, I have to be the real me, not a made-up, public-relations version of me dictated by a couple of New Yorkers. I can't fake who I am."

"You're making a mountain out of a molehill. All I am asking is for you to follow Graham's advice on the length of your hair and what you wear to court. That's not faking who you are."

"Mr. Duval, there's way more to it than that."

If she had learned anything so far about Sparks Duval, it was that there was no arguing with him.

***

The next morning after her run and shower, her cell phone rang. She looked and saw it was her father.

She anxiously answered. "Papá, are you calling to say you will come to Dallas and help me defend Sparks Duval" Gabriela needed for her father to come back to Dallas. He was the one who enabled her to feel confident in herself. He was the one with whom she could brainstorm ideas. Most importantly, he was the one who could act as a foil when Deborah Snow told her what to do.

"I told you I can't help you now. I told you I want you to come home."

Gabriela understood that in the MexicanAmerican culture, when a parent was ailing, the youngest unmarried child came home.

"No Papá no. Quitting now is no longer an option. I'd be forever known as the lawyer who quit defending the richest man in Texas after her photo was on the front page of a tabloid."

Gabriela could not go home a failure. She couldn't face all the people who had questioned whether she was smart enough to go to the University of Texas in Austin, smart enough to get into a law school and capable enough to practice law in a big city. She was certain everyone who knew her in the Rio Grande Valley had seen her photos in the National Tabloid Journal.

Gabriela decided to change the subject.

"Papá, we've made a motion to get Lawrence's rehab records and all of his texts, emails, and other correspondence with the FBI."

"Has Judge Comstock ruled?"

"Not on the rehab records, but he has directed Daniels to provide us with all of the text, emails and other correspondence between Lawrence and the FBI."

"Great work. You just might see what Lawrence and the FBI agents were thinking and saying to each other."

Gabriela hoped from her father's compliment that he really wanted to be in Dallas helping her.

"From the look on Daniels' face, there must be some helpful materials in those documents. He was frowning and shaking his head like he dreaded giving them up."

"What could he fear?"

"We'll soon find out."

"That's good, the back and forth with the FBI may give you plenty to confront Lawrence with when you cross-examine him. There just might be notations in the exchange that exonerate Sparks Duval."

"That's where I want your help. You are the only one I can trust to give ideas and give me honest feedback. I can't stomach the idea of getting ideas and feedback from the PR team."

"You can call me anytime."

"Sparks Duval told me I had to get you back on the trial team."

"Tell him you tried, and I declined. He can use you as his Hispanic prop, but he's not using me. I don't like Duval's public relations team. You'll learn that you can't successfully defend someone if you aren't calling the shots. Plus, they got you into trouble with their campaign. Their attempt to make you look like Mother Teresa led to the *exposée*, proving you're not."

"Papá."

"I've got to go. Tell Duval I'll think about whether I can leave your mother, but I don't like what your defending him has done to our family."

Gabriela knew from those words that no matter what else he said, he couldn't stay away. She allowed herself a faint smile. For the first time in days, she believed he'd be there when it mattered.

Chapter 24

A week before the trial, as she was sitting down for dinner, her doorbell rang. When Gabriela opened it, she was at first startled.

"I'm here to sit with you and help you."

She had been right. He wanted to help her after all. Gabriela reached out and hugged Roberto Sanchez tighter than ever before. She wondered if Sparks Duval had gone through with his offer to give $100,000 of her fee to her father.

"Papá, I'm so happy to see you!"

After her father sat down in his favorite chair, Gabriela called Chuck Green. She whispered, "He's back to help me."

Green sounded relieved. Now he could get back to work for other clients.

A week later, Gabriela went to bed early, knowing that the next day she, her father, and Sparks Duval would sit at the counsel table looking over the potential jurors.

Going to bed was one thing. Sleeping was an entirely different story. Early in Gabriela's career, her father had told her that he had never slept well during a trial. Gabriela hadn't either, but this time it was worse. It was the trial of the century. Top lawyers, the press and Deborah Snow would pass judgment on everything she did each day of the trial. As Vince Lombardi had once said, *"Winning isn't everything. It's the only thing."*

Gabriela feared losing. She understood that all trial lawyers are afraid of losing, but it was a painful feeling. If she failed, an innocent man might go to prison, and his reputation would be destroyed forever. *But was Sparks Duval truly innocent?*

That night she tossed and turned until, near four o'clock, she gave up on sleep. Faces of jurors drifted through her mind. In one dream she couldn't remember the password for her iPad—the one with every note and document she'd need at trial. Each mistake she imagined played out in front of Judge Comstock, the jurors, and the local, state, and national media camped outside the courthouse.

Gabriela tried to turn the fear into fuel. *I've got this. I can do this. I've prepared for this my entire life. I will win.*

She'd managed pressure in college, in law school, and working beside her father, but nothing eased the tightness in her chest. When she finally sat at her desk, she read her opening statement again and again until she knew every word.

She remembered something the famous trial lawyer Gerry Spence had said in an interview: *Every trial is a case about betrayal.* Jurors understand betrayal, he'd said, because everyone has lived it. In this case, Don Lawrence had betrayed Sparks Duval, and Gabriela intended to make that the heart of her defense.

In the morning Gabriela dressed for the courtroom in one of the black Armani suits Steven Graham had picked out for her. According to

Graham, the slight flare at the hem supposedly drew attention away from her figure. A week before the trial, despite her protest, Graham had pressured Gabriela to go to a salon where the stylist could cut her hair to shoulder-length. Gabriela had refused.

On the first day of trial, Gabriela wore four-inch heels, another sign of standing up for herself. In those heels, she looked taller than Jason Daniels.

***

When Gabriela and Roberto Sanchez arrived at the courthouse, a line of media reporters and cameramen greeted them. Reporters barked questions at her while cameras recorded her every move. Gabriela ignored them and walked quickly into the courthouse.

This is your dream case. You are prepared to win. Gabriela ignored any feelings of doubt or anxiety. Her father had once told her that before a big trial, most nervous lawyers make one last trip to the bathroom. She followed that routine.

Two minutes later, as they walked down the courtroom aisle, Gabriela looked for Chuck Green in the packed courtroom. She sighed. He wasn't there. She looked again, and found Green sitting a few benches behind the rail.

Prior to the trial, her father and Deborah Snow had carefully studied the eighty potential jurors' answers to the questionnaire each submitted prior to the trial. Almost every potential juror knew the name William Thomas "Sparks" Duval. Green and Snow each had strong opinions on which potential jurors would favor the defense.

Gabriela had been surprised that several potential jurors earned over 4100,000 a year and that nearly thirty held college degrees. Chuck wanted those jurors, but Deborah wanted more blue-collar workers who had been left behind during the Obama years.

Most of the jurors over forty claimed to be regular churchgoers. Chuck thought they would not make the best jurors. Deborah wanted as many regular churchgoers as possible. That had been a significant part of her PR campaign.

Gabriela and her father had done their own research of the potential jurors. They checked out each prospective juror's' social media pages to discover any bias that might deny Sparks Duval a fair trial. They discovered a great deal about each prospective juror from his or her online personas. Many of the potential jurors had posted their political views on social media sites. She also found two prospective jurors who were environmentalists. Each had posted negative comments about fracking.

When Gabriela arrived at the counsel table, she looked down and found a folder. She opened it and saw a document titled: *Trial Objections Cheat Sheet*. She looked at the yellow Post-it Note, and read, *I use this. Remember, jurors will not get the nitty-gritty details. They will focus on fundamental fairness. You should also. Chuck.*

She turned back. Green smiled.

During the jury questioning, several potential jurors automatically concluded that Sparks Duval was guilty solely because he was rich.

Gabriela struck some of them for cause, but their bias made her question whether Duval would have gotten a fairer hearing from Judge Comstock.

Too late now. That ship has sailed. We're stuck with a jury.

Daniels chose young jurors, especially any young juror who supported Bernie Sanders in 2016. Each chance he had he excused middle-aged and elderly jurors. He must have also wanted jurors that used social media. He had asked each potential juror to describe their social media use and how they received the news of the day.

Gabriela believed the youngest jurors, especially those who spent their time using social media, would have the shortest attention spans. She hoped Daniels would bore them and put them to sleep.

After several hours and challenges, the lawyers had finally selected twelve jurors and two alternates. They had selected seven women and five men, comprised of one black man and one black woman, one Hispanic man, two Hispanic women, and seven white jurors. Their ages ranged from early twenties to late fifties. One thing was certain: None of the jurors lived in affluent neighborhoods like Highland Park or Preston Hollow or hung out in any other places that Sparks Duval frequented.

When Gabriela entered the courtroom after the lunch recess, she noticed more than a dozen reporters seated in an area Judge Comstock had reserved for them. The one reporter who attracted her attention was Aubrey Gall, the *National Tabloid Journal* reporter. She recognized him from photos she had found from a Google search. There was clearly tension in the air.

When the jurors were seated, Judge Comstock said, "Mr. Daniels, you may address the jury."

Gabriela looked over at his counsel table. She saw several filing cabinets within reach behind his chair. Melinda Swanson handed Jason Daniels a legal pad, and he rose and strode to the podium, with head held high and pages of notes.

"May it please the court. Ladies and gentlemen of the jury. My name is Jason Daniels." Gabriela saw his head move slightly up as if he was looking at the wall behind the jury. Right from the start, he appeared to be nervous. Despite his swagger, Daniels had little jury trial experience.

Gabriela looked at the jury. She suspected the jurors knew right away from Daniels' accent that he was not a Texan.

After introducing himself and Melinda Swanson, Daniels seemed to settle in and get more comfortable.

As Gabriela expected, Daniels began by telling jurors that Sparks Duval was arrogant and greedy and that the reason he decided to take his fracking operation to Mexico was because he wasn't satisfied being the largest natural gas driller in the United States.

Then Daniels went right to the bribery and claimed that "we know Duval bribed the PetroMex officials because Don Lawrence pleaded guilty and is obligated to tell the truth."

Roberto Sanchez elbowed his daughter in the ribs. Gabriela knew he must want her to object, but she didn't know the grounds for an objection. She stood and looked as her father hurriedly wrote.

Her pulse quickened. Every juror was watching. She looked down at the paper. "Your Honor, we object to Mr. Daniels suggesting Mr. Lawrence has done anything honorable and object to his statement that Mr. Lawrence is obligated to tell the truth. He can't bolster his witness's testimony."

"Your Honor, I couldn't understand Ms. Sanchez. Could you have her repeat her objection?"

"Mr. Daniels, I understood what Ms. Sanchez said. Her objection is sustained. I shouldn't need to remind you not to bolster your witness's testimony. Just tell the jury who will testify and skip bolstering. Do you understand?"

"Yes, Your Honor. I do."

"Ladies and gentlemen, when I sustain an objection, that means you should disregard what was said," Judge Comstock said while shuffling papers in front of him.

That rebuff seemed to shake Daniels' self-confidence, and he started talking faster. He brought up Lawrence's plea agreement and what it said if Lawrence 'didn't tell the truth.

That brought another objection from Gabriela and a rebuke from Judge Comstock, who said, "The objection is sustained. Mr. Daniels, I have warned you once. We are not going to have you bolstering Mr. Lawrence's testimony before we even hear from him. And I am warning you not to try it after he testifies."

Daniels glared at Gabriela. He apparently had missed the point, because when he turned to the jury again, he said, "Ladies and gentlemen as Judge Comstock has told you, you'll hear from Mr. Donald Lawrence, one of the top energy lawyers in Texas, and the former Duval Energy general counsel. Mr. Lawrence has firsthand knowledge of the deal Duval struck with PetroMex and entered into a plea agreement requiring him to tell the truth."

This time Judge Comstock interrupted. "Mr. Daniels, you must have a hearing problem or an inability to comprehend what I have told you. Do you want me to conclude your opening statement right now?"

It is very unusual for an opening statement to draw so many objections. Gabriela chalked it up to Daniels' lack of jury trial experience. A lawyer has only one chance to connect with a jury, and so far, Gabriela thought Daniels was blowing it.

Daniels turned to explaining how Duval Energy had paid José Lopez a thirty percent fee. Then he said, "The government will prove that the defendant, William Thomas Duval, either knew, or purposely chose not to know that José Lopez planned to take a portion of the thirty percent commission Duval Energy paid him and bribe, yes bribe, the PetroMex officials.

"At the conclusion of the trial," Daniels told the jury, "we will ask you to find the defendant, William Thomas Duval and his company, Duval Energy, guilty of bribing Mexican officials to win a fracking contract in violation of the Foreign Corrupt Practices Act."

Judge Comstock looked over at Gabriela. "Ms. Sanchez, you may address the jury."

Gabriela had learned that an opening statement is more important than a final argument because a number of jurors made up their mind at the start.

One time before a big trial in the Valley, she had told her father she was nervous and afraid. He had grimaced and shaken his head.In a stern voice, he had said, "Gabriela, look at me." She had looked him in the eye. "It's okay to be nervous and afraid. If you weren't, I'd worry about whether you care enough to win. The jurors are also afraid. They are also nervous. They have a big responsibility. Be yourself in the courtroom. Act the same way you would if you were having coffee with the jurors. They'll respect you for respecting them."

She left her iPad and notes on the counsel table and stepped to the lectern. That distinguished her from Jason Daniels. She started by letting the jurors get to know her, and hopefully like her.

"Thank you, Your Honor. Good morning, ladies and gentlemen. When I was a little girl growing up in the Rio Grande Valley, my father, Roberto Sanchez." She turned and looked at her father. "He was a lawyer, and he took me to court with him. Each time when we were alone in the courtroom, he would have me sit where you are in the jury box. One day I asked him, 'Why do you have me sit there?' He said, 'If you ever become a lawyer, you'll want to see what the courtroom looks like as a juror.' So, I've sat in your seats and I know from my father what it is like to be a juror.

"Before I discuss what I believe the evidence will show in this case, I want to give you a sense of what it is like for me now to be defending Sparks Duval. I wish I wasn't so afraid. I'm afraid that a man who started with nothing and worked hard and became a huge success and made lots of money cannot get a fair trial no matter what I say or what the evidence shows.

"Long before the CSI television show, a famous television detective described how he solved crimes. He said, 'You look at the science and look at the motive.' CSI has made the science famous.

"You might wonder, what's the science in this case? There is more science than you might imagine. But you won't hear or see much science in this case. If Mr. Duval was guilty, he would have unwittingly left a paper trail. The only paper trail in this case exonerates Mr. Duval. Sparks Duval emailed Donald Lawrence, asking his lawyer, one of the top energy lawyers in the country, to make sure there were no legal issues with the deal.

"The science is following the flow of the money from Duval Energy to José Lopez. The government must prove that money paid by Duval Energy made it to the pockets of the PetroMex officials."

Gabriela paused and looked at the jurors to make sure they understood what she had just told them.

"Let's turn to motive. Powerful people at the justice department in Washington, including Mr. Daniels, went after Sparks Duval." She counted to five while she turned and stared at Jason Daniels.

"They sent more than fifty FBI agents in kevlar vests and extra clips of ammunition in a raid of Duval Energy's offices and Mr. Duval's home. Were they looking for terrorists? No, they did that to terrify Duval's employees.

"Why? Could it be because Mr. Duval was one of the most ardent supporters of the newly elected President Trump?"

As she expected that brought Jason Daniels to his feet. "Your Honor, I object to the notion this is a political vendetta."

Judge Comstock glared down at Daniels. "Mr. Daniels, that is not what Ms. Sanchez said. Your objection is overruled."

"Is it because Mr. Duval grew up poor and worked hard to develop one of the most successful oil and gas businesses in the country? If the government in Washington can come down here to Dallas and do this to Mr. Duval, they can do it to you or to me, or to anyone sitting behind me."

She turned and faced the packed courtroom.

"We live in Texas. Unlike Mr. Daniels, who has to report to his boss in Washington, you don't have to answer to anyone in Washington, DC.

"The government must prove that Mr. Duval acted 'corruptly' and 'willfully'; and that Mr. Duval authorized the payment 'while knowing' that Mr. Lopez planned to direct the money, in whole or part, to a foreign official.

"The evidence will show that Mr. Duval wasn't even interested in investing in Mexico. So, why did Duval Energy enter into a contract with PetroMex?

"Donald Lawrence. Mr. Duval depended on Mr. Lawrence for advice. The only evidence in this case that even suggests Mr. Duval knew some of the money paid to Lopez went to PetroMex officials will come from the mouth of Mr. Lawrence. Mr. Daniels left out one critical fact in his opening statement.

"Mr. Lawrence betrayed his client, Mr. Duval. The code of ethics for lawyers required Mr. Lawrence to be loyal to his client. Mr. Lawrence broke that code of ethics when he secretly received a two-million-dollar bonus from Mr. Lopez. Why did Mr. Lopez give Mr. Lawrence two million dollars?"

Gabriela took a moment to let it sink in.

"Think about it. Why do you suppose Mr. Lopez put two million dollars in an account in Panama for Mr. Lawrence? Why did he pay Mr. Lawrence anything? Lawrence worked for Mr. Duval—"

Jason Daniels leaped to his feet. "Your Honor. Ms. Sanchez is making a closing argument not an opening statement about the case. There is no evidence on why Mr. Lopez put two million dollars in an account for Mr. Lawrence."

Judge Comstock responded. "Mr. Daniels, you're right. There is no evidence why Mr. Lopez put two million dollars in a Panama bank account for Mr. Lawrence. As I understand what I have heard, Ms. Sanchez is asking the jurors to question why Mr. Lopez gave Mr. Lawrence the money. Ms. Sanchez may do that in her opening statement."

Gabriela looked over at Daniels and smiled. He was shaking his head. Gabriela turned back to the jury.

"Ladies and gentlemen, the government found the secret account several months ago. That's when the FBI approached Mr. Lawrence and asked him to wear a recording device and try to get Mr. Duval to admit to the crime. Can you imagine, Mr. Duval's lawyer, the person he trusted to advise him, betrayed his client when he wore a recorder to entrap Mr. Duval. You will hear the recording. Mr. Duval never once said he knew or expected José Lopez to bribe PetroMex officials. Near the end of the recording, you'll see Sparks Duval knew something was wrong. His face turns red and he glares at Lawrence and says, "Don, you're wearing a wire, aren't you?" Lawrence shrugs, turns and walks out of the room.

"Let's turn back to motive. Who had a reason to make a deal in Mexico? Who knew where the money paid to José Lopez was going? Ladies and gentlemen, you will learn the answer. You will learn that Sparks Duval depended on the advice he received from his lawyer, Mr. Lawrence. As you listen to the evidence, I want you to ask yourself, 'Who benefited from Duval's contract with PetroMex?'"

Gabriela looked the jurors in the eyes. She could tell they were thinking about the answer to her question.

"As you hear the evidence, you will discover the obvious answer and on that basis return with a not guilty verdict."

As she walked back to the table, Roberto Sanchez greeted her with a smile and a quick wink. That was all she needed.

Judge Comstock looked over at the jurors. "Let's adjourn until tomorrow at 10:00 a.m. At that time, Mr. Daniels will call the first government witness."

When they reconvened, at the Parker & McEvoy office, Deborah Snow started attacking Gabriela.

"I looked at the jury," Snow said. You were nervous, and they saw it. Some jurors could not understand you, because you spoke softly with an accent. You've got to make a better connection with the jury."

Before Gabriela could respond, Roberto Sanchez said, "Ms. Snow, you don't know what you are saying. Daniels looked nervous. Gabriela looked confident. Daniels barely gave jurors eye contact. Gabriela connected with each juror, even the young ones who you could see were bored when Daniels spoke to them. You need to keep your mouth shut and let Gabriela be Gabriela."

"Mr. Sanchez, Gabriela started her opening statement fine, but as she went through it, she started speaking faster and with more of a Spanish accent, like she couldn't wait to return to her seat."

"That's how I speak," Gabriela responded.

Deborah Snow glared at Gabriela, took one step toward her, and pointed her finger. "Then you need to change. You can't be nervous, and you have to speak slower now."

Roberto responded, "Gabriela can't defend Sparks if you are pushing her to think of her speaking mechanics. She connected with the jurors. The jurors paid close attention to her and liked her. You are damaging our defense, and you must stop now."

Snow walked toward him. "Good try Mr. Sanchez." She looked over to Gabriela. "Pay attention Gabriela, this is the most important trial in

Texas since Enron, and the local, national and international media are all watching and reporting. Get with it."

Chapter 25

Roberto Sanchez heard his daughter tossing and turning all night. He understood; he'd tossed and turned many nights after the first day of a trial. She was still nervous and couldn't get the jury, and likely Deborah Snow, out of her head.

At 5:00 a.m., he woke up and turned on the Keurig coffee maker. She came into the kitchen in her running clothes. Roberto saw her nose had bled during the night, and he knew that was a result of her anxiety about the trial. He handed Gabriela his handkerchief, and she wiped her nose.

"Papá, my cell phone has been ringing all night. I finally turned it off. When I woke up this morning, I saw over one hundred voicemail messages."

"Who called you?"

"Environmentalists spouting hate about me defending a person who is destroying the environment."

"How did these people get your phone number?"

"I'm not sure, but someone who hates Sparks Duval must have posted it on social media. I don't know how that person found out my cell number."

After drinking coffee, Gabriela went out for a run to clear her head.

Three hours later, she came back to the kitchen dressed for her day in court. She wore a white blouse with three strands of pearls, a black blazer, and a black pencil skirt.

Roberto Sanchez thought his daughter looked professional in her power suit.

"Jessica Pearson."

"What?"

"Steven Graham did not want me to wear this skirt. I told him that if the lawyer character Jessica Pearson wore this outfit to court on the TV show *Suits,* then I should wear it."

"I'm not familiar with that show."

"But you know who Gina Torres is, right?"

"Sure."

By the time Roberto drove them to the federal courthouse, his daughter looked confident and ready to go. As Roberto had suggested, she had focused on what she wanted to accomplish that day.

At 10:10 a.m., after the jury was seated, Jason Daniels called Thomas Barnes as the first government witness.

Barnes looked like he was born to play the role of an FBI agent or a Cowboys tailback. Roberto Sanchez marveled at how clean-cut FBI agents looked. Barnes was at least six feet three inches tall, with a powerful build. His hair was dark and slicked straight back. That day, he wore a navy blazer with a white shirt and a red, vertically striped tie.

Gabriela had learned a great deal about Barnes. His father had been shot down and killed in the Vietnam War. His mother was a professor at Texas A&M, and she raised Thomas Barnes in College Station. In high school, he was an all-state football player and track star. In his senior year, he had blown out his knee and decided not to play football at A&M. Instead, he went to school year-round and graduated in three years.

He went to law school at Southern Methodist University and completed his law degree in two calendar years. He went right from law school to the FBI and had been an agent for twenty-two years.

Gabriela thought Barnes was full of himself. According to people who went to law school with him, Barnes always thought he was the smartest guy in the room. She believed Barnes was smart, maybe too smart. Defense lawyers told Gabriela that Barnes was a little sloppy in his investigations. Apparently, he was a big-picture guy who paid less attention to details. Gabriela planned to take advantage of that when she cross-examined him.

After Barnes took the oath, Daniels began his questions. He spent the first fifteen minutes going over Barnes's education, background, and experience—all things Gabriela already knew.

Roberto looked over at the jurors. Barnes had captivated them. He wrote a note and showed Gabriela.

They like him.

Over the next fifteen minutes, Daniels asked Barnes about the Foreign Corrupt Practices Act and about bribery and corruption in Latin America. Barnes testified that Mexico was the Latin American country involved in the most Foreign Corrupt Practices Act settlements.

When Daniels asked, Barnes testified that approximately two-thirds, or sixty-seven percent, of the Mexico FCPA cases involved illegal payments made through business partners—such as joint venture partners, sales representatives, and distributors—who interacted with government agencies on behalf of the prosecuted companies, and that half of those business partners were sales agents.

When Gabriela looked over at the jury, she thought the younger jurors had already zoned out from boredom. "Your Honor, I would like the witness to have a document in front of him, and we can project it on the screen for the jurors."

Finally, Daniels turned to the oil and gas industry.

"When did you first learn that U.S. energy companies were paying bribes to receive lucrative oil and gas deals in Mexico through a sales representative?"

Roberto elbowed Gabriela.

Gabriela popped up from her chair. "Your Honor, I object. Mr. Daniels has presented no evidence that any U.S. energy company bribed anyone."

"Sustained." Judge Comstock stared at Daniels. "Mr. Daniels, you know better than that."

Roberto wrote on his legal pad.

Daniels is testing you. Better to object and be wrong than to let it go.

"Yes, Your Honor, let me rephrase the question. What prompted the FBI to start an investigation of U.S. energy companies doing business in Mexico?"

"We received leaked information that a Colombian law firm, which specialized in setting up secret bank accounts for the rich and famous around the world, had set up accounts for José Lopez. The law firm helps its clients keep their dealings private, no matter how shady or corrupt."

No elbow needed this time. Gabriela rose again. "Your Honor, the government has presented no evidence showing that any of the leaked accounts involved shady or corrupt business dealings."

"You're right, Ms. Sanchez." Judge Comstock turned toward the witness. "Mr. Barnes, you are not a newspaper reporter; you can only testify to facts you know. Do you understand?"

"Yes, sir."

"You may continue, Mr. Daniels."

"From whom did you receive the leaked information?" Daniels asked.

"The main FBI office in Washington."

"What records were leaked and to whom were they leaked?"

"We never figured that out. The leaker exposed offshore shell companies used by the rich and famous to evade taxes."

Gabriela spoke as she was getting out of her chair. "Your Honor, there he goes again."

"Do you object, Ms. Sanchez?"

"Yes, Your Honor."

"Please say so and give your reason. No need to editorialize here."

"Yes, Your Honor."

Judge Comstock crossed his arms and leaned forward. "Mr. Barnes, I shouldn't have to repeat this again. Just testify to what you personally know, not what you read in the paper or saw on television."

"Yes, Your Honor. The leaker provided us with many files that included bank records and invoices. The leak included details of accounts of several United States and Mexican citizens."

Daniels then had Barnes explain offshore accounts to the jury and asked what type of people set up those accounts.

Gabriela stood again. "Your Honor, I object. Mr. Barnes is in no position to get into the heads of U.S. citizens who open accounts outside the country."

"Sustained. Mr. Daniels, ask questions about what he knows."

Barnes explained that the FBI discovered that thirty-six Americans had created offshore shell companies and accounts. Some of those

Americans had already been convicted of fraud. Others were under investigation. Still others were using the offshore accounts to avoid paying taxes.

Roberto elbowed his daughter again, but Gabriela let that one go.

Barnes testified that José Lopez had an account for his corporation, Albueno Company. The FBI had traced when Lopez had deposited funds and when he spent money from the account. Barnes noted that Lopez had made a deposit into that account from Duval Energy and that he transferred funds from that account to another offshore account he had set up for Donald Lawrence.

"Did you learn anything else from those records?"

"Yes, we saw Mr. Lopez made a deposit into the Albueno Company account from funds American Energy had paid him, and we saw Mr. Lopez used funds from that account to pay for BMW automobiles given to Rafael Garza and Rodrigo Villa and to pay tuition for Garza's daughter to attend college in the U.S."

"When did Mr. Lopez purchase the BMWs?" Daniels asked.

Barnes looked at his notebook.

"December 12, 2014."

"And when did Mr. Lopez pay the tuition for Garza's daughter?"

"August 25, 2014."

Daniels had Barnes explain that shell companies exist mainly on paper. They have no physical presence, they employ no one, and they produce nothing. They have no phone number, email address, physical address, company logo, contact person, or federal identification number. People create and use shell companies to avoid identifying themselves as the true owner of the account.

After explaining, Barnes testified, "It normally takes investigators a long time to trace funds to the real owners. In this case, the data breach of the Colombian law firm provided us with the names of the true owners of the accounts."

"What did you do next in the investigation?"

"We brought Donald Lawrence in for an interview."

"What did he tell you?"

Barnes looked again at his notes. "At first, he acted like he couldn't understand why we wanted to interview him. We told Lawrence he had failed to report his offshore bank account as required by law. Lawrence acknowledged he had negotiated the Duval–PetroMex deals as Duval's lawyer, but at first he denied any knowledge of the shell company and the account Lopez had created for him."

"Then what happened?"

"We explained to Mr. Lawrence that we had discovered account records showing a payment from Duval Energy to Albueno Company, owned by José Lopez. Mr. Lopez deposited two million dollars of those funds to a Cayman bank where he set up an account for Slo Trading

Company, a shell company owned solely by Mr. Lawrence. We also explained to Lawrence that while the two million dollars represented income to him, he had failed to report that sum on his income tax return. It was at that point that Mr. Lawrence began to cooperate with us."

"What did you learn from Mr. Lawrence?"

"He told us—"

"Your Honor, I object to what Mr. Lawrence told the FBI. It is hearsay."

"I agree. Your objection is sustained."

"Your Honor, the government is not presenting what Mr. Lawrence told the FBI to prove it is true. We are presenting it to show how it figured in the course of the investigation."

"Mr. Daniels, I sustained the objection. It is hearsay. Put Mr. Lawrence on the stand and he can testify."

Daniels was clearly flustered. He turned a page from his notebook and then another.

Daniels stammered, "What happened next?"

"We worked out a deal for Mr. Lawrence to plead guilty to one count of tax fraud and to wear a wire and a shirt-button video camera and go back and capture what he had told us on tape with Mr. Duval."

"What is a shirt-button video camera?"

"It is the latest technology for surveillance and the smallest camera available. It slides into a shirt buttonhole and records with the press of a button."

"Did Mr. Lawrence agree to wear the buttonhole camera?"

"Yes, he went to Mr. Duval's vacation home in Wyoming, and we taped a conversation with him."

Daniels looked up from his notes. "Your Honor, at this time we would like to play the video conversation."

"Ms. Sanchez?"

"We continue to object. Mr. Lawrence was Mr. Duval's lawyer and trusted advisor, and as such, conversations between them are confidential and privileged."

Judge Comstock looked from Gabriela to Daniels. "I understand your objection, Ms. Sanchez, and it is denied. Mr. Daniels, while your assistants are setting up the video, I will give the jurors a break. Ladies and gentlemen, you have fifteen minutes."

During the break, Deborah Snow cornered Gabriela in the defense room. "The jurors all love Thomas Barnes. You must change their feelings about him."

Gabriela pulled back and didn't respond.

Twenty minutes later, after the jurors were seated, Daniels began playing the video.

After exchanging pleasantries and after Mr. Duval's wife left the room, they talked for ten minutes about the state of the oil and gas industry. Then the conversation turned to the PetroMex deal.

Donald Lawrence: "Last week the FBI came to visit me."
Sparks Duval: "What about?"
Donald Lawrence: "The PetroMex deal."
Sparks Duval: "What about it?"
Donald Lawrence: "You directed me to pay José Lopez, so he could pay the PetroMex officials. If you tell me to lie to the FBI, I would do that for you."
Sparks Duval: "That's bullshit and you know it. Are you wearing a wire?"
Donald Lawrence took off his sports coat and turned around. "No, I'm not wearing a wire. I would never do that."
Sparks Duval: "You need to get your story straight. I was never in favor of paying José Lopez. His fee was outlandish, and I didn't trust him. You were the one who kept pushing the deal, not me. I asked you to make sure there were no legal problems with the deal."
Donald Lawrence: "But, Sparks, in the end you gave the okay for the deal."
Sparks Duval: "Only after you assured me there were no legal problems. I said if you and Christopher believed it was worth pursuing, you could go for it. I still didn't like paying Lopez thirty percent."
Donald Lawrence: "That's why I'm concerned. We paid Lopez the thirty percent fee."
Sparks Duval: "I don't think there's anything to be concerned about. We paid a guy. We paid a consultant."
Donald Lawrence: "I don't know, I'm just—"
Sparks Duval: "You're paranoid. Stop worrying so much."
Donald Lawrence: "I mean, you told me to make the payment. I made the

payment."

Sparks Duval: "You paid a consultant."

Gabriela looked at Roberto. He smiled and looked at the jury. It could have been his imagination, but he believed the jury had been waiting for the bombshell that never came in the tape. He sighed in relief.

Daniels picked back up with questions. "Agent Barnes, in the tape, Mr. Lawrence and Mr. Duval discussed Duval Energy paying José Lopez a thirty percent fee. In your investigation, did you determine what percentage commission is customary?"

Gabriela stood. "Your Honor, I object again. Mexico just opened up its oil and gas market. There has not been enough time to determine what is and what is not customary."

"Ms. Sanchez, those are points you can make in your cross-examination and final argument. I'm going to allow the question."

Judge Comstock looked at Thomas Barnes, who began to answer.

"We determined that fifteen percent is the customary commission paid by companies outside of Mexico to brokers there."

"Did you look at the Duval Energy books and records to determine how the company reported the commission?"

"Yes, we found Duval Energy initially reported the thirty percent as a commission. We discovered Mr. Duval wrote a note directing the accountant to change the accounting entry to fifteen percent commission and fifteen percent outside services."

"When you searched the Duval Energy premises, did the FBI ask Mr. Duval what the thirty percent commission was for?"

"Yes."

"What was his response?"

"He said he didn't know, and he didn't want to know."

"Did you determine the source of the funds in Mr. Lopez's Albueno Company account?"

"Yes, the funds that came from Duval Energy were commingled with the funds that came from American Energy."

"And were those commingled funds used to buy BMW automobiles for Garza and Villa and to pay tuition for Garza's daughter to attend college in the United States?"

"Yes, the money came from that account."

With that, Daniels concluded his direct examination, and Judge Comstock said, "Ms. Sanchez, you may cross."

Roberto wrote a note. *Tomorrow.*

"Your Honor, it's ten minutes before five o'clock. I would like to start my cross-examination in the morning."

"I'll allow that." Judge Comstock glanced over at the jurors. "Ladies and gentlemen of the jury, I instruct you not to discuss this case with anyone overnight—not with reporters, not with your friends or family, and not with each other. I'm sure you understand."

Chapter 26

Jason Daniels and Thomas Barnes walked out of the courtroom together.

"They liked you. Good work. We need to stay together and prepare for your cross-examination," Daniels said.

"Sure. Want to go upstairs to the office?"

"No, that's not necessary. I've already given you the outline of what I expect Sanchez to ask you. Let's go to T-Bone Prime."

The bar at T-Bone Prime was known as the most exclusive spot in Dallas for older men to meet younger women. Some businessmen arrived with women, while others came alone, hoping to meet someone. Either way, it was clear the women had left work, gone home, and changed into something elegant before heading to T-Bone Prime.

Barnes had made the mistake of taking Daniels there several years ago. He knew the bar was loud, which meant they would spend little or no time preparing for his cross-examination.

"You don't think we should prepare in your office and go to T-Bone Prime when we're ready for tomorrow? This isn't like the other times I've taken you there. This time we have work to do."

"Barnes, you have the outline. Just study it. Sanchez has no clue what she's doing, and unless her daddy writes down each question, she won't ask anything that's not in the outline. Besides, you know I love to check out the young women at T-Bone Prime. We don't have women like that in D.C. Who knows, you might get lucky."

On the drive from downtown to T-Bone Prime, Barnes asked, "What main areas do you think Sanchez will focus on?"

"That's easy. She'll ask why the FBI didn't trace the funds from Duval to Lopez to the bribes."

"What makes you think she'll ask that?"

"This isn't my first rodeo. I have a sense about these things."

"Okay, how do I answer that?"

"Tell her it's impossible to trace the funds."

"But that's not true."

"Did you try to trace them?" Daniels asked.

"No."

"Then you don't know whether it's true or not. Understand?"

Barnes clenched his jaw, determined not to lie while testifying.

Finally, he said, "What else will she ask?"

"I expect her to focus on Don Lawrence and how you turned him against his employer and client. She may ask about José Lopez. She thinks the FBI knew about the bribes and did nothing, and she'll want the jury to think the government orchestrated the PetroMex deals. She'll also want to know why we didn't pursue an indictment and bring Lopez to the United States for trial."

"And what do you expect me to say?"

"You can answer that the FBI hasn't found Lopez. That's true."

"That's not true. We knew when Lopez was in the United States, and we know where to find him now. We just haven't searched for him."

"Quit trying to be a boy scout. Don't volunteer anything."

"What if she specifically asks if we knew he was in the United States and didn't arrest him? Are you suggesting I lie?"

"Did you see Lopez or talk to him while he was here?"

"No. My agents told me Lopez was in the country and we could have easily arrested him."

"You didn't see him or talk to him, so you can honestly answer that you didn't know he was here."

"What if Sanchez asks if I know where he is now?"

"At the moment she asks, you won't know where he is. You can honestly answer that you don't know."

Barnes gnashed his teeth. He disliked Daniels and couldn't wait for him to go back to Washington. "But I do know that you have Lopez hidden away and plan to call him as a rebuttal witness."

"I haven't decided yet. So, you don't know where Lopez is, and you don't know whether I'll call him."

Barnes sighed. "Okay. Anything else I should be prepared to answer?"

"She'll try to get you to change what you told the grand jury about the percentage of funds Lopez paid to Garza and Villa that you traced back to Duval. You told the grand jury that ninety percent came from Duval, and we know it wasn't that much. You need to say the ninety percent was an estimate—close to ninety percent."

"Okay."

"Barnes, remember we must prove that Duval knew Lopez planned to use some of Duval's payment to bribe Garza and Villa. Duval may or may not have known, but we know he turned a blind eye because he wanted to do the deal."

They pulled into the parking lot and stopped at the valet stand. Daniels' rental car, a Ford Taurus, looked out of place among the Porsches, BMWs, and Mercedes. Barnes even spotted a bright red Lamborghini at the front of the line. A tall blonde climbed out of the passenger side, followed by a man in his fifties from the driver's seat.

Daniels gawked and said, "Let's go look for a couple just like her."

Inside, Barnes saw Daniels slip a twenty-dollar bill to a waiter who led them to a sofa with two chairs. Barnes had seen this before. By nine o'clock, the bar would be packed. Daniels wanted seats ready for any two attractive women.

After reserving the spot, they went into the restaurant for dinner. The dining area buzzed with noise.

"Don't you think we should spend more time prepping for my cross?" Barnes asked. "Won't Sanchez ask about the lewd email exchanges with Lawrence?"

Daniels smirked. "Sure. Just look at the jury and tell them you were playing along to get more information about the deal. Quit worrying. You've done this a dozen times. You're up against the Latina Rising Star—a rookie who barely knows how to find the courtroom. You'll be fine. The jury loves you."

Barnes took a deep breath. "Whatever you say."

After dinner, they returned to the lounge and took their seats. Just as planned, at 9:20 four women walked up and asked to join them. Barnes noticed the grin on Daniels' face.

By 10:45, Barnes had had enough small talk. Daniels was busy with a blonde, so Barnes ordered an Uber. Three minutes later, a driver in a Toyota Camry picked him up.

The next morning, Barnes picked up his *Dallas Morning News*, unfolded it, and read while drinking coffee.

Headline: *Duval Changed Accounting Records.*

The first line read: *In a surprise development on the first day of testimony, jurors learned that billionaire Sparks Duval directed his bookkeeper to change the accounting entry for the commission paid to José Lopez...*

Barnes was certain Daniels had fed the story to the reporter as part of his trial strategy. Daniels was a master at getting the media to advance the government's version of events. So far, so good.

Later, at the courthouse, Barnes saw Daniels.

"Good work getting that headline," Barnes said.

"That was nothing. I've been feeding that writer for weeks. The *Post*, the *Times*, and MSNBC picked up the story. We've also mounted a social media campaign."

"Social media?"

"Yeah. We have at least a thousand tweeters and Facebook posters spreading ugly things about Sparks Duval. You shouldn't have left last night. Things were just getting interesting. You could have taken one— maybe two—young women home."

When Judge Comstock entered the courtroom and took his seat, Barnes returned to the witness stand. The judge looked down at Gabriela.

"Ms. Sanchez, you may begin your cross-examination of Agent Barnes."

Barnes watched as Gabriela stood tall, adjusted her black skirt, grabbed her iPad, and walked to the podium. She looked calm and focused, not like the young, inexperienced lawyer Daniels had described. He took a deep breath and waited.

"Mr. Barnes, you led FBI agents in a raid of Duval Energy's offices, isn't that true?"

"Yes."

"How many agents raided the Duval offices?"

"I'm not sure."

"Isn't it true you led more than fifty agents in that raid?"

"I could have led that many."

"And your agents had weapons, didn't they?"

"Yes."

"Were you expecting to encounter terrorists?"

Jason Daniels stood. "Your Honor, I object to that question."

Judge Comstock frowned. "Sustained, Ms. Sanchez. You know better."

"Were you trying to scare the Duval Energy employees?"

"No."

"You threatened several employees, didn't you?"

"No, Ms. Sanchez. I didn't threaten anyone."

"Your agents told Duval employees they could go to jail if they didn't cooperate, isn't that true?"

"No, Ms. Sanchez. I didn't say that, and I'm confident none of my agents did either."

"Did you sit in when Mr. Daniels rehearsed with Mr. Lawrence?"

"I sat in, but Mr. Daniels wasn't rehearsing his testimony."

Gabriela smiled and looked at the jury. Several jurors smiled back. "Would you call it practicing?"

"No."

She raised an eyebrow. "Did Mr. Daniels ever tell Mr. Lawrence questions he planned to ask?"

"Yes."

"Did Mr. Daniels ever suggest that Mr. Lawrence change the wording in an answer?"

"Yes, but—"

"Did Mr. Daniels ever suggest you change the wording of an answer?"

"No."

"Mr. Barnes, isn't it true you can't be sure Mr. Lopez deposited any of his Duval Energy commission into accounts belonging to PetroMex officials Garza and Villa?"

Barnes knew she was following the money, hoping to convince jurors Lopez hadn't used any of Duval's commission to bribe PetroMex officials.

"I'm almost one hundred percent certain José Lopez deposited a substantial amount of Duval Energy's commission in Garza's and Villa's accounts and bought them BMWs."

"Almost one hundred percent certain? So, it's possible Lopez deposited none of Duval's money into those accounts, isn't that true?"

"That's possible, but highly unlikely."

"It could be Lopez deposited only American Energy funds and used that commission to buy the BMWs, correct?"

"It's possible, but I'd say the chances are one in a thousand. Even if that were true, Duval still intended to bribe Garza and Villa when he paid Lopez's commission."

"In your direct examination, you said the money to pay for the BMWs came from Mr. Lopez's Albueno Company, correct?"

"I believe I said that."

"Isn't it true Mr. Lopez owns both Albueno and Sierra Verde?"

"Yes."

"And isn't it true Lopez deposited none of the fee Duval Energy paid him into the Albueno account?"

"I can't say that's true. I don't know where Duval's commission went after Lopez received it. We believe Lopez commingled Duval's funds with the American Energy commission."

"The FBI could have traced those funds, right?"

Barnes hesitated, hoping Daniels would object. "I can't say whether we could have traced Duval's funds."

She glanced at her iPad, then looked up. "Mr. Barnes, the FBI purposely chose not to trace Duval's commission funds to see if Lopez put any of that money into accounts for Rafael Garza and Rodrigo Villa, isn't that true?"

"No, that's not true. We didn't feel it was necessary. The funds were commingled in Lopez's Albueno Company account."

"Commingled with what other funds?"

"The payment to Lopez by American Energy."

"And when was the Duval Energy payment made?"

"March 10, 2014."

"And when was the American Energy payment made?"

"August 2, 2014."

"Mr. Barnes, isn't it true that Lopez's Albueno account had a balance of less than five thousand dollars in May 2014?"

"Yes."

"And the BMWs cost substantially more than that, didn't they?"

"Yes, but—"

"So Lopez couldn't have used Duval's money to buy the BMWs, could he?"

"No, Ms. Sanchez. That's not true. As I said, Lopez commingled funds and moved money from account to account to make it impossible to trace."

"When did Mr. Villa come to work for PetroMex?"

"In July 2014."

Gabriela looked at the jury. Barnes followed her gaze and hoped they hadn't caught the date conflict.

"Who made the decision not to trace the funds?"

"I don't remember."

"You were in charge of the investigation, weren't you?"

"Yes."

"So, you made that decision?"

"I don't remember."

"Did you discuss it with anyone?"

"I didn't discuss the decision with colleagues."

"But you knew Duval and American paid Lopez months apart?"

"Yes."

Barnes exhaled when Gabriela changed direction and moved to legal ethics, suggesting the FBI acted unethically by having Don Lawrence record Sparks Duval.

First, he made her show him the ethical rules, hoping to bore the jury. After reading the rule on loyalty to a client, he looked at the jury. "I believe a lawyer also has a duty to the public not to help clients commit illegal acts. That duty is greater than loyalty to a client."

Gabriela rubbed her face. Maybe Daniels was right about her, Barnes thought. He smiled at the jury.

She pressed again. "He continued working for Duval Energy while secretly working for you, didn't he?"

"Yes."

"And you knew that?"

"Yes, but it wasn't at our request. While we investigated Duval, we saw no harm in Lawrence continuing. I didn't demand or ask him to stay on."

Barnes chose the word *I* instead of *we*, hoping she wouldn't notice.

"It was up to Mr. Lawrence?"

"Yes. I told him he should decide for himself."

"If you didn't demand he continue, do you know if anyone else in the FBI or Justice Department did?"

"I can't be sure."

"Mr. Barnes, I notice that when you answer some of my questions, you look over at the jury. Is that something you learned in FBI school when they taught you how to testify?"

Daniels stood. "Objection, Your Honor."

"Sustained. Ms. Sanchez, stay with the facts."

"Mr. Barnes, when you interviewed Mr. Lawrence, you didn't record the interview, correct?"

"That's correct. The FBI believes recording interferes with our effort to build rapport with witnesses."

"Instead, you had someone take handwritten notes?"

"Yes. That's standard procedure."

"College and law students take notes on computers, yet the FBI still relies on handwritten notes?"

"Yes."

Barnes noticed two jurors smiling.

"So the accuracy of what a witness says depends entirely on the note-taker, correct?"

"Yes, but that agent is trained."

"And that agent can change words or stop writing if the witness says something the FBI doesn't like?"

"No. Our rules don't permit that."

"You know judges have chastised the FBI for changing or stopping notes, don't you?"

Daniels was up. "Objection, Your Honor. What judges have done in other cases isn't relevant."

Judge Comstock waved him off. "I'll allow the question. Mr. Barnes?"

"I've been told some judges found that agents changed or stopped notes. That's why we emphasize accuracy in training."

"And those handwritten notes become 302 Reports, correct?"

"Yes."

Barnes was relieved when the judge called a break, stopping Gabriela's momentum.

During the recess, Daniels scolded him. He told Barnes he was letting Sanchez score points and needed to take control. Fifteen minutes later, Barnes was back on the stand.

"Mr. Barnes, you don't have any evidence proving Mr. Duval knew Mr. Lopez intended to use part of his payment to buy cars for Garza and Villa, do you?"

Barnes smiled. The question gave him a chance to slip in hearsay he couldn't use before. "That's not true. Mr. Lawrence told us Mr. Duval knew and approved."

"But in your investigation, including the seized Duval computers, you found no documents corroborating that, right?"

"No. People committing bribery don't leave a paper trail."

"There were no emails from Mr. Duval showing he knew Lopez intended to use part of the commission to bribe officials, correct?"

"True, but we found Duval rarely used email."

"You did find an email from Mr. Duval to Mr. Lawrence complaining the Lopez commission was too high, right?"

"Actually, Duval's assistant sent the email. But yes, he complained about the amount."

"And another email asking Lawrence to make sure there were no legal problems with the deal?"

"Once again, the assistant sent it. Mr. Lawrence told us Duval wanted to cover his tracks in case of legal trouble."

Gabriela turned to the judge. "Your Honor, please instruct Mr. Barnes to limit his answers to facts he knows, not what others told him."

Judge Comstock nodded. "You're right. Agent Barnes, testify only to what you know. The jury is instructed to ignore what Mr. Lawrence told the FBI."

Barnes hoped they wouldn't.

"Those were the only emails between Mr. Duval and Mr. Lawrence about the PetroMex deal, correct?"

"That's true."

"Isn't it true, Mr. Barnes, that those emails refute your claim that Mr. Duval knew Lopez intended to use part of his payment for bribes?"

"No."

"When you seized Duval Energy's computers, did you check for emails about other oil and gas deals?"

"No. PetroMex was the only one we were investigating."

"Did you find it strange there were only two emails on a deal this big?"

"No. I've already testified that Duval rarely used email."

"You found no notes showing Duval knew Lopez intended to use part of his payment for bribes, correct?"

"No notes. Criminals don't leave written evidence of bribery."

"The only evidence you have is Mr. Lawrence's unsubstantiated statement, correct?"

"Yes."

"Did the FBI have a code name for Don Lawrence?"

That caught him off guard. He looked at Daniels, waiting for an objection that didn't come. "I'm not sure what you mean."

"When you sent emails or texts, you didn't use his real name, did you?"

"We called him several names, including Lawrence, Donald, and Don."

"You called him *Big Daddy*, didn't you?"

"Yes, sometimes."

"And did you choose that name because it reminded you of someone else called Big Daddy?"

"No. We just thought he was always sharply dressed."

Gabriela tilted her head. "Isn't it true you called him Big Daddy because he used money to attract young women in Mexico?"

"No. It was a joke about his expensive suits."

"Didn't you once describe him as a heavy drinker and womanizer?"

"That's possible."

"Possible? You either did or didn't."

"I'm not sure I used those exact words."

"Didn't you once say he used his money to talk young women out of their clothes?"

Barnes frowned at Daniels, who again stayed silent. "I likely said something like that. I wasn't particularly fond of him."

"Why not?"

"I'm not fond of lawyers who help their clients commit illegal acts."

"And you say the nickname Big Daddy referred to his suits?"

"Yes."

"Isn't it true your agents joked about sex in emails and texts with Mr. Lawrence?"

Daniels jumped up. "Objection, Your Honor."

"On what grounds?"

"Relevancy."

"I'll allow it."

"Yes. Some agents joked with him until I found out and stopped it."

"He sent your agents links to sex websites?"

"Yes."

"And your agents encouraged him to send more?"

"They were trying to get more information. It was an investigative technique. When I found out, I stopped it."

"If it was investigative, why stop it?"

"I thought it was unprofessional."

"Didn't you think Don Lawrence was sleazy?"

"I never used that term."

"But after the FBI gave him the name Big Daddy, you wanted him to continue as Duval's counsel so he could manipulate Mr. Duval for your investigation, isn't that true?"

Barnes paused before answering.

After several seconds, Gabriela said, "That's all I have at this time, Your Honor."

"Okay, let's break for lunch. We'll be back at 1:30."

When they returned to Daniels' office, Barnes asked, "How did Sanchez know about the Big Daddy code name?"

"I don't know. It wasn't in the documents we gave her. Did one of your agents slip? I can't let the FBI mess this up for me."

Chapter 27

At lunch, Deborah Snow sat beside Gabriela and began critiquing her performance. She claimed Gabriela had confused the jury.

Roberto Sanchez once again came to his daughter's defense. "Ms. Snow, I watched the jurors. They understood the FBI purposely didn't trace the funds. If you want to critique Gabriela in the middle of a trial, share it with me."

Snow looked over at Sparks Duval. When he said nothing, Snow got up and left the room.

Gabriela had paid no attention to Snow. She was already thinking about the next witness. To her surprise, Jason Daniels planned to call Vivian Dandridge to testify. Gabriela had spent hours with Vivian and her lawyer. Gabriela believed Vivian was ready for anything Daniels might throw at her. Supposedly Vivian was a cooperating government witness, but Gabriela expected Daniels to declare that she was a hostile witness right away.

After the jury took their seats, Judge Comstock said, "Mr. Daniels, you may call your next witness."

"Thank you. The government calls Vivian Dandridge."

Vivian walked through the courtroom doors escorted by a US marshal. All eyes turned to watch her. She wore a stylish black business-casual dress and heels, looking very professional.

After Dandridge was sworn in and stated her name Jason Daniels began his questioning. After establishing where she worked and her position at Duval Energy, Daniels asked about her salary.

Vivian Dandridge answered, "I earn two hundred fifty thousand dollars a year."

"Do any other Duval executive assistants earn that kind of money?"

Gabriela stood. "I object, Your Honor. What other executive assistants earn is irrelevant."

"Overruled. I will allow her to answer," Judge Comstock replied.

"I don't know how much Duval Energy pays the other executive assistants."

"Does Christopher Duval have an executive assistant assisting him?"

"Yes. His assistant's name is Karen Clark."

"How much does Duval Energy pay Karen Clark?"

"I told you I don't know how much Duval Energy pays other assistants. It's none of my business. You would have to ask Karen Clark."

"How long have you worked for Mr. Duval?"

"Seven years."

"How much did Mr. Duval pay you when you started?"

"Sixty-five thousand dollars."

"In seven years, your salary has gone from sixty-five thousand to two hundred fifty thousand dollars. What have you done for Mr. Duval to justify that increase?"

"I have been a loyal employee. I work many hours, and I have many years of experience in the oil and gas industry."

"Are you so loyal that you would lie for Mr. Duval?"

"Not after swearing to tell the truth, sir."

"Judge Comstock, I believe Ms. Dandridge is adverse. I want permission to examine her as an adverse witness."

"Mr. Daniels, I'm not sure you have shown Ms. Dandridge is adverse, but I will allow you to cross-examine her."

Gabriela watched Vivian take the stand and wondered how she would handle Daniels' questioning. They had practiced for this moment, but now it was game time.

"Thank you, Your Honor. Ms. Dandridge, if the jury convicts Mr. Duval, you will lose your two hundred fifty thousand dollar a year job, right?"

"I don't think so." Dandridge looked over at the jurors. "I know Mr. Duval. He would find a place for me in the company."

"Mr. Duval has become a rich man through Duval Energy."

"I'm not sure his wealth comes all from Duval Energy. I believe Mr. Duval has made other investments, but I don't know all of them."

"You know Mr. Duval very well, don't you?"

"I'm not sure what you are getting at Mr. Daniels. We have a professional relationship, not a personal relationship. I know Mr. Duval focuses on his family, especially his grandchildren. Mr. Duval also focuses on his work for the company he founded."

"You have good instincts and anticipate what Mr. Duval needs, right?"

"I do my best to anticipate what Mr. Duval needs. I believe that is the first trait any executive assistant should have."

"You are Mr. Duval's voice to the public, true?"

"I'm not sure what you mean. I do my best to react to people with whom we do business in the way I believe Mr. Duval would react. In that sense, I am his voice."

"You are Mr. Duval's loyal assistant and you keep every aspect of your work for him to yourself. Right?"

"Yes. I never say anything to others about Mr. Duval, and I would never betray his confidence."

Daniels surprised Gabriela by pursuing this line of questioning. He was allowing Vivian Dandridge to show that she was an excellent executive assistant.

"Ms. Dandridge, did you meet with Mr. Duval's lawyer before your testimony today?"

Vivian uncrossed her legs and answered in a soft voice, "Yes."

Daniels jumped on her soft answer. "I don't believe the jurors heard you Ms. Dandridge, please answer more loudly."

"Mr. Daniels, I said yes. I wasn't any different than each of your witnesses who met with you before their testimony."

Gabriela smiled. She and Vivian had practiced that response and Vivian had pulled it off.

Daniels stepped back from the podium and several jurors laughed out loud.

Daniels turned to Judge Comstock. "Your Honor, please instruct the witness to simply answer the question."

"I thought she did answer, Mr. Daniels. She's entitled to explain her answer."

If the jurors could have cheered, they would have. Daniels was coming across as a jerk over an issue that didn't matter. Gabriela was surprised when Daniels continued down that path.

"How long did you meet?"

"We met more than one time. I believe we met for about eight hours total."

"Did the lawyers tell you that Mr. Duval took compliance with the law very seriously?"

"No, I told them Mr. Duval takes compliance with the law very seriously. Before he hired Mr. Lawrence, he was on the phone constantly with the company's law firm. I know. I saw the monthly bills."

Vivian looked and acted comfortable now. Her voice was stronger, she looked at Mr. Daniels when he asked a question and at the jury when she answered, and she sat straight in the witness chair with an air of confidence.

"Did you talk with the lawyers about the PetroMex deal?"

"Yes, I told the lawyers Mr. Duval was dead set against drilling in Mexico. I overheard him arguing with Christopher and with Mr. Lawrence."

"But he finally agreed to do the deal?"

"He reluctantly agreed to do the deal. He tried to talk Christopher out of wanting to drill in Mexico."

"As Mr. Duval's executive assistant, would you say he knows everything about each drilling project?"

"Mr. Daniels, I don't believe anyone could know everything about each drilling project." Vivian answered.

"Wouldn't you say Mr. Duval is insatiable when it comes to each and every detail of each project?"

"I don't use the word insatiable. I do agree he pays attention to the details."

"He personally was involved in the PetroMex contract, don't you agree?"

"I disagree. Mr. Duval let Christopher and Mr. Lawrence negotiate the PetroMex contract. Mr. Duval told me he—"

Daniels looked agitated. "Ms. Dandridge, what Mr. Duval told you is hearsay. Just testify to what you witnessed."

Daniels' interruption brought frowns from several jurors.

"Okay, Mr. Daniels. I witnessed Christopher and Mr. Lawrence taking responsibility for the PetroMex deal."

"Ms. Dandridge, please look at page seventeen of your grand jury transcript. Question: Mr. Duval is personally involved in each drilling contract and knows the details of each one, correct? Answer: Correct. Did I ask that question and was that your answer?"

"Yes, sir."

"Did you tell the truth to the grand jury?"

"Yes, but the contracts you showed me were all US contracts. You didn't show me the PetroMex contract, so I thought you were referring only to the US contracts."

Daniels frowned.

"Isn't it true that Mr. Duval asked you to send two emails to Mr. Lawrence so he would have a record to cover himself?"

"I don't know. Mr. Duval didn't say he wanted me to send the emails to have a record to cover himself. He told me that entering into a drilling contract in Mexico concerned him and he relied on Don Lawrence to make sure the agreement had no legal issues."

"Has he ever asked you to send an email to Mr. Lawrence on any other drilling contract to make sure everything was legal?"

"No, but every other drilling contract was in the United States. Mr. Duval knows the potential legal issues on US contracts. We had never entered into a drilling contract in Mexico."

Gabriela looked at the jury to see if that answer had hurt their defense. She couldn't tell.

"That's all I have Your Honor."

"Ms. Sanchez, do you want to cross-examine?"

Gabriela had heard Judge Comstock use those words before typically to signal to the lawyer he didn't think cross-examination would be helpful.

"I have no questions of this witness, Your Honor."

When they left the courthouse for the day, Deborah Snow started in on Gabriela again.

"No questions. No questions. Daniels got her to say that Duval was concerned about drilling in Mexico. That means the jury can easily believe he either knew about the bribe or should have known since he expressed concern. You could have had Dandridge clarify what she meant by that statement."

Gabriela had finally heard enough. "Deborah, you think you know juries and how jurors think. I'm not so sure. Had I asked Vivian questions and had her clarify, that would have given Daniels another bite at the apple. Asked the right questions, Vivian could have hurt us."

She'd had enough of Snow's criticism. This was her courtroom now, not Snow's.

Chapter 28

Donald Lawrence had rarely testified in court, but he was sure he'd outmatch the young Hispanic lawyer waiting to cross-examine him.

The day before Lawrence was to testify, the media campaign started. Several national newspapers featured articles about him. One headline read: *Noted Energy Lawyer Takes Stand*. Another headline read: *Duval Star Witness Lawrence to Take Stand*. He perused the article.

It's showtime tomorrow in Dallas, when one of the top energy lawyers in the world takes the stand. All attention will be focused on the Dallas courtroom when the man known for his international oil and gas expertise testifies for the government. "What's at issue, in this case, is whether Sparks Duval knew that José Lopez planned to use a portion of the thirty percent fee Duval's company paid to him to bribe PetroMex officials," said Dallas trial lawyer, William Bolling. "I expect Mr. Lawrence to address the email he received from Sparks Duval asking about the legality of the PetroMex deal." Lawrence is expected to testify the email was a ruse to cover Mr. Duval.

#StarWitness quickly trended on Twitter as bloggers posted praise for Donald Lawrence. He found only one news article that mentioned he had received two million dollars from José Lopez that he did not report on his income tax return.

That headline read: *$2 million Tax Evader Takes Stand Today.*

He read the first paragraph:

The government's star witness, Donald Lawrence, takes the stand today in the case against his former boss, Sparks Duval. At the time he was paid $2 million by José Lopez, Lawrence was Duval Energy's general counsel, hired to help the firm legally expand its oil and gas business outside the United States. The defense will portray Lawrence as the mastermind behind the PetroMex deal, which netted him the $2 million. Lawrence has pleaded guilty to income tax evasion and faces sentencing after the conclusion of the Duval trial.

As Lawrence started reading the second paragraph, his phone rang.

When he picked it up, he could tell Daniels was angry just by his tone.

"Lawrence, Gabriela Sanchez filed a motion in court today to get some documents specifically about you."

"What?"

"Is there something you've been withholding from me?"

"No."

Lawrence heard Daniels exhale sharply. "Yes, there is, Mr. Lawrence."

"What's that?" Lawrence asked, knowing that Gabriela Sanchez must have found out about his alcohol rehab.

"You went to rehab in Minnesota while negotiating the PetroMex deal. Why didn't you tell me?"

"I told you and Barnes I had a drinking problem."

"You didn't tell us about needing rehab. Sanchez will raise it in cross-examination and make you look like a flaming alcoholic who can't possibly remember the details of the deal."

"I remember it clearly." That was easy to say since he believed no one could contradict his testimony.

"Were you drinking at the time?"

"Yes, so was José Lopez."

"Have you been drinking recently?"

He lied. "No."

"Then, you damn well better be as sober as a judge when you testify."

"I'll be fine." Lawrence said, knowing it was a lie. "I've testified many times, and I've been cross-examined by the best trial lawyers in Texas." While that was not true, he figured he could easily handle any questions from Gabriela Sanchez.

At 9:30 a.m., Donald Lawrence was in the witness room going over in his mind what he would tell the jury.

Finally, Jason Daniels walked in from the hall with Melinda Swanson by his side. He didn't look happy, but that wasn't unusual. Nor did Thomas Barnes, who followed them into the witness room. They sat down at the conference table across from Lawrence.

"Before we get started, I need for you to know something Barnes and his FBI pals did that may come up when you are testifying."

"What's that?"

"Why don't you be the one to tell him, Barnes?"

Lawrence looked over at him. He saw him swallow hard.

"Tell him, Barnes."

"During our investigation, our agents gave you the code name 'Big Daddy.'"

"Why?"

"I guess you reminded them of a ladies' man."

Lawrence thought for a moment. He remembered "Big Daddy," but couldn't place where he had heard the term. He and the FBI agents had joked about sex, Mexican prostitutes and booty calls in texts and emails, but was the FBI making fun of him?

Lawrence turned and heard Jason Daniels say, "So, prepare an answer if Sanchez brings it up in your cross-examination."

"Okay, but what am I supposed to say if she does?"

"Sanchez may ask if you knew of that code name, and you can say no. She may ask if you know of any reason the FBI agents would call you that, and you can say that you don't know. I would think that would be the end of it."

"Okay."

Even though the FBI had gone through Lawrence's emails, Daniels asked, "Did you go through all the personal emails you sent and received while employed at Duval Energy?"

"Yeah."

"Did you find anything the defense can use to attack your honesty and integrity?"

"I've told you, I'm an alcoholic."

"Yes, we'll try to keep that excluded from evidence."

Melinda Swanson asked, "Is there anything in your emails about your alcoholism?"

Lawrence thought about whether he should bring up emails the FBI had not seen. He decided it would be best. "Yes, I was three sheets to the wind most of the time. I wrote plenty of emails to José Lopez of a personal nature."

Daniels grimaced. "Damn, Lawrence. We have not seen any of the emails you sent to Lopez or received from him. Did you discuss the PetroMex deal in any of the emails you hid from us?"

"Yes. I told Lopez that Sparks Duval did not want any part of the deal, and I doubted I could convince him to change his mind. I asked him to give me a two-million-dollar bonus if I persuaded Sparks."

"And why haven't we seen that email and others between you and Lopez?" Daniels asked raising his voice.

"Because Christopher, Lopez, and I set up a secret email account, and we posted emails there as drafts, and we deleted emails after we read them."

"What? You son of a bitch. You, Christopher, and Lopez kept a secret email account from us? Do you have any other last-minute bombshells for us?"

"No."

"There damn well better not be any more, or you can get ready to do as much time as I can get the judge to order."

Lawrence nodded.

Jason Daniels was quiet for more than a minute. Lawrence just sat waiting.

Finally, Daniels said, "Does Sparks Duval know about the secret email account?"

"I never told him, and I don't believe Christopher told him."

"You're sure?"

Lawrence shrugged his shoulders. "I'm sorry. What can I say? Don't worry. If Sparks knew about it, you would have heard long before now."

"Whatever you do, don't mention it. If Sanchez asks, deny it flat-out. Do you understand?

Lawrence wanted to tell Daniels where he could stick it, but he kept his mouth shut.

Melinda Swanson stood up.

"Jason, may we go into the next office for a moment?"

After they walked out and closed the door, Don Lawrence started talking to Thomas Barnes.

"Damn Barnes, Daniels is a jerk. He'll screw up my testimony. I'm a confident guy, but Daniels is spooking me out."

Lawrence looked at Barnes, hoping for support. Barnes finally said, "Don, Daniels won't screw it up. You're our star witness. Just tell the jury what you told me, and you'll be fine."

Jason Daniels came back into the office. Melinda Swanson was not with him.

"Where's Melinda?" Lawrence asked.

"She had to take a call."

Daniels looked over at Barnes and rolled his eyes.

At 10:05 a.m., after Judge Comstock seated the jury, and the courtroom was quiet, he looked down from the bench.

"Mr. Daniels, you may call your next witness."

"The government calls Donald Lawrence."

As he walked to the witness chair, Lawrence caught Gabriela Sanchez looking back at him. Sanchez shook her head, once slowly. Lawrence wondered why. Maybe it was because he was wearing an inexpensive sports coat, and slacks.

Daniels had told him to dress and look like he was auditioning for the role of a friendly uncle.

After Lawrence was sworn in and stated his full name for the record, Jason Daniels went right to the arrest and his agreement to plead guilty.

Lawrence saw Roberto Sanchez write something on a legal pad and show it to his daughter. That stopped him for a moment, and he stared down at the two of them until they finished.

Over the next several minutes, Lawrence admitted he had pleaded guilty and described his crime to the jury.

"I dealt with José Lopez who was a broker. During our negotiations, I strongly suspected that Mr. Lopez planned to use part of the fee we paid him to bribe PetroMex officials."

"What caused you to suspect this?"

Daniels had told Lawrence that his freedom depended on how he answered these questions. They had practiced questions and answers for hours.

"My first suspicion was because of the amount of the fee we were to pay Lopez. It was thirty percent. I know from years of experience working on international deals that no one legally earns a thirty percent commission by doing nothing more than introducing people to one another."

"What happened?"

"I told Sparks Duval that Lopez wanted thirty percent and that I thought he didn't deserve that much."

"What did the defendant say?"

"At first he agreed. He said that no deal was worth that. At that point, I thought the deal was dead."

"Then what happened?"

"Mr. Duval asked me to find out if the big three oil companies were paying middlemen thirty percent." That part of his story actually happened.

"Were they?"

"Yeah, I called the lawyers I knew from each company. They each told me their company planned to pay José Lopez thirty percent of the amount of their contract. They each joked that we should be in the business of brokering deals."

"Did you report this to the defendant?"

"I sure did."

"What was his response?"

"He told me he refused to let the major oil companies beat him in Mexico. Since they were paying thirty percent commission, I was to do whatever it took to get a drilling contract for Duval Energy." Those weren't Duval's exact words, but Lawrence thought it was close enough to be at least partially true.

Across the room Sparks Duval say motionless.

"Whatever it would take. Did the defendant put that in writing or an email to you?"

"No, Mr. Duval rarely sends email and prefers not to use mobile devices. When he sends emails his assistant typically types them for him. His cell phone is one of the retro flip phones. He just told me to take care of it for him."

"What did you do?"

"I met several times with Mr. Lopez. Eventually, I paid the thirty percent fee, and we won the contract."

Lawrence was distracted again when he saw Gabriela Sanchez write something on her legal pad and show it to her father.

"Mr. Lawrence, Mr. Lawrence." Lawrence's head jerked back. *Don't let her distract me.* "And how did you end up with two million dollars in an offshore account?"

"Mr. Lopez and I developed a personal relationship. We became friends. At first, I wasn't aware Mr. Lopez had set up an offshore account for me."

Lawrence looked over and saw Gabriela Sanchez's crossed arms and eyes rolling.

Daniels then turned to the plea agreement. Lawrence acknowledged he had agreed to plead guilty, give up the offshore funds, and tell the truth in this trial.

"What happens if you do not tell the truth?" Daniels asked.

Before he could answer, Gabriela Sanchez rose and objected. "Your Honor, Mr. Daniels is trying to bolster the informant's testimony again."

"I'm going to allow it. Mr. Lawrence, you may answer."

"I'll go to prison for perjury and income tax evasion."

At that point, Daniels started asking Lawrence questions about his education and experience, including his several years as an energy lawyer working with the Ellison and Grayson Law Firm.

Lawrence expected these questions. They were the softball questions. Daniels had explained that he planned to put the boring stuff in the middle.

Daniels then asked how Lawrence had met the Duvals and begun working with them.

Lawrence testified that he had heard Duval Energy was looking to hire a general counsel with international oil and gas experience. Christopher had contacted him and invited Lawrence to dinner to discuss the opportunity. Lawrence testified that he tried to convince Christopher to hire him as an outside lawyer rather than a company general counsel. That was when Christopher had sweetened the offer.

"Christopher said if I came on board as general counsel at Duval, I could have five percent of any deals I brought to the company or negotiated. That attracted my interest, and I told him I was interested."

"And when did you begin work as general counsel with Duval Energy?"

"January 2, 2014. I know that because December 31 was my last day at my law firm."

Over the next twenty minutes, Jason Daniels questioned Lawrence about each of the deals he had worked on for the company. Finally, he returned to the PetroMex deal.

Daniels pointed at Sparks Duval. "Did the defendant know that José Lopez planned to bribe Rafael Garza and Rodrigo Villa with some of the funds Duval Energy paid him?"

"Yes."

"How can you be sure?"

Lawrence turned to look at Duval and raised his right arm. "Because I told Sparks Duval before we signed the contract."

"Your Honor, can we have a break at this point?" Daniels asked.

"Yes, Mr. Daniels, let's break for lunch. Let's reconvene at 1:30."

As soon as they walked into his office, Jason Daniels turned to Lawrence. "Look at the jury. They won't trust you if you don't look at them."

"I forgot. I'll keep my eyes on them from now on. I'm hitting it out of the park, right?"

"You've done well so far. This afternoon, we'll drive the point home and deal with the email he sent you.."

Chapter 29

Gabriela Sanchez had dreamed of cross-examining a government star witness from the time she first watched her father cross-examine a star witness in the Rio Grande Valley.

Cross-examining an experienced lawyer like Donald Lawrence would pose challenges. His polished self-assurance was just a façade, and she needed to crack it.

Steven Graham had demanded that she practice her cross-examination with him. Roberto Sanchez had sat through those practice sessions. Graham wanted to make sure Gabriela had the right rhythm, cadence, and sequence of her questions. Gabriela had argued those couldn't be precisely determined until the actual cross-examination.

"Lawrence has certain things he wants to remain secret. He is in debt to the casinos. This trial is a war, Gabriela, and Don Lawrence wants to kill our client," Roberto had said. "Think of him as the devil. He's a bad person who got caught with his hand in the cookie jar and betrayed Sparks Duval when he cut a deal with the government."

"Yes, Papá, but—"

"No buts, you've got to take him down to win this case. You must show he is lying."

"Yes, Papá, but what if the jury is sympathetic toward him?"

"They better not be sympathetic when you finish with Lawrence. Make them think he's the sleazy guy the FBI believes he is."

Her father was right, but the task would be a challenging one.

As they walked back into the courtroom, Gabriela took a deep breath when she saw Jason Daniels standing in the aisle with papers in his hand.

"I have a motion to give you, Gabby." He handed her the papers.

Gabriela immediately caught the title: motion *in limine*, trying to exclude something from coming into evidence. As Gabriela skimmed the motion, Roberto looked over her shoulder, and they both saw that Daniels wanted to exclude any mention of Lawrence's alcohol rehab.

"I've alerted Judge Comstock, and he will hear our arguments before he calls the jury back to the courtroom."

"But I've had no chance to review your legal argument and prepare a response."

"Gabby, Judge Comstock does not want to delay the trial. He told me he would hear the argument now."

"You, you talked to him without us?" Gabriela asked.

"Yes, Gabby. Only to tell him we had a motion to file and for him to consider before Mr. Lawrence resumes his testimony," Daniels replied sarcastically.

Roberto Sanchez whispered when they were alone. "We'll be okay. When you argue, stay calm, stand straight, speak slowly."

"Papá, you sound like Deborah Snow. I can handle this."

"Sorry, you're right. Go for it."

Daniels came up from behind and startled Gabriela. "Gabby, Judge Comstock wants us in his chambers now. Maybe he'll give you the fifteen minutes."

After everyone took a seat, Judge Comstock looked at Jason Daniels.

"I understand you have a motion for us, Mr. Daniels. May I see it?"

"Yes, Your Honor." He handed a copy to Judge Comstock.

Judge Comstock put on his glasses and began reading. "Have you given a copy of this motion *in limine* to Ms. Sanchez and Mr. Sanchez?"

"Yes, Your Honor. I gave Ms. Sanchez a copy before we came back to your chambers."

"Your Honor, may I have another copy of the motion and brief for my co-counsel?" Gabriela asked.

Daniels reached over and gave her another copy and whispered. "Here you go, Gabby."

"Before we get into the substance of the motion, do you have anything to say, Ms. Sanchez?"

"Your Honor, I filed a motion requesting that the government turn over any Brady material that would reflect upon the credibility, competency, bias or motive of government witnesses, including any health problems or substance abuse issues Donald Lawrence might have.

You requested that Mr. Daniels give you Lawrence's medical records for an *in-camera* inspection. After reviewing them, you ruled that we are not entitled to review Mr. Lawrence's files because the material was available to us in our exercise of reasonable diligence. We discovered that Mr. Lawrence's alcoholism and medication could have impacted his perception of reality and his ability to recall. We are prepared to question him on his perception and ability to recall events. Just before we are to cross-examine Mr. Lawrence, Mr. Daniels hands this motion and his brief to us. It came out of the blue. We've had no chance to consider his argument and prepare a response."

"Judge Comstock, Ms. Sanchez and her co-counsel have known for at least a month that Mr. Lawrence was an alcoholic who spent time in rehab. They even know what medication Mr. Lawrence is taking. Certainly, they did not think we would just let them tear into Mr. Lawrence and violate his right to privacy."

"Mr. Daniels, why did you file this motion at this late date?"

"Your Honor, we believe Mr. Lawrence is entitled to keep his health issues private, and we believe Ms. Sanchez plans to make it an issue in her cross-examination."

Gabriela spoke. "Your Honor, how could he possibly know that? Mr. Daniels would have to have accessed my computer to know that."

"Your Honor, Ms. Sanchez has read too many spy novels. You don't have to be a rocket scientist to figure out she plans to make Lawrence's health an issue when she cross-examines him."

"For now, I'll take them at their word," Judge Comstock said. "But you could have filed this motion this morning before calling Mr. Lawrence. Why didn't you?"

Gabriela looked over at Daniels and waited for him to respond.

"Mr. Daniels, you can't find the words to answer my question because you wanted to have it both ways. You wanted to bring up his condition in your direct examination if you thought that would work to your advantage, and you wanted to spring this motion on the defense if you decided it was not."

"I wouldn't say it that way, Your Honor."

"You just did. I don't like your tactics. As a result, I will excuse the jury for the afternoon and give the defendant that time to prepare a response to the motion. We'll take it up tomorrow morning with the court reporter here before we seat the jury."

***

When they returned to the office, an associate handed Gabriela a brief.

Gabriela turned to her father. "We're going to lose on this motion, aren't we?"

"I think so. We must show that Lawrence's alcohol and drug use either affects his memory of the PetroMex deal or his ability to testify honestly now. Even though it is likely true, I don't think we can show that."

"Okay."

After she looked at him, the associate volunteered, "Gabriela, I'll have the brief ready for you and an outline of an oral argument." Gabriela directed her associate to file the brief that afternoon before Judge Comstock left for the day.

Gabriela had spent weeks preparing to cross-examine Don Lawrence about his alcoholism and show the jury it had distorted his memory of events. In truth, Gabriela wasn't sure Lawrence's drinking had tainted his memory. She thought he was like every other government snitch, lying to save himself. That said, she wanted the jury to learn about his heavy drinking.

Roberto Sanchez agreed. He had observed something he thought Gabriela would find helpful: Lawrence rarely looked at the jury. Roberto suggested that when witnesses do not look at the jury, it is because they fear jurors will see they are lying.

Gabriela expected to be up all night, re-working her cross-examination. When she got home at three o'clock, she gulped down an energy drink and went for a run to get the endorphins to kick in. She worked all night and was more prepared than ever for her big moment in court.

***

In the morning over coffee, Roberto Sanchez asked, "Are you ready?"

"Yes, I was up most of the night going through my cross-examination and eliminating the questions on Don Lawrence's alcoholism, drug use, and his visit to rehab."

Two hours later, Roberto and Gabriela walked into Judge Comstock's chambers. The judge sat behind his desk, and a court reporter was at his side. Jason Daniels, Melinda Swanson and Thomas Barnes sat in chairs facing the judge. Roberto and Gabriela took seats to the judge's side.

"Okay, let's go on the record. Ms. Abernathy," the judge said. "Let the record reflect the parties are present. The United States is represented by Jason Daniels and he is accompanied by Assistant US Attorney Melinda Swanson and Special Agent Thomas Barnes. The defense is represented by Gabriela Sanchez and Roberto Sanchez. I am prepared to rule on the government's motion, and I don't need oral argument by either of you. With those thoughts, do either of you have anything to add?"

"No, Your Honor," Jason Daniels replied, staring at Gabriela.

"No, Your Honor," Gabriela said.

Judge Comstock picked up some papers and said, "Okay, I have before me a motion *in limine* filed by the government to restrict the scope of cross-examination of a cooperating witness, Donald Lawrence regarding his alcoholism and his treatment. The government seeks to limit the cross-examination of Mr. Lawrence on the ground that his alcoholism is a mental condition, and its existence and treatment are protected from disclosure by the psychotherapist-patient privilege. Is that a correct statement, Mr. Daniels?"

"Yes, Your Honor."

That brings us to Ms. Sanchez's argument, right, Ms. Sanchez?"

"Yes, Your Honor ."

"The defense argues that at the time of the PetroMex deal, Mr. Lawrence's alcohol and drug use impaired his judgment and memory and to not allow cross-examination on that subject would deny the defendant due process to confront the witness against him. Did I get that right, Ms. Sanchez?"

"Yes, Your Honor."

"As the parties are aware, I have reviewed Mr. Lawrence's medical records from his visit to the rehab center, and an affidavit from his doctor. I have found Mr. Lawrence was drinking heavily during the PetroMex Duval Energy contract negotiations."

Jason Daniels winced.

Judge Comstock continued. "The defendant has the right to confront, cross-examine, and impeach the witness against him. That right is especially important when the witness is a cooperating government witness."

So far so good, Gabriela thought, but she knew from experience what was coming next.

"However." Judge Comstock paused.
Jason Daniels turned and grinned, already sensing the win.

"The problem for the defense in this case, is that they have not shown Donald Lawrence's drinking and alcoholism treatment can be used to impeach his testimony. The defendant has pointed to several memory lapses, and what the defense contends is abnormal behavior. I find none of those behavior issues are relevant to attack his credibility in this case. However, alcoholism, by itself, is not a badge of incompetence or dishonesty. Ms. Sanchez, you must show incompetence or dishonesty first. Do you understand?"

"Yes, Your Honor."

"The court will grant the government's motion *in limine* and restrict the defense from cross-examining Mr. Lawrence about his alcoholism and treatment."

Jason Daniels was smiling ear to ear now. "Thank you, Your Honor. I'm certain Mr. Lawrence appreciates you not allowing Ms. Sanchez to delve into his most personal and private health issues."

"Is there anything else for us to go over this morning?"

"Yes, Judge, there is one more thing."

"What is that, Mr. Daniels?"

"It has come to our attention that Christopher Duval, the defendant's son, has taken to Twitter to intimidate Donald Lawrence or prejudice the jury's view of him."

"What?" Gabriela asked.

"We have learned Christopher Duval has so far called Mr. Lawrence a liar, turncoat, drunk, druggie. Those are from the PG-rated tweets. I won't burden you with the X-rated tweets. Here's one of his tweets. *#DonLawrence top energy lawyer lied about PetroMex deal. #liar #turncoat*'"

"Ms. Sanchez, I take it you were not aware of Cristopher Duval's tweets. Is that what they are called?"

"Yes, Your Honor, they're called tweets, and I was not aware of them."

"Your Honor, Christopher Duval is threatening our witness. You must order him to stop."

Gabriela responded, "Your Honor, I didn't read any threatening tweets. He's just exercising his First Amendment right to free speech. He has the right to offer his opinions about Mr. Lawrence."

"Your Honor, with all due respect, her suggestion is bogus. Christopher Duval is threatening Mr. Lawrence because he knows about his alcoholism and some of his resulting behavior. You have ruled that Ms. Sanchez cannot use Mr. Lawrence's alcoholism and treatment in this trial. Christopher Duval is violating Mr. Lawrence's right to privacy. We request you order him to stop."

"I have to say this is a first for me. I've never had this question before, and I don't know what other judges have done. The tweets are disgusting, but I am not sure they are threatening."

"Your Honor, what he is doing in these tweets is telling Donald Lawrence he knows the most personal and private things about him, and he will disclose those to the world if Lawrence testifies negatively against his father. Consider the timing of the tweets."

"Ms. Sanchez, what do you say?"

"Your Honor, we don't represent Christopher Duval. We represent his father and the company. I—"

Daniels jumped in. "You also represent the company. Christopher Duval is an owner of the company."

"Your Honor, if Mr. Daniels will let me continue, as I've said, I don't believe they are threatening. To order him to stop would violate his First Amendment right to free speech."

"Anything else?"

"Yes, Your Honor," Gabriela said. Someone is creating blogs and using social media to post all kinds of negative things about our client and about me. In particular, one specific handle, @nofrackingtx. Could that person possibly be on Mr. Daniels' prosecution team?"

"That's an insult." Daniels barked. "How could she suggest such a thing?"

"Using social media to tarnish the other side is all new to me. Mr. Daniels, I take it you assert that no one on your prosecution team has posted negative things about Mr. Duval or Ms. Sanchez on any social media sites?"

Gabriela looked over at Daniels. He was staring at the judge.

"Yes, Your Honor. To tell you the truth, I don't have any time to be on social media. If you have someone look, they won't find any social media accounts in my name."

That's an odd choice of words.

"What about DOJ lawyers and staff who are not part of your team?"

"Your Honor, you know they are more professional than to be tweeting about Mr. Duval or Ms. Sanchez."

"Okay. For now, I will take your word. I'm in uncharted waters here. I have never used Twitter or any other social media sites and I don't know how they work."

"We can show you, Your Honor," Jason Daniels volunteered.

"That's not necessary."

"Okay."

"Here's how I see it. I agree with Mr. Daniels. The tweets communicate to the witness and the world that Christopher Duval knows about Mr. Lawrence's medical condition. I have ruled that the psychotherapist and patient privilege protects Mr. Lawrence's medical condition from disclosure. I will issue an order directing Christopher Duval to not put anything about Donald Lawrence on any social media site until this trial concludes. And even though you do not represent Christopher Duval, I expect you to advise him immediately I have ordered him to stop. I will give you thirty minutes to advise Christopher Duval of my admonition. Ms. Sanchez, can you be ready to cross-examine Mr. Lawrence in thirty minutes?"

Gabriela straightened up in her chair and replied. "Yes, Your Honor. Most definitely."

As they walked out of the judge's chambers, Jason Daniels stopped, turned, and stared at her like a boxer trying to psyche his opponent.

"Gabby, I bet the Rising Star had a sleepless night worrying about Donald Lawrence. You're not ready for prime time, and he's ready to eat your lunch."

When they were alone, Gabriela turned to her father. "He's lying. He or someone in the justice department is using social media to destroy Sparks Duval and me. And I think they are spying on me."

"Easy to say, harder to prove," Roberto said.

Chapter 30

When Gabriela Sanchez walked back into court, reporters and spectators packed every seat. Gabriela understood over one hundred people had stood in line for hours to gain access to the few remaining seats. The spotlight was Donald Lawrence and her. The media wanted a show for their viewers and their readers. Gabriela just wanted to win.

She knew she had to walk a fine line no man in her position ever faced. Be too aggressive, and they'd call her abrasive. Hold back, and they'd see her as weak. Gabriela took a deep breath and reminded herself she had never been more prepared.

"Ms. Sanchez, you may cross-examine now."

Lawrence smiled, glanced at the jury, sat up in his chair, and sneered at her. She had expected it. She stood and straightened her jacket, feeling more self-confident having heard Lawrence's direct testimony.

"Yes, Your Honor." Gabriela picked up her iPad and several eight-by-eleven photographs she hoped Lawrence would believe showed him with José Lopez in Mexico. She looked back at her father as she walked to the podium. The night before, she'd outlined two versions of the cross-examination, one packed with questions and the other lean and surgical.

When Gabriela reached the podium, she put her left hand at her side, straightened her back, and slowly picked up the photos, making sure

Lawrence saw her going through them. She started by introducing herself.

Donald Lawrence slyly smiled at her like she was a little kid on a playground. "I know who you are Ms. Sanchez. I've read about you recently. I think it was in the *National Tabloid Journal*."

She wanted to wipe the smile off his face. She had plans to do just that later. *Score one for Lawrence.*

Lawrence scored his second point when he told the jury he worried Gabriela would ask him to change his testimony when she asked why he wouldn't speak to her before the trial.

"Mr. Lawrence, isn't it true that Mr. Daniels had instructed you not to talk to me?" Gabriela asked.

Lawrence smiled as if he had expected the question. Before he could answer, Jason Daniels leaped to his feet.

"I object, Your Honor."

"Mr. Daniels, Ms. Sanchez is entitled to an answer on whether you told Mr. Lawrence not to talk to her. You may answer, Mr. Lawrence."

"Ms. Sanchez. He didn't need to advise me not to talk to you. I'm a lawyer. I knew I didn't need to and shouldn't talk to you." Lawrence glanced over at the jury and smiled.

Gabriela's goal was to show that Lawrence was in Daniels' hip pocket, willing to do whatever he directed. She wasn't sure she had accomplished that goal, so she changed the subject.

"Mr. Lawrence, isn't it true that you approached Christopher Duval about coming to work for Duval Energy?"

"No. I didn't contact Christopher Duval. He contacted me."

Gabriela pulled out a sheet of paper. "Your Honor, could I hand this to the witness?"

"Go ahead, Ms. Sanchez."

After she handed the paper to Lawrence and gave a copy to Daniels, Gabriela asked, "Isn't it true you sent this email to Christopher Duval, suggesting Duval Energy pursue international oil and gas deals?"

"Yes, it's true. I sent this email to Christopher Duval. It was after he heard me speak on the subject at an energy conference, and he asked me about international deals."

"Isn't it true that when Christopher Duval offered you the position of general counsel at Duval Energy, you told him you wanted to use your legal expertise and contacts on deals outside of the United States?"

"I don't remember my exact words, but you are correct. As I have testified, he told me he wanted to do deals outside the United States, and that is what I wanted to do. I told Christopher he could count on not only my expertise and experience but also my contacts in the oil and gas business around the world. He thought I would be an invaluable asset."

Gabriela turned to Judge Comstock. "Your Honor, would you instruct the witness to answer the question asked and not testify to what he believes someone else was thinking?"

"Mr. Lawrence, you know you can't testify to what Christopher Duval was thinking. Just answer the question."

"Yes, Your Honor." Lawrence shrugged his shoulders and wo jurors laughed.

"Mr. Lawrence, isn't it true that Duval Energy hired you to make sure the company followed all legal requirements on deals outside of the United States?"

"Ms. Sanchez, Judge Comstock just instructed me not to speculate on what others like Christopher and Sparks Duval were thinking."

"Isn't that what they told you, Mr. Lawrence?"

"I don't specifically recall."

"How many years have you practiced international energy law?"

"As you undoubtedly know, twenty-seven years."

"And isn't it true, you have the highest rating possible in international energy law?"

"Yes, I've worked hard to earn and keep that rating."

"How much money did your law firm pay you the last year you worked there?"

"That's personal information. I won't answer," Lawrence replied.

Gabriela looked at Judge Comstock. Finally, he said, "Mr. Lawrence, you must answer the question."

"Okay. I'm not sure, Ms. Sanchez."

"Was it over one million dollars?"

"Yes."

"Was it over two million dollars?"

"I've made that much in the past, but the year before I joined Duval Energy, I made about one-point-six million dollars."

"And you thought you could make more money with Duval Energy?"

Knowing no juror made 4100,000, Gabriela hoped the jurors would see Lawrence was greedy and always going after more money.

"Yes, Ms. Sanchez."

"Even more than two million dollars."

"Yes, Ms. Sanchez. Even more than two million dollars."

Gabriela got Lawrence to admit that before he was hired, Duval Energy had never drilled for oil and gas outside the United States. Then she got Lawrence to acknowledge that he had turned down the company's offer of one-point-six million dollars plus a signing bonus of two hundred fifty thousand dollars and had accepted only after the company sweetened the deal by offering him five percent of the profits and any deals outside the United States he found, negotiated, and gave his legal opinion on. She then turned to problems he had working at his law firm.

"You had been a partner in your law firm before you joined Duval Energy, is that right?"

"Yes, Ms. Sanchez."

"Did your law firm partners ever vote to dismiss you from the firm?"

Lawrence raised his eyebrows and pulled his head back.

Score one for me.

Daniels stood. "I object Your Honor."

"On what grounds?"

"Relevance," Daniels replied.

"Overruled. You may answer, Mr. Lawrence."

Lawrence had regained his composure. "No, Ms. Sanchez. I was a top rainmaker in my firm. My partners never threatened to dismiss me."

"Isn't it true that your legal assistant complained that you had sexually harassed her?"

"No, Ms. Sanchez, she came with me to Duval Energy. She never filed a complaint when we worked at my law firm."

"How much did you have to pay her?"

Daniels leaped to his feet. "Your Honor, I object."

Before Judge Comstock responded, Gabriela said, "I'll withdraw the question."

Gabriela hoped the jury would find it odd the way Lawrence had dealt with the sexual harassment questions.

"Did any other companies offer you a job?"

"Ms. Sanchez, in my long career, I probably received at least one job offer every month. I'm certain you know companies frequently make offers to successful law firm partners."

"So, with job offers coming from companies every month for twenty-seven years, Duval Energy was the only one you accepted, correct?"

Lawrence looked puzzled. "Yes, I guess that is true, Ms. Sanchez."

Gabriela took a quick look over at the jury. She saw jurors writing in their notebooks.

"Mr. Lawrence, you were Duval Energy's general counsel, right?"

"Yes, you and the jury already know that."

"Do you consider yourself to be an ethical lawyer, Mr. Lawrence?"

"Yes, certainly." He stared at Gabriela. "My integrity and professionalism are the hallmarks of my law career."

"And you know the ethical rules about loyalty to your client?"

The smirk on Lawrence's face took Gabriela by surprise. It was as if he had been looking forward to this line of questioning.

"Yes, I do. I told you I believe all lawyers should conduct themselves ethically and with integrity."

"Your Honor, may I approach the witness and hand him the Texas State Bar Rules of Professional Conduct?"

"Yes, you may hand it to Mr. Lawrence."

Gabriela noticed that Lawrence fidgeted when he took the copy of the rules. That seemed odd after the smirk she saw. As she approached him, she thought she smelled alcohol on his breath.

Has he been drinking?

Gabriela had Lawrence read the rule requiring a lawyer to be loyal to his or her client.

"Duval Energy and Mr. Duval were your clients, right?"

"Yes."

"And. As their lawyer, loyalty to them was your ethical obligation, right?"

"Yes." Lawrence started speaking slower and looked over at Jason Daniels. "Ms. Sanchez, I realize you haven't practiced law that long, so you may not be aware that as lawyers, we also owe a duty to the public. So, when the FBI directed me to remain general counsel and wear a recorder and camera, I was exercising my duty to the public."

"Very noble on your part."

Jason Daniels stood. "Your Honor, Ms. Sanchez knows better than to characterize Mr. Lawrence's testimony that way."

"He's right. Ms. Sanchez, watch your commentary on his testimony."

"Mr. Lawrence, you have testified that Thomas Barnes directed you to remain Duval Energy's general counsel. If Mr. Barnes testified that he told you to leave the company, he'd be wrong?"

"I wouldn't say Agent Barnes is wrong. I would say his memory is faulty."

"Did he also tell you to stay employed by Duval Energy as a requirement of your cooperation agreement with the government?"

"Yes."

"Mr. Lawrence, were you aware of the code name the FBI gave you during the investigation?"

"Agent Barnes told me that the FBI code name for me was 'Big Daddy.'"

"So, the FBI thought you were whose Big Daddy?"

As Gabriela expected, Jason Daniels quickly rose to his feet. "Your Honor, I object, this witness can't testify to what the FBI thought."

"I agree, Mr. Daniels. Objection sustained. Ms. Sanchez, can you rephrase the question?"

Gabriela wanted to show the jury that Lawrence was a liar, so she rephrased the question.

"Do you know why the FBI gave you the code name "'Big Daddy?'"

"No."

"Had you ever been called "'Big Daddy?'"

"No. Not that I can remember."

"Your Honor, may I approach the witness and give him an exhibit?"

"Yes, Ms. Sanchez."

Gabriela handed Lawrence a document and gave a copy to Daniels.

"Mr. Lawrence, what is the exhibit I handed you?"

Daniels was up in a flash. "Your Honor, I object, this document is totally irrelevant and will unfairly prejudice the jury."

That had been Gabriela's plan—to prejudice the jury against Lawrence.

"Mr. Daniels, Ms. Sanchez is entitled to impeach the witness. I will allow the exhibit."

"Mr. Lawrence, describe the exhibit."

"It is an email I sent to José Lopez."

"What did you say in the highlighted part of the email?"

Lawrence looked sheepish.

"Alejandra calls me her 'Grande Papi.'"

"Tell the jury what that means in English."

"Alejandra calls me her 'Big Daddy.'"

"And, who was Alejandra?"

"A woman I met in Mexico."

"Did you also tell the FBI what Alejandra called you?"

Lawrence's face had grown red. He grimaced.

"Mr. Lawrence, did you send emails and texts to Agent Barnes about your sexual escapades?"

"Ms. Sanchez, I sent emails and texts to Agent Barnes as a joke. I was trying to get him to lighten up. They weren't serious."

"You thought it was important for Agent Barnes to lighten up?"

"Yeah, he just seemed too serious. I joked with him that I would send him a video of the strippers in Houston during an energy conference there. I knew he would be appalled. What I wrote in the emails and texts never happened. It was just a joke."

Gabriela looked over at the jurors. A few were frowning. She had Lawrence read the ethics rule regarding the conflict between his or her client's interest and the lawyer's own interests. It included an example, that a lawyer should not allow related business interests to affect representation, for example, by referring clients to an enterprise in which the lawyer has an undisclosed interest.

After he read the comment, Gabriela looked back at Donald Lawrence. "You say that at the time Duval Energy paid you to be its general counsel, you were close friends with José Lopez. Did you tell Mr. Duval or Christopher Duval about your friendly relationship with Mr. Lopez?"

"No. I'm certain they knew that I became close to Mr. Lopez, and spent a lot of time socializing with him, to win the contract for Duval."

"Did Mr. Lopez invite you on trips with him to Cabo San Lucas while you were negotiating the Duval Energy PetroMex contract?"

"Yes, but those were work-related trips."

"Oh, I see. You never told Mr. Duval or Christopher about those work-related trips?"

"No."

"Mr. Duval and Christopher didn't know you were in Cabo San Lucas working on the Duval Energy PetroMex contract?"

"No."

"What work did you do in Cabo San Lucas?"

"I was building a relationship with Mr. Lopez."

"Did Mr. Lopez pay for your hotel room, restaurant, and club visits on these trips while you were building your relationship with him?"

"Yes."

"If you were building a relationship with Lopez, why did he pay for your hotel, restaurant, and club visits?"

"He wanted me to persuade Mr. Duval to do a deal with PetroMex."

"Was that work-related?"

"Jason Daniels stood up. "Your Honor, she's badgering the witness."

"Mr. Daniels, I'm going to allow it."

"No, Mr. Lopez was entertaining me. He entertained me in Cabo many times."

"Did Mr. Lopez take you to play golf in Cabo while you were negotiating the Duval Energy contract?"

"Yes."

"Did he take you fishing while you were in Cabo?"

Lawrence's face was red.

"Yes. Ms. Sanchez, we spent hours on a fishing boat together. We got to know each other better."

"Did Mr. Lopez pay for you to fly first class on these personal trips to Cabo?"

"Ms. Sanchez, the airlines do not offer first class on flights between Dallas and Cabo."

Gabriela smiled. "Did Mr. Lopez pay for you to fly in business class on your flights to Cabo?"

"Yes."

"What else did Mr. Lopez buy for you or pay for you while you were negotiating the Duval Energy contract?"

"Mr. Lopez bought me this pair of cowboy boots." Lawrence lifted the leg of his trousers and showed a pair of alligator skin boots.

"How many days and nights did you and Mr. Lopez spend together in Cabo?"

Donald Lawrence looked puzzled.

"Mr. Lawrence, how many days and nights did you and Mr. Lopez spend together in Cabo?"

"I don't recall."

"Did you spend more than ten nights?"

"I'm not sure."

"One hundred nights?"

"Not that many."

"So, somewhere between ten and one hundred, right? Gabriela asked.

"Probably."

Jason Daniels stood. "Your Honor, can we take a fifteen-minute recess?"

"Your Honor, Mr. Daniels wants this recess so he can coach his witness and break my momentum," Gabriela said loud enough for the jury to hear.

"Ms. Sanchez, you may be right, but it is time for a recess. When we get back, you can continue your cross-examination."

After Judge Comstock left the bench, Gabriela peered over at her father and whispered, "The son of a bitch wanted to break my momentum. I hope the jury got my message."

When they sat in their assigned conference room, Deborah Snow said. "Speed it up Gabriela. The jurors look bored."

"Deborah, I just showed the jury he lied about the code name. They weren't bored."

"Gabriela, one rule of cross-examination is to be concise. That is particularly important with jurors whose longest conversations are in short text messages. Get to your points and finish."

Chapter 31

Thirty minutes later, Donald Lawrence returned to the witness stand.

Gabriela had considered starting with a brief recap for the jury, maybe shifting to a few neutral questions before returning to ethics. But to satisfy Deborah Snow, she abandoned the idea and went straight to the bribery testimony.

"Mr. Lawrence. Your story now is that Mr. Duval knew that José Lopez planned to bribe Rafael Garza and Rodrigo Villa using the commission Duval Energy paid him. Is that true?"

"It's no story. I specifically told Mr. Duval."

"When did you tell him?"

"Before we closed the deal in March of 2014."

"You didn't put it in writing, did you?"

"No, Mr. Duval told me not to put it in writing. He wanted no written record."

Gabriela should have anticipated that response. Chalk another one up for Lawrence, she thought quickly.

"When did he tell you not to put it in writing?"

Lawrence started twisting his watch. Gabriela thought he didn't know how to respond.

"I don't remember."

"Was it before or after he sent you the email asking you to assure him there were no legal problems with the deal?"

"It was before. Mr. Duval sent me the email shortly before the deal closed so he could claim he relied on my legal advice."

"And you didn't make any written note of that, isn't that true?"

"I don't recall making a note of it."

"So, you claim that Sparks Duval told you to commit a crime, right?"

"That's right."

"You didn't think it was important to make a note after you received Mr. Duval's email to protect yourself from a legal malpractice suit, or disbarment?"

"No, I never expected we would get caught."

"If you never expected to get caught, why would Mr. Duval send you the email saying he was relying on your legal advice?"

Lawrence shook his head and shrugged. "Maybe he thought we would get caught."

Score one for Sanchez.

"That's your story. Mr. Duval sent you the email because he thought you would get caught?"

"That could have been the reason."

"Did you ever meet Rafael Garza and Rodrigo Villa?"

"I met PetroMex officials, but I'm not sure whether I met Rafael Garza or Rodrigo Villa."

"And you did not know Mr. Lopez planned to give either of them gifts or money, did you?"

"Maybe not those specific names. Lopez told me that to win the PetroMex contract for Duval Energy, he would have to do favors for PetroMex officials to grease the skids. He didn't give me the specifics."

"When did he tell you?"

Lawrence raised his head and put his hand on his chin. After a moment, he answered. "I believe it was about a month before Duval paid his commission."

"Mr. Lawrence, when the FBI contacted you for the first time, were you afraid?"

"No. But I wasn't sure what they wanted."

"Was Mr. Barnes the FBI agent who first contacted you?"

"Yes."

"Did you ask him what the FBI wanted?"

"I'm sure I did."

"What did Mr. Barnes tell you?"

"Mr. Barnes told me I was in trouble for not paying taxes on the two-million-dollar bonus José Lopez had paid me."

"Mr. Lawrence, didn't you originally tell the FBI that the PetroMex deal had been your idea, and that Mr. Duval was totally against the idea?"

Gabriela scanned Lawrence's face carefully for clues on whether he believed Gabriela had a source for that statement. Lawrence crossed his arms. Bingo, that convinced her he was uncomfortable.

He's worried about what I know.

"I tried to protect Mr. Duval. He knew about the bribe, but he was smart enough never to mention it."

Gabriela held a paper in her hand and asked, "And you told the FBI in your first interview that the only thing Sparks Duval said about the commission paid to José Lopez was that the amount was outrageous, isn't that true?"

Daniels stood. "Your Honor, I object, none of this is in the FBI 302 interview reports we furnished Ms. Sanchez."

Gabriela was prepared with an answer. "Your Honor, that's the problem. The FBI purposely did not include in the FBI 302 interview report anything Mr. Lawrence told them that was favorable to the defense. We have discovered it through other sources."

Gabriela stared at Don Lawrence to make sure he understood what the other sources were.

"Mr. Daniels, I will allow the question," Judge Comstock ruled.

Gabriela stared again at Lawrence. He crossed his arms again, clutching them to his chest. Once again, he seemed confused.

"Would the court reporter repeat the question?" Gabriela asked.

The court reporter looked back at her sheet and repeated the question.

"Yes, I believe so. I suspect you already know that Mr. Duval purposely didn't want to know anything else about the commission."

"Judge, please instruct the witness to testify to facts he knows."

"Mr. Lawrence, I shouldn't have to tell you to stick to what you know."

"Yes, Your Honor."

Gabriela turned to the plea agreement. She had Lawrence admit he pleaded guilty only after the FBI discovered he had two million dollars in an offshore account. He admitted he agreed he had not paid tax on the two million dollars, and he admitted he had not been sentenced.

Gabriela asked, "And the government will recommend a sentence based on your performance in this trial, isn't that correct?"

"Based on me telling the truth in this trial, yes."

"When the FBI asked you to wear a camera with a microphone and videotape your conversation with Mr. Duval, you were still the Duval Energy general counsel, is that correct?"

"Yes."

"The FBI directed you to entrap Mr. Duval in the conversation, didn't they?"

"Yes."

"How did you feel when the government demanded you inform on your own client, the one who gave you an opportunity after your law firm booted you?"

Daniels was up in a flash. "Your Honor, I request that you admonish her for that question. It was totally inappropriate."

Judge Comstock stared at Gabriela. "Ms. Sanchez, you know better than to use that language."

"Yes, Your Honor," Gabriela replied while watching jurors take notes.

Judge Comstock continued. "Ms. Sanchez, you may continue, but watch your step."

"Mr. Lawrence, did the FBI give you a script to study and tell you what to say to Mr. Duval?"

"Yes. Agent Barnes gave me a script to study."

"And they told you the purpose of the script was to entrap Mr. Duval to admit that he knew about the bribes, isn't that right?"

"Yes."

"Did you rehearse?"

"Yes."

"With a camera?"

"No. I wasn't going to be on camera."

"And you never objected to what the FBI agents wanted you to do?"

"No"

"You were Mr. Duval's lawyer and you agreed to wear a button camera to record and entrap him."

"I didn't like the idea and I told Agent Barnes."

"You did. But, you wore the camera anyway because Agent Barnes told you that if you refused, you would not have the plea agreement, isn't that true?"

"Yes."

"And Agent Barnes told you to get Mr. Duval to admit he knew Lopez planned to bribe PetroMex officials, isn't that true?"

"I don't remember his exact words, but that was the gist of what he said."

"During the recording, Mr. Duval never said he knew about the bribes, did he?"

"No. Sparks knew I was recording what he said. He even asked me if I was wearing a wire."

Gabriela looked at her iPad. She had planned to ask Lawrence about the dichotomy of using his office email for all US deals, but not using his office email account for the PetroMex deal. She saw no value in that line of questions at this point.

"Your Honor, may I have the witness examine this document?"

"Yes."

Gabriela handed Lawrence the document, and she gave a copy to Daniels. Gabriela noticed Lawrence's hands were shaking.

"Mr. Lawrence, I have handed you your cell phone records for the period from the beginning of the PetroMex discussions to six months after you closed the deal with Mr. Lopez. Are there any calls to or from Mexico?"

Lawrence looked over the document.

"No."

"There is no record of any calls between you and Mr. Lopez, is there?"

"No. I didn't communicate with Mr. Lopez on my cell phone. I used another prepaid phone for phone calls with him."

"You used a burner phone like drug dealers use?"

As she expected, Daniels stood. "Your Honor, I object to her characterization."

"Sustained."

Gabriela didn't mind Judge Comstock sustaining the objection. She had made her point.

"You used a burner phone?"

"I used a prepaid phone."

Gabriela was tempted to ask the why question, but she knew better. Instead, she just let the jurors reach their own conclusions.

"Do you recall the date you wired 30 percent of the contract price to Mr. Lopez for his commission?"

"It was in March 2014, but I'm not sure of the exact date."
"And when did Mr. Lopez deposit the two million dollars …".."

"I don't remember the exact date, but it was around the time we closed the deal."

"Your Honor, may I approach the witness and hand him an exhibit?"

"You may."

After she handed Lawrence the exhibit and gave a copy to Daniels, Gabriela paused while Lawrence looked at it. "Mr. Lawrence, look at the document and tell the jury what date Mr. Lopez deposited two million dollars in an offshore account for you."

"The date shown here is March 12, 2014."

"Just a couple of days after you wired his thirty percent commission, right?"

Lawrence's hand trembled as he put the exhibit down, avoiding her eyes.

"Mr. Lawrence, did you hear my question?"

Finally, he responded, "I'm not sure of the dates. What could it possibly matter?"

"And Mr. Lawrence, you claim Lopez paid you the two-million-dollar bonus for successfully convincing your client, Duval Energy, to enter into the PetroMex contract?"

"Yes, it was a bonus from José Lopez."

"You asked Mr. Lopez to pay you a two-million-dollar bonus, isn't that true?"

"We mutually agreed to the bonus. I can't remember who brought it up first."

Gabriela looked at the jury and concluded most of them weren't buying what Lawrence had just said.

"You told Lopez that you needed the money to take care of some problems, isn't that true?"

"No, I didn't have any money problems. As you know, I earned a lot of money."

"Do you have a gambling problem, Mr. Lawrence?"

Daniels jumped to his feet. "Your Honor, may we approach the bench?"

"Yes, Mr. Daniels."

When they stood together in front of Judge Comstock, Daniels whispered, "Your Honor, this gets into the evidence you said she could not bring up."

Judge Comstock turned to Gabriela. She did not whisper. "Your Honor, you've not allowed me to question Mr. Lawrence about his drug and alcohol problem and his rehab, but you've not excluded his gambling issues."

Daniels whispered. "Your Honor, he's an addict, and gambling is one of his addictions."

"Mr. Daniels, I'm going to permit Ms. Sanchez to inquire about his gambling."

Daniels slowly walked back to his counsel table. Gabriela returned to the lectern.

"Mr. Lawrence, are you known as a high roller in Las Vegas?"

Lawrence smirked. "Yes, Ms. Sanchez, I am one of the preferred customers there."

"You've lost lots of money in Las Vegas, haven't you?"

"And I've won lots of money there."

"As a high roller, you were allowed to go into debt while gambling in Las Vegas, isn't that true?"

"Yes, the casinos allowed me to borrow money to gamble."

"And you visited Las Vegas at least once a month and sometimes twice a month, isn't that true?"

"I don't remember specifically."

"You were in debt to the casinos at the time of the PetroMex deal, weren't you?"

Lawrence paused and cleared his throat. "No, Ms. Sanchez, I wasn't in debt."

Gabriela's eyes swept to the jury box. She saw Juror Seven give a subtle, yet unmistakable headshake, followed by Juror Eleven's quiet, skeptical frown. Score one for Sanchez.

At that point, she had planned to ask Lawrence about meeting Lopez several times in the United States to show the FBI could have arrested him at any time. After a moment of thought, she decided it would be better to catch Lawrence in one last misstatement.

"Mr. Lawrence. Isn't it true that you asked Mr. Lopez to assure you he would not use any of the Duval Energy fee for gifts or payments to PetroMex officials?"

"I don't remember doing that."

"Do you remember telling anyone you did that?"

Jason Daniels rose. "I object, Your Honor, she's getting into the matter you have excluded."

He must have told the alcohol rehab group.

"Your Honor, we are entitled to know if Mr. Lawrence told anyone that he had asked Mr. Lopez to assure him that he would not use any of the Duval Energy fee for gifts or payments to PetroMex officials Rafael Garza and Rodrigo Villa."

"I agree," Judge Comstock ruled. "Mr. Lawrence, you may answer the question."

Lawrence peered over first at Daniels, turned, and stared at the jury.

"Ms. Sanchez, that never happened. I know that for sure because prior to our closing the deal, Mr. Lopez specifically told me that to win the deal, he would use part of his thirty percent commission for gifts and money for Rafael Garza and Rodrigo Villa."

Gabriela was surprised because Lawrence had earlier testified that he didn't remember the names. "You're sure of that, Mr. Lawrence, and you're sure it was before you closed the deal with Mr. Lopez?"

"Yes, Ms. Sanchez. I remember it clearly."

"And that was in March of 2014?"

"Yes."

"Mr. Lawrence, Mr. Villa wasn't even working on foreign contracts at PetroMex in March 2014, so you're remembering something that never happened, aren't you?"

For the first time, Donald Lawrence slumped in his chair. After looking at Jason Daniels, he finally responded. "Maybe, ah maybe I got the names wrong."

"I have no further questions."

As she turned, she saw Deborah Snow shaking her head. When she sat down at the counsel table, Gabriela saw a note from Sparks Duval.

Well done.

"Judge Comstock, could we take another fifteen-minute recess?" Daniels asked.

"Let's make it ten minutes."

As Gabriela stood, Deborah Snow walked up still shaking her head, and said, "I told you at the break. Too damn long. Too damn boring. I watched the jury. They have no earthly clue what you were trying to accomplish."

When they were alone, Roberto grabbed Gabriela's arm.

"Don't pay any attention to that woman."

"Easier said than done. What do you think Daniels wants to clear up on redirect?"

Chapter 32

Don Lawrence slid into his chair, pushed himself back, and sat straight up, the leather creaking beneath him. He glanced at Jason Daniels, Melinda Swanson, and Thomas Barnes. Daniels glared at him.

"You've screwed this up, do you know that? I have the biggest trial of my career, and my star witness screws it up."

Lawrence smiled and stood to leave.

"Did you hear what I said to you?"

Lawrence stayed silent, eyes fixed on the floor.

"Damn it, Lawrence, did you hear what I said to you?"

"Yes, Mr. Daniels, I heard what you said." He pointed at Daniels. "Screw you. You're the one who screwed it up when you told me what to say, and it turned out to be wrong.

"No. You had it wrong. You told the jury that Agent Barnes here directed you to continue working for Duval Energy after the FBI arrested you."

"That's because he did."

That's not true," Thomas Barnes said. "I told you to quit after a few days. I have it right here in my handwritten notes."

Daniels spoke sharply. "I want you to go back in there. When I ask, tell the jury you made a mistake when you testified that the FBI directed you to continue working for Duval Energy and wear a wire after your arrest."

Lawrence looked at Melinda Swanson, who stood with her arms crossed and a deep frown. He shook his head, trying to catch her eye.

"You want me to lie? You people from Washington are something else. Can I record this?"

"I never directed you to keep working for Duval Energy," Barnes said. "Your memory may be faulty because you were drunk. You stayed on because you needed the money."

Lawrence didn't know what to say. He was angry but tried not to show it. His face flushed, and he wiped his forehead with a handkerchief.

"I don't think you'll want to put me back on the witness stand."

"We have to. You've made the FBI look like a pack of liars, and you made it sound like you and Lopez were doing a drug deal rather than a gas deal."

"I'm not a good liar, and what you're asking me to do is lie. You made me look like I was dealing drugs with Lopez using that prepaid phone. You screwed me when it turned out Villa wasn't working with PetroMex when we closed the Duval deal."

Melinda Swanson looked from Lawrence to Daniels. "Jason, I'm not sure you want to put Mr. Lawrence back on the stand and ask him to lie."

"Swanson, I didn't ask for your opinion. We're not asking him to lie. We've never asked him to lie. We're asking him to refresh his memory since he was half-drunk most of the time during the investigation."

"My memory was fine when I was on the witness stand. The problem was your memory of what Barnes told me to do and your memory about when Villa came to work with PetroMex. Are you sure you want to put me back on the stand?"

"You've given us no choice, Mr. Lawrence. Maybe you should at least let the jury know you were drinking at the time and may not have remembered the details clearly."

"Mr. Daniels, if I mention my drinking, Sanchez will destroy your case by showing how alcohol distorts memory."

"Just tell the jury you were mistaken when you testified that the FBI directed you to continue working for Duval Energy, and you were mistaken about Lopez mentioning Villa."

"But I wasn't mistaken, and it'll make me look bad as a witness."

"You are a bad witness, but you need to fix your mistake. You agreed to cooperate and testify. If you don't get back on the stand and clarify your testimony, I'll recommend the maximum sentence and ask the State Bar of Texas to debar you from practicing law again."

"Is that a threat?"

"No. I'm telling you to follow your agreement and tell the truth."

"You mean what you need to be the truth."

Outside, Gabriela waited for the marshal to signal that the jury was ready to return.

***

Gabriela watched as Donald Lawrence walked to the witness chair. His posture wasn't as straight as when he had left earlier. When he sat down, he kept his eyes on the table.

"You may redirect, Mr. Daniels," Judge Comstock said.

Daniels stood and walked to the podium. His jaw was tight.

"Mr. Lawrence, do you recall being asked if the FBI directed you to continue working for Duval Energy while you were cooperating with the government?"

"Yes."

"And you testified that the FBI directed you to continue working for Duval Energy?"

"I believe so."

Gabriela wrote a note and slid it to her father. *Impeaching his star witness?*

"Do you wish to clarify your answer?" Daniels asked.

Lawrence looked down at the table. His fists clenched, then he raised his head and sat tall in his chair, still not looking at the jury. "I may have been mistaken or misunderstood what I was told to do."

Roberto slipped his daughter a note. *Daniels made him change his testimony.*

"Didn't Agent Barnes tell you it would be better if you quit working for Duval Energy?"

"He may have. I'm not sure."

"Why did you continue working for Duval Energy while you were cooperating with the FBI?"

"I liked my work, and Duval Energy paid me well."

"Were you mistaken when you testified that Mr. Lopez told you he planned to bribe both Rafael Garza and Rodrigo Villa with part of the Duval Energy commission payment?"

"I had to be mistaken. Rodrigo Villa wasn't working for PetroMex at the time we closed the deal."

"That's all I have, Your Honor."

"Do you wish to cross-examine again, Ms. Sanchez?"

Gabriela felt a lump in her stomach. It wouldn't get better by asking more questions. It might even give Lawrence a chance to redeem himself. Deborah Snow stood, leaned over the rail, tapped Gabriela's shoulder, and handed her a note. *He's down. Now knock him out.*

Gabriela whispered to her father. "We need to leave this where it is." He nodded in agreement.

"Ms. Sanchez, do you have any more questions for Mr. Lawrence?" Judge Comstock asked again.

"Mr. Lawrence, I only have a few questions." Gabriela saw Lawrence's face brighten. He sat up straighter, as if he welcomed the battle to come.

Gabriela glanced at her iPad.

"I previously asked you about being loyal to Duval Energy and Sparks Duval. Do you recall that specific line of questioning?"

"Yes."

"What did you state in response?"

"I don't specifically remember my answer.."

"You claimed you owed a duty to the public. Isn't that what you replied?"

Gabriela turned to the jury certain they remembered Lawrence's answer.

Lawrence paused, looking toward Daniels and Barnes. When neither came to his aid, he replied, "If that's what's in the transcript, that's what I said."

"I then asked if you were absolutely certain the FBI directed you to remain as general counsel to Duval Energy after your arrest. Did that happen?"

"Not word for word, but something like that."

"And you said the FBI told you that the only way the government could convict Sparks Duval was for you to get him to admit he knew of the bribe. Is that right?"

"Yes."

"So, the FBI told you the only way the government could convict Mr. Duval was for you to get him to admit he knew of the bribe?"

"That was the substance of what they told me."

"I asked who told you that. Did you identify the agent?"

"I previously asked you about being loyal to Duval Energy and Sparks Duval. Do you remember that?"

"Yes."

"Do you remember your answer?"

"Not the exact words, but I remember saying I owed a duty to the general public."

"You claimed you owed a duty to the public. Do you remember that testimony?"

Lawrence paused, looking toward Daniels and Barnes. When neither came to his aid, he replied, "If that's what's in the transcript, that's what

I said."

"I then asked if you were absolutely certain the FBI directed you to remain as general counsel to Duval Energy after your arrest. Do you remember that question?"

"Not word for word, but something like that."

"And you said the FBI told you that the only way the government could convict Sparks Duval was for you to get him to admit he knew of the bribe. Is that right?"

"Yes."

"So, the FBI told you the only way the government could convict Mr. Duval was for you to get him to admit he knew of the bribe?"

"That was the substance of what they told me."

"I asked who told you that. Do you remember?"

"Yes."

"And you answered, 'Thomas Barnes,' right?"

"And that exchange took place only a few hours ago. Now, after meeting with Mr. Daniels and Mr. Barnes, you're telling the jury a different story. I wrote down what you said just now. You testified, 'I may have been mistaken or misunderstood what I was told to do.' Mr. Lawrence, do you occasionally suffer from memory loss?"

Daniels stood. "Your Honor, I object based on what we discussed this morning."

"Mr. Daniels, I'll let the witness answer."

"Yes," Lawrence said.

Gabriela paused for a moment.

"Mr. Lawrence, did Mr. Daniels tell you what to say when you returned to the witness chair?"

"Mr. Daniels refreshed my memory."

"Do you fear that an answer you give in this trial might alienate Mr.

Daniels or Mr. Barnes because of the control they have over the rest of your life?"

"I object," Daniels said, rising from his chair. "Your Honor, she's badgering the witness."

"I disagree," Judge Comstock said. "You opened the door to that question in your redirect."

Gabriela looked again at Lawrence. He was smiling. He looked at the jury and said, "No, Ms. Sanchez. I'm beyond that. I'm doing my best to remember what happened, what I said, and what the FBI agents said to me."

"Then did you stay on because Duval Energy paid $100,000 each month, which enabled you to maintain your lifestyle?"

"That's what Christopher Duval agreed to pay me."

"So now you say it wasn't because the FBI directed you. It was because you liked Duval Energy—the company you betrayed—paying you over one $100.000 a month?"

Daniels shot up. "Your Honor, she can't characterize what Mr. Lawrence did that way."

"Ms. Sanchez, please keep the characterizations to yourself. You may raise that point in final argument."

"Yes, Your Honor," Gabriela said, knowing the jurors had understood her point.

"Mr. Lawrence, did you spend over $100,000 each month?"

"No, Ms. Sanchez. I invested some of the money."

"That's all I have, Judge Comstock." Gabriela walked back to the counsel table and sat down. She saw Jason Daniels glare at Donald Lawrence as he stepped down from the witness chair.

Judge Comstock looked at the jury. "We've had enough for one day. Mr. Daniels, do you plan to call any more witnesses tomorrow?"

"Judge, I'm not sure. I'll know in the morning."

Judge Comstock turned to Gabriela. "Well, Ms. Sanchez, if he doesn't, you'll begin your defense in the morning."

Chapter 33

As soon as they returned to the Parker & McEvoy conference room, Gabriela's phone rang. The caller ID flashed *Christopher Duval*.

"What's going on, Christopher?"

"I just got off the phone with my lawyer. He told me Jason Daniels said that if I testify for the defense, he'll use my testimony against me and might charge me with perjury if he thinks I'm lying. I'm heading to my lawyer's office now."

Gabriela motioned for Chuck Green to step out of the conference room and told him what Christopher had said.

"Can Daniels bully Christopher like that? Can we ask Judge Comstock to give him immunity so he can testify if we need him?"

"Under the Sixth Amendment, Sparks has the right to call Christopher as a witness, but Judge Comstock can't grant him immunity."

"I don't think we should call any witnesses," Gabriela said.

"I agree," Green replied. "If there was ever a case with reasonable doubt, this is it."

When they returned to the conference room, Chuck Green told the group about Christopher's call, then turned it over to Gabriela.

"Mr. Duval, I know you've wanted from the beginning to tell your story to the jury, but I strongly believe it would be a mistake for us to put on any evidence."

Deborah Snow frowned. "Why keep the jury from hearing from Sparks?"

"Deborah, Chuck and I believe that when we walk into court tomorrow, Judge Comstock will ask Daniels if he has any more witnesses. Daniels will say, 'The government rests.' He's setting us up."

"How so?"

"He wants us to call Sparks. Then, after we rest, he'll bring in a witness who makes Sparks look like a liar. And we won't be able to call anyone to counter it."

"So, Ms. Mind Reader, who do you think he'll call?"

"Good question. Daniels could call José Lopez and grant him immunity. He could call a former Duval employee with a grudge. He could even call Garza or Villa—he doesn't need to give them immunity."

"Why not?"

"Because the Foreign Corrupt Practices Act doesn't cover the foreign recipients of bribes."

"Okay, but Judge Comstock ordered Daniels to identify his witnesses. How could he get away with that?"

"Because it's rebuttal. He doesn't have to disclose witnesses who'll contradict Sparks' testimony."

Deborah scoffed. "Our defense is that neither Sparks Duval nor Christopher knew Lopez would use the thirty percent fee to bribe PetroMex officials, right?"

"Yes, in part," Gabriela said.

"There's no evidence supporting that. If the jury doesn't hear Sparks deny knowing about the bribery, they'll assume he did and told Lawrence to pay Lopez."

"There is evidence," Gabriela replied. "Sparks didn't want to drill in Mexico. He knew corruption was a risk, so he sought legal advice from one of the top international energy lawyers in the world, and that lawyer betrayed him. Everything I just said is already in evidence."

"I watched the jury," Deborah said. "They believe Lawrence. They think Sparks sent that email to cover himself if the deal turned out illegal. They don't believe he legitimately relied on his lawyer."

Green stood. "Sparks, what Gabriela told you is true. Jason Daniels would love nothing more than to spring a witness who makes you look like a liar. The jury would crucify you for it."

"I won't have lied when I testify," Sparks said.

Green tried another approach. "You remember what I always say in our trials?"

"Not word for word, but I know you never wanted me to take the stand."

"Our case peaks when the other side rests. It will never be stronger than it is right now."

"I know, but the jury will hold it against me if I don't tell my story. They need to hear from me."

"You're hardly the ideal witness. The same traits that made you the richest man in Texas could be your undoing. On cross, you might look evasive or, worse, forget something important."

"I understand."

"How many times have you lost your temper under cross-examination?"

"Every time. But those cases were about money. This one is about my integrity. I can control myself."

"That's what Ken Lay told his lawyer in the Enron trial. You remember how that ended."

"The jury didn't like him, didn't believe him, and convicted him."

"Exactly. And since 2002, every CEO who has claimed ignorance of what his people were doing has been convicted. The only one who walked free never took the stand."

"I know, I know."

"Donald Lawrence was a disaster for the government, and Vivian helped our case. It is not going to get better than this."

"I thought you planned to move for a judgment of acquittal once they finished," Deborah Snow said. "If you're right, Judge Comstock will throw it out, and Sparks won't have to testify."

Gabriela's chest tightened. "I know Judge Comstock. He won't grant it. At best, he will defer the ruling until after we present our side or even after the jury verdict. If we rest now, he might still find Sparks not guilty."

"Judge Comstock could even acquit Sparks after a guilty verdict," Deborah said. "So what do we lose by letting him testify?"

"Deborah," Gabriela said evenly, "have you heard anything we've said?"

"I've heard you. I just don't agree."

"If Sparks testifies, we lose the reasonable-doubt advantage. Right now the jury must decide if Daniels proved beyond a reasonable doubt that Sparks knew Lopez planned the bribes. Once Sparks takes the stand, it is no longer about the evidence; it is about whether they believe him and whether they like him. His credibility becomes the case."

Duval stood. "I agree with Deborah. I have to tell my story. I can explain that email. I can make them believe me. I'm testifying. That's final."

"Okay," Gabriela said quietly. "Every time Daniels asks a question that rattles you, stop and say 'Ken Lay.' Do not lose it."

"That's a good idea," Duval said.

Green looked at her, arms crossed, and shook his head when no one else was watching.

When they were alone, Gabriela whispered, "We need Daniels to think we're not calling Sparks. It might be the only way to keep him from preparing rebuttal."

"I agree. How do you plan to do that?"

"I'll send you an email. Daniels will see it."

"How?"

"Because I'm convinced the government has hacked my computer the same way they hacked the CBS reporter's."

During the break, Gabriela opened her office laptop and typed a short email to Chuck Green.
Chuck, great work convincing Sparks he shouldn't testify. That's a much safer plan.

Within an hour, Scottie Johnson brought her a motion asking Judge Comstock to grant Christopher Duval immunity so he could testify for the defense. As Chuck had said, Judge Comstock wasn't the one who could grant it.

An hour later, Gabriela received Jason Daniels's response. He denied threatening or pressuring Christopher and argued again that Judge Comstock lacked authority to grant immunity.

When she looked up, Katy Roberson, a firm associate, was handing papers to Chuck Green.

"Here's a motion and brief arguing that Jason Daniels's threat to prosecute Christopher if he testifies violates Sparks Duval's Sixth Amendment rights," Katy said. "I made a point about Daniels reconvening the grand jury and issuing a subpoena for Christopher right after he saw our witness list."

After reading both documents and signing them, Gabriela handed them back. "File these right away."

When the room cleared, Roberto asked quietly, "Did you really plan to call Christopher?"

Gabriela smiled. "I'm not sure. He can be persuasive, but he doesn't always know when to stop talking."

Sparks Duval knew Gabriela, Roberto, and Chuck Green were right. If the defense rested, the jury might find reasonable doubt, and Daniels would have no chance to change that. But Duval still worried they would convict him if he didn't stand up and deny bribing PetroMex officials.

That morning Deborah Snow called.
"It's all over Twitter."
"What's all over Twitter?"
Star witness buries Duval.
Star witness testifies Duval told him to bribe PetroMex officials.
Star witness takes down Duval's Latina lawyer.
Sanchez no match for Donald Lawrence.

"I hope you understand now why I criticized Gabriela's cross-examination and why I told you to testify. You're the only one who can convince the jury Lawrence lied."

After hanging up, Duval opened the *Dallas Morning News* and stared at his picture on the front page. The headline read: *Can Sparks Duval Dazzle the Federal Jury?*
Damn. *Dazzle.* As if he planned to charm the jury and lie his way out of a conviction.

He kept reading.

Should William Thomas (Sparks) Duval testify? That is the question facing Gabriela and Roberto Sanchez in the criminal bribery case against Mr. Duval, founder and billionaire owner of Duval Energy.

Mr. Duval may be the only person capable of convincing the jury that Donald Lawrence acted alone when two PetroMex officials received favors in exchange for awarding a drilling contract to Duval Energy.

Duval's friends describe him as supremely confident, a man who believes he knows more than any lawyer and who has used his charisma and drive to build one of the largest oil and gas companies in the world. But confidence can cut both ways. "A man like Sparks Duval thinks he's invincible," one Dallas lawyer said. "That's what could get him in trouble with a jury."

When Duval arrived at the Parker & McEvoy office, Gabriela and Roberto were finishing a conversation with Chuck Green in the conference room.

"Is he telling you how to handle me this morning?" Duval asked.

Gabriela gave him a half smile. "No. We're going over the social media barrage about the trial. Twitter lit up overnight with attacks against you."

"I heard that from Deborah."

"Someone using the handle *@TXJusticeman* has sent out ten tweets overnight, each one calling you a liar, a crook, or guilty. There are even tweets about me: *'Duval's rising star lawyer is sinking fast. Not ready for prime time.'* I'm convinced someone is trying to manipulate public opinion."

"What makes you think that?"

"Each tweet has been reposted more than a hundred times, and national outlets have picked them up. That doesn't happen by accident."

"How can an anonymous person influence the trial?" Duval asked.

"I don't think this person is anonymous. Whoever it is knows things they couldn't have learned just by sitting in the courtroom. Someone is orchestrating this."

At 10:00 a.m., the jury was seated.

"Mr. Daniels, do you have any more witnesses at this time?"

"No, Your Honor. The government rests."

"Does the defense have any motions?"

Gabriela rose. "Yes, Your Honor."

"Ladies and gentlemen of the jury, I'll excuse you while the lawyers and I take up some legal matters. This may take a while, but please stay in the jury room."

After the jury left, Gabriela handed Judge Comstock the defense motion for judgment of acquittal and the supporting brief.

"Mr. Daniels, do you have a response?"

"We do, Your Honor."

Judge Comstock adjusted his glasses. "I'll take an hour to read both briefs before ruling. We'll reconvene then."

Gabriela glanced back at her father, who gave her a thumbs-up. During her clerkship, she had never seen Judge Comstock take an hour to review a motion for acquittal or allow argument before denying one.

At the prosecution table, Jason Daniels flicked his pen and shifted in his chair. He clearly hadn't expected the judge to take the motion seriously.

An hour later, Judge Comstock returned to the bench.

"I've reviewed the briefs. I rarely consider a motion for acquittal at this stage, but I wanted to give both sides a fair reading. At this point, I will not take the case away from the jury. However, Mr. Daniels, I'm giving you notice that I see some problems with your case."

Jason Daniels forced a smile and mouthed, *Nice try, Gabby.*

Judge Comstock looked down at his notes. "I understand there is also an issue regarding Mr. Christopher Duval's testimony for the defense. Do you wish to address that now?"

Christopher Duval's lawyer, William Donoghue, walked to the podium.

"Your Honor, I'm William Donoghue, counsel for Christopher Duval. My client was on the defense witness list and fully expected to testify."

"Yes, Mr. Donoghue. I've read your motion and brief."

"Thank you, Your Honor. I shouldn't have to be here today. Yesterday, Mr. Daniels called me. He asked whether Sparks Duval planned to call Christopher as a witness. I told him I didn't know. Mr. Daniels then reminded me that the investigation into Christopher was still open and that the grand jury could indict him at any time. I took that as a threat that if Christopher testified for the defense, the government would pursue an indictment and use his testimony against him. Mr. Daniels also implied that Christopher could face perjury charges. That's why I filed a motion asking you to grant him immunity so he could testify freely."

"Mr. Donoghue, as you know, I cannot grant immunity unless the government requests it. Mr. Daniels, do you intend to make that request?"

Jason Daniels stood. "No, Your Honor."

Judge Comstock leaned forward. "Even so, I'm troubled by your approach. The Supreme Court has made clear that a defendant has the right not only to confront witnesses against him but also to present witnesses in his defense. Your comments appear to have compromised that right."

"Your Honor," Daniels said, "Mr. Donoghue has mischaracterized our call. I contacted him, not Christopher Duval."

Gabriela felt her father's elbow in her ribs and stood. "Your Honor, when we listed Christopher Duval as a witness, Mr. Daniels issued a subpoena requiring him to testify before a grand jury. When you questioned him about it, he claimed it was for a new matter. You specifically ordered that he could not use anything from that proceeding in this trial."

"May I continue, Your Honor?" Daniels asked.

"Go ahead, Mr. Daniels. I'm eager to hear why you called Mr. Donoghue now."

"Yes, Your Honor. I called in good faith to confirm whether Christopher Duval still intended to testify."

"You could have asked Ms. Sanchez."

"I understand, but I also wanted to remind Mr. Donoghue of his client's duty to testify truthfully."

"And you thought the best way to do that was to mention the grand jury?" Judge Comstock asked. "Are you saying that if Christopher testified, you intended to seek an indictment?"

"I didn't say that, Your Honor. I simply told Mr. Donoghue to remind his client of his obligation to tell the truth."

"Mr. Daniels, Mr. Donoghue is one of the most respected lawyers in Dallas. Are you suggesting he needs your reminder on how to advise his client?"

"No, Your Honor. That wasn't my intent."

"Then it was unnecessary. And that makes me believe you made the call knowing it could affect the defense's ability to present its case."

Judge Comstock turned to Gabriela. "Ms. Sanchez, do you wish to add anything?"

"Yes, Your Honor. Mr. Daniels's conduct has violated Sparks Duval's Sixth Amendment rights, and he did it knowingly. After receiving our witness list, he immediately subpoenaed Christopher Duval before the grand jury—his first attempt at intimidation. Now, on the eve of our case, he calls Christopher's lawyer to 'remind' him to testify honestly. Mr. Donoghue doesn't need that reminder. Mr. Daniels's message was clear, and it worked. Mr. Donoghue has told us Christopher will no longer testify."

Judge Comstock nodded slowly. "Suppose I agree with everything you've said, Ms. Sanchez. What remedy are you seeking? A mistrial? If I grant that, the government will simply reindict Mr. Duval."

"Your Honor, we renew our motion for judgment of acquittal. Mr. Daniels has failed to prove that Sparks Duval or Duval Energy committed any crime. He's shown only that a rogue lawyer betrayed his client for money. And now, he's denied Mr. Duval a fair trial."

Daniels clenched his jaw. "Your Honor, that's ridiculous. Even if you accept Ms. Sanchez's account, you can't acquit a defendant because I made a phone call. That would be a rich white-collar criminal walking free on a technicality."

"The problem, Mr. Daniels," Judge Comstock said, "is that the harm may be irreparable. If you were acting in good faith, you could fix this by granting Christopher Duval immunity. Are you prepared to do that?"

Gabriela knew Comstock wasn't asking; he was warning. Daniels's arrogance had worn thin.

Daniels hesitated. "Your Honor, I'd need to call Washington and get approval."

"Then call them," the judge said. "And tell your boss that I may enter a judgment of acquittal—either before or after the defense presents its case—if your office refuses to grant immunity to Christopher Duval."

When they walked out of the courtroom, Gabriela wanted to take one more chance to persuade Sparks Duval to let the defense rest. Before she could speak, Chuck Green called her aside.

"I have some bad news."

Her pulse quickened. "What is it?"

"William Donoghue came to see me. When Christopher learned the government might give him immunity, he told Donoghue that he and Donald Lawrence created a secret shared email account."

Gabriela stopped walking. "A secret account?"

"Yes. They used the address **Duvlawr8111@gmail.com**."

She stared at him. "How did they use it?"

"When one of them wanted to send a message, he left a draft in the account. The other could open the draft, read it, and delete it."

"Why would they do that?"

"Donoghue said it started as a way to hide messages from Christopher's father. But once the PetroMex deal began, they used it for company business."

"What kind of messages?"

"According to Donoghue, they wrote that they either knew or suspected Lopez planned to buy gifts and pay PetroMex officials to win the contract."

Gabriela rubbed her temple. She hadn't slept well since the trial began, and it took her a moment to process what he had said. "That might help show Sparks didn't know."

"Maybe, but it would hurt the company. If Daniels gives Christopher immunity and asks the right questions, Christopher can't lie about it."

"Daniels doesn't know about the secret account," Gabriela said. "If he did, he would have already called Christopher."

"I agree."

She looked toward the elevators. "Still, this puts us in a difficult spot. Bringing it up might help Sparks Duval but could destroy the company. Can we represent both?"

"I'm not sure," Green admitted. "Christopher said they only used personal devices, not company computers, so the government probably hasn't found anything."

"Assuming that's true. I don't believe Lawrence told Barnes or Daniels. If he had, we'd have heard about it."

"You're probably right. But if Daniels grants immunity and asks Christopher how he and Lawrence communicated, Christopher might tell the truth, protect himself, and sink the company."

"No. He'd lie first," Gabriela said. "The company is his livelihood. He won't jeopardize it."

"Maybe not," Green replied. "For now, Daniels is on the defensive with Judge Comstock. Let's see if we can use that to our advantage."

"I like that idea," Gabriela said. "That arrogant Ivy League bastard deserves to squirm."

When they reconvened, Judge Comstock asked, "What did Washington say about granting Christopher Duval immunity?"

"They declined," Daniels answered.

"That surprises me, Mr. Daniels. You chose not to indict Christopher Duval, yet now you have threatened to indict him if he testifies for the defense."

"Your Honor," Daniels said, "I didn't threaten Mr. Duval's son. I only told his lawyer to remind him to tell the truth."

"Yes, Mr. Daniels. I heard that earlier."

Judge Comstock turned toward the clerk. "Bring in the jury."

Once the jurors were seated, he said, "Let's proceed. Ms. Sanchez, call your first witness."

Chapter 34

"The defense calls William Duval," the clerk announced.

Gabriela glanced at Jason Daniels. His face drained of color, and a gasp rippled through the courtroom. As she walked to the podium, Daniels rifled through his notebooks.

After Duval was sworn in, Gabriela began with what she called softball questions to help him relax before the jury. She asked him to tell his life story.

He described growing up poor, his father leaving, and how he had gotten his start in the oil and gas business. Ten minutes later, she asked if he was a billionaire.

Duval admitted he was a billionaire and explained that he had started with nothing and worked twelve- to fifteen-hour days, sometimes seven days a week. He told the jury he felt fortunate and blessed and used his money to give back to the community.

Daniels stood. "Your Honor, I've sat here patiently through this rags-to-riches biography, but isn't it time to move on to the PetroMex contract?"

"Ms. Sanchez, can we move along a little faster, please?"

"Yes, Your Honor." Gabriela turned back to Duval. "Mr. Duval, when did you first meet Donald Lawrence?"

Duval told the jury that his son, Christopher, met Lawrence at a 2012 energy conference and introduced him later.

"Did you interview Mr. Lawrence?"

"Not at first. Christopher wanted to hire him as general counsel because of his international experience and connections. I had no interest in foreign deals, so we didn't need him then."

"Why did you later agree to meet with him?"

"Christopher still wanted to expand abroad, so I agreed to the interview."

Duval explained that Lawrence had claimed to be an expert on both U.S. and international energy law and promised to keep every transaction legal and ethical.

"What was your impression of him?"

"I questioned his integrity."

"Why?"

"He spent our first meeting bragging about deals, about clients he shouldn't have named. No lawyer with integrity does that. But he was smart and confident, and I didn't want to undermine Christopher's judgment."

"So you agreed to hire him?"

"Yes. I told Christopher I'd trust his decision. Lawrence was respected in the industry and knew the law, which mattered to me."

"You mentioned concerns about his integrity. Anything else?"

"Yes. I'd heard rumors about his drinking and gambling."

Daniels rose. "Objection, Your Honor, it's hearsay and previously ruled inadmissible."

"Your Honor," Gabriela said, "Mr. Duval isn't offering it for truth, only to explain his concerns and what he did about them."

"I'll allow it," Judge Comstock said.

"I'd heard his firm threatened to fire him over alcohol issues and harassment complaints," Duval said.

"Did you ask him about it?"

"Yes. He said he'd quit drinking entirely. I took him at his word."

"Describe Mr. Lawrence's performance after you hired him."

Duval told the jury that Lawrence seemed competent and issued legal opinions on every deal.

"Mr. Duval, how did you first learn about potential oil and gas deals in Mexico?"

"Like everyone else, I read about the 2014 reforms that opened exploration to foreign companies."

"Were you interested?"

"No."

"Why not?"

"Prices were down. We'd never operated outside the U.S. We didn't speak the language, knew nothing about Mexican regulations, and I'd heard about the cartels. Too risky."

"But you did go forward. What changed?"

"Lawrence went to a Latin-American Energy Conference. He came back talking about huge opportunities. He and Christopher kept pressing me to consider it. I said no, but Christopher accused me of never letting him lead. He was right—I'd always kept control. He said even the U.S. State Department encouraged American companies to invest. That eased my mind."

"What happened next?"

"I finally said fine, look into it. They started meeting with José Lopez, the broker they said could guide us through the process."

"What did they tell you about him?"

"I asked why we needed a middleman. They said Lopez was essential—he'd been married to the former PetroMex CEO's daughter and knew everyone there."

"Did they tell you anything else?"

"Christopher said Lopez told him the only way to win was to pay a thirty-percent commission."

Daniels shot up. "Objection, hearsay on hearsay."

"I'm not offering it for the truth," Gabriela said. "Only to show what Christopher relayed to his father."

"I'll allow it for that limited purpose," the judge said.

"What did you do after hearing that?"

"I asked Donald Lawrence if there were legal problems. I was looking for a reason to say no."

"What did he say?"

"He told me it was normal in Mexico to use a middleman and that Lopez assured him everything was legal. He said American Energy paid a similar commission."

"Did he put that opinion in writing?"

"No, and I wish he had. He just showed me a Google search about commissions being standard practice there."

"Did Mr. Lawrence ever tell you that part of the commission would be used to bribe PetroMex officials?"

Duval faced the jury. "No. If he had, I'd have shut the deal down immediately. We didn't need it."

"Did you suspect Lopez would use part of the commission to bribe anyone?"

"No way. I've spent my life building a company on integrity. I wouldn't risk it."

"Did you know Lawrence and Lopez were friends—golfing, fishing, clubs in Mexico?"

"No. If I had, I'd have taken Lawrence off the deal."

"Did he ever tell you Lopez promised him a two-million-dollar bonus?"

"No. I assumed his five-percent profit share was enough."

"Did he tell you Lopez opened an offshore account for him?"

"No. Any of that would've stopped me cold."

"Did you ever meet Mr. Lopez?"

"I don't remember meeting him. I went to Mexico for the signing but didn't go to the PetroMex building. That was Christopher and Don's meeting, not mine."

"Is it possible you met him and forgot?"

"I suppose, but unlikely."

"Did you know the government had arrested Donald Lawrence?"

"No. They kept it secret."

"Had you known?"

"I'd have fired him immediately."

"Did you know he was wearing a camera when he visited you in Wyoming?"

"No, but I suspected something. He'd never come there before."

"What did he say about the visit?"

"He told me he'd received a grand-jury subpoena and didn't know what to do. Odd thing for a lawyer to say."

"Do you remember Agent Barnes testifying that you said you didn't care what Lopez did with the money?"

"Yes."

"Why did you say that?"

"One day dozens of FBI agents raided our office wearing bulletproof vests. It was humiliating. I was angry. What I meant was I didn't care anymore about the Mexico deal—I'd opposed it from the start. I never said I didn't care about bribery."

"Your Honor, that's all the questions I have."

Gabriela looked over. Daniels was still flipping pages.

"Mr. Daniels," Judge Comstock said, "would you like to break for lunch?"

"Yes, Your Honor."

"Very well. We'll resume at 1:30."

Gabriela turned and saw Deborah Snow mouth the words *Well done.*

As she left the courtroom, Daniels brushed past and muttered, "You've screwed this up, Gabby. Your client's going to hang himself on cross. He's toast."

Chapter 35

Over lunch, Deborah Snow showered lavish praise on Sparks Duval, telling him he would do a great job handling Jason Daniels's cross-examination. She urged him not to let Daniels intimidate him. Gabriela listened quietly. She was more worried that Duval would not be intimidated but kept her thoughts to herself.

At 1:35, after Judge Comstock seated the jury, he said, "Mr. Duval, please come back up and take your seat in the witness chair."

Sparks Duval rose and sauntered toward the witness stand. His confident manner was not a good sign.

"Okay, Mr. Daniels, you may begin your cross-examination."

Daniels glanced down at his notebook. "Mr. Duval, you have a lavish lifestyle, don't you?"

As Gabriela had instructed, Duval paused before answering.

"Your Honor, I object," Gabriela said. "Mr. Duval's lifestyle isn't relevant."

"Your Honor, Ms. Sanchez made it relevant," Daniels replied.

"I agree," Judge Comstock said. "Mr. Duval, you may answer."

"I'm better known as the man who grew up dirt poor, raised by a single mother, and worked hard to build a successful company. Once I became successful, I've been known for what I've done to help people in Dallas and across Texas."

"Your Honor, please instruct him to answer the question," Daniels said.

"I answered the question," Duval replied.

"Mr. Duval," Judge Comstock said evenly, "when Mr. Daniels addresses me, let me respond."

"Yes, Your Honor."

"Mr. Daniels, perhaps you should rephrase your question if you didn't like his answer."

Daniels grimaced. "Mr. Duval, how many planes does your company own?"

"We don't own any planes."

"How many does your company lease?"

"I'm not sure."

"More than a half-dozen?"

"It could be. You'd have to ask Christopher."

"Mr. Duval, isn't it true you flew friends to France just to watch the Monaco Grand Prix and the cost was over $100,000?"

"I don't remember the cost."

"Whatever the cost, you wrote it off as a business expense, didn't you?"

"I'm not an accountant. Ours assured me it was legitimate. The guests were oil-and-gas executives and their families."

"You mix personal and business expenses to get more write-offs, don't you?"

"No. Absolutely not."

"Do you attend other Grand Prix races?"

"Yes, I'm an enthusiast."

"Do you claim a business expense when you and Christopher go alone?"

"I don't think so."

Gabriela braced, expecting Daniels to produce Duval's tax returns. When he moved on, she exhaled quietly.

"Mr. Duval, how many homes do you own?"

"I own three."

"Where are they?"

"One in Dallas, one in Wyoming, and one in Ireland."

"How much did you pay to build the Dallas home?"

Duval looked to Gabriela. When she didn't stand, he said, "Forty-two million dollars."

"Forty-two million?"

Gabriela watched the jurors' faces and didn't like what she saw. Most probably owned homes worth a fraction of that.

"Yes," Duval said. "It was my way of helping construction workers when the economy tanked in 2008."

"And you claim to help people in Dallas. How much have you donated to Dallas causes in the last ten years?"

"I'm not sure, but well over two million."

"And isn't it true that one million of that came after your indictment?"

"I'm not sure of the amount."

Daniels displayed a photo. "Tell the jury how big your house is."

"Twelve thousand square feet."

"That seems excessive. Are you and your wife the only residents?"

"Yes."

"Your Dallas property sits on how many acres?"

"Ten."

"And it has a tennis court?"

"Yes."

"So, you and your wife play?"

"No. Our grandchildren do. We built it for them."

"You also have an outdoor pool?"

"Yes."

"You and your wife swim?"

"Occasionally, in summer."

"Do you have a pool house?"

"Yes."

"How large is it?"

"I'm not sure."

"It has a living room?"

"Yes."

"A kitchen?"

"Yes."

"Three bedrooms?"

"Yes."

"Who sleeps there?"

"Our children and grandchildren when they visit. Mr. Daniels, I grew up with nothing. I worked hard, succeeded, and want to provide for my family."

"That's noble of you," Daniels said, glancing at the jury. "Your son Christopher owns his own home in Dallas?"

"Yes."

"Over eight thousand square feet?"

"That sounds about right."

Gabriela rose. Duval mouthed, *About time.*

"Your Honor, we've heard enough about houses. Mr. Duval isn't on trial for owning property, and Christopher Duval isn't on trial at all."

"Your Honor," Daniels said, "Mr. Duval's greed and motive to strike the PetroMex deal are the focus of this case."

"I'll allow questions about Mr. Duval's property," Judge Comstock said. "But limit them to what Mr. Duval owns."

Daniels nodded and displayed another photo. "Your Wyoming home has an indoor pool, correct?"

"Yes."

· "Do you swim there?"

"Not for years, but our grandchildren do."

369

"How many people maintain your ten acres?"

"Four."

"Full time?"

"Yes. I try to give opportunities to Mexican Americans."

"Mr. Duval," Judge Comstock said, "just answer the questions, please."

"Yes, sir. He's trying to embarrass me in front of the jury."

"Ms. Sanchez, instruct your client to answer questions only," the judge said.

"Your Honor, may I have a short recess to speak with him?" Gabriela asked.

"Your Honor," Daniels objected, "he knows the rules."

"Mr. Daniels," the judge said, "no lectures. Ms. Sanchez, your client knows what's expected. Continue."

Duval took a deep breath, following his doctor's advice.

"Mr. Duval, how many cars do you have in Dallas?"

"Five."

"All kept at your house?"

"Yes."

Daniels projected another photo. "Is one a red Ferrari Testarossa?"

"Yes. You've already shown I like fast cars."

"And this one—a Bentley?"

"Yes."

"Not exactly fast, is it?"

"No."

"And the others?"

"One's a Ford F-150 pickup I use for work."

"You need five cars and a truck to get around Dallas?"

"No. I'm a car enthusiast."

"Your Wyoming house—about six thousand square feet?"

"Roughly."

"On the mountain?"

"Yes, in Jackson Hole."

"So, you and your wife ski?"

"No. We're too old. Our children and grandchildren ski in winter and fish in summer."

"How often are you there?"

"Two to three weeks in summer, sometimes Christmas."

"And vacant the other fifty weeks?"

"No. Our family uses it. Someone looks after it the rest of the year."

"You have a caretaker on payroll full time?"

"Yes. But none of this relates to PetroMex."

"Mr. Duval," Judge Comstock warned, "just answer the questions."

"What prompted the house in Ireland?"

"My wife's family is from Ireland. She loves visiting."

Daniels showed another photo. "It's a historic castle, isn't it?"

"Some call it that, yes."

"You also own a yacht?"

"Yes."

"Where do you keep it?"

"In Florida."

"How much did it cost?"

"I don't remember."

Daniels displayed a photo of a massive yacht. "About fifty million?"

"I'm not sure."

"And a full-time crew?"

"Yes."

"How many crew members?"

"I'm not sure."

"How many weeks a year do you use it?"

"It depends. When we sailed the Mediterranean, we were aboard six weeks."

"You didn't sail from Florida to the Mediterranean, did you?"

"No. We met the yacht in Monte Carlo."

"You and your guests flew there in your jet?"

"In the company's leased jet, yes."

Daniels switched topics. "Isn't it true you called Mr. Lawrence nine days before the trial started?"

Duval glanced at Gabriela and saw her frown. He hadn't told her about that call.

"Yes. I called Don, but I'm not sure when."

"You called to get your stories straight, didn't you?"

"No. I called because I couldn't remember if I'd ever met José Lopez."

"Didn't you tell Mr. Lawrence you had never met Lopez?"

"I told Don I didn't remember meeting him."

"And you told him to testify that you never met Lopez, didn't you?"

Duval's jaw tightened. He drew a breath. "No. I told him to tell the truth. I only asked if he remembered me meeting Lopez."

"What did Mr. Lawrence say?"

"He said he was afraid of you."

"What did he say about meeting Lopez?"

"He said I met Lopez when we closed the deal. I remember going to Mexico with Don and Christopher, but not meeting Lopez. Why does it matter?"

"Mr. Duval," Judge Comstock said, "let Mr. Daniels ask the questions."

"Yes, Your Honor. I don't remember meeting Lopez."

"If you had, wouldn't you have asked what he planned to do with his thirty-percent commission?"

"Maybe, but I don't recall meeting him. It was Don's and Christopher's deal, not mine."

"You credit your success to attention to detail, correct?"

"I think I've been fortunate and blessed."

Daniels handed Duval a document and another to Gabriela. "What is that?"

"An interview I did for the Oil and Gas Journal in 1997."

"Read the highlighted question and answer."

"Mr. Duval, you're the most successful privately owned energy company. What makes you so successful?"

"My answer: 'I see things others miss because I'm insatiable about research and every detail of potential deals.' "

"In the same article, your son said you're on top of every project, correct?"

"He may have said something like that."

"So, your success comes from attention to detail?"

"In part. I like doing things my way, but I've also been lucky," Duval said, glancing at the jury. "I was twenty years younger when I gave that interview. Times change."

"Duval Energy is one of the top fracking firms in the country, true?"

"We've done more fracking than anyone."

"And contaminated more water than anyone, isn't that true?"

"Dead wrong. That's fake news. We've done thousands of jobs, and the EPA alleged contamination only a handful of times—a record better than airline safety."

"Yet you settled with homeowners?"

"Yes, like airlines settle after crashes. No industry is perfect. Fracking is safe when done right, and we do it right."

"Do you treat landowners as badly as airlines treat passengers?"

"Your Honor," Gabriela said, "irrelevant and meant to inflame the jury."

"I agree," Judge Comstock said. "Mr. Daniels, stay within the case."

"Yes, Your Honor."

A juror raised her hand. Judge Comstock said, "We'll take a fifteen-minute break."

"Your Honor, I don't want him coached during the break," Daniels said.

"Your Honor," Gabriela objected, "that's improper. Please instruct the jury to ignore it."

"I will," the judge said. "Ladies and gentlemen, ignore Mr. Daniels's comment. We'll resume shortly."

In the hallway, Deborah Snow grabbed Gabriela's arm. "You're letting Daniels get away with too much. You should object to half his questions."

"Deborah, I'd love to. The problem is, I need grounds—and the jury won't like repeated overruled objections. A jury expert like you should know that."

When they reached the conference room, Gabriela began while her father kept Deborah occupied in the hallway.

"Sparks, don't let him get under your skin. Don't argue. Don't raise your voice. The jury will think you're hiding something."

"I'm trying to stay calm, but he's twisting everything and quoting lies. I have to correct them—and Deborah says you should be objecting."

"Sparks, the jury has to like you. If they don't, they'll convict you. Stay calm. I'll object when I have solid grounds."

"Okay, okay. I'll stay calm."

Gabriela turned as the U.S. marshal appeared at the door.

"Judge Comstock is ready."

Chapter 36

Duval took his seat in the witness chair and Judge Comstock looked out from the bench. "You may continue, Mr. Daniels."

Daniels got Duval to admit that when he invested in Barnett Shale in Texas, he was involved in every detail of the transactions.

"And you didn't pay a middleman to help you reach agreements to drill, isn't that true?"

"I guess arguably we did. We paid a lawyer to negotiate the deals and prepare the paperwork."

"And you received many emails about the details of those transactions, didn't you?"

"I received some emails from our lawyer and from Christopher, yes."

"Did your outside law firm provide you with a legal analysis on those deals?"

"Yes."

Duval then refused to admit he had been involved in every detail of the Bakken Shale deals in North Dakota. He said Christopher handled a lot of the details.

"And those people, including Christopher, reported every detail to you, didn't they?"

"I'm sure they did."

"And you received many emails about those transactions, didn't you?"

"I don't know what your definition of many is, Mr. Daniels. Perhaps you can define how many is many."

Daniels laughed out loud and so did several people in the courtroom audience. After Judge Comstock restored decorum, Daniels continued. "You received several emails from the law firm you hired, didn't you?"

"Again, I remember receiving a few, not several."

"And you paid your lawyer, but you didn't pay a middleman to help you win any of the deals in Bakken Shale, right?"

"No, we didn't pay a middleman on any US deals. It wasn't necessary."

"Did your outside law firm provide you with a written legal analysis?"

"Mr. Daniels, we get a legal opinion on every deal we do."

"You have reserves of over 1 billion barrels in North Dakota, isn't that true?"

"Yes."

"A major business magazine called you 'America's most reckless billionaire,' isn't that true?"

Sparks Duval felt the blood rushing to his head again. He hesitated again. "That magazine is liberal rag. It's a left-wing environmentalist's publication, claiming to be a business magazine."

"The magazine reported that you almost went broke in 2008 after the oil crash because you had borrowed so much money, isn't that true?"

"That is what the liberal rag magazine reported, but what they reported was fake news. It was untrue. The fall of 2008 was a big blow for our company, just as it was for our entire country." Sparks Duval looked at the jury. "I was broke, but we survived it and came back even stronger, despite liberal media efforts to destroy me."

"One magazine compared Duval Energy to Enron, isn't that true?"

Sparks Duval glared at Jason Daniels, and in a raised voice, he started to answer, "We are—"

Gabriela stood, hoping to signal Duval.

"I object, Your Honor."

"On what grounds?"

"Hearsay." Gabriela looked at Duval and gently shook her head.

"Your Honor, we have the evidence right here." Jason Daniels handed Gabriela a blog post from a left-leaning white-collar crime blog.

Before Gabriela could respond and before Judge Comstock ruled on Gabriela's objection, Sparks Duval answered.

"This is a blog posted by a liberal blogger hell-bent on smearing me and destroying me. Nothing could be further from the truth. Enron executives committed fraud and the company went broke because of it. We thrive because no government agency has ever accused us of doing anything illegal until you took us on this witch hunt."

Gabriela sighed and sat down.

"Do you vilify anyone who disagrees with you, Mr. Duval?"

Before Gabriela could object, Sparks Duval retorted. "Are you including yourself?"

"Mr. Duval, you are welcome to include me on the list of people who disagree with you, but let's turn to another subject. Duval Energy now owns rights to far more acres than you can ever drill, isn't that true?"

"No, we plan to drill every acre we own," Duval replied with pride while sitting up in the witness chair.

"And you have never been satisfied that you have enough, isn't that true?"

"I would be bored if I wasn't looking for other opportunities."

"When interviewed, you said, 'We are constantly on the search for new plays that could be even better than the plays we have,' isn't that true?"

"Yes, what you read is true. So, I believe I said it."

"Which is why you wanted to drill Mexico, isn't that true?"

"How many times do I have to tell you I was dead set against drilling Mexico? There was little upside and a great deal of downside."

"Because you knew about the corruption there?"

"I was more concerned about the cartel. They were stealing from PetroMex and would steal from us if we drilled in Mexico. I also envisioned labor problems. We had no reason to drill in Mexico. I was happy just doing business in the US."

"American Energy and other competitors were seeking contracts in Mexico. Didn't that influence you?"

"That didn't influence me. Those are public traded companies. What they and other competitors do has never influenced my decisions."

"You claim Mr. Lawrence and Christopher wanted Duval Energy to drill in Mexico. Who decided what markets to enter in the United States?"

"Me. I made each decision."

"You spoke to the media after Donald Lawrence testified, didn't you?"

"Yes, I'm asked for comments every day when I leave the courthouse."

"You called Mr. Lawrence a liar, didn't you?"

"Yes, but I believe you coerced Don and told him what he had to say."

"What did I tell Mr. Lawrence to say?"

Sparks Duval's voice grew louder, and he started to rise from the witness chair. "You threatened Don. You told him to testify that he told me what Lopez planned to do with his commission, and I told him I didn't want to know."

"You didn't want to know, did you?"

"No, I didn't want to do the deal. I only wanted to know that the deal had no legal problems. That's why I sent the email asking Don for his legal opinion."

"Unlike every other project, your lawyer, Mr. Lawrence did not provide you with a written legal opinion, did he?"

"No, he gave me assurance that there were no legal problems, but it wasn't in writing."

"Whatever misgivings you had about doing business in Mexico, you ultimately reached an agreement with PetroMex, didn't you?"

Sparks Duval was frowning. "That's correct. I wanted my son, Christopher to know I respect his judgment. Then, unlike any other deal, I stood back and let Christopher and Don Lawrence negotiate the agreement."

"On this one and only deal, you stood back and let Christopher and Donald Lawrence put your company at risk?"

"Don was our lawyer. When I hired him, I made clear his primary job was to make sure our company was not at risk. It was right in his contract. He assured me he would identify any risks and help us evaluate them. I trusted Don, and he assured me the company would not be at risk on the PetroMex deal."

Jason Daniels picked up the *Texas Monthly* issue with Sparks Duval on the cover. "Mr. Duval, you remember giving the interview to *Texas Monthly*, don't you?"

"Yes."

"And in the interview you said, and I quote, 'I don't need a lawyer. I know more about energy law than any lawyer I've met.' Is that true?"

"Yes, but that was in jest, and it was before we had hired Don Lawrence as general counsel. I was making fun of lawyers, like you, who think they know it all."

"Lawyers like me?"

"Yes, Mr. Daniels, you've never negotiated a drilling deal, and yet you think you're an expert. Like other lawyers, you second guess what businessmen do."

"Do you think I would need to be an energy law expert to know whether a middleman planned to use money we paid him to bribe PetroMex officials?"

"No, Mr. Daniels. You'd just need to know what the middleman planned to do with his commission."

"Mr. Duval, you never asked José Lopez what he intended to do with his commission, did you?"

"I didn't ask because I understood that Don Lawrence had asked and was satisfied with Lopez's answer."

"Why did you travel to Mexico when the deal was closed and choose not to meet with the man you paid a thirty percent commission to help you win the contract?"

"I didn't want to meet the guy we paid a thirty percent commission just because his ex-wife was the PetroMex CEO's daughter."

"Mr. Duval, weren't you aware that in Mexico, bribery of public officials is well known?"

"Donald Lawrence assured me that the Mexican government was cracking down on corruption. That was one reason there was an auction for the oil and gas contracts."

"Mr. Duval, look at the screen and tell the jury who is in the photo."

"I am in the photo with Christopher and Don. I don't know the other man in the photo, and I don't remember this photo being taken."

"Mr. Duval, the other man is José Lopez and the photo was taken the day Christopher signed the contract."

Sparks Duval covered his mouth with his hand, looking dazed and confused. Gabriela knew that was not a good sign. Had he purposely forgot meeting with Lopez?

Finally, Duval answered, "Like I said, Mr. Daniels, I don't remember that photo being taken."

"Mr. Duval, one last thing. Duval Energy was the only company who bid on the contract you won and American Energy was the only bidder on the contract they won. Did your two companies have an agreement on who would win each contract?"

Sparks Duval laughed. "Mr. Daniels, your question proves how little you know about oil and gas, and our company. American Energy bid on a deep-water contract. Our company only drills on land. We never considered bidding on the contract they won."

Daniels put his hand on his throat as if he had choked. Apparently, he hadn't known the difference in the contracts.

"Your Honor, that's all I have."

Gabriela looked at her father for a signal on whether she should try to clear anything up on redirect. He put his finger and thumb close together, which she took to mean do very little redirect.

When she stood, she had Duvel repeat that he had not known that Lopez would use any of the Duval commission to bribe PetroMex officials, that Lawrence had assured him that everything about the deal was legal, and that he had relied on Lawrence's legal advice.

"Your Honor, that's all I have," Gabriela said. "And the defense rests."

Judge Comstock looked over at the jury. "Okay, Ms. Sanchez. Ladies and gentlemen of the jury, the defense has rested. Mr. Daniels has the right to present rebuttal evidence if he desires. Mr. Daniels, have you decided whether to present rebuttal?"

"No, Your Honor. We'll think about it tonight."

Gabriela asked, "Your Honor, can Mr. Daniels at least identify who he might call as a rebuttal witness so we can prepare?"

Daniels responded, "Your Honor, we don't know if we will call any witnesses, and we don't know who we might call."

"Okay, Mr. Daniels. Let's break for the day."

When they were on the street, Roberto Sanchez's cell phone rang, and he answered. His face immediately turned pale. When he hung up, Gabriela asked what was wrong.

"José Lopez told me they plan to call a witness who taped a conversation with Rafael Garza and Rodrigo Villa, during which they described how to win a PetroMex contract. The mysterious man will be their rebuttal witness."

Chapter 37

.Gabriela asked her father for more details about Lopez's call.

"Lopez told me a private investigation company secretly recorded Rafael Garza and Rodrigo Villa describing bribery as the only way to win a PetroMex oil or gas contract."

"How did Daniels learn about the recording?"

"Lopez said he didn't know."

Gabriela worried Garza and Villa might have claimed that Duval Energy bribed them to win the drilling contract. She called the number Lopez had used to reach her father, but no one answered and there was no voicemail.

She spent the night re-working her final argument, trying to strike a balance between what she believed would persuade the jury and what Deborah Snow insisted she emphasize.

After rewriting, Gabriela practiced in front of the mirror, then set up a video camera and filmed her closing. She studied her gestures, listened to her tone, adjusted her inflection, and practiced pausing at key moments. Through the night she memorized every line until she could deliver it with conviction and restraint.

While she worked, her phone vibrated constantly with new tweets about Sparks Duval's testimony:

#GreedyDuval didn't want to know about PetroMex bribe.

#GreedyDuval deceptive to save himself.

#GreedyDuval defiant, defensive, defeated.

#GreedyDuval indignant, incensed, infuriated.

#GreedyDuval stuck head in sand.

#GreedyDuval sorry attempt to cover with bogus email.

The next morning, Gabriela opened *The Dallas Morning News* on her iPad and saw a photo of her and her father leaving the courthouse with Sparks Duval.

The headline read: **Duval's Fiery Testimony**

Sparks Duval, known around Dallas as the real-life Jock Ewing, may have turned into J. R. Ewing in court two days ago, engaging in one fiery exchange after another with Washington D.C. prosecutor Jason Daniels. Trial experts and friends expected Duval to remain calm and composed during testimony, and he was—until cross-examination. The usually cool billionaire lost his temper almost from Daniels's first questions. Duval seemed offended that the prosecutor would ask about his three houses, airplanes, and yacht, and compare their cost to his charitable contributions. Daniels didn't do the math for the jury, but the News did—and Duval's lifestyle spending exceeds his donations by roughly a hundredfold.

The fireworks didn't stop there. During an intense cross-examination, Daniels accused Duval of tampering with the government's star witness, Donald Lawrence, claiming Duval called him days before trial to influence his testimony. Duval denied it, saying he was only trying to refresh his memory. Whether his performance helps or hurts his case will soon be up to the jury.

***

Before court that morning, Duval and Deborah Snow came by Gabriela's office.

"Gabriela," Snow began, "the media and the bloggers think Donald Lawrence wiped the floor with you. They're also attacking Sparks's testimony."

"What?"

"You heard me. I've seen dozens of blogs, tweets, and Facebook posts—all showing a woman's rear end with a footprint on it. The most-retweeted one says: *Legal experts agree Donald Lawrence dazzled Duval's lawyer.* The runner-up: *Legal experts claim Duval's lawyer off the rails in her defense.* Then there are the others—*Duval guilty, Duval testimony proves guilt.* We can't keep up with the barrage."

Gabriela's mouth fell open. "Those liars. None of them were in the courtroom."

"That doesn't matter," Snow said.

"Ms. Snow," Roberto Sanchez asked, "has it occurred to you that one of your PR competitors might be creating those posts to influence the jury? The language matches what's been used all trial."

"Sure," Snow replied. "We've tried to counter it. It's called trolling. We use strategic trolling in politics and business all the time to shape public opinion."

"It isn't against the law?" Roberto asked.

"In England, yes—but not yet here."

"Donald Lawrence is the only thing standing between Sparks Duval and an acquittal," Snow said. "It's his word against Duval's."

"Maybe," Gabriela replied, "but you're the jury expert. You can see the jury doesn't like either of them. If Sparks hadn't testified, they'd only dislike Lawrence. Now we'll see who Daniels brings in for rebuttal."

"Well, the jury better not like Lawrence," Snow shot back, "and they'd better like Sparks when you finish your final argument. And you'd better handle whoever Daniels calls today."

"That's what I intend to do."

"Hope isn't good enough," Snow said sharply. "You need to show Lawrence for what he is—a narcissist, a drunk, and most importantly, a liar—and you need to destroy the rebuttal witness."

"Deborah, I can't mention his drinking. I'll tell the jury he lied and that Daniels coached him, but I can't call him a drunk."

Sparks Duval finally spoke. "Daniels can't win without Lawrence. He's their star witness. You need to make sure the jury sees he lied to save himself."

Gabriela had heard enough. She wanted to tell them both to leave. Instead, she said evenly, "I have it under control. I'll show the jury Lawrence lied."

"You'd better," Duval said.

"It damn well better be a winner," Snow added, "or you'll never see another courtroom."

"The two of you need to go," Gabriela said, standing. "Before we get to closing arguments, we still have to hear from a rebuttal witness who could change everything."

Chapter 38

After seating the jury the next morning, Judge Comstock asked once again whether Jason Daniels had any rebuttal evidence.

"This time I do, Your Honor," Daniels said. "The government calls Kira Gregoreva as a rebuttal witness."

Gabriela turned and saw a tall, blonde woman, likely in her thirties, walk down the aisle. She was striking—high cheekbones, pale skin, and sharp green eyes—dressed in a gray pinstripe suit that looked tailored for intimidation. After Gregoreva took the oath, Daniels began his direct examination.

"Ms. Gregoreva, tell the jury a little about yourself."

With a soft Russian accent, she said she lived in Moscow and worked for a private investigation company called Spider Security.

"Did there come a time when a Russian energy company hired Spider Security for an investigation?"

"Yes."

"What was the name of that company?"

"Petrovichgas."

"What did Petrovichgas hire Spider Security to investigate?"

"Why PetroMex had not awarded Petrovichgas an oil or gas contract."

"How did you become involved?"

"Our head of investigations assigned me to lead the case."

"What did you do?"

"First, I researched the oil and gas industry in Mexico. I learned that in 2013 Mexico opened its energy sector to foreign investment for the first time since 1938. I studied the contracts PetroMex had awarded to international companies."

"What, if anything, did you discover?"

"I discovered that Rafael Garza and Rodrigo Villa were the PetroMex officials responsible for awarding drilling contracts."

"What did you do then?"

"I flew to Mexico City with a young associate and contacted Garza. I invited him and Villa to dinner at an upscale restaurant."

"Did they accept?"

"Yes."

"Tell the jury what happened during that dinner."

Gregoreva explained that she bought a bottle of expensive tequila, and the two officials began drinking immediately. After ordering appetizers, she told them she represented the largest oil and gas producer in Russia and had been sent to learn how her company could enter the Mexican market.

"What did Garza and Villa tell you?"

"By the third glass of tequila they were talking freely. They said our company must hire José Lopez and pay him a thirty-percent commission. I asked what Lopez did with that commission, and they both pointed to themselves and laughed."

"What happened next?"

"I asked how Lopez paid them. Garza said Lopez had created companies in their children's names and opened offshore accounts for them. They also said Lopez paid bribes to the PetroMex CEO."

"What else did they say?"

"I asked how the bribes were disguised. Garza said Lopez handled everything and called the bribes a 'third-world tax.'"

"Did you record your conversation with Garza and Villa?"

"Yes."

For the next hour, the courtroom was silent as the jury listened to the recording of Garza and Villa describing an elaborate pay-to-play scheme.

When the tape ended, Daniels said, "Your Honor, that's all I have for this witness."

"Thank you, Mr. Daniels," Judge Comstock said. "Ms. Sanchez, you may cross-examine."

"Thank you, Your Honor." Gabriela rose. "Ms. Gregoreva, are you a Russian spy?"

"No. I work for a private company in Russia, not for the government."

"Do you know why you were chosen for this operation?"

"I was told PetroMex officials would be more likely to open up to a young woman than to a man."

"Did you seduce either Mr. Garza or Mr. Villa to get information?"

"Ms. Sanchez," Gregoreva said with a faint smile, "you have watched too many movies. I didn't need to seduce them. After a few glasses of tequila, they shared everything you just heard."

"At no time did either Garza or Villa say they had been bribed by Duval Energy. Isn't that true?"

"They never mentioned any specific company. They said everyone knew a bribe through Mr. Lopez was the only way to win a PetroMex contract."

"And they never said Lopez used any of the fee Duval Energy paid him to bribe them, correct?"

"Yes. They only said which PetroMex officials Lopez paid and how large the bribes were."

Gabriela paused, searching for another angle, but found none. "Your Honor, I have no further questions."

When she turned, Daniels smiled faintly.

"No redirect, Your Honor," he said.

"That will conclude the rebuttal," Judge Comstock announced. "Ladies and gentlemen, I'm releasing you for the rest of the day. During that time, the lawyers and I will go over the law applicable to this case. I'll give you the final instructions tomorrow, and then each side will present closing arguments. Mr. Daniels will argue first, followed by Ms. Sanchez, and then Mr. Daniels will have the last word.

"Remember—do not discuss this case with anyone. Do not read, listen to, or watch any coverage of it. You'll be ready to deliberate tomorrow. Do you all understand?"

In unison, the jurors answered, "Yes."

After the jury exited, Gabriela stood. "Your Honor, we renew our motion for a directed verdict."

"Ms. Sanchez," Judge Comstock said, "I'm going to let the jury decide whether Mr. Duval and his company are guilty."

After half an hour of discussion about the jury instructions, the real dispute emerged: whether Sparks Duval had to have actual knowledge of bribery to be convicted, or whether the jury could find him guilty if there was a high probability of bribery that he chose to ignore.

Following twenty minutes of argument, Judge Comstock ruled. "Ms. Sanchez, I'll instruct the jury that they may infer knowledge if Mr. Duval purposely avoided learning what Mr. Lopez intended to do with the money. The jury can decide the importance of the email."

Gabriela sat silently, considering how she might turn the "blind-eye" or "head-in-the-sand" instruction to her advantage.

"Ms. Sanchez, did you hear me?"

"Yes, Your Honor."

She glanced toward Daniels. He was smiling, hand raised in a V-for-victory sign.

"Looks like I got you on that one, Gabby."

"I guess so, Jaybird."

Daniels laughed as she walked out.

Chapter 39

In the morning, while drinking coffee, Gabriela read the headline:

Bribery the Norm on PetroMex Contracts

The government called Kira Gregoreva as a rebuttal witness yesterday. The Russian investigator testified and provided a secretly taped conversation she had with Rafael Garza and Rodrigo Villa. On tape, Garza and Villa told Gregoreva that the only way an international company could win a PetroMex energy contract was to pay José Lopez and let him bribe Mexican officials. Final arguments will be this morning. Afterward, the jury will retire to reach a verdict.

Three hours later, after the jury had been seated, Judge Comstock looked down from the bench. "Mr. Daniels, you may address the jury."

Gabriela watched Daniels. He looked more confident and strident than he had during his opening statement. After thanking the jury, he began by talking about Duval's greed. Photos of each Duval house appeared on the screen with the purchase price at the bottom, followed by images of the Duval yacht and the Duval Energy aircraft.

Then Daniels turned to the PetroMex contract and the bribery. He told the jury they should care because the money could have been used to help the poor in Mexico—or the poor in Dallas. Gabriela saw several jurors nodding, which meant they agreed.

With the jury leaning his way, Daniels argued that Duval either knew or purposely chose not to know that Lopez planned to bribe

PetroMex officials to win the contract. He reminded them that Kira Gregoreva testified the only way to win a PetroMex deal was to hire José Lopez, who paid bribes to officials. He replayed the theme of the Garza and Villa recording that laid out how the corruption worked.

Next, Daniels attacked what he called Duval's "ostrich defense." He projected an image of an ostrich with its head buried in the sand. "Remember Enron and WorldCom," he said. Gabriela noticed puzzled looks among the jurors. She doubted many of them remembered those scandals, but Daniels pressed on, building to his conclusion.

"Sparks Duval," Daniels said, turning and pointing at the defense table, "was suspicious about the size of José Lopez's commission. He realized it was so large that some of it might be used to grease the skids, so to speak, with PetroMex. He purposely chose not to learn the truth. Even worse, just before the deal closed, he sent an email to his lawyer solely to give himself an excuse if anything went wrong. If you're not sure about that, ask yourself why he sent that email days before the deal closed rather than months before."

Gabriela glanced toward the jury. Every juror was focused on Daniels. She could tell some had accepted his argument that Duval's email was written to cover himself in case of trouble.

"I want you to compare the demeanor of Donald Lawrence—who stood up, acknowledged his wrongdoing, and took responsibility—with that of William Thomas Duval. This greedy, narcissistic, and extraordinarily arrogant defendant played games with you. He played the blame game—blaming his lawyer for his lapse in judgment. He played the memory game—claiming he couldn't remember key facts. And he played the excuse game—making excuses for his lack of involvement in the PetroMex transaction."

Listening to Daniels, Gabriela was convinced again that she had been right: Sparks Duval should never have taken the stand. His demeanor, not his words, could easily be his undoing.

"William Thomas Duval was deeply involved in every single detail of every deal his company made. Yet he claims to have been hands-off on the one deal outside the United States—the one deal where his company paid a thirty-percent commission to a middleman. It was also the one deal where his company bribed PetroMex officials to win a drilling contract. It makes no sense. It's absurd. It's a lie. Don't buy what he's trying to sell you. Go into the jury room and bring back a guilty verdict."

Jason Daniels returned to his seat.

Judge Comstock addressed the jury. "Ladies and gentlemen, we'll take a break now for lunch. Remember, you are not to discuss the case or view anything on social media."

During the lunch recess, Gabriela and her father sat at a separate table. She wanted to avoid Deborah Snow and Sparks Duval and focus on her own argument.

After lunch, the Duval team walked back to the courthouse. The media had surrounded the building—TV trucks, cameras, and reporters speaking into microphones. It looked like coverage of the Super Bowl. When reporters spotted Gabriela, they shouted questions about what she planned to say in her closing argument.

Environmental protesters were there too, waving anti-fracking signs and shouting at Duval. The security detail Duval had hired managed to push them through the crowd and into the courthouse.

Inside, the lobby was packed. The U.S. marshal saw Gabriela and escorted the defense team through security.

As soon as they reached the conference room, Deborah Snow started in again.

"Gabriela, some trials turn on the final argument. That's especially true when jurors don't know who to believe. You must convince them to believe Sparks."

"You told me that yesterday, Deborah."

"Let's hear what you plan to say."

Gabriela crossed her arms. "Deborah, I need to focus on my final argument. You're distracting me, and that's not helping."

She looked at her father and caught a faint gleam in his eye.

Snow folded her arms. "It better be good, because you haven't persuaded them so far. What you say—and how you say it—will be judged on every local and national media outlet tonight."

That was not what Gabriela wanted to hear.

There was a knock on the door. Gabriela opened it.

"Judge Comstock is ready," the marshal said.

Chapter 40

As Gabriela walked into the courtroom with her father, she saw that even more reporters from local and national outlets filled the gallery. Since cameras weren't allowed in Federal Court, two spectators sat sketching scenes that would appear on television that night and in newspapers the next morning.

When she reached the defense table, Gabriela looked back at the crowd behind her. In the second row sat several Catholic priests in clerical collars, including Father Anthony, who had once worked with her helping undocumented children. He smiled warmly at her.

Farther back, she spotted Chuck Green standing in the last row. He gave her a slight nod—his signal to go for it. A low murmur drifted through the courtroom.

Judge Comstock entered, settled into his chair, and looked down from the bench. "Ms. Sanchez, you may address the jury."

Gabriela rose and walked to the podium without her iPad or any notes. She hated standing behind a podium in federal court—it created distance between her and the jurors. She wanted to move closer, to speak to them as people.

"Ladies and gentlemen," she began, her voice steady, "this is the last time I will speak to you on behalf of William Thomas 'Sparks' Duval."

She turned toward him. Duval smiled.

"Remember, in my opening statement I told you this case was about the word *why*. The government hasn't answered many of the *why* questions, because the answers would exonerate Sparks Duval and Duval Energy.

"The big *why* staring you in the face is this: Why would a man who started with nothing, who worked and sacrificed to build one of the most successful energy companies in the world, knowingly risk everything by bribing PetroMex officials to win one minor contract in Mexico?"

Gabriela looked each juror in the eye, one by one.

"I trust you agree—it makes no sense. But there are many more *why* questions the government hasn't answered.

"Why did the FBI purposely fail to trace the money flowing into and out of José Lopez's accounts? Why didn't they simply ask Lopez if he used any of Duval Energy's commission to bribe PetroMex officials? Why didn't the government arrest José Lopez or call him as a witness?"

Several jurors leaned forward. Gabriela knew she'd struck a chord.

"Isn't the answer obvious? The FBI already knew the truth—and they didn't want *you* to know it. They knew José Lopez never used Duval Energy's money to bribe Rafael Garza or Rodrigo Villa. They didn't trace the money because they knew the bribe money came from Lopez's American Energy commission. You heard the evidence: Rodrigo Villa wasn't even working for PetroMex when the Duval deal closed in March 2014."

Jason Daniels was on his feet immediately. "Your Honor, the government doesn't have to prove where the bribe money originated. It's enough that Mr. Duval intended or knew it would go to PetroMex officials."

Gabriela glanced at the jurors. She saw frowns—Daniels's objection had only confused them.

"Mr. Daniels, the argument is proper," Judge Comstock said. "You may continue, Ms. Sanchez."

"Thank you, Your Honor."

Gabriela turned back to the jury. "The FBI could have arrested José Lopez when he visited the United States. They could have extradited him from Mexico. They didn't—because they knew Lopez would exonerate Sparks Duval and Duval Energy."

She paused. "Why did Mr. Duval hire Donald Lawrence as his company lawyer and trusted advisor?

"Both men testified that Mr. Duval hired Lawrence to protect the company from legal entanglements. That duty was written into Lawrence's own contract."

Gabriela paused again—one, two, three—then continued.

"Why did Mr. Lawrence push Mr. Duval to pursue the PetroMex contract? Because Lawrence had millions to gain. He insisted that José Lopez pay him two million dollars if he persuaded Mr. Duval to agree to the deal. On top of that, Lawrence would receive five percent of Duval Energy's profits.

"Mr. Daniels talks to you about greed. Donald Lawrence is the greedy one, not Sparks Duval."

Gabriela saw nods from two jurors.

"If Mr. Duval knowingly paid Mr. Lopez to bribe PetroMex officials, why was he so opposed to doing business in Mexico and so against paying any commission at all?

"If he intended to bribe PetroMex officials, why did Donald Lawrence testify that Mr. Duval complained about paying the commission—and complained that it was thirty percent?

"And if Mr. Duval knowingly paid a bribe, why couldn't Donald Lawrence get him to admit it when he secretly recorded their conversation wearing a wire for the FBI?"

She turned back toward the jury box. "Let's talk about Mr. Lawrence's role. He met José Lopez at an energy conference. Lopez told him about the PetroMex opportunity. Lawrence brought that deal to Sparks Duval and his son Christopher.

"Sparks Duval wanted no part of it. But Lawrence persuaded him—because Lawrence was chasing a two-million-dollar bonus. He deceived Sparks Duval. He deceived Duval Energy. And he tried to deceive *you*."

Gabriela's right hand struck the air for emphasis, each phrase landing like a hammer.

She asked why Lawrence kept the two-million-dollar payment hidden in an offshore account and failed to report it to the IRS. The answer was obvious: he thought he could get away with it.

"Donald Lawrence was so smug he believed no one—other than José Lopez—would ever know about that bonus. If the Panamanian law firm hadn't been hacked, no one would have discovered his secret account."

Her voice rose slightly. "Lawrence was caught in the government's web, and he became their pawn. The government demanded that he keep working for Duval Energy—while secretly wearing a wire and camera to record his client. Lawrence violated his ethical duty of loyalty."

Gabriela paused, letting the silence settle.

"Why did he become the government's pawn? Because they promised leniency if he cooperated—and threatened him if he didn't."

Daniels jumped up. "Your Honor, there's no evidence the government promised Mr. Lawrence leniency or threatened him."

"Mr. Daniels," Judge Comstock said, "Ms. Sanchez may argue reasonable inferences. You can address it in your rebuttal."

Gabriela nodded. "Thank you, Your Honor."

Turning back to the jury, she said, "When you watched Donald Lawrence testify, what did you think? At first, he seemed confident—even self-righteous. But that was easy. He was reading a script the government gave him.

"Then he slipped. The government forgot its own timeline. They forgot when Rodrigo Villa became a PetroMex official. You saw Lawrence caught in a lie because he followed the script too closely. Do you remember when Mr. Daniels suddenly asked for a recess?"

She looked again at the jurors. Nine of the twelve nodded.

"Mr. Daniels demanded that Lawrence 'clarify' his testimony to match what Agent Barnes said. After that recess, Lawrence returned to the stand claiming a memory lapse."

Gabriela let that sink in. "In a nutshell, Donald Lawrence spearheaded the PetroMex deal—not to benefit Duval Energy, but to line his own pockets with two million dollars and five percent of the profits. He needed that money to pay off a gambling debt. He hid it offshore until the FBI found out. Then he flipped—becoming an informant to save himself.

"He deceived Sparks Duval then, and he deceived *you* now. He lied to save himself from prison."

Gabriela turned to her final theme—reasonable doubt. "To convict Sparks Duval or Duval Energy, the government must prove beyond a reasonable doubt that they bribed PetroMex officials. They haven't.

"They must prove beyond a reasonable doubt that Sparks Duval knowingly and willfully joined that bribery. They haven't.

"They must prove beyond a reasonable doubt that Donald Lawrence didn't act alone for his own gain. They haven't."

Her right hand punctuated each point. "The government hasn't even proved that a single dollar of Duval Energy's money was ever used as a bribe. They can't—because Sparks Duval hired Donald Lawrence to protect him from legal problems abroad. They can't—because Sparks Duval specifically asked if there were any legal issues, and Lawrence said no. They can't—because Donald Lawrence acted alone to get his two million dollars."

Gabriela took a step back. "The only person the government has proved guilty beyond a reasonable doubt is Donald Lawrence. He took a bribe—from José Lopez."

She turned toward her table and, while walking back, looked at Jason Daniels. His hands gripped the table edge, knuckles white. Christopher Duval, sitting beside his mother in the front row, smiled and nodded.

Many later said Gabriela's closing was one of the best they had ever heard. She nailed it when she told jurors that Donald Lawrence was the only proven criminal in the courtroom.

"Mr. Daniels," Judge Comstock said, "you may make your closing argument now."

Daniels strode to the podium. As Gabriela expected, he turned her "why" questions back against her.

"While you're asking *why*," he said, "ask why Ms. Sanchez never mentioned Kira Gregoreva, or her recording of the two men José Lopez bribed to win the contract for Duval Energy. You heard it. The only way to win a PetroMex contract was to pay a thirty-percent commission to José Lopez—money he used to bribe Mr. Garza and Mr. Villa."

He pivoted toward Duval. "Ask why the defendant who built a billion-dollar company by knowing every detail now claims ignorance on the one foreign deal where his company paid a thirty-percent commission.

"Why does he suddenly know so little? Because he lied to you.

"Why does a man buy a forty-two-million-dollar home in Dallas, and others in Wyoming and Ireland? Because he's greedy. Because having a billion dollars wasn't enough.

"The defendant has no conscience. He can take land from farmers. He can poison water through fracking. He can bribe PetroMex officials—and it doesn't bother him.

"He's gotten away with it his whole life. Now you have the chance to tell him he's no better than anyone else. You have the chance to send a message to big oil companies that they are not above the law. Send that message. Find Sparks Duval and Duval Energy guilty as charged."

***

Thirty minutes later, after Judge Comstock excused the jury, the defense team filed out. Roberto Sanchez smiled, clasped his daughter's hand, and mouthed, *You knocked it out of the park.*

Gabriela's pulse still raced. *No way twelve jurors could find Sparks Duval guilty.*

Chapter 41

Four days later, they were all back in the crowded courtroom. Reporters from every local TV station filled the benches. *The Dallas Morning News* had two reporters present, and each major cable network had sent correspondents.

"Ladies and gentlemen, have you reached your verdict?" Judge Comstock asked.

The white-haired man in the first chair stood. "We have, Your Honor."

"Please hand your verdict to the marshal."

A uniformed U.S. marshal walked to the jury box. The foreperson passed him the verdict form, and the marshal carried it to the bench.

Roberto watched Judge Comstock's face, searching for any sign of disagreement. When the judge's expression hardened, Roberto's stomach dropped.

He turned toward his daughter and gently touched her arm.
If only Sparks Duval hadn't testified. If only Judge Comstock had granted Gabriela's motion for acquittal.

He was her father, but he could still be objective. She had handled the case even better than he'd expected. The jury had clearly liked her— but he wasn't sure they liked Sparks Duval.

Roberto Sanchez had stood beside defendants through more verdicts than he could count, but he had never felt the pressure he felt now. The jury held his daughter's future in their hands. If she won, she'd be recognized as one of Texas's top trial lawyers. If she lost, she might never get another chance.

Then he heard Judge Comstock read the verdict: **guilty**—on each of the five counts of violating the Foreign Corrupt Practices Act.

He touched Gabriela's arm again. He knew she wanted to cry but couldn't. Her shoulders slumped as the judge repeated the word *guilty* again and again.

He thought back to her junior-golf days. When she won, he'd been proud. When she lost, he'd been just as proud—but he knew how deeply she took defeat. Today's loss, though, cut deeper than any missed putt.

Jason Daniels walked over and shook Gabriela's hand, a broad smile plastered across his face.

The two PR consultants brushed past her to reach Sparks Duval. When Gabriela turned, Deborah Snow shoved her aside, eager to make sure no one blamed her for the loss.

When the courtroom finally emptied, Gabriela and her father walked slowly toward the exit. Her head was down, her steps heavy. Roberto placed a hand on her arm. When they reached the hallway and were alone, he lifted her chin and spoke softly.

"Gabriela, there's nothing I can say to make you feel better. I know how painful losing a case is. I've lost too."

She looked at the floor.

"You gave Sparks Duval the best defense possible. I watched you every day in court and brainstormed with you every night. I'm proud of the trial lawyer—and the woman—you've become. This loss doesn't change who you are. You know who you are. Hold your head high."

"But, Papá—"

"You didn't push Sparks Duval into the Mexico deal. You didn't alienate the jurors during cross-examination. Duval knew exactly what he was doing. He understood the corruption in Mexico. He's the reason the jury found him guilty."

"Papá, you might think I'm devastated, that I'm afraid my career is over. I thought I'd feel that way too. But I don't."

He looked surprised. "You don't?"

"No, Papá. I'm just relieved it's over. I'm exhausted. From the day Duval hired me, I've been under a microscope. I never imagined being on TV every day. I never imagined reporters camping outside my house, following me on my morning runs. I never imagined strangers attacking me just for doing my job."

"That was Duval's fault. He hired Deborah Snow and let her dictate how you defended him. She shouldn't have interfered with your trial strategy—and she never should've persuaded him to take the stand."

"Maybe. But people would've tried to tear me down with or without her. I needed to convince the jury to believe in me so they'd believe in Duval. They didn't."

"The jury didn't find *you* lacking," Roberto said. "They found Sparks Duval guilty. They convicted him because Judge Comstock instructed them that Duval could be guilty for consciously choosing not to know what Lopez was doing."

As they spoke, a reporter approached and handed Gabriela a Department of Justice press release. She began reading aloud.

DALLAS, TEXAS – Duval Energy, a Dallas company, and its founder and CEO, William Thomas Duval, were convicted by a federal jury on all counts for their roles in a scheme to bribe officials of PetroMex, Mexico's state-owned energy company. Evidence showed that Duval Energy paid José Lopez a 30-percent commission and that both Duval and his company knew Lopez intended to use part of that money to pay bribes. The jury reached its verdict after four days of deliberation, following a two-week trial.

"Today's guilty verdicts mark an important milestone in our Foreign Corrupt Practices Act enforcement efforts," said Department of Justice prosecutor Jason Daniels. "Duval Energy is only the second company ever tried and convicted under the FCPA—but it will not be the last. No matter how wealthy or well-connected, no one is above the law."

Roberto drove Gabriela back to her office. When they arrived, Lucia met them with a message. Chuck Green wanted to see her right away.

She knocked on his door.

"Come in," he said.

Chuck Green looked up from a pile of papers. "We're preparing a motion for judgment of acquittal. We have several arguments."

"What are they?" Gabriela asked.

"First, we still believe PetroMex employees don't meet the definition of *government officials,* especially since the Mexican government opened drilling to foreign companies. Second, there was insufficient evidence to convict. Daniels never proved Sparks knowingly paid a bribe. Judge Comstock was ready to rule when Daniels finished his case."

Gabriela shook her head. "Donald Lawrence testified that he told Duval. And Duval bombed on the witness stand."

"Maybe so," Green said, "but that's not what Lawrence originally told the FBI. They coerced him into changing his story."

"I'm not sure Judge Comstock will buy that."

"Maybe not," Green admitted. "But we have another argument."

"What's that?"

"The one Lopez mentioned to you. Daniels never proved that Lopez bribed Garza or Villa with any of the money Duval Energy paid him."

"That might be stronger," Gabriela said. "But some courts have ruled the government doesn't have to prove the bribe actually happened."

"How do we get Judge Comstock to overturn the verdict?" Green asked.

Gabriela leaned back, thinking through everything that had happened—from jury selection to the verdict. Then her expression changed. A slow smile spread across her face.

"I think I may have something," she said.

"Prosecutorial misconduct?" Green asked. "You're not planning to argue that Judge Comstock should dismiss the case because the government hacked your computer, iPad, and phone, are you?"

"No," she said, shaking her head. "I thought about that, but Daniels would just deny it and make me look paranoid. Judge Comstock would never believe the government would stoop that low."

She smiled again. "No, Chuck. I have another idea."

Chapter 42

Something had always troubled Gabriela about the social-media tirades and the front-page tabloid article. While reviewing trial transcripts, she noticed that many of the same phrases Jason Daniels used in court had appeared earlier in the online posts.

That night she opened her laptop and began a Google search on how governments, corporations, and political campaigns used social media to influence the public and discredit opponents. What she found stunned her. She learned that automated accounts could shape opinion and spread narratives at scale. It had a name—*manufacturing consensus.*

Could the Department of Justice have done that? Could they have used social media to *manufacture consensus* and convince potential jurors that Sparks Duval was guilty before the trial even began?

Gabriela kept reading. She found a 2011 quote from a public-relations firm boasting that it could "create and maintain third-party blogs and spruce up Wikipedia profiles and Google search rankings." The practice was called *astroturfing.*

One article cited *Merriam-Webster's* definition: *an organized activity intended to create a false impression of a widespread, spontaneous grassroots movement in support of or in opposition to something—but actually initiated and controlled by a concealed group or organization.*

Another journalist described how astroturfing had been used by both sides during the 2016 presidential election to destroy the opposing candidate's public image.

Gabriela read that more than two-thirds of Americans now get their news from social media, while only one-third watch cable or network news and just one-fifth read newspapers. No wonder Daniels had asked potential jurors how they got their news.

It finally hit her. Duval's PR team had focused on traditional media—newspapers, cable, evening broadcasts—the sources one in three or one in five people might see. Daniels had targeted the platforms used by *two-thirds* of Americans.

Wow.

She picked up the phone. "Papá, someone who hates Sparks Duval tried to influence the jury against both him and me. I think Daniels and the Department of Justice had something to do with it."

"No way," Roberto said. "Federal judges have condemned DOJ lawyers for dirty tricks before, but this would be beyond anything I've ever heard."

"We'll see."

***

Four weeks later, Gabriela and her father returned to court to argue their motion for judgment of acquittal. Sparks Duval sat between them; Deborah Snow occupied the first row behind the rail.

Gabriela had avoided Snow since the verdict, knowing she'd been deflecting blame onto everyone but herself. Reporters once again packed the courtroom. Jason Daniels didn't speak to Gabriela or her father. He didn't even call her "Gabby." He sat silently, jaw tight, shaking his head. Judge Comstock adjusted his glasses and looked down from the bench. "Ms. Sanchez, we're here on your motions for a judgment of acquittal—first, for insufficient evidence to convict, and second, for alleged prosecutorial misconduct. I've read both briefs."

He turned a page. "Let's start with the first motion. As you know, when Mr. Daniels rested the government's case, you raised this same argument, and I seriously considered granting it. But judges rarely overturn a jury verdict for insufficient evidence. If I granted your motion here, the Fifth Circuit would almost certainly reverse me.

"You argue the government failed to prove that José Lopez used any of the commission Duval paid him to buy the BMWs for the PetroMex officials or to pay Garza's daughter's tuition. You say Lopez's Albueno account had less than five thousand dollars after Duval Energy's payment and before those purchases. You also contend that Rodrigo Villa wasn't even a PetroMex official at the time of the contract. Is that correct, Ms. Sanchez?"

"Yes, Your Honor. And we reassert that Villa and Garza were not public officials as required under the statute."

Judge Comstock nodded. "You also claim that, based on the evidence, no reasonable jury could have found that Mr. Duval knew Lopez intended to use any of the commission to buy cars or pay tuition in return for the contract award. Is that right?"

"Yes, Your Honor," Gabriela said, though she knew it was their weakest argument.

The judge turned to Daniels. "Mr. Daniels, your position?"

"Yes, Your Honor. The law doesn't require us to trace every dollar. The Foreign Corrupt Practices Act prohibits the *offer, authorization, or promise* to make a corrupt payment—not just the payment itself. Even if the money was co-mingled, the intent was clear."

"And regarding the officials?"

"Even though PetroMex does business with U.S. companies, Garza and Villa remain public officials under the Act."

Judge Comstock leaned back. "And finally, you rely on Mr. Lawrence's testimony that he told Mr. Duval about the bribes—and, at minimum, that Mr. Duval turned a blind eye."

"Yes, Your Honor."

The judge set down his pen. "Ms. Sanchez, although I agree the government's evidence was thin, I won't overturn the verdict. To do so, I'd have to find that no reasonable juror could have convicted Mr. Duval, and I can't say that here."

Gabriela had expected that. "Yes, Your Honor."

Daniels allowed himself a small smile.

Judge Comstock looked up again. "Mr. Daniels, I wouldn't celebrate just yet. Ms. Sanchez's second motion alleges prosecutorial misconduct—specifically, that you or someone in the Department of Justice engaged in a secret public-relations campaign using social media to influence public opinion and the jury. Is that correct, Ms. Sanchez?"

"Yes, Your Honor."

"She contends the Department used a strategy called *astroturfing* to sway public opinion, setting up thousands of social-media accounts and dozens of blogs, including one under the Twitter handle **@nofrackingtx**, which began posting before the indictment and continued through jury deliberations.

"She further alleges that you, Mr. Daniels, were @nofrackingtx, based on a forensic linguistic analysis by Dr. Gregory Austin of Texas A&M University, who found your syntax, phrasing, and word choices in briefs and arguments to be strikingly similar to the posts. Is that correct, Ms. Sanchez?"

"Yes, Your Honor," Gabriela said. "Dr. Austin's analysis identified repeated linguistic markers unique to Mr. Daniels's writing style."

"Mr. Daniels?"

"Yes, Your Honor," Daniels said stiffly.

"You've denied posting anything about this case on social media and expressed outrage at the allegation. Yet, after Dr. Austin issued his report, I ordered the Department of Justice to provide IP-address data for @nofrackingtx and any internal communications with public-relations firms. The Department's production was incomplete. You continue to deny knowledge of any posts. Correct?"

"Yes, Your Honor. I deny ever posting about this case or authorizing anyone to do so."

Judge Comstock's gaze hardened. "Did you, or anyone at the DOJ, communicate with outside strategic-communications firms? Were any media outlets paid to report selectively or publish false statements about Mr. Duval or Ms. Sanchez?"

"I can honestly say I did not," Daniels replied.

"What about your colleagues?"

"I can't speak for every DOJ employee, but each lawyer and staff member who worked on this case told me they made no social-media posts."   "Mr. Daniels, that's not good enough," Comstock said. "In the age of cyberspace, fake news, and algorithmic manipulation, the courts have tried to anticipate potential abuses. But I never imagined someone in the Department of Justice would use these tactics to influence a jury.

"Someone smeared both William Duval and his lawyer. If anyone at the DOJ participated, it would violate professional and ethical obligations, as well as federal regulations. I've reviewed hundreds of posts. I strongly suspect a coordinated campaign. Therefore, I am issuing an order directing the Attorney General to appoint a Special Counsel to investigate whether anyone at the Department of Justice was involved."

Daniels straightened. "Your Honor, without admitting anything, you know Mr. Duval also engaged a PR firm to influence public perception. We were on the receiving end of that. Ms. Sanchez and her client were on television daily proclaiming his innocence. They inflamed public opinion, not us."

"Mr. Daniels," Comstock said sharply, "the Department of Justice is held to a higher standard. The DOJ must serve *truth* and *justice*, not publicity. Federal regulations prohibit the release of information intended to influence a trial—and that is precisely what I suspect happened."

"Your Honor," Daniels shot back, "you and I both know the defendant was guilty as charged."

"Perhaps," Comstock said evenly, "but if the DOJ tried to sway the jury with social media, it may have succeeded. I instructed the jurors to avoid all coverage, but we can't know if they did. The jury wasn't sequestered. And given your voir dire questions, I have every reason to believe they were social-media users. It's entirely possible some followed @nofrackingtx."

"Even if that's true," Daniels said, "Ms. Sanchez's motion goes to the fairness of the trial, not guilt or innocence. She hasn't proved any juror was actually influenced."

"Then you can raise that on appeal," Comstock replied. "For now, I'm ordering a full review."

Daniels exhaled sharply. "Yes, Your Honor."

"Thank you, Your Honor," Gabriela said quietly.

As she left the courtroom, Deborah Snow caught up with her.

"Good work," Snow said. "I guess our PR campaign worked. You're going to win."

Gabriela forced a polite smile. "Thank you."

You almost destroyed my relationship with my mother, she thought. "But I didn't win. The jury convicted Sparks Duval. Daniels won the smear campaign. The only good news is that Judge Comstock might grant a new trial."

"If it hadn't been for our massive PR campaign," Snow said, "the DOJ never would've mounted its own. We deserve credit for luring them into the trap."

Gabriela laughed softly. "That's all well and good, but if Comstock grants a new trial, who's going to defend Duval?"

"I'm already working on that."

"You'll need to find a new lawyer," Gabriela said. "Because it won't be me."

Outside the courtroom, Roberto approached. His face was tense.

"I just got a troubling voicemail," he said.

"Troubling?"

"It was from Aubrey Gall."

That bastard again.

"He's planning a *National Tabloid Journal* story—about me, my law practice, and corruption in the Rio Grande Valley."

"Oh, no," Gabriela said.